Where the Silent Ones Watch

Where the Silent Ones Watch

Edited by James Chambers

Hippocampus Press
———————
New York

Selection and introduction copyright © 2024 James Chambers
All stories and poems © 2024 their individual authors.

Published by Hippocampus Press
P.O. Box 641, New York, NY 10156.
www.hippocampuspress.com

All rights reserved.
No part of this work may be reproduced in any form or by any means without the written permission of the publisher.

Cover art and design © 2024 by Daniel V. Sauer, dansauerdesign.com
Hippocampus Press logo designed by Anastasia Damianakos.

First Edition
1 3 5 7 9 8 6 4 2

ISBN 978-1-61498-443-6 (paperback)
ISBN 978-1-61498-458-0 (ebook)

Contents

Introduction: The Pulse of the Master-Word	7
The Events at Apoka Station	15
Peter Rawlik and Sal Ciano	
Hangman's Coming	27
L. E. Daniels	
Resistant to Change	36
Adrian Ludens	
A Disturbance in the Field	42
Steve Rasnic Tem	
Death and the Goddess Yet Seen	55
Linda D. Addison	
Our Lady of Morocco	57
Robert E. Waters	
The Ship on the Sea of Nightmares	75
Lisa Morton	
All That Lies Below	87
Tim Waggoner	
The Call	100
Stephanie M. Wytovich	
The Shellback's Tale	101
Lee Murray	
The Captain's Wife	105
Nancy Holder	
Latitude Dark	117
Teel James Glenn	
From the Bowl of the Gods	131
Wendy N. Wagner	
Going, Going	145
Meghan Arcuri	
Little House on the Borderland	155
Todd Keisling	
That Colossal Wreck	172
John Langan	
A Bodyless Thing	185
Sam Rebelein	

This House 197
    L. Marie Wood

Where the Silent Ones Smile 198
    Patrick Freivald

Night Landing 206
    Ann K. Schwader

Night Hearing 208
    Michael Cisco

The Battlements of Twilight 224
    Kyla Lee Ward

Death Knocks (Someday Soon) 238
    Maxwell I. Gold

Bellow of the Steamship Cow 241
    Aaron Dries

The House on the Scannerland 255
    David Agranoff

Out in the Night with the Memphis Dead 261
    Andy Davidson

About the Authors 269

About the Editor 278

Introduction: The Pulse of the Master-Word

> "And as it was with the Road Where The Silent Ones Walk, so it was with all those other monstrous things ... whole libraries had there been made upon this and upon that; and many a thousand million mouldered into the forgotten dust of the earlier world."
>
> —William Hope Hodgson, *The Night Land*

William Hope Hodgson, born on November 15, 1877, in Blackmore End, England, may be the most powerful—and most neglected—fantasist and horror writer of the twentieth century. So vast and original are his creations and mythologies that Hodgson's name should spill seamlessly from readers' lips when they speak of Bierce, Chambers, Howard, Lovecraft, Machen, Tolkien, and so many better-known and well-loved founders of modern horror and weird fiction. Yet contemporary readers seem to know him best only in piecemeal fashion. This one has read *The House on the Borderland*. That one knows his Sargasso Sea stories. Here one has read *The Boats of the "Glen Carrig"* and *The Ghost Pirates*, while another recalls his tales of Carnacki the Ghost-Finder. On rare occasions there is a reader who has devoured in full Hodgson's most stunning and most challenging work, *The Night Land*. Outside the realms of fantasy and horror, Hodgson is known for naval tales and suspense stories, the former of which he wrote with remarkable authenticity and detail based on his near decade spent at sea.

With so many accomplishments across so many genres and subgenres, why is Hodgson not better remembered and more widely read today than his contemporaries and followers? Where is the seemingly endless stream of books, comics, games, movies, toys, and other spin-off media and merchandise that ride the wake of Howard, Lovecraft, and Tolkien? The history of horror and weird fiction is paved with past editions and iterations of their works as well as those of Bierce, Chambers, and Machen. Yet not until 2003–2009, when Night Shade Books published the five-volume edition of *The Collected Fiction of William Hope Hodgson,* did a publisher undertake a comprehensive gathering of Hodgson's works. In the early 2000s, inspired by reading the graphic novel adaptation of *The House on the Borderland* by Simon Revelstroke and Richard Corben, I searched my local bookstores high and low for a copy of the source novel, eventually landing a brittle, beat-up mass-market paperback (which I ultimately had to bind together with rubber bands) in a small batch of books I purchased from the late Stanley C. Sargent, himself a master of cosmic horror and weird fiction.

When I approached authors to submit stories for this anthology, I found the same fragmentation. Some immediately lit up at the prospect of playing in the sandboxes of *The House on the Borderland*, *The Night Land*, or the Sargasso Sea. Others recalled having read this or that piece by Hodgson long ago and dove into reading and re-reading before choosing a thread to pull and follow, perhaps leaning first toward the Borderland before falling in love with *The Ghost Pirates* or the monstrous creatures of the Sargasso Sea. A few had not yet read any of Hodgson's writing previously and dove in as novitiates.

How could the works of such an immense imagination remain so obscure, especially in 2024 when no one need hunt for his books and stories, all in the public domain, many readily available online? The answer, I believe, lies in three facts. One, Hodgson sought constantly to find the literary footing that would support him and his family, attempting to launch several different story series with commercial appeal rather than working consistently in a single genre. Two, Hodgson tried on different writing styles, from detailed technical accounts of ocean navigation in many of his sea stories to the dense, repetitive, archaic, and anachronistic language of *The Night Land*, challenging readers to follow him from one work to the next. And, three, Hodgson's writing life spanned only fourteen years from the publication of his first story, "The Goddess of Death," in 1904. He died young, age forty, obliterated by an artillery shell at Ypres, Belgium, in April 1918, leaving his literary legacy in a fragmented and formative state.

Had Hodgson lived to write for another ten, twenty, or thirty years, perhaps he would have found his singular voice as a writer—the voice that makes it impossible to forget the works of other speculative and seminal writers of his era. Perhaps he would have produced a work of such grand imagination and literary magic that it would have dragged all his other writing into focus for modern readers. Maybe not. Hodgson tried his hand at many things to make a living: sailor; photographer; proprietor of a school for physical fitness; challenger of master escape artist Harry Houdini; writer; and, ultimately, soldier. In that sense, Hodgson's fiction mirrored his life, leaping from one possibility to another to find one that fit and proved rewarding. Who can guess what possibility, other than writing, might next have inspired him had he returned from Ypres?

For contemporary readers, Hodgson's works can be off-putting. *The House on the Borderland* switches from weird horror to cosmic fantasy to borderline science fiction, as does *The Ghost Pirates,* which strikes surprisingly modern, science-fictional notes in its ideas about alternate dimensions and mirror realities. Some Carnacki stories are purely supernatural, while others are grounded entirely in reality. *The Night Land,* with its post-apocalyptic landscape of Ab-Humans, the Last Redoubt, the House of Silence, the Master Word, and Monstruwacans, contains some of the most startling ideas and imagery in the entire history of fantasy literature—but one must patiently peruse long, repetitive passages to experience them (or embrace *The Dream of X,* Hodgson's much abridged version of the novel). It is no surprise that Hodgson's most ardent readers today are students of the horrific and the weird, writers and readers with much more than a passing interest in fantasy and horror literature and its history. Of all Hodgson's creations, only Carnacki has found steady traction among current readers and writers, thanks to the series' established formula and readers' undying interest in occult investigators.

Which brings me to *Where the Silent Ones Watch*. The book was originally proposed as a gathering of stories to reimagine the concepts of *The House on the Borderland* in various times, locations, and domiciles, but I expanded its scope at the advice and encouragement of Derrick Hussey. I'm very glad I did. The poems and stories here draw upon a wide swath of Hodgson's concepts, settings, and themes, and from them one aspect of Hodgson's work emerged as a unifying element: its liminality, its preoccupation with remote places and spaces where the rules of the known, physical world seem not to apply, allowing for all manner of strange phenomena.

To those familiar with Hodgson's work, some of these tales may read like exciting visits to new corners of his realms, while others present bold and daring interpretations of his ideas. All, I hope, especially for those who have not yet read much of Hodgson's work, will strike a dark note of "Hodgsonian horror," whether they delve into the Borderland, the Ghost Seas, the Night Land, the Sargasso Sea, or even Hodgson's first, grim story, "The Goddess of Death." All, I hope, will awaken or reignite interest in Hodgson among contemporary readers. As he wrote in the opening lines of *The House on the Borderland*: "The inner story must be uncovered, personally, by each reader, according to ability and desire." The contributors to this anthology have accomplished this. I hope its readers will as well.

The title of this book, *Where the Silent Ones Watch,* is inspired by dangerous and enigmatic denizens of the Night Land, described by the narrator of the novel: "Before me ran the Road Where The Silent Ones Walk; and I searched it, as many a time in my earlier youth had I, with the spy-glass; for my heart was always stirred mightily by the sight of those Silent Ones. And, presently, alone in all the miles of that night-grey road, I saw one in the field of my glass—a quiet, cloaked figure, moving along, shrouded, and looking neither to right nor left. And thus was it with these beings ever." That image of the protagonist spying from the massive edifice of the Last Redoubt at these mysterious figures always makes me wonder if the Silent Ones looked back. Did they, like so many other odd beings of the Night Land, like the Watchers to the North-West, South-East, South-West, and South, stare back at the miles-high pyramid that provided humanity's last refuge and watch the people therein? If so, did they wonder about them, covet them, hate them, or pity them? Did they observe them with indifference as their time on earth drew to its end? Did they see into the liminal spaces that inhabit so much of Hodgson's work? Perhaps only William Hope Hodgson knew the answer.

I am much indebted to Derrick Hussey of Hippocampus Press for his unflagging support for this anthology and the creative freedom and encouragement he has afforded me to edit it. If you are not already familiar with the Hippocampus catalogue, I encourage you to explore its wealth of wonderful books—fiction, nonfiction, and poetry—which capture the soul of horror and the weird in all its historic glory.

Much gratitude goes to the contributors to this book, who not only took the theme and ran with it, but delivered stories and poems of dark excellence and imagination that, in my opinion, honor Hodgson's ideas of horror and the weird. They have my gratitude too for their patience during the long road to publication. Many thanks as well to you, the reader, for without your interest and support all our writings and editings would amount to little.

As always, special thanks to my family for their steadfast encouragement, indulgence, support, and understanding of all the time and effort I dedicated to this book.

JAMES CHAMBERS
Northport,
January 2024

I read, and, in reading, lifted the Curtains of the Impossible that blind the mind, and looked out into the unknown. Amid stiff, abrupt sentences I wandered; and, presently, I had no fault to charge against their abrupt tellings; for, better far than my own ambitious phrasing, is this mutilated story capable of bringing home all that the old Recluse, of the vanished house, had striven to tell.

Of the simple, stiffly given account of weird and extraordinary matters, I will say little. It lies before you. The inner story must be uncovered, personally, by each reader, according to ability and desire. And even should any fail to see, as now I see, the shadowed picture and conception of that to which one may well give the accepted titles of Heaven and Hell; yet can I promise certain thrills, merely taking the story as a story.

William Hope Hodgson,
December 17, 1907
The House on the Borderland

The Events at Apoka Station

Peter Rawlik and Sal Ciano

I have told this story three times now, and three times those in authority have called me mad. I beg them to talk to Ash, the conductor, or the station master, or to examine the evidence themselves, but they just shake their heads and ask me to repeat what I heard and saw. But there are only so many ways to tell the same story. So here it is again, I hope for the last time.

We were ten hours behind schedule when we pulled into Apoka Station for the second time in two days. I was having breakfast as the train slowed, and I was careful to place my coffee back on the table before the train stopped and then lurched back. Over the last few months I had become adept at the finer points of rail travel, and learning how to imbibe had been one of the first skills I had mastered. It is not merely compensating for the occasional deceleration, acceleration, or braking. There are rhythms to the movement of a train, the cars shimmy and shake in response to the curves and straights both at the front of the line and toward the rear, and if one pays attention one can feel the shift and anticipate the corresponding lurch back and the accompanying vibration of the cabin on top of the axles and rails. It was in this manner that I was able to keep myself stain-free while the other less-traveled passengers wore their experience—or lack thereof—on their shirts.

I took the pause in movement to finish my cup and then refresh it. This was not my preferred Kenyan blend, but rather a brew from beans grown on the slopes of certain Jamaican mountains. These near-shore sources were making gains as international relations and trade had been strained by conflict, politics, and virulence; the same reasons that air travel had become so unreliable and travel by rail, even with its inherent delays, had become a necessary compromise. Commuting by Pullman—with the ability to open windows for fresh air or to step outside while freight, baggage, and passengers were loaded and unloaded—had become more desirable than being trapped in a flying tin can, breathing the recycled air of a hundred other passengers.

There were even spur stations, where the train stopped and took a detour off the mainline to a dead-end station, only to return hours later then rejoin the mainline. Such stations were a boon to those well-seasoned travelers who knew to take advantage of them, for they represented a rare opportunity to disembark and spend some time stretching one's legs, partaking of local fare, and wandering the various shops that populated the colorfully diverse towns that dotted the landscape. I and my partner, V——, had often taken advantage of such stations and had found such regions to be full of serendipitous surprises, both culinary and bibliophilic.

The investigation of various small towns—their bookstores, library sales, and flea markets—and the extraction of treasures therefrom were the primary purposes of our travels. We would ride the train overnight, from one region to the next, spend a day or two treasure hunting via hired car, and then catch a train to the next town, while our purchases would be properly crated up and shipped back to our residence, via trains going in the opposite direction.

It might seem an odd arrangement, but we found it rather enjoyable, and it allowed us to travel while we slept and arrive at our destination without being weary from driving the highways, byways, and backroads of the nation. There were, of course, occasional rural stops—like Apoka Station—that had little more to offer than a lonely station and stale baked goods in the middle of wastelands long since abandoned by the locals. One would not think such regions would be prime for railways and their stations, but in such areas land is cheap, almost disposable, and no one raises a voice of opposition to the rails and the speeding silver cars.

Apoka Station itself was an underwhelming affair made up of a platform of crumbling concrete and rebar atop that sat an even less inviting building of brick with a faded copper roof. The station—which was distinctly both rurally located and a spur station—nestled itself between the faded and forgotten town of Apoka on one side and the limestone rock pit that had once provided the town with employment on the other. It was hard to tell how long the quarry had been abandoned. Evidence that it had once been a thriving industry included huge, rusting cranes, decaying conveyor belts, and other pieces of equipment in various states of disrepair dotting the background. Whatever precious resource had once been hidden within the earth had long since been clawed away and sold, leaving behind a blighted black-water pit that stretched toward the horizon. I frowned at the damage done and the equipment left to rot, and thought of a quotation from Lovecraft:

> The nethermost caverns are not for the fathoming of eyes that see; for their marvels are strange and terrific. Cursed the ground where dead thoughts live new and oddly bodied, and evil the mind that is held by no head . . . Great holes are digged where earth's pores ought to suffice, and things have learnt to walk that ought to crawl.

It was then that the cabin door slid open and our conductor, Ash, rushed in. She was a tall woman with dark features and a strong personality that fitted her chosen profession. She had been working the rails for many years and had finally settled into a position on the southeastern line that served the town that we called home. Thus we knew her well, and she us, and that familiarity had proven mutually beneficial. We tipped her well, in cash and found delicacies, and she made sure that we were well served in both the dining car and our sleepers.

"Mr. S——," she whispered as she reached my table, "Miss V—— has returned. I thought you should know." A puzzled look crossed my face, and she, realizing that I must have thought V—— to be on board and in her cabin all this time, explained further. "Last night when we pulled into Apoka Station Miss V—— decided she would get off and stay at the station for the two hours that it would take to reach the Shoals and then come back. She said her legs were giving her problems. But when we started back there was a tree down on the line, and when we tried calling the station no one answered." She paused and let the situation sink in. "I'm so sorry Mr. S——, Miss V—— has been out there all night. She must be in a terrible state. Could you go check on her?"

I nodded and took a glance at my phone, saw no new notifications, and quickly surmised that the situation had not been dire: "Bring us a pot of coffee and a plate of this morning's special." I could tell she was genuinely concerned. "And don't worry, V—— has been through much worse than being stuck for the night on a train platform."

And this was true: V—— and I may have chosen books as our recreation, but it was out of necessity to undertake less stressful endeavors. I had spent three decades collecting biological specimens among the mangroves and salt marshes of the tropics, while V—— had spent about the same time as an engineer on polar research vessels. She had incredibly long and supple fingers, delicate yet skilled at working with tools on ships where space was at a premium. One cool night was not going to be much more than an inconvenience to V——. She might be tired and hungry, but that would pass. She was a durable sod. I expected that by the time we reached our destination she would be ready to go out into the world and rummage through the literal mile of books that awaited us.

Our cabins were three cars back. The train resumed its journey as I made my way back through the various rows of private compartments. One larger unit was occupied by a couple with two small children whose bathroom habits had earned them a rather coarse reprimand from Ash. Another was occupied by a reclusive college student who was apparently working diligently on some assignment or other. Then there was the vociferous woman whose position on family planning seemed to favor the complete lack thereof—a position V—— found particularly abhorrent. My partner, despite her age, had a few years back become pregnant, but suffered a tragic miscarriage that ultimately ended her marriage. As a result, V—— had developed very strong feelings concerning the proper need and access for all manner of family planning.

In due course I came to my compartment, slid the door to the side, and then gently rapped on the adjoining cabin door that my partner supposedly occupied. "V——," I called through the partition, "are you there? Ash told me you spent the night at the station. She's bringing you some breakfast. Are you all right?"

There came from the other side a sudden whining noise, as if some animal had sucked in some air. This was followed by a heavy almost labored breathing that finally resolved itself into a voice. "S———, is that you? It is so good to hear your voice. I thought perhaps I might never hear it again."

"What? Of course, it's me, who else would it be?" Her voice seemed thin and haggard. "Stop being so melodramatic." I tried the door, but it was bolted. "Unlock this door."

There then came that sound again, as if something was whining or struggling to breathe. "No, not yet. I want to explain, to prepare you. You need to understand what has happened before you see me like this."

"What are you talking about?" I tried the handle once more with no success. I was growing concerned. Had she been injured in some manner? "Open this door. Whatever has happened, we need to deal with it."

"No, my friend. No, we don't. At least not yet. At least not until I tell my story." She took a thin gasping breath. "Sit down and listen, not for long. Just sit and listen, I won't be long at all."

And so, having little choice in the matter, I did as I was told.

"The sun was low in the west when I stepped off the train. The sky above the setting sun was gray, but the weather did not seem threatening. If it had been, perhaps I would have not decided to linger, but it was a pleasant evening and we had been in the train for so long that I had an overwhelming desire just to get out and get some fresh air; to walk, and to feel the earth beneath my feet. I had checked the timetable and knew that the round trip to the Shoals and back was only a couple of hours. The sign on the station clearly showed the hours of operation to be well past the time of return. It seemed a trivial thing then, to step off the train and walk about for a time, so I did just that. I stood there as the train pulled away, in my good woollen coat, my navy dress, my leather boots, and my clutch, which held a modicum of money, my watch, and a few other odds and ends. One might ask why I had not brought my mobile phone, but as you and I have learned, despite advertisements to the contrary, wireless service throughout the country is not as reliable as one is led to believe, and so my phone was left behind as essentially useless.

"I suppose I should have gone and spoken to the station master, told him that I had disembarked and would be rejoining you on your return. Yes, that would have been the prudent thing to do. It would have prevented much that would come later. But I didn't, and I am damned because of it.

"I walked off the platform, down a set of crumbling concrete stairs, and onto a cracked and weathered pavement that led in the general direction of the small town the train had just skirted on the way in. I thought I might wander down, see what sights Apoka had to offer, and hopefully do a little window shopping. It seemed only a couple of blocks, not a long walk at all. Unfortunately, the first buildings I encountered were decrepit shells, long since abandoned. Undeterred, I continued to walk, hoping that I might eventually encounter some remnant of commercial civilization; yet to my utter dismay, no matter what street I turned down I was met with the same urban blight with shattered windows, broken sidewalks, and rutted streets.

"If all this seems superfluous to my tale, I assure you it is not. As is my habit, I checked my watch and found that I had somehow already used up more than an hour of my allotted time. The train should have completed its run to the Shoals and should have been on the way back. Flabbergasted that I had somehow underestimated the length of my exploration of the blasted streets of Apoka, I began my return to the station at a quickened pace. The sun was now well set, and the streetlights, or what there were of them, had flickered on and attracted the usual influx of flying insects. Those pale flickering lights and the swarms of insects that danced in front of them cast queer and swirling shadows.

"As I approached the station, I caught sight of a man in a faded pea coat bent with age mounting an old-style bicycle. For some reason or other I thought that this must be the station master, though I can't say why—after all, I had never seen the man—and I called out to him and asked him if he was such. He confirmed his identity, and I rushed over to meet him. I can't remember the exact conversation we had, but he informed me that my train had been delayed—a tree or something had fallen on the tracks, and it would take hours to clear. With no passengers waiting for the train, he had closed early and was heading home. I assured him that I was a passenger on that train and explained how I had disembarked for a brief constitutional while the train ran to the Shoals and back. He asked to see my ticket, but of course I had left it in my portfolio on the train. He made it quite clear that without a ticket he could not help me. I offered to buy a new one, just until the confusion could be cleared up, but he shook his head and cast a glance over his shoulder at the moldering station. When I protested and asked if I could spend the night in the station, I swear to you the look on his face was indescribable, as if what I had suggested was something horrifically terrible. Without another word, he pushed his bike into motion and then peddled away as fast as his old legs could move.

"Confused, and more than a little frustrated, I continued back to the decrepit and decaying station platform. I tried one door to the lounge and another to baggage storage, hoping against hope that one or the other had been left unlocked or easily forced, but to no avail. Thwarted, I settled into a wrought-iron bench and began the unenviable task of waiting.

"Surprisingly the bench was rather comfortable, worn in just the right places from years of use, and this combined with the warm embrace of my woollen coat apparently lulled me into a light sleep, from which I barely stirred, at least until I was rudely awakened by a queer barking noise. I shot up immediately, for the sound was not one to which I was accustomed. As I stood there on the platform I heard it again: it was a low-pitched croak or bark that I was sure had not been produced by any bird or amphibian I was familiar with. Indeed, to my ear it was most definitely mammalian in origin, though certainly not any sound made by a dog, cat, or any bovine for that matter. I thought perhaps it might be the product of some species of deer, or their heavier relatives, but when it came a third time I dismissed these possibilities in favor of something far more dangerous. Thinking that I could at any moment encounter a bear, I shrank back into the frame of the door and did my best to remain still and silent.

"It was but a moment later that I heard something large and heavy shuffling about the far end of the station platform, rummaging through the accumulated leaves and trash. It made a curious snuffling sound, and its feet clicked as they walked on the poured concrete. As I listened there seemed to be far too many feet to be just one animal, and so I concluded that there must have been at least two, if not more, making their way toward me. Inevitably, the scrounging, snuffling creatures were, it seemed, just feet from my hiding spot, and as I watched, wisps of hot breath came swirling through the rapidly cooling night air. They were so very close, and I could smell the mephitic stink of musk and garbage that exuded from their bodies. I clamped a hand to my mouth and prepared to run, and fight if need be. But just then there was a snort of surprise, and the creatures seemed to skitter away in the direction they had come.

"Cautiously, I peeked from my hidey-hole to see what beasts I had just avoided. To my surprise it was not a pair of bears, but rather something completely different, something both fascinating and revolting. It was the size of a dog and covered in a sickly pale skin pocked with thick gray bristles and occasional splotches of sickly pink. Its head was not in any manner ursine, but was instead reminiscent of something porcine, particularly of the Indonesian babirusa, with its small ears, oversized curling tusks, and beady crimson eyes. But as strange and wondrous as this pale monstrosity was, the most terrible thing about it was the eight spindly legs that ended in small, clawed hooves. It danced away from me on those queerly numbered appendages. I had mistaken the sound of these as coming from multiple animals rather than a single monstrous individual.

"It was an impossible creature, and I immediately concluded that I was still asleep, trapped in some deeper realm of slumber and enduring some phantasmagorical nightmare. Emboldened, I stepped out to get a better look at the creature, and it dashed off the platform and onto the tracks. It bleated at me with that horrible low-pitched bark and then turned to amble away. My mind at once went to work trying to name such a creature. You will recall my fondness for archaic words, and from my lexicon I recalled an old word for hog, *mucc,* and another for spider, *cob,* and thus the creature was quickly given the name mucc-kob, or muckob. The fact that this was a near homophone with *macabre* made the naming even more appropriate.

"Intrigued, I followed the muckob as it skittered down the tracks. It was aware of me but did not seem particularly concerned about my presence. Indeed, if anything it seemed annoyed, not with me following it, but rather with the slow pace at which I was moving. It would on occasion dash forward and then snort at me as if urging me on. I was rather cautious and kept my distance, fearful that the thing might turn and charge. It was a fascinating thing to watch, for it had a strange rhythm to the placement of its legs, one over the other but somehow never tripping over the number of appendages that it moved with grace and fluidity.

"About one hundred yards from the station, the beast left the tracks and made its way down a rough trail into the pit mine that dominated the landscape. Having nothing better to do and assured by the sheer wonder of the thing that this was a dream, I followed it down the descending path carved by centuries of men plundering treasures of the earth. The path cut through limestone rock laid down by some ancient ocean, the walls crowded with shells of long-extinct bivalves and whelks and conchs of titanic proportions. As fascinating as this was, it paled before the wonder of the thing that galloped and pranced down the trail in front of me.

"We followed that serpentine path, ever deeper, and I paused to glance back and up at the hint of artificial light left still seeping over the edge of the pit. I thought that now was the time to turn back, but then the damned thing bleated out once more, and like Odysseus to the siren I turned and followed. This was an apt analogy, for it wasn't but a few minutes later that we reached a large plateau strewn with rocks and boulders, and my erstwhile guide dashed up the side of one, skittering like some giant tarantula before turning and bellowing. There then came another bellow, then a third, and fourth, and again more skittering. Before long I was surrounded by four of the monstrous things, all holding positions high above my head.

"Cautiously I bent down and picked up a good-sized chunk of limestone and made a show of tossing it up and down in my hand. I thought this would act as a deterrent, but instead it seemed to galvanize them into action. In strange unison they shrieked, and as they did so their hindquarters rose and bent up over their heads and I could see a strange cluster of black and chitinous teats between their thighs dangling in the air above their heads. I steeled myself for the worst, but at that exact moment there came another horrific noise, deeper and louder than the bellows of the quartet of muckobs. They paused in their imminent attack and then scattered off into the darkness beyond, their multipronged hooves like some cacophonous, hellish tap dance.

"I turned to face the direction of the noise that had scattered my attackers and saw a man of some stature, cloaked in a tattered robe. He had the physique of a roughneck or a miner, with broad shoulders and massive thick legs that rippled in the dim starlight as he stalked intently forward. I hefted my rock once more, but at the same time called out a word of thanks to my rescuer. He said nothing, but carefully and deliberately kept walking toward me. His stride was immense, and he closed the distance quickly despite my taking several cautious steps backwards. It was only when he was within arm's length that I saw those beady red eyes and the tusks that framed his jaw and recognized him for what he was. I caught a brief glimpse as the tattered cloak fell away and his six spindly arms reached out to grab me with hoof-like claws, before I collapsed into blessed unconsciousness.

"I know it was only hours for you, but I lived an entire, tortured lifetime in that wasteland, and I need you to know that when I awoke after He took me . . . everything was different, I had a purpose. I will spare you all the grotesque details, but you need to understand that for decades we lived by the dim light of distant and dying stars and a sickly moon. We ate infrequently, scavenging the grotesque fungal growths that seemed to gestate like tumors in this strange twilight desert, and we drank the thick soupy dew that gathered inside the gills and crevices of fat toadstools. I endured unimaginable pains and fought for our survival more than once. Then one day I by chance caught a glimpse of the rim of the pit, and the artificial light that glowed weakly from beyond—and I remembered! I remembered my life from before the pit and resolved that we should return to it. It took us what felt like days, but I finally made my way up and out, and scrambled down the tracks just before the sun rose. I found the station and the old wrought-iron bench and, burden in hand, I fell asleep briefly before the arrival of the train woke me and I dashed aboard."

"Gods, what a nightmare!" I said. "But you're back now, and safe. Ash is on the way with food and coffee."

"A nightmare," V—— repeated, "I wish it had been." And then I heard her rise and unbolt the door before she fell back down into the chair. Again I heard that queer wheezing noise.

I opened the door carefully, and there was my friend, barely alive, her face pale and thin, her hair gone iron-gray with age. She was wrapped loosely in what looked to be her woollen jacket, though it was threadbare and torn and stained with age. I could see that her neck and shoulders were covered with dozens upon dozens of thick scars, and her once delicate fingers were worn, calloused, and bent at improbable angles.

She smiled at me and revealed a mouth full of shattered teeth. "Hello, my friend," she whimpered with her dying breath. "I had hoped to see you one last time."

I rushed to her side, but only in time for her to clutch my hand. Then she exhaled and there was this terrible death rattle, and my friend and companion closed her eyes and died. I wish that was the end of things, but it wasn't, for as I knelt beside her I heard again that queer wheezing sound. It was coming from beneath her coat. I stared, frozen with fear over what might be found beneath the now ancient leather, and that fear grew greater when I saw something shift beneath. I lifted the flap of her coat and was astounded to find that she wore an outfit made of strange skins, crudely stitched together, from which hung something squirming wrapped in a makeshift blanket or tarp.

I turned back into my own cabin just as Ash came in. She had set the tray down on the table behind me. She must have seen the thing in the blanket move, for she commented on the fact that animals were not allowed on the train. I realized as she moved forward that she had heard none of what V—— had said and did not know my friend had expired.

Then her hand reached out and she drew part of the blanket away. The thing was almost exactly as V—— had described, and it shrieked as it bolted from my hands. Its beady eyes were filled with hate as it screeched at us. Although so young, there were still thick and ugly bristles scattered all over its body. It skittered up the wall and hung in the corner as it worked its jaws with their tiny tusks to try and threaten Ash and me. I was livid with fear and frozen by the horrific spectacle of what I was witnessing. Thankfully, Ash was of sounder mind than I. She pulled the heavy metal tray off the table, sending the coffee and food crashing to the floor, and then in the same fluid movement arced that makeshift weapon over her head into the corner, smashing the monstrous thing off the wall.

It fell, stunned as it hit the floor, and curled up into a little ball, mewling in fear or pain. Ash was pitiless and unrelenting. Showing no fear, she stepped toward the window and with a single hand unlatched it and let it drop open. Then, with the tray acting as a makeshift shovel, she scooped up the monstrous thing my friend had called a muckob and flung it out the opening. In a last desperate act, it grabbed the frame with one of its long, spindly appendages and tried to claw its way back in, but Ash smashed those delicate fingers with the metal tray and the creature lost its grip and was lost to the landscape as the train sped away.

Ash closed the window and turned to me, clearly attempting to maintain a sense of composure and decorum in the face of the bizarre. "Are you all right, Mr. S——? It's over now. Nothing to worry about."

But there was something to worry about, something the thought of which gnawed at me. V—— had described the monstrous things—the muckobs—as having hooves, but this thing had fingers, long delicate fingers. Fingers that were reminiscent of V——'s own graceful hands. Why did it have her fingers? And why—why had she wrapped it in a blanket and clutched it so dearly to her breast?

And why, when I ask such questions, do none dare answer?

Hangman's Coming

L. E. Daniels

June 1891, Sargasso Sea

Two weeks into her transatlantic voyage from Napoli to New Orleans, the *S.S. Algiers* sat dead in the water for hours, propellors tangled in an arterial mat of seaweed thick as cable and the color of jaundice.

Sixteen-year-old Grazia sat sweating on a bench with a cluster of Sicilian mothers, all with fussing children in their laps. Across the table, two women passed a whimpering four-month-old from one to the other to breastfeed him, as his own mother couldn't produce enough milk. More than two hundred steerage passengers were gathered at the long tables of the humid dining area, nearest to the ventilation of the stairs and away from the stench of seasickness wafting from the bunks lining the vast, windowless space.

"The gulf weed. You see it out there," said Peter, an old Norwegian sailor. Letters in faded blue ink spelled H-O-L-D and F-A-S-T across his knuckles. "Between the warmer water and the weed, our engines overheat. The weed grabs the propellors." He gestured with his fists. "It's in the machines."

Grazia had been on the steerage deck for sunlight and fresh air when the engines' familiar drone choked to a stop. From the rail she saw that ochre weed, so dense that she wondered if she could walk to New Orleans from here.

Beside Peter, a lineup of men translated in turn into Russian, Turkish, Spanish, and Hungarian for their groups, their ticket class apparent from the way their best clothes now hung damp and loose.

Nearby, Grazia's older sister, Maria, translated for the Italians. Grazia and Maria's uncle, Zio Ernesto, a teacher who had lived for a decade in America, had taught his nieces some English—another reason to leave their withering Sicilian village. With their mother's death and their father taken by illness years ago, Zio paid for their passage with the little he had. He used his connections to find them work at a New Orleans *pasticceria* and *caffè* where they would make biscotti, *sfogliatelle,* and tiramisu, just as their mother had taught them. The owners, also Sicilian, would pay them in real American money, not Elodie cigar bands as some opportunists did. The same day Zio showed the sisters their steerage tickets, news broke from New Orleans: a mob of ten thousand angry men shot and hanged eleven Italians from lampposts in the street and mutilated their bodies. When the news reached Sicily, Zio and the sisters knelt on the floor and wept, but still they packed.

Each of the translators finished their descriptions and looked at Peter.

"The engineers are fixing it," he said, scratching at his beard, "but they need time. Now we wait. Maybe one day, maybe two. Don't overheat down here. Go out and get some air but come back inside at night. There's plenty of food and water."

Grazia watched sweat bead on the sailor's furrowed brow. Most of these passengers had brought their own provisions and carefully rationed them, but nearing the end of their voyage supplies had dwindled.

"And for the last time, yes, the water is safe." Anger flashed in Peter's ice-blue eyes as he spoke slowly, deliberately. "The food . . . is safe."

Back home, while Grazia and Maria had struggled to fit everything they could into two suitcases each, the sisters gathered as much bread and hard cheese as they could carry. Zio had warned them that immigrants weren't wanted, even as steamship fares were cordially collected. All they had to do was enter "fever" on the ship's manifest and . . . *è finita. Sepoltura in mare.* Burial at sea.

"You need to eat," the old sailor said. "Stay healthy. When we get to New Orleans, if you look sick, they turn you right back."

The translators took it in turns and Peter continued, "The first- and second-class passengers up top are going to march right off this ship into the streets with someone carrying their bags. You must look well when you get into port. Understand?"

Peter looked down at the baby being passed back to his mother and said, "Look." He pointed. "Which one is the mother?"

Maria hesitated to translate. The baby's mother, Agata, clutched her infant, Antonio. She was Maria's age, eighteen, and traveling alone to a husband who waited for her in New Orleans. Now her hair was stringy and askew. Her chin and cheekbones looked sharp.

Peter repeated his question and flattened his palms on the table.

Maria shot a pained look at Grazia and slowly translated.

Several of the older women locked eyes with Peter. One drew an arm protectively around Agata and Antonio. The young mother looked as if she'd been shaken from a dream, the circles under her eyes suddenly savage. One of the older women stood, and Peter backed off until she reclaimed her seat.

"You must eat," Peter said. "That is all I am saying. All of you."

In that dampening lamplight Grazia felt the room shift, and she grew more aware of the water beneath them. The passengers' faces looked more shadowed in that instant; they seemed to age before her eyes. She turned to Peter's face to see him twitch, take another step back, and fold his arms around a proud belly.

Across from Grazia, an American stockman in his thirties named Frank dropped his elbows on the table and sighed with some force.

"They're not gonna eat your food," he said. "They'll die first, and you know it. Besides, the water stinks."

"Is this how you help them?" Peter tilted his head. "We're stuck. Look at them all. The babies."

"So fix the problem." Frank scowled. On his shoulder a black raven puffed and panted, its breast feathers plucked in patches, a long leather cord wrapped around its feet. It spoke occasionally and was a welcome mascot when *balalaika* notes had strummed over the drone of the engines. Now the bird chittered weird incantations, and Grazia wondered how Frank could stand it.

Grazia remembered Frank's warmth at the start of their voyage. He had charmed the Sicilian mothers, but not too much, and they let him sit with them, so long as he didn't get too cozy. Early on, Grazia noticed how Frank had gravitated toward anyone who spoke English. He told the sisters he preferred the community of steerage, but once the seasickness started and people withdrew into themselves, Grazia and Maria knew something hadn't worked out for him in Europe. This was all he could afford to get home.

The sailor clapped his hands together, startling the raven, and said, "Righto, that's everything then. Report any fever or pox. We'll send down fresh food and drinking water within the hour."

The raven grumbled, an earthy mix that sounded like an old man considering murder. Frank stroked the bird's beak into silence.

Peter wiped the sweat from his forehead and had started to climb the stairs when the Russian translator tapped his arm.

"Aye." The sailor sucked in a deep breath. "We'll send another mop and bucket for the seasick."

With little more than a rustle the passengers dispersed, and Maria took a seat next to Frank. Grazia wanted now only to creep out of this potbellied stove up to the steerage-class deck where she could breathe. If it was packed with passengers, she could watch the sunset from the promenade railing as she dangled her feet over the sea—anything for a breeze.

But she had to wait. The mothers were still convening about the food situation and watched over the sisters like a ring of owls. Grazia and Maria followed all Zio's instructions, the first of which was to embed themselves with a group of nursing mothers for safety. At sixteen and eighteen, they needed protection; and few things in this world were as fierce as a pack of Sicilian mothers with babes in arms.

Maria rested her chin on her palm. Frank opened a book. The raven preened under its clipped wings. Grazia pulled her worn Tarot deck from her dress pocket and shuffled the cards absently. The women watched her vaguely, then looked away to comfort Agata, none of them asking her to *"Mi leggi le carte,"* to read cards for them like before. Maybe they were tired of seeing all those swords. They knew life ahead of them would be anything but easy.

Just then a card slipped from Grazia's hands and fell onto the table.

L'Appeso. The Hanged Man. 11.

On the card a lone figure faced away from her—strung up from a tree by a noose, hands bound, shoeless, his coat as blue as the sea.

Grazia looked up to see an opaque sadness clouding Maria's eyes.

The raven fluffed its feathers and looked sideways at the table. In a low, graveled voice it said, *"Hangman's coming."*

Just before midnight Grazia sat along the promenade at the rail, bare feet dangling. Peter had told everyone to come in at night as they couldn't hear or see anyone go overboard, but the heat below was stagnant and the smell unbearable. Passengers' bodies soured in the heat below and babies howled. If anyone slept, it was desperate and fitful.

Frank and Maria joined Grazia under the lights at the rail and the raven held its jagged wings aloft and seemed to imagine a wobbly flight. Agata and Antonio joined them, and Maria gestured Agata to turn her back to her and braided her hair. For a moment everything that felt so dangerous in their world dissipated as the night air slid over the Sargasso Sea like silk. The tide rolled softly against the hull below them, and a half-moon hung in a deep, starry sky and a streaked river of milk unfurled overhead.

No one spoke. No one needed to.

And Grazia was grateful for their company.

The baby dozed on Agata's shoulder while Maria finished the braid with a *"Perfetta."*

Suddenly Agata held Antonio tighter and stood. She waved her free hand before her nose and asked, *"Lo senti, quello? Cos'è quell'odore?"* Do you smell that? What's that smell?

Maria laughed and said she truly had a mother's nose. Mothers can smell anything from miles away.

Agata shook her head and insisted something foul was on the air.

The raven grumbled and called out, as if it sensed something too. Frank put a hand on the bird to settle it, his fingers tangled up on the cord that bound it to him.

Grazia stood and looked out into the dark sea. Maria and Frank lined up at the rail, silent.

"*Sì, sì,*" Grazia said. "*Eccolo.*"

"I smell it now." Maria winced, clutching the rail.

"Oh, there it is." Frank stroked the raven. "Sweet Jesus, it smells like death. Where's it coming from?"

"*Hangman's coming,*" the bird cried out, dropping feathers in the salty breeze.

"Shush, Edgar!" Frank whispered, patting its beak, but the bird struck out and stabbed his hand. "Ouch! Calm yourself now." He examined his hand in the light. The bird had drawn blood.

Maria took Frank's hand, but he pulled it away, saying, "It's all right."

Out on the horizon lightning flashed, illuminating a distant silhouette.

"*Che cos'è?*" Agata pointed into the vast darkness.

"What is that?" Frank craned his neck. "I saw something. A ship?"

Grazia wasn't sure. A crackle hung in the air, and the scent of ozone bled into the stench, stronger now.

Just then a groan traveled over the roll of the tide, something primal and throaty like a birthing mother, and Grazia felt a chill comb over her bones. The passengers had heard whales earlier on the journey. A large, melodious orchestra began one night around the dinner hour that swept through the hull and frightened everyone, but Peter came down and explained so they could enjoy it. Those rumbling purrs rattled Grazia's innards, and the round, swirling squeaks made the babies laugh.

But not this. This was something else.

No one made a sound. Even the bird was still as a stone, beak aimed at the void like a compass needle shining in the steamship's shivering lights.

Another flash on the horizon, and something appeared closer this time—a hulk of some sort, an old ship from a forgotten time. It looked broken. Gaping holes in the hull flowed with foamy seawater, sloshing it back to its source. It didn't make sense. Then it was gone, swallowed by the dark.

The water beneath them pooled as they waited; poised, silent. The baby stirred and let out a weak cry against his mother's shoulder.

Another flash, and the hulk had drawn closer again before it disappeared in the darkness.

A score of terrible sounds rippled over the black sea, this time clearer. Layers of cries and twisted moans shattered the air.

"Mi sento male." Agata said she felt sick.

"What was that? Are we moving?" Maria clung to Grazia's arm. "I did not think we were moving."

"We're not moving," Frank said, holding the bird now. "It's moving. Toward us."

Grazia's fingers tightened around the rail. Again a flash of lightning and the hulk was closer and the smell, like a wet, gray eruption of decay, peppered the air.

The bird shouted, *"Hangman's coming!"*

With just enough moonlight now, the hulk emerged from the shadows and grew into its stature as some kind of battered, early-century wooden sailing bark. It cut though the current without wind or sail. Of its three masts, the foremast and rear mizzen were splintered and half gone. From the middle mainmast objects swung like fruit, and they were not tattered sails. The rigging and shrouds supporting that mast gleamed wet in the gloom, and all around where the ship met the water a fog boiled like steam.

The ship was moving at speed. Not just toward the *S.S. Algiers,* but the hulk's body itself was writhing with movement. Like bugs. Sea lice. The skin of a horse shaking off flies. Nothing made sense. All four of them stood staring at its approach. Grazia's eyes burned from refusing to blink.

The *Algiers'* horn blared overhead, and both the raven and infant screamed.

Closer still, the bark was headed for them. It was clear what was moving on board.

Instead of wood, the ship was composed of bodies. Groaning, stinking bodies. Human arms and legs and torsos and faces blended together as the patchwork flesh of the ship. All colors of flesh, slick with seawater, barnacled and crusted with salt. The ship was locked onto the *Algiers,* shrieking and headed swiftly to impact the steamer.

All four of them clutched the rail, no chance to retreat below where they might have been safe. The bark turned about rapidly, sidelong to the steamer, and slammed into it.

Grazia was knocked off her feet. Maria, Frank, and Agata were strewn about the promenade, the infant squalling in his mother's grip. A series of splashes and bumps reverberated along the side of the steel ship, and a deafening scraping sound squealed as the hulk bashed and slid against the steamer. The devilish stench exploded.

Grazia looked up. From the remaining mast's shimmering yards—eye-level in the lamplight now—half a dozen bodies swung, bloated, gull-pecked, and spinning in the night air.

Where Grazia had hung her feet and along the rail, there was movement. Disjointed fingers slid. Then hands. Arms reached over the side, and when Grazia looked down, bodies formed chains like ant bridges and were reaching into the ship. Lightning cracked as the slapping sound of flesh filled her ears.

The sisters huddled against the promenade floor. Frank shielded Agata and her baby. Grazia grabbed Agata by the elbow to pull her and Antonio back.

Peter shouted in Norwegian and appeared behind them. He clamped his thick hands on the sisters and tried to drag them from the scene, but Agata was seized about the shoulders by ghoulish, tremorous limbs. Grazia held on, even as tissue dripping with seafoam slipped around both the mother's and baby's throats. It tightened. And pulled.

Agata whipped around, eyes pleading with Grazia. Antonio opened his mouth but didn't make a sound. The raven flapped about until Frank released the leather cord and the bird toppled over the rail, tail spinning into the seething deck below.

Snaking limbs rode up Frank's trouser legs and wound up around his neck.

Peter tugged hard on Grazia, and she let go of the young mother.

"Agata!" Grazia screamed as mother and infant were dragged, flailing over the rail, Frank kicking and close behind them.

Maria sobbed an ungodly wail, something that reminded Grazia of home, of their father's fists, of burying their mother in the dusty churchyard without their father beside them.

With a hard shove, Peter pushed the sisters toward the stairs and slammed the door.

By morning, the crew counted eleven steerage passengers missing—Agata, her baby Antonio, and Frank among them. No mark was left on the *Algiers* and not a single passenger from the upper decks was touched.

By noon, the steamship's engines burst back to life and black smoke poured once again from the stacks without celebration. With a heave, they were on their way to New Orleans.

Peter sat, hands on his knees on the steerage deck. Grazia and Maria were perched on wooden deck chairs beside him, bruised all over, their eyes puffy and sore.

Grazia hadn't said a word since she called Agata's name. She turned to Peter. "What was it? Tell me."

The old sailor shook his head and said nothing. Overhead a seabird kept up with the ship, a sign they were already closer to shore.

"Prego," Grazia said. "Please, Peter."

"The Sargasso." Peter breathed the word. "The water, it goes round and round. Things get caught in it and we can see things . . . a terrible, unknowable dark. My years at sea tell me it has a taste for the terrors we create. It is not a good place."

"But where is Frank? Where is Agata?" Grazia couldn't say the baby's name.

"I don't know." Peter dropped his head into his hands and slipped into his native language. *"Beklager,"* he said. *"Beklager,* Grazia. I'm sorry."

Grazia stood and went to the rail alone.

Behind them, the Sargasso sparkled and spun like an eye; a wide, cruel eye seeing everything and reflecting it for those who made the real darkness in the world.

Resistant to Change

Adrian Ludens

"I've just returned from debunking a supernatural legend," our host announced without preamble. We sat in silence, knowing our host would take his time in the telling of his tale. Such was his habit, much as we were accustomed to serving as his attentive audience.

"Some years back I gained secondhand knowledge of a remarkable journal discovered by fishermen among some fallen ruins that lay on the cliffs of a remote location of the Irish coast. Among the fantastic revelations, the author claimed horrible human-sized pig creatures with dead-white skin emerged from a nearby fissure in the earth and carried out a series of assaults on his home.

"After my harrowing ordeal in the case of The Hog, I felt a keen desire to locate and read the journal for myself. Unfortunately, I was never able to learn the journal's current whereabouts. I found I had the opportunity to visit the site of the purported events and did so without the benefit of my electric pentacle, or anything else that could be carried with me. Instead, I spoke a protective incantation from the pages of the Sigsand Manuscript and approached the ruins.

"Precious few traces remain of the journal writer's home. I could just make out the uppermost blocks of stone from my position at the edge of the precipice. Mossy growth gave the stones a stunning emerald hue. I got the impression the earth was swallowing the remnants into itself, as if eager to be rid of any remaining trace of the structure's existence.

"Imagine my surprise when I turned from the chasm and found myself face to face with an elderly woman. She had the harried countenance of a spinster tasked with maintaining a large household, and a frame that spoke of a lifetime of hard work.

"'I suppose you've heard the stories,' the old woman said.

"I admitted that I had and inquired her name.

"'Catherine Byrne,' she replied. 'I lived here for many years with my brother, Martin. People in the village said he was mad. They were right.'

"I asked her to elaborate, and she willingly complied."

"My brother always had his eccentricities" (the old woman said), "but after his betrothed broke their engagement and left the country with a foreign suitor, Martin took a sharp turn for the worse. He used all his savings to purchase this remote residence and withdrew from human contact. Worried about his welfare, I moved in with him. I kept the house clean, cooked meals, and received supplies from the village once a month. I purchased a dog for Martin to serve as a companion. Pepper, her name was. Very perceptive dog. She learned to tell when one of his dark spells threatened to overtake him and would bark to alert me.

"Regrettably, his dark spells rarely cleared, and Martin seemed to be living in a world of his own creation. I know he kept a journal though I never invaded his privacy to read its contents. I gained enough understanding of his delusions just by interacting with him each day.

"He claimed the room changed colors around him, and that he floated like a bubble across time and space. Martin said he visited a land where our home was hewn of jade stone and a red-wreathed sun hung in the sky. My brother spoke of mountains encircling us on all sides, and huge stone idols of ghastly horrors crowning the mountaintops.

"A quick glance around us shows nothing of the sort, as you can see. I learned not to argue or try to coerce him into talking sensibly. The times I challenged him he grew very agitated, even violent. This set Pepper into a frenzy; the poor girl didn't know which of us to side with. So I kept silent, feigning confusion or ignorance whenever Martin questioned me while in the throes of his madness.

"I did what I could for him. I kept him fed and crushed herbs into his tea to help him sleep. But one day the situation took a dramatic turn for the worse. I'd been picking vegetables in the garden, and when I returned to the house I found the door locked. I knocked gently at first, but having received no response, I pounded on the door. I pressed my face to the glass and shielded my eyes from the glare of the sun. Martin stood in the foyer. He saw me, but in his eyes I saw only fear and madness. His clenched fists and rigid posture conveyed his revulsion toward me. I retreated to the yard. My brother raised a window in his study. As I watched, he pushed a closed umbrella through the opening and shrieked. I heard Pepper barking wildly. My only desire was to calm them both, so I sat down in the grass. I wanted to appear as non-threatening as possible. This seemed to placate Martin. He closed the window and Pepper quieted. But when I rose, my brother was right back at the window with the umbrella, and intuition told me he believed he was shooting a weapon. I perceived then that he viewed me as some sort of threat, an invader. I kept sitting down every time he screamed. Finally I gave up and hurried away to the village.

"When I returned at sundown, Martin, to my great relief, let me inside the house. He seemed more lucid, but aghast that I'd been out. He warned me of 'hideous pale Swine-Things' that had tried to invade the house. This would have wounded my self-pride had I not made peace with myself regarding my looks in my younger years.

"Several days passed before he gathered up the courage to explore the yard and garden with Pepper. I watched surreptitiously from an upper window. He seemed fascinated by a small crevice in the yard between the house and the cliffs above the sea. It was simple erosion, you see. But Martin busied himself with its exploration like a child at play. At last he raced into the house and down the stairs to the root cellar dug into the basement floor. I eavesdropped from the stairwell and heard him muttering about water-filled tunnels and a deep abyss.

"His final descent into permanent madness came rapidly. He raved day and night, refused to eat, and most of the time seemed to forget I was even in the house with him. From his ravings, I gleaned several pieces of information. He believed his former love was dead and thought she had somehow visited him; he believed he had either seen the future or traveled forward in time; and he also convinced himself that Pepper had died, and that he'd acquired a new, nameless dog. He loved Pepper, you understand. I believe the sudden dissolution of their camaraderie and his refusal to call her by name hurt all three of us in varying ways. It was as if he had taken a step toward separating himself from his own humanity.

"I don't claim to be a martyr. I did my best to coexist peacefully, making him comfortable and going about the daily household chores as unobtrusively as possible. I found, in keeping with my habits, a technique to cope with Martin's prolonged descent into madness.

"One afternoon Martin happened upon me petting Pepper, and he flew into a rage. I realized he took me for one of his imaginary Swine-Things again and that he intended me harm. My love for my brother overruled my sense of self-preservation. I grasped his thrashing arms and tried to talk sensibly, imploring him to recognize me. It didn't work. He struck my face, and I admitted defeat and fled to my bedroom, locking the door behind me.

"I heard Martin pacing and lamenting about a 'luminous fungus' growing on his arms before he must have retired to his study. He quieted, and I guessed he was writing again in his mad journal. Not content to hide in my room, I crept to the cellar to retrieve some jars of canned fruit and vegetables to restock the kitchen pantry. I craved normalcy, as I have said. When I climbed out of the cellar, Martin was standing there waiting for me. He'd broken the leg off a wooden chair and brandished it, as if to strike.

"For the first time I truly panicked. I dropped the jars, and they shattered. My brother approached, and in his eyes I saw a tortured soul longing for release. I stooped and retrieved a large glass shard with which to defend myself. But I'd decided I also wanted to help him.

"We both lunged simultaneously . . ."

"The old woman trailed off and I understood her tale had reached its end," Carnacki said.

"So the contents of the journal were nothing more than morbid fancies?" Jessop asked.

"Just so." Our host sat ruminating in his customary chair, though someone had draped it with a white dust cloth in his absence.

"What of Martin Byrne, then?" Taylor stood near the empty hearth.

"His spirit did not present itself," Carnacki said. "I can only surmise he has moved on."

"At least this Byrne fellow is finally at peace," Jessop offered.

"One hopes."

I thought our host was being evasive about something. Then it struck me. "Wait a minute," I said. "How old is this journal?"

"It dates back many years," Carnacki said.

"How is it possible this old woman survived her brother's attack, survived the subsequent collapse of the house, and was conveniently waiting for you at a remote location just at the time of your arrival?"

"I wondered who would notice first, Dodgson," Carnacki said. He favored me with a wan smile over his tented fingers. "In my professional opinion, the entity that spoke to me at the ruins was not a living human being."

"Good heavens!" Jessop said. "You mean to say a ghost debunked the legend?"

"A spectral manifestation of Catherine Byrne, yes." Carnacki gave a small nod.

"Why hasn't her spirit moved on?" I wondered aloud. It was true that Catherine Byrne might have found peace after speaking with Carnacki, but I have no way of knowing.

"Somehow she must be resistant to what I can only describe as The Change," Carnacki said. "Perhaps she is still on a quest for earthly knowledge."

"She still has stories to tell," Taylor said.

"Questions to be asked and answered," Jessop added.

"Possibly she is simply not yet ready to move on," I said.

"Because there is still much to learn about the living side of the human condition," Carnacki finished.

We mused in contemplative silence. One by one our eyes drifted to the cloth-covered armchair that had been Arkwright's customary place.

As if reading our collective thoughts, Carnacki said, "Do you suppose Arkwright has achieved a greater understanding of The Change now that he is apart from us?"

Perhaps it was meant as a rhetorical question, perhaps not. None of us hazarded a reply.

The silence in the room unwound like thread from a spool.

Change isn't easy to accept. I believe this to be true for many people. I considered Catherine Byrne and Arkwright. They seemed to me to be placed on opposite sides of the same coin. Her spirit seemed to look backward. Did our old friend look forward?

Someday, perhaps we'd all be reunited and I'd get a chance to ask him. After all, Arkwright couldn't live forever.

A Disturbance in the Field

Steve Rasnic Tem

He never anticipated how cold it would get during the spring nights. He was tempted to leave the fire burning, but what if there was a mishap while he was sleeping? There might be danger from smoke inhalation, although he wasn't familiar enough with fireplaces to know for sure. It seemed ironic to worry about fire or smoke taking his life.

Darkness came quickly up here, and then the cold. The air was thinner than it was in Denver. Sometimes he woke up in the middle of the night, afraid he couldn't breathe. The world itself felt sheer, the tops of the trees ragged with disintegration, the fields and mountains only slightly more substantial than the fog.

While he slept, threats multiplied, spread abnormality throughout his world, and destroyed time.

Late in the afternoon, as Rhys gazed across the broad expanse of upland valley, he imagined himself walking through that interminable park of sagebrush and tall grasses, crossing the shiny thread of stream, then hiking up the steady incline into the dark green bands of spruce and fir and the snowy peaks beyond. Of course, he didn't have the stamina, not even when he was younger. He added one more item to his list of things he would never do.

His cabin was tucked into the forest along one elevated edge of the park. On his final phone call to his sister he'd tried to explain that in Colorado a mountain park was the term they used for those wide-open stretches between peaks. From his front window he could see elk and fox, deer, and the occasional bobcat. This view was his alone. His closest neighbors lived on the other side of the mountain.

"Rhys, you've always complained about not having enough friends, and now you've decided to become a hermit?"

"I'm fine, Sis. I'm not aiming to be a recluse. At least not permanently." He paused. He hated lying to her. "I need time away from all the noise."

He changed the subject, chattered on about the Ute and Arapaho tribes who might have traveled through here, how an inland sea once covered this land during the Cretaceous before the mountains rose, and his hopes of finding dinosaur fossils, which were abundant in Colorado. He never got around to telling her his news, the main reason for the call.

His cancer diagnosis wasn't a shock. This was the end phase he'd anticipated all his life. If anything, he'd expected it sooner. Both their parents died from the disease, different types but with the same derangement of cells. Rhys and his sister never talked about death, or their health, or anything potentially frightening. He hoped she was okay. She was the only person in the world who loved him.

After his diagnosis it took a few months to find the right property, a wilderness plot with a burned-out cabin abandoned since the eighties. The previous owner died in the fire. Given his own circumstances, that bit of information didn't bother him. Much of the old foundation was reusable and his builders could follow the original layout of the rooms. Upgrading the road, restoring the well, and extending electrical and phone lines cost more than rebuilding the cabin itself. Rhys drove up to the property in an old camper where he lived until the work was complete.

Rhys stayed friendly with the laborers working on his new home. Maybe he was a pain in the ass. He didn't have enough social smarts to tell. But he wanted them to know how important this project was to him.

One of those workers, a short stocky guy sporting a bushy gray beard, came to him carrying a battered metal box. "It was hidden behind one of the foundation stones. I reckon the fire still got to it."

The box was the only thing they found from the cabin's previous existence. At least they didn't find any of the former owner's bones, for which Rhys was grateful.

The contents stank. Inside was a handmade sketch book, a warped leather cover wrapped around loose pages cockled and discolored, the bundle tied with brittle leather cords that broke when he tried to untie them. Fire had singed the cover, and many of the pages were moldy.

He peeled the pages apart one by one. Some were blank, whatever they'd had on them washed and faded, but if he held those at a certain angle he could see the impressions of pencil marks. He couldn't quite make out whatever they were meant to portray: long necks and massive bodies on some animal species he did not recognize? It was hard to say. The pages did conjure some bizarre imagery in his imagination, even with little visible. And on one page another one of those long-necked creatures with long flippers, and a scrawled word, *Plesiosaur.*

He studied the sketchbook the whole of one afternoon, trying to decipher more, then threw it in the trash due to the smell.

Once the cabin was done and the workers gone, Rhys was grateful to be able to move in. He had a few pieces—a bed, a nice table to go beneath the big window, a long sofa—delivered for an exorbitant fee. The empty camper, an eyesore, squatted on one side of the cabin. He could plant a few bushes to disguise it.

He spent the first few days reading from the box of books he'd brought from the city, all that remained of a once extensive library. It seemed foolish: he should be exploring this beautiful new environment. But he was nervous about going outside, venturing into these woods, and he found comfort in these volumes of Tolkien, Eddison, Burroughs, Hodgson, and others. He'd also brought along *A Guide to Colorado's Dinosaur Fossils.*

He had a journal for capturing his thoughts about his final days. He'd always kept a journal. But although he sat down to write every day, the words refused to come. This was seriously disappointing; he'd been denied words at the very time they were most important.

He'd brought a few art supplies: pencils, pens, watercolors, a stack of good-quality paper. He wasn't particularly good, but he enjoyed sketching. One morning he grabbed a sheet and made a few lines, which led to other lines, shapes, foreground, middle ground, and background. He found these spontaneous compositions oddly satisfying. He sketched the nearby trees, and an elk, and then he attempted to draw the wonderful landscape spread out before him, using ink and watercolor. It wasn't easy to capture. His hand kept wandering around, drawing vague shapes, gestures, suggesting objects which weren't there, or at least weren't there when he looked up to check their position.

Thinking of the sketchbook he'd thrown away, Rhys went into the camper and cut a big piece of leather from a bench cushion, wrapped it around his stack of paper, and tied it with two of his leather boot laces.

Every morning the valley filled with fog, often burning off by noon but sometimes not. It was what they called upslope, or "Cheyenne" fog. The sloping terrain lifts the air, cooling it until the fog forms at the higher elevations then builds downward into the valley. Some days Rhys couldn't see the wooded ridge on the opposite side of the park until midafternoon.

This was disappointing as much of the attraction of his final home was the view. He tried venturing out in the mornings, wearing a jacket because the fog had a cooling effect even during the first days of summer, but he felt uncomfortable with the limited visibility, and the color of the fog, which was reddish, like wildfire smoke. When he gazed upward the fog looked tumultuous, aggressive, and appeared to be eating the trees.

Living in the final stages of cancer, in the mountains in near isolation, was an exercise in delicate balances. Some unfortunate change could tip the balance and create inconvenience, discomfort, or disaster. A persistent ache, disguisable with medication, was what first sent Rhys to the doctor, and for a time afterwards he still felt little pain, which magnified the surrealness of his diagnosis. Now, months later, the pain had increased, along with a pronounced fatigue, and Rhys found himself dipping into his "magic sack"—a black mesh bag containing a variety of swallowables, edibles, and injectables (not all legally obtained)—with increasing frequency. The last thing he wanted to do was diminish this experience, but he also didn't want to suffer.

The first sign of trouble in his environment was a change in the well water. What had once been clear and refreshing developed an increasingly bitter aftertaste, and one afternoon while he filled a pot in the sink, the fluid coming out of the faucet resembled a darkening bruise. Startled, Rhys poured it down the drain. But worse, there appeared to be a thickening, and odd signs of resistance as the water disappeared. He went into the bathroom, gazed into the toilet, and flushed it. More corrupted water filled the bowl, this time with definite signs of swimmers, although he couldn't quite make out their exact forms in the dark water until one raised its slender head and stared at him. He flushed and flushed again until he could find no more evidence of the slippery invaders.

Rhys kept a list of local service people by his phone. The recorded message at one plumber's number indicated he was away for the season. The other, a woman this time, answered but apologized because it would be at least three weeks before she could get to his job.

Perhaps if he'd been thinking clearly he would have hired someone to drive up from Denver or Grand Junction. Luckily, Rhys kept a month's supply of purified spring water in his larder. Although the idea was unpleasant, relieving himself outside was always an option.

A few days later the kitchen faucet became unmoored, spraying that nasty liquid everywhere. Rhys drenched himself shutting off the water supply to the sink, but not before his kitchen floor was an inch deep with a viscous, moving pool, alive with curious swimmers, their heads bobbing up to look at him, their long tails whipping. He opened the kitchen side door to the outside and began pushing the flood out with a broom, which allowed some of the reddish fog to pour in as if waiting for the opportunity.

There was nothing Rhys could do to prevent that. He wielded the broom frantically, sweeping the flood and its inhabitants outside, brushing at what remained until the floor appeared only vaguely stained with shadow, then stripping off his contaminated clothing and throwing that out as well. A fan and an open window cleared the air. Rhys wondered if it would be possible to avoid the bathroom and the kitchen until the plumber came. At least the larder contained food which didn't require cooking.

Over the next few days Rhys attempted to depict the swimmers in his sketchbook, but his memory of them had become unreliable. Were their heads rounded or angular? Was his cancer beginning to affect his brain?

Every version of the creatures he drew appeared equally plausible/implausible. He ventured outside looking for evidence of their remains, but found no sign of them. He did, however, find his clothes, which he burned in the fireplace.

Rhys didn't have enough time left to invest in such distractions. Still, the swimmers continued to make random guest appearances in his sketchbook, curled in the corners of his landscapes, dropping out of trees, on the backs of elk or deer.

He was taking more frequent dives into his magic medicine sack. He didn't always think about it until he caught himself popping something into his mouth. He wasn't always aware of the increased pain, but then, that was the goal, wasn't it?

One morning Rhys woke up to a brilliant white mist thickening the closer it got to the ground. He went outside to investigate, and found the ground covered with frost, hard frozen layers of it that wouldn't have seemed atypical in the late fall or winter, but it was now the middle of July.

He remembered something his mother used to say when his behavior crossed an invisible line. "You're on thin ice, buddy." He wasn't always sure what he'd done, what mistake he'd made, but he was definitely in jeopardy.

He crouched down and put his palm on the ice. The thin windowpane layers were bitter cold and painful to the touch. He lifted one and saw it had a stem, or root, an icicle descending into the ground, as if it had grown there.

He retreated inside and disinfected his hands. An hour later he heard a loud cracking noise. He went to the window and watched as the layers of frost exploded under the heat of the sun.

He went out later that afternoon to see if there were any other peculiarities. He'd been in considerable discomfort most of the day, chewing on painkillers and sipping wine because he was trying to conserve his water supply. He became aware of a general humming sound that decreased when he retreated into the shade, only to rise again when he stepped into the sun's heat. Was the sun making this noise, or had he overdone his self-medication?

Rhys had seen few animals during the past several days. A deer. At least he'd gotten a glimpse of its antlers. A distant elk galloping into the dark cover of the trees. But no rabbits or squirrels or other small animals. He wondered if they'd chosen to stay in their dens out of a sense of caution.

He thought he saw his sister walking through the sagebrush on the far side of the rapid stream, then standing and talking with two older people who resembled their dead parents. But there was no route she could have taken to get there. He turned away. He felt dizzy and ill.

When next he looked the human figures were gone, but dozens of dark shadows were crouching in the sagebrush, visible above the vibrating tops of the tall grass. The humming was back, louder than before. At first Rhys thought these were prairie dog mounds, the entrances to their burrows. Then he saw their gleaming eyes as they moved in staggered fashion in his direction.

He heard a tremendous rumbling from somewhere over the distant ridge, coming closer and gathering speed until it was right overhead. It shook the earth and made him dizzy, pounding his head and pushing its way deep into his belly. He fell to his knees and vomited shapes that scrambled away as soon as they hit the ground. He raised his head and saw thrashing shadows flooding out of the distant line of trees. They would be on him in seconds.

Doubled over in pain, Rhys managed to make his way back into the cabin and lock the door. He threw his shoulder into one end of the couch, moving it inches at a time until it blocked the door. He collapsed into its soft cushions and fell asleep waiting for the attack.

Rhys woke up on the floor buried beneath the couch cushions. He managed to push himself up and surveyed the damage. The table was overturned, and the pages of his sketch book were scattered everywhere. The rug was twisted around his feet.

Streaks layered the window, but no evidence anything had gotten inside. The park had become like a loud and troublesome next-door neighbor, but he was apparently safe if he kept his door shut.

Except for his state of mind. Once he accepted his illness, Rhys understood he would be embarking on a strange journey. He had no idea. He thought he knew the destination. Sometimes it felt as if he were already there.

Naturally, he thought about leaving. He no longer owned a car, but there was gas in the camper and the tires were in reasonable shape. He wasn't sure how much money he had left in his accounts, but enough to end his days holed up in a cheap Denver hotel with his magic sack of drugs. What else did he really need?

But maybe the cancer had reached his brain, and these experiences would follow him out of the mountains all the way to Denver, assuming he was able to stay on the road long enough to get there. This was *his* terminal experience, his expedition across the borderlands. Shouldn't he stay with it all the way to the end?

He straightened up the living room and sat with his sketchbook before the front window. He had his food, his wine, and his drugs nearby. His biggest challenge would be staying alert. He'd never felt so tired.

Little changed during his first day of observation. Still, he filled page after page with images from recent dreams, fearful anticipations, things only vaguely glimpsed. He wasn't sure when and how he'd glimpsed them. He took periodic naps, but believed his watches should be both day and night. During the second day there was a change in the light, certainly inside the cabin where everything had become bluish, as if he were wearing colored lenses, while outside everything was bright and definitive, like a movie set. Out in the fields the sagebrush began to ripple, but not in its usual random way blown by the wind, but as a series of solid waves, as if it were a straw-colored sea. The broad valley between his cabin and the distant trees became a liminal region, liquid and otherworldly, lightning strikes illuminating worn places in the landscape, allowing another scene, another world to bleed through: an ocean of deep grays and shining greens rising to the edge of the window. He expected the glass would break and he would drown, but that didn't happen. He watched as his camper was swept away from the cabin, rocking unsteadily as it floated out into the liquid valley, spinning around, then disappearing beneath the ocean's surface, taking with it all Rhys's notions of escape.

A dark shadow crossed the window, and only as it moved away did Rhys recognize it as the model for the plesiosaur he'd seen in the old sketchbook. It must have been at least seventy feet long, and the four long flippers attached to its shoulder and pelvis enabled it to fly through the water with their powerful strokes.

It took a sudden dive at a coiled shell over a dozen feet across, snatching out a squid-like creature who'd just emerged.

Rhys sketched furiously trying to capture it all, his drawings devolving into quick, desperate strokes. He scribbled the name "plesiosaur" at the bottom of the page for identification.

The ocean surged away from the window in one giant tidal wave emptying the sea and revealing vast acres of marsh land featuring great swirls of rotting seaweed pushed out of the dwindling pools by giant serpents eager for more space. Several hundred yards away lay a sprawling cemetery of dying behemoths feebly flapping their nearly transparent fins in the gray muck.

Beyond those, where once Rhys witnessed elk and deer and a bobcat or two venturing shyly from a ridgeline crowded with evergreens, he saw indications of a stranded armada of ancient ships, but even with his binoculars he could obtain no definitive proof.

Night fell over this Sargassian nightmare, just as it would over any normal landscape, which provided Rhys with some small comfort. He peered into the dark looking for signs of life, and he may have found some glimmers of silver off a sea creature's scales, subtle indications of movement within the inky dark, but he could not be sure. Eventually he couldn't keep his eyes open and succumbed in his chair.

* * *

The next morning, Rhys recalled dreams in which he talked to his sister, his parents, people he used to work with, romantic partners (none enthusiastic or lasting). They were like shadows, and of no consequence to his journey. He had regrets but felt too far along to back out now.

He felt empty, and yet without hunger. He doubted he could eat another bite for the rest of his life. He gazed down at his belly, lifted his shirt. His abdomen was swollen, his skin stretched and firm to the touch. He thought back to those long, slippery creatures, the swimmers, and wondered if they might have made a nest inside his belly. It seemed unlikely, but Rhys was now living an unlikely life.

It might have been a progression of the cancer, of course, spreading into his stomach, creating fluid. He might be filling up with cancer. No wonder he wasn't hungry.

He suffered from a raw ache, yet he was reluctant to take more drugs. He wanted to stay awake and experience everything. He discovered that if he moved carefully he could avoid the pain.

He had little strength, however, and it took him considerable time, broken with several rest periods, before he could push the sofa away from the door. Once that was accomplished he stumbled outside.

The landscape was much as he first encountered it: limitless fields of golden sage and other grasses backed by the evergreen-covered ridge and those snow-capped peaks in the distance. A perfect portrait of Colorado's higher elevations. The local fauna were not out. Perhaps they had evacuated. There wasn't a single bird in the sky as far as Rhys could tell.

He stomped around the front of the cabin thinking he might find mud, or soft spots left from the recent flood. With that volume of water there had to be soft spots, at least a puddle or two, but Rhys uncovered nothing of the sort.

His doctor told him his cancer might metastasize to his brain. No doubt that was what had occurred. He wondered how long it would be before all coherent thought escaped him. Those sketches he'd made were indicative of a mind on the brink.

He turned around to look at his cabin, certainly normal in every way. He loved this home, but perhaps he wasn't good for it. What damage might he do to it if he remained much longer? A house was like a head. It was only as good as what you put into it.

His camper was gone. Of course. He'd seen the waves carry it away.

Rhys spent the rest of the day traipsing around his property, searching for anomalies or evidence of what he had witnessed the past few days. Nothing appeared out of place. If anything, it all seemed a bit too perfect—the shape of the trees, the distribution of undergrowth, the lack of the sort of random debris generally found in an old-growth forest. It was like a scene in some well-curated diorama.

He looked for animal life, insect life, anything living that wasn't plant-based. He couldn't find so much as a beetle or an ant.

Now and again he had a sense of something changing beyond his peripheral vision, a shift in gravity, movement, something opening or closing. But when he turned his head in that direction nothing appeared amiss.

He tried blinking his eyes rapidly. Something changed between those blinks, but with the next opening of his eyes the change—whatever it was—was gone.

Rhys thought he could hear things off to the side or faintly in the distance. It looked as if the shadows were changing shape and direction.

He returned to the cabin and was about to go inside when he heard the rumble. He turned around. The ground was heaving, or maybe it was the sky. Then he saw the birds, thousands of them pouring from beyond the ridge, flashing overhead, and disappearing.

Five hundred miles northwest of here lay the Yellowstone caldera. He wasn't sure why he should think about the super-volcano now, except he had been having nightmares about it for years.

It wasn't a realistic fear. The odds of an eruption during his lifetime were infinitesimal, assuming it might happen at all. But if it did occur, hundreds of thousands of years into the future, thinking of all those people in Colorado and the western states it would kill, Rhys would wonder if it mattered how little he'd accomplished in his life, when all such accomplishments could be so easily erased.

He felt the ground move again, this time the vibration passing through his entire body, his internal organs shifting their position relative to his rib cage, and he thought he might die right there in front of his cabin. He hugged himself and ran against the door, twisted the knob, and pushed inside.

He fell into his chair in front of the window. The glass provided no protection, of course. If anything, this was the most dangerous place in the cabin to be. But the perfect place for observing the end of his life.

Outside the rumbling continued, although things within the cabin remained motionless. He imagined the earthquakes gathering, swarming into some kind of collective effect.

The ground in front of the cabin rose suddenly and everything beneath exploded, sending black smoke and fire miles into the air, the dark cloud spreading into a huge umbrella shape over everything. He covered his ears trying to stop the noise. Another explosion made him dive onto the floor, though his window didn't shatter. It barely vibrated.

He lay there waiting for something worse to occur. He was in terrible pain. This would be a good time to die, he thought, before he was forced to endure more.

After a few minutes Rhys thought he heard it raining outside. He struggled to his feet and saw the burning ash falling, glowing flakes of splintered rock and glass, rapidly covering everything.

He caught a glimpse of the nearby trees. They'd been decapitated, now a ragged line of burnt fence posts.

He was strangely tempted to go out there. Somehow he felt protected. If he was safe in this small cabin he might be safe out in the open. But that was a delusion, wasn't it? Either he would suffer a burning death or his lungs would fill with cement and he would suffocate.

His beautiful parkland was buried in ash to a depth of at least three feet. Hundreds of blackened figures rose out of the ash and stood like ruined statues, staring, waiting for him to join them. This was not the ending he'd expected.

The telephone on the wall began ringing, louder and louder until it was shaking, louder still until it shook itself into nothing and disappeared.

He heard the rustle of pages behind him, felt the frantic energy of the figure trying to get the sketchbook into its metal box. Rhys turned and watched himself prying stones out of the wall and shoving the box inside the cavity, then hastily packing smaller fragments around it to fill the space.

The other Rhys turned and gazed at him in dismay. He looked worse than Rhys had expected—gaunt, frail, and eaten. The other Rhys smiled wanly and then began to burn.

Flaming timbers and great chunks of ceiling crashed to the floor. Rhys reached for the window thinking he could push his way out, but the glass shattered around him. He lost the skin covering his left hand. All that was left was muscle and bloody bone. There was a word for that. He tried to remember. *Degloved.* Such a peculiar term, and a fitting final thought.

Freed from his brain, these memories slipped through the invisible cracks in the fabric of our world: ice and fire, water and ash and the difficult calculus of being.

Death and the Goddess Yet Seen

Linda D. Addison

Ah, you clever, clever human animal
using logic in your monkey brain,
 figuring it all out, feeling safe, as
 bullets made one of my mightiest
 bleed, did you notice the slight smile
 under the white mask, his death mask?

You thought the lake washed away
 blood released from holes you made,
 but not seen in those last moments:
 my many arms embracing him,
 I lapping the outflowing essence,
 giving life eternal for his devotion.

Tonight when celebrations are done,
 wine glasses empty, you stumble in
 the bedroom, wondering at dainty
 wet footprints, hoping a villager
 wants to lay with you, you hero,
 you protector of mere mortals.

For you, gods and goddesses live in the
 realm of superstition, while you fake
 belief in the Garden, the Fall from
 grace. I am your Serpent, uncoiling
 in shadows of your naked deception,
 revealing the true duality of logic.

But what of things yet seen?
> You won't live to see humans prove
> our existence in other dimensions,
> but as I feast on your soul, tightening
> reasoning around your neck slowly,
> we will become One, you will see All . . .

Our Lady of Morocco

Robert E. Waters

In the summer of 2020 I received an anxious message from Ashland Grace, an old college friend. He wanted me to attend him at his home in Virginia. "Things are getting ugly here, Paul," he texted. "I need your help!" He didn't tell me what was getting "ugly," which I found surprising. Being a history major from the University of Colorado, Ashland was always a stickler for detail. That summer saw the height of the COVID-19 pandemic and the rejuvenation of the Black Lives Matter movement due to the murder of George Floyd at the hands of Minneapolis police officers. Given Ashland's politically conservative views, which could sometimes border on crackpot conspiracy theories, I figured it was either one or both of those issues. Despite my misgivings about traveling across the country via aircraft, I agreed. Regardless of his political views, Ashland was a friend, and I have so few of those in my life.

He picked me up at baggage claim at the Richmond International Airport. He wasn't wearing a mask.

"You don't need no goddamn mask," he said to me with a hearty laugh, giving me a strong bear hug. "This whole COVID thing is a bunch of bullshit. Come on," he said, tossing my bag into his truck bed and opening the passenger door. "Let's get going."

"How are you, Ash?" I asked as he pulled away from the curb. It had been six years since I had last seen him. "Your message was . . . vague. What's going on?"

He paused, and I could always tell when he was anxious, nervous. His eyes watered, his face grew red, and he rubbed his cheeks vigorously. Since I'd last seen him, his light brown hair had grown long and he sported a shaggy, unkempt beard with a touch of gray.

He sighed deeply, with a hint of beer on his breath. "They want to take it away, Paul. They want to tear it down and take it away."

"What?"

"Captain Uriah Bridgeport's monument."

I shook my head. "Not familiar with it."

"It's Rivertown's only Confederate statue, and the SJW goons want to tear it down."

I refrained from snapping back at him about the misplaced social justice warrior insult, sighed deeply as well, and said, "I appreciate you inviting me for a visit, Ash. It's good to see you again. But was it necessary to bring me all the way here from Denver just because of a statue?"

He turned to me, stared for a good while, then pulled the truck over onto the shoulder before we exited the airport. "Paul, there's more to it than just a statue."

"Okay," I said, shrugging, "what else?"

Ash stared through the windshield, his eyes glazed over as if he had seen a ghost. "There's been a murder."

He took me to see the statue. It stood in the middle of Rivertown in a small park square with a couple of wooden benches and a walkway around and up to the monument. When we arrived, there were several people around the statue, waving signs and chanting in protest against, I assumed, its very existence. Police had erected a small barrier between the protesters and the statue, but I could see it hadn't protected the tall figure, in marble, standing erect on the base, all kitted out in a stone-gray Confederate officer's uniform.

"You see what they've done," Ash said, as we sat in his truck across the street, away from the protestors.

Paint had been thrown onto the statue, black, red, and white, all across the legs of the figure. It had run down the legs, over the base, and onto the ground. Someone had tried to clean it up; you could see where a high-pressure spray had been applied; it had done little good. The statue was marked, in protest, and as long as the people continued to march it would remain so.

"See all the black protestors?" Ash said, pointing out various people in the crowd. "They want it torn down 'cause they believe that it was put up decades ago as an intimidation tactic, as a way to scare the black civilians in the area to behave themselves." He huffed. "Bullshit! I'm a history major. You know me well. I always do my research. There's no proof anywhere I can find that suggests that Captain Bridgeport's statue was put up to scare the hell out of black folks. None!"

Ash was clearly agitated, and in his own mind I suppose he considered himself correct in his assessment of the situation. He'd been a near straight-A student in college, so I didn't doubt his claim of research. But sometimes the truth is not documented. I mean, does a gangster state publicly what he wants his goons to do with the body of a rival boss?

"Okay," I said, "but surely you can understand their frustration? I mean, a lot of Confederate statues have been constructed, particularly around the South, for that very reason."

Ash rubbed his face, growing annoyed. "As I said, I've done my research, Paul. Captain Bridgeport's statue was put up to commemorate his defense of Rivertown, nothing more."

Ash paused, and I knew he was about to go into one of his legendary lectures. I considered stopping him, but in truth I wanted, needed, some context to this whole affair. "Uriah Bridgeport was a Confederate raider. Kind of like a John Singleton Mosby, a.k.a. Mosby's Raiders?"

I'd heard of Mosby's Raiders but wasn't all that familiar with them.

"Bridgeport and his men," Ash continued, "about twenty to thirty, helped defend Rivertown against the Union attack here on the Peninsula back in the early years of the Civil War. Per the public record, he and his men held off two full companies of Union Zouaves for twelve hours before reinforcements arrived." He slapped the dashboard of his truck. "That's why his statue sits there, not because of some trumped-up, racist reason."

He stopped talking. I was surprised that he didn't continue with the entire history of the Peninsula Campaign or explain to me what Zouaves were; he had a propensity for long-windedness, especially when it came to history. Clearly, his passions and, dare I say, overzealous emotions about current events were focusing his attention. I could almost see the rage in his eyes as he stared at the protesters through his cracked windshield.

I changed the subject. "You said there was a murder?"

Ash snapped to, rubbed his face, and nodded. "Right. Let me take you to the scene."

We pulled out into the road. As we passed the statue, he said, "You know, rumor has it that Captain Bridgeport's ashes are in an urn inside the statue, and at night his spirit comes out of the marble to protect the town, to this day, from all threats, foreign and domestic. You believe that?"

Yeah, right! It didn't surprise me that my friend would say, and believe, such a thing. I was about to express my skepticism, but I paused. For as we passed the line of protesters in front of the statue I couldn't help but notice that the statue's eyes, dark, deep, and inset, were watching me all the way down the street.

I'm a forensic pathologist. Well, an assistant to one in the Denver Crime Laboratory. Where Ash decided after college to return home, I instead decided to stay in the Rockies and accept the position after my internship. I've been an assistant for four years now.

"Here's where the murder happened," Ash said as we parked the truck and walked about a quarter mile into the woods.

"We shouldn't be here," I said, holding back from the tree that he was pointing to and approaching. "It's a crime scene."

Crime scene tape had been put in place, but it had fallen over in many spots and was covered in mud and water in others.

Ash scoffed and waved his hand at me. "It happened over a month ago. The police don't give a shit about this place anymore. They've closed the case, abandoned the site. Come on."

I followed him to the tree. He knelt and ran his hand over bark that had been chipped away from the trunk. "Self-inflicted gunshot wound to the head," Ash said. "The man lay right up against this tree and shot himself . . . or so say the police."

"Who?"

"Michael Span. Leader of the SHPS, the Southern Heritage Preservation Society, in charge of ensuring that Bridgeport's statue remains in place."

I knelt and looked at the tree. I'd seen marks like that before. The product of a gunshot, for sure. My guess was that this Michael Span placed his head against the tree, put the gun to his head, and pulled the trigger. The recoil of the pistol caused a glancing blow. Poor fellow probably didn't die instantly, but sat slumped over, twitching, bleeding out, before anyone noticed him. I checked the tree and ground for blood. Nothing, although if I had had my forensic equipment and chemicals with me, I'm sure I would have found traces.

"Okay, the man shot himself," I said, clearing my throat before offering a possible explanation. "If he was the leader of this SHPS, perhaps he was feeling guilty about trying to save the statue. Perhaps he couldn't live with the guilt."

Ash shook his head so vociferously that he nearly fell over. Instead, he rose and walked away from the tree and into the sunlight. "Bull. I knew the man well. He was just as dedicated to protecting the statue on his last day as he was on his first. No. He was murdered, Paul. Someone brought him here and shot him. And, I think I know who."

He waved me over. I joined him. He knelt again and wiped away a swath of dried leaves. "I covered these 'cause I didn't want those lefty protestors finding them and hiding their crime, but look here." He pointed to a set of muddy footprints. "Those aren't Mike's shoes. He was a heavyset man. His foot would have sunk further into the mud. No. Someone followed him here and pulled the trigger."

I looked at the footprints. Small and light. More of an indent at the toe of the shoe, but even that was sparse. Oddly enough, they weren't the only prints.

"Is that a hoof mark?" I asked, plucking away a leaf.

Ash shrugged. "You're the forensics guy. You tell me."

I studied it closely; it certainly looked like one. I stood and turned my head left, right. "Are we on a farm?"

"Nope," Ash said gleefully, as if he were pleased at the strange combination of markings. I guess he looked at them as a justification for his propensity for conspiracy theories. "Odd, isn't it? That a crime scene would have three sets of footprints: the victim; a very small, light person; and a goat. Don't you think that's weird?"

I did, though I wasn't about to stoop to Ash's level and start yapping about conspiracies without further information. Quite honestly, these prints could have been here long before the suicide—or murder—took place. "What did the police report say about these prints?"

Ash shook his head. "Nothing. As far as I know, they didn't even notice them. I have friends on the police force; from what they tell me, there was nothing in the report about these prints. Mike Span's death was ruled a suicide, and that's how they left it. They're wrong, Paul. Dead, dead wrong."

"Okay," I said, my patience about to give out, "I'm willing to play ball here. You say he was murdered. By whom?"

Ash rubbed his face, moved closer to me, and spoke in hushed tones, as if we were being watched. "About two months before Mike committed suicide, he and his wife separated." He shook his head, whistled. "A beautiful woman, I must say. And not white. No, sir. She was from somewhere in the Middle East. Olive-skinned, radiant eyes. Man, oh man."

He paused, looked out into the woods as if he were fixed on a vision. Then he shook his head and continued. "She left town, and Mike went into a kind of depression."

I nodded. "Understandable. I've had my fair share of breakups. If the man was deeply depressed, the breakup, plus his work with the preservation society, might have—"

"No, I'm telling you, Paul, he didn't kill himself for either of those reasons. He was as strong as granite. As strong as—well, Captain Bridgeport's statue. Mike Span was tough as nails. He didn't kill himself." Ash leaned in and whispered, "His wife did it."

I leaned away from him, raised my eyebrows. "I thought you said she left town."

Ash shook his head. "That's what everyone thinks. But no. She never left. I've seen her. And I saw her on the night Mike died."

After looking over the crime scene, Ash and I grabbed lunch, and then he took me to his house, which was close to the square and the Bridgeport statue. In fact, I could see Bridgeport's marble image through the kitchen window. Shortly thereafter, Ash set out to meet with the SHPS to help organize a counter-protest for later in the week. I took time to recover from my trip. I showered, shaved, and then headed out myself.

The police station was a couple of blocks from the square. I was intrigued by Ash's insistence that Span had been murdered. I needed to see if I could find some clues that might point to that theory.

Unfortunately, I acquired little information, despite flashing my forensic pathology credentials. Since I was out of my jurisdiction, the chief of police refused my request to see the case file. But, because of my credentials, he did provide me with a verbal description of the crime scene and revealed one photo of the victim.

Michael Span's body leaned left against the tree, as I had suspected. The right side of his head was a mess, with blood all down his body. A pistol lay in his right hand, which I found peculiar. Normally, when someone shoots himself in the head, the recoil from the pistol is so great that the hand opens and the pistol is thrown to the ground. Not here. Span's fingers were curled around the grip. Even his trigger finger was firmly in place. It was impossible to know for sure if he had died immediately or, as I had suspected, had died thereafter in the throes of agony. What was most curious, however, was the expression on his face.

His eyes and mouth were wide open. The look of terror on his face was not necessarily abnormal under these circumstances, but it wasn't a look of death, or the cold, vacuous stare of a man already dead. This was a man dying, bleeding out, who was staring at something, someone, standing right in front of him. Maybe Michael Span had killed himself as stated in the official police report, but if so, someone was standing in front of him, giving him encouragement to do so. Encouragement he could not refuse.

I finally asked the police chief if he had seen or spoken to Michael Span's wife. He looked at me like a confused dog. "Michael Span didn't have a wife."

I left the police station with even more questions. To satisfy those questions, I went to the library.

Ash was a good researcher, but under the circumstances I believed that he was suffering from confirmation bias: the tendency to seek out information that confirms and supports your beliefs and values. He did his research on Captain Bridgeport's Civil War activities up to a point, then stopped when the facts confirmed his beliefs. I intended on digging deeper.

Rivertown's library was small. It didn't have the kind of information I was looking for. It did, however, confirm what Ash believed: in 1862, near the beginning of the Union Army's campaign up the Peninsula, Captain Bridgeport and his men defended Rivertown from Union forces for more than twelve hours. In fact, the data suggested that they had protected the town for twenty-four, though some scholars dispute that claim. Nevertheless, on this information alone one could understand why the local citizenry might object to the statue's removal. But again, I wasn't convinced that this was the definitive word on the matter.

The library had good Internet access, so I went online and kept digging. Here's what I discovered.

The so-called "Zouaves" that Ash mentioned had been a Civil War fighting force modeled after a light infantry regiment of the French Army in Northern Africa. They were introduced to the United States by a fellow named Elmer E. Ellsworth, who created a drill company called the "Zouave Cadets." They toured nationally and became popular. During the Civil War, Zouave companies were mustered on both sides of the conflict.

Most striking about them was their distinctive uniforms. Instead of the typical Civil War blue or gray, the Zouaves wore traditional North African clothing: a short, open-fronted jacket with red baggy trousers (called *serouels*), sashes, and a red fez-like cap called a *chechia*. Their uniforms were beautiful, bright, and expressive. I watched some video of modern Zouave re-enactors at Gettysburg to get a feel on how a full company of these men would have looked on the march. Most impressive.

Digging deeper, I discovered that two companies of these Zouaves—one from Pennsylvania, one from New York—had indeed attacked Rivertown, but the story that Captain Bridgeport had held them off with a mere handful of men was exaggerated. What really happened was that the townsfolk also rallied to defend their homes. So the battlefield odds were close to even by the time the fighting commenced.

That was all the public record stated. I spent another hour digging deeper and could find nothing further on Bridgeport's defense of Rivertown.

So I called a friend of mine at the University of Colorado, a librarian in their extensive research facility. She had far better access to obscure historical data than I. If anyone could find the truth of this matter, it was her.

I left the library, and for the next couple of days I spent time walking around town talking with various people: some on the pro-Bridgeport side, some on the protest side. The battle lines were fully drawn, neither side willing to yield. I asked them questions about their cause, the statue. I asked many of the pro-statue folk about Michael Span's death, what they believed to be the cause, and about his ex-wife. Some thought it a suicide; others didn't. Like Ash, some thought he had been killed by BLM protesters, while others thought it was a government plot. And, like the chief of police, most of them had no recollection of his wife.

On my second day of investigation, as the sun began to set and the crowds around the square grew, I paused to look at the statue. The base was a perfectly formed block of marble, pitch black with veins of white running everywhere. The statue of Bridgeport itself was perhaps seven or eight feet tall. Pure dark gray, a pristine Confederate uniform formed perfectly around his thin body. Bridgeport himself was staring into the sky as if he were looking upon the face of God. In his left hand was a pistol; in his right he held the pole of a Confederate flag that had been savaged by red and white paint.

What struck me the most were the statue's eyes. As they had done earlier in the week, they looked into the sky, and yet, they seemed to stare directly at me as I walked around the base. Deep, powerful, soulful eyes, piercing my heart, calling to me.

"It's an abomination, isn't it?"

I turned to the voice. There stood a short, olive-skinned man, grinning broadly.

I cleared my throat before answering. "Yes, I suppose so. Although some around here would disagree."

The man huffed, shook his head, and walked past me toward the statue. "They are ignorant of the true history of it."

"Do you know the true history of it?" I asked.

From a pocket of his loose trousers he pulled a handkerchief, leaned toward the statue, and wiped a portion of the marble clean. "I know enough to know that it is an abomination."

"Who are you?"

He turned and flashed another smile from ear to ear. "My name is Richard, and I have been the groundskeeper of this square and the statue for thirty years."

"And yet . . . you call it an abomination."

He nodded. "And so it is. But how can I, a black man and a loyal, obedient member of the community, express my hatred for this wonderful bit of local heritage? How can I do that and not find the same fate as the much-revered Michael Span?"

I wanted to ask him further questions, but the expression on his face told me to stop. He seemed as if he was about to blow, to bark, to scream out his disdain for all to hear. I said nothing further about the statue.

"You knew Michael Span?" I asked.

He nodded. "I did. He, too, was an abomination."

"Some think he was murdered." I squinted. "Do you think he was murdered?"

Richard shrugged. "Who can say? Regardless, he died from his own hubris, his own guilt." He snorted and ran his fingers over a portion of the granite base. "The world is better off without him."

"Did you know his wife?"

Richard lowered his arms and shaped his back like a dome. His jovial expression turned quizzical. His nostrils flared; his eyes widened. "Wife? What wife?"

As Ash and I were sitting down to dinner, my source from Colorado called.

"Paul," she said, "I looked into the situation, and unfortunately there isn't much more to add to the public record."

"Nothing?"

"Well, other than Captain Bridgeport being an über-secessionist and one quote confirming his pro-slavery credentials, but that isn't surprising. Many officers of the Confederacy were both. There's nothing in the record indicating any action suggesting criminal activity on his part, other than, of course, being a secessionist."

"Damn!" I said, in full frustration. "Thanks for the help anyway, Dee. I owe you one."

During dinner I told Ash what I had discovered about Bridgeport (nothing). He, naturally, was elated and kept trying to convince me to march with him that evening at the protest. I refused, and finally I had to put my foot down by stating that I would never, ever lend my voice to such nonsense.

"I knew you were against all this," he said, throwing down his fork and pushing away from the table. "You're on their side, aren't you?"

I shook my head. "There's something else going on here, Ash. Dee may not have found anything in the record, but Bridgeport did something, something bad. I can feel it." I felt it when the statue's eyes had followed me.

"Oh, bullshit! You're just like those mealy-mouthed libs out there: on the edge of your seat with a bag of popcorn, like you're watching a movie, just waiting for any Southerner like me to open his mouth and speak, so you can accuse him of racism or sexism or homophobia or whatever else to make yourselves feel morally superior. Yeah, you're just like them."

I was getting annoyed. "Ash, don't accuse me of something you know nothing about. I am who I am, and I've always been this way. What's changed is you. You were never like this in college. You were always a very thoughtful, diligent researcher and a critical thinker. What the hell happened to you?"

"I got wise!"

He grabbed his jacket and left. I called to him; he ignored me. I watched him walk toward the square. The crowds were gathering. Tonight was going to be a dangerous night in Rivertown. I considered going after him, hoping that I could persuade him to stay home. Neither the statue nor the cause was worth getting hurt, or killed, over.

Instead, I stayed inside and watched from the kitchen as things unfolded.

I used a pair of Ash's binoculars to view the growing protest. It was dark. Some were holding candles, some torches. The crowds ebbed and flowed in and out of my view, but I could see enough to know what was going on.

Both sides were quite animated, waving signs such as HERITAGE OF HATE, BLACK LIVES MATTER, PRESERVE OUR HERITAGE, and TOUCH THE STATUE AND DIE. Much heated shouting and taunting reverberated around the statue as police, a local force supported by SWAT from Richmond, encircled the statue wearing riot gear, holding shields and batons. A local news crew was on site. Things were chaotic, tense.

But through this chaos I saw Ash. He was on the pro-statue side of the protest, of course, waving his fists, most assuredly barking obscenities at the "SJW goons" who were barking right back at him. The lines wavered back and forth, and the police had to pepper-spray a few on both sides and drag them away. But not Ash. Though his protestations were as strong as anyone else's in the line, he did not condescend to commit any violent acts. He stayed above the fray, and for a moment I was proud of him. Violence begets violence, they say, and my friend was behaving himself; physically, at least.

Then he disappeared. I refocused the binoculars and searched through the crowd. I figured it was just the fact that there were so many people, and perhaps he had simply shifted to the other side of the square. It was dark, the light was faint, with shadows everywhere.

He reappeared minutes later alongside his truck, which he had parked near the protest. He stood on the passenger side. With him were two people: Richard, the groundskeeper I had spoken to earlier in the day, and a woman. From my vantage point I could not see them clearly, but they were talking quietly. Both Richard and the woman seemed to be consoling Ash. Ash was listening to what they were saying, apparently nodding agreement. And then it seemed as if he broke into tears. He leaned over, and the woman, her hair pitch black, her skin the same olive tone as Richard's, let his head rest on her shoulder. She rubbed his hair as if he were a sobbing child wanting affection. Ash stood like that for several minutes, then pulled away. He nodded, and they all walked off together, up the street, around the corner, and out of my view.

I dropped the binoculars and went after them. The pursuit was difficult, with so many people in the streets. I passed through mostly BLM protesters who mistakenly took me for a pro-statue fellow. They threw a few expletives my way, but otherwise left me alone. One tried to trip me, but I jumped his leg and kept going, desperate to keep Ash and Richard and the woman in my view. I lost them a couple of times in the hot, humid haze of the evening, but I found them finally, moving off the road and down a gully into woods.

"Ash!" I called out. He didn't reply.

I followed them. I could hear Ash sobbing and the woman's smooth, comforting voice through the trees. The faint muffle of the protest was behind me; I tried ignoring it as I made my way up and down gully walls, trying to avoid slipping into mud. Ash's sobbing grew stronger, the woman's voice now even more soothing and pleasant, almost angelic, as I made my way up the last gully and through underbrush.

I knelt and crawled quietly to a place where I could see them through the brush. They stood under a large tree, its branches big and brooding like the legs of a spider. Ash stood in front of the woman, Richard behind him. The woman was speaking words that I could not understand, in a language that was . . . Arabic, Berber? I could not tell. But that didn't seem to matter, because Ash nodded at every word, wiping tears from his eyes while the woman spoke, while the small man behind him laid his hand on Ash's shoulder to provide even more support.

Ash nodded again, said, "Okay." Then Richard reached into the pocket of his jacket, pulled out a pistol, and handed it to Ash.

My heart ached, and for a moment I froze. I could not speak or shout. None of it seemed real, and I wondered if I were dreaming. Maybe I had fallen asleep at the kitchen table while watching the protest. Maybe I was still in Colorado in my comfortable bed.

Ash put the pistol to his head and cocked the hammer. I knew then that this was no dream.

"No!" I screamed. I cared not what Richard or the woman was doing; I focused my attention on Ash, leapt out of the brush, and struck him square in the chest.

But not before he pulled the trigger. Luckily, my strike pushed the pistol away such that the bullet merely grazed his head. Ash fell against the tree, the pistol fell to the ground, and the woman was on me immediately.

She—it—was no woman. It had the shape and form of one, but its black, luxurious hair now began to thin and go gray. Its pleasant face turned sour, with wrinkles scarring its dark flesh. Its fingernails grew longer. It screamed at me, bared its wet, bloody mouth with fangs sharp along blood-red gums, and tried to bite my neck. I held it off as best as I could while Richard cackled like a hyena.

"Good, good," he said, nodding approvingly. "Feast on his neck, Qandicha. Feast! Show these abominations the truth. Make them regret their choices."

I didn't know what he was talking about, and I didn't bother to pause and ask questions. Spittle from the creature's razor fangs dripped on my neck. I held the creature firmly in place with my left arm while I searched the ground for the pistol.

"The statue is coming down," Richard said, stepping closer. "You and your racist friend will die, and Bridgeport will fall."

"I'm not a racist," I said, trying to keep from gagging on my own stomach acid. "I'm not a—"

"Oh? Good friends with one, and yet you claim you are not. Interesting. Very well." He waved his hand over the creature, wiggled his fingers. "Show him, Qandicha. Look into his eyes and educate him."

Despite my abject fear, I turned my head, opened my eyes, and stared into hers. I knew then that the eyes of that statue had indeed been hers. This Qandicha had been watching me the whole time, and now I was watching her as she revealed the truth through her eyes as if they were windows into the past.

After the Zouave companies from New York and Pennsylvania retreated, Bridgeport and his men formed a counter-attack. They went after the Zouaves to exact revenge against their brutal assault on Rivertown. They pursued, found them, attacked, and took prisoners. What they didn't know, however, was that Louisiana had sent a Zouave company of its own to the Peninsula to help support the Confederate cause. Simply put: Bridgeport and his men attacked the wrong company. It was dark, and Zouave uniforms were similar on both sides at that time of the war. They made a terrible mistake. Once they realized their error, they released the prisoners. All but one: a Sergeant Daoud Tuhami, whom the Louisiana soldiers called "David." He was a Moroccan who had fought with French forces in North Africa and had come to America to help train the Louisiana Zouaves. They did not release Daoud Tuhami. Instead, they lynched him, at the order of Captain Bridgeport himself. Hanged him by the neck from a tree, like the one I was lying under right now.

"Do you know the truth now?" Richard asked. He waved his hand again over the creature. "Kill them both, Qandicha. Kill them now."

As the creature refocused her efforts on ripping out my throat, I groped the leafy ground where Ash lay. I could see the blood-matted hair on his head, the trickles of blood down his face, and I wondered if perhaps I had miscalculated my leap. Was he dead? I could not tell, but the thought of it made me angry. I reached out, under his body, and found the pistol.

I gripped the handle, pulled the pistol free, clicked the hammer, and pointed it at the beast on top of me. I paused, hoping that it would see the gun and withdraw. It didn't. I closed my eyes and pulled the trigger.

The shot echoed through the woods, then silence. I opened my eyes. The creature was still on top of me, seemingly unharmed by the shot. But Richard, who stood nearby, was not so lucky. His smile disappeared, and in its place there was shock and horror. I looked down at his stomach. The bullet had punctured his side. Blood poured through his fingers as he gripped the wound. He looked at me, his eyes wide, dark, hollow, filled with shock and, perhaps, regret. He tried speaking, but all that escaped his mouth was a groan.

He fell, face first, to the ground. The creature rose into the sky and gave such a bloodcurdling shriek that I cocked the gun again, thinking that perhaps it would deliver the killing blow. Instead, it wavered in place, shaking like an earthquake. Its motions were so violent that it began to fall apart. First its legs, then midsection and chest, then arms and face. Like a pixelated image on a computer screen, bits and pieces falling to the ground and vanishing like fog in sunlight. Finally it dissolved, its last scream so loud I was compelled to cover my ears and watch as the creature faded away.

It was gone, and so too Richard. I had been so fixated on the creature that I forgot about the groundskeeper. Like the creature, his body was gone as well. Had it dissolved like the beast? Or had he wandered away injured but alive, without my knowing?

Those questions did not concern me at that moment, because Ash stirred at my side. He coughed. He lifted his head, his hands balled into fists. I couldn't help but lean over, lay my head on his back, and cry.

Ash and I were still alive.

The Rivertown police found and took us to the local hospital. They wanted to charge me with attempted murder, but Ash, having recovered enough from his head wound, made an impassioned plea on my behalf. He told them that he had pulled the trigger, that he had been suicidal, and that it wasn't my fault at all. They accepted his statement and let me go. But I knew it wasn't a suicide attempt; at least, not in the strict sense. Yes, Ash had pulled the trigger, but his desire to do so had been motivated by supernatural forces.

At my request, the Denver FBI sent a couple of their paranormal investigators, both experts on the Sigsand Manuscript and certified in the Carnacki Method, to Rivertown to investigate the groundskeeper and his vile creature. Turns out that Richard's full name was Raoud Tuhami, a direct descendant of Daoud Tuhami, the Louisiana Zouave that Bridgeport had executed. From this information, it was clear to me that his reason for killing Michael Span and then attempting to kill Ash was motivated by vengeance, anger. The controversy swirling around Bridgeport's statue was just the justification he needed to put his rage into action. Raoud's plan was clear: kill the leadership of the pro-Bridgeport movement, thereby weakening its resolve. Michael Span had been the first, Ash was to be the second, and the killings would most certainly have continued if he hadn't been stopped.

The creature that Raoud "Richard" Tuhami had deployed against Span and Ash was a female Moroccan cryptid called Aicha Qandicha. Similar to a jinn, but beyond beautiful, she would befriend a man and sometimes marry him under the guise of being human. And then drive him insane or, as noted, kill him. The Aicha Qandicha is often portrayed as having the hooves of a goat or a camel, so that answered the question about the hoof marks where Michael Span had been found dead. The smaller, lightweight footprints alongside the hooves had been Raoud Tuhami's. They had stood there, watching Michael Span die, just as they would have done with Ash.

The investigators also found a small, cleverly hidden door at the base of the statue wherein lay a small corked vial. Nothing was in the vial, though they suspected that was where Raoud had held the Moroccan jinn. She in effect lived inside Bridgeport, which explained the statue's wandering eyes. Raoud's plan seemed pretty cut and dried.

But it had failed. Ash survived. The fired bullet had placed a severe cut along his head, and he had suffered a concussion. However, he would live. I'm not a praying man, but I thanked God for that. Ash was a nutjob, one who had fallen into the life of a conspiracy monger, but he was my friend, and he hadn't been wrong about everything. Michael

Span did indeed have a wife, and Ash was the only one who had seemed to notice. Another supernatural twist in Tuhami's murderous plan.

The matter has now concluded. The mayor of Rivertown, at the behest of Richmond officials, has finally ordered Bridgeport's statue to be removed. In a twisted, evil manner, Raoud Tuhami has gotten his wish.

But, as I stand here now, watching as the statue is removed from its base and put into a truck where it will be taken to Richmond and put into storage, I can't help but wish my friend all the best. In the hospital, Ash seemed to express genuine remorse for the role he played in the violence that struck Rivertown. He asked for my forgiveness, which I humbly gave, for I knew that he, like many others, was struggling to find their place and meaning in a rapidly changing world. Their violence in response to that changing world was inexcusable, but I hoped that he would find purpose and peace in that new world. Someday, at least.

I stand here now, watching the crane place Bridgeport's statue on the truck, and I'm reminded of an old Civil War hymn that, ironically, my friend Ashland Grace used to hum to himself in our dorm room . . .

> Lord, may the bonds of the captive be broken,
> O may this struggle bring sweet liberty.
> Teach us that love is a heavenborn token,
> and that the truth can alone make us free.

The Ship on the Sea of Nightmares

Lisa Morton

"Here. This is where he died."

Berry gazed at his new friend, losing himself in the way the setting sun outlined Tonnison's pale face in crimson. Berry imagined how it would be to lean in and kiss that almost delicate mouth, but he knew Tonnison was here for other reasons. They'd only just met, but somehow Berry already thought that time was a long road they might be traveling together. He could wait.

"How do you know?" Berry asked. "I mean, how do you know *exactly* where it happened?"

Tonn smiled, turned his hazel eyes on Berry. "I don't, but it was somewhere around here, on the east slope of Mont Kemmel." He scanned the horizon of open fields and heavy woods, dotted below with the occasional farmhouse and the one small military cemetery they'd passed. In the slanting rays of the dying sun, the woods had turned from vivid green to muddy brown. "Of course it didn't look like this during the War—the woods were almost all gone, the hillside just . . . ugly. Another victim of war."

It was April, and Berry knew night in the Belgian countryside would soon turn cold, but it was less than a mile's walk back to the bus stop and then just a few minutes back to Ypres, where a warm train would return them to Brussels.

"Tell me," Berry asked his friend, "how he died."

"It was the Fourth Battle of Ypres, during World War I. He was a lieutenant in the British Army; they were trying to keep the Germans from taking this area. His commanding officer had sent him to a forward observation post, but he and another man took a direct hit from a German artillery shell and were blown to bits."

"Fuck," Berry muttered. Then: "And you said today was the anniversary of his death?"

Tonn nodded, said, "Yes. William Hope Hodgson died on the nineteenth of April, 1918. He was forty."

"That's too young."

"It is." Tonn hesitated before adding, "He left behind plenty of short stories, but just four novels. Imagine what he would have produced had he lived."

"And you wanted to be here today because it's the day he died?"

"Yes," Tonn said, before chuckling in slight embarrassment. "It sounds quite fanboyish, doesn't it."

"It's nice. A way of honoring him."

"Good. I'm glad you understand."

Tonn looked across the landscape around them as if absorbing some part of it. Despite his silence, Tonn's passion shone, leaving Berry hoping to share it.

They'd met in a bookstore in London: Tonnison, the British scholar obsessed with a horror author Berry had never heard of, and Berry, an American architecture student with a return ticket to Atlanta in four days trying to make the last of his funds stretch until then. When Tonn (who had explained his name as belonging to a distant ancestor) had invited Berry to join him on a trip to Belgium to research the place where William Hope Hodgson had died, Berry's wallet told him he shouldn't, but his instant attraction to the twenty-four-year-old Brit had swayed him easily. Who needed to eat, after all? Berry had even taken a secret profile photo of Tonn that he'd texted to his sister back home, who'd responded with a heart-pumping avatar.

On the Eurostar from London to Brussels, Tonn had talked of Hodgson for almost the entire two-hour trip, but he was a good storyteller and Berry was fascinated. Tonn spoke of Hodgson's novels, his life at sea, how he'd transformed his body to avoid bullying, and the legacy he'd left behind after his too-early death. He'd told Berry about the book he was writing: a critical study of Hodgson's work that he hoped would be published by a university press.

"Bullying at sea," Berry had asked at one point, thinking of the photos of Hodgson that Tonn had brought up on his phone. "He was a handsome dude, and you said he was like sixteen when he left home. Do you think . . . ?" He trailed off, uncertain how to phrase the question.

Tonn grasped his meaning. "Well, Winston Churchill said that the traditions of the British navy were 'rum, sodomy, and the lash.'"

Conversation trailed off then, each lost in thought. A haze had filmed the western horizon, causing the sun's last light to turn ruby red. Berry squinted into the crimson glare, saying, "Strange . . . wonder if there's a fire somewhere causing that—"

Tonn's gaze turned upward—even the air overhead was scarlet. "It *is* strange. Reminds me of something . . ."

Berry shivered, although not completely from the cooling temperature. "Maybe we should be heading back to the bus stop."

Tonn nodded, turned . . . and turned again. "Do you know which direction it is?"

"Yeah, it's—" Berry broke off when he saw that the landscape around them was lost in a thick, reddish fog that blanketed even the concrete path they'd walked.

"It's okay," Tonn said, reaching into a pocket, "we'll just use GPS." He looked at his phone, and frowned before peering up at Berry. "It's dead. It had a seventy percent charge ten minutes ago."

Feeling the first tingle of alarm, Berry dug out his own phone, tapped the screen, thumbed the power button. "Mine's dead, too. What the fuck?"

They stood close together, not moving, waiting, as the atmosphere around them didn't darken, but *deepened*. The red light was now so dense that even Berry's dark skin was blood-hued. It wasn't just the visual quality of the light; the air *felt* strange, too, both weighty and charged. Berry didn't like the way his adrenaline was rushing; he tried to force himself to breathe easily, to stay alert but calm, to figure out a solution.

"Okay," he said, "we just have to find the paved path and follow it." He broke off as he looked down and saw that his feet rested on something that might have been either grass or long-dead brush. "Did we really walk this far from the path?"

He heard Tonn's gulp followed by, "No, I'm fairly certain we didn't."

A sound intruded then: a deep, resonant creak that echoed through the miasma like an old giant's bones. "What is that?" Tonn said, the pitch of his voice climbing with his fear.

Some intuition told Berry they had to *move*, and he grabbed his friend's arm, running any direction, just *away*. After a few seconds the sound came again, from behind them this time—where they'd just been—and they turned.

An object appeared slowly in the denseness, moving—or, perhaps, *forming* as they watched. It took Berry's mind a few seconds to assemble what appeared: curved wood, weathered to what was probably gray, fraying ropes, low railings, hanging canvas—

"It's . . . a ship."

Tonn, whose shuddering Berry could feel against his own, blurted, "That's impossible."

"I know it is, but—"

It *was* a ship, of a kind long obsolete. Berry knew more about buildings than boats, but he knew enough to recognize this as something from more than a century ago, when vessels still plied the seas by virtue of sail-power alone. Berry could smell brine, although whether it came from actual water or from the old stained and chipped sides of the ship he couldn't say.

The ship, with its long bowsprit preceding it, floated before them. At first it seemed to be unmanned, but as Berry squinted through the gloom he thought he saw movement—*stealthy* movement—somewhere near the center.

Tonn started forward, walking slowly. Berry gasped and leapt to stop his friend. With low urgency, he asked, "What are you doing?"

"I saw something . . ."

"Isn't that even *less* reason to go towards that thing?"

Tonn's eyes glinted in the red air. "Don't you want to know?"

Yes, Berry almost shouted, *I do want to know—I want to know how to get out of here, get back to Ypres, or Brussels, or London, or best of all Atlanta, but I'd like to get out with YOU, because what I feel for you is stronger than my fear.* Instead, he said, "If you're going, so am I."

Tonn smiled at him, and when he took Berry's hand the fear diminished. Then they were approaching the ship together, watching its bulk loom before them, growing as they neared.

At a distance of six feet, they walked along the hull; the railing was still several feet over their heads ... *as if,* Berry thought, *we were walking on the surface of the ocean.* They made their way to the bow, but saw no easy way to climb aboard. As Tonn reversed and began striding back to the center, Berry said, "I could boost you."

Tonn stopped, visually assessing. "That might work."

Berry caught sight just then of something moving directly overhead, and he instinctively pulled Tonn aside as a long wooden gaff with a rusted metal hook slashed through the air where Tonn had stood. They staggered back, and Tonn cried out incoherently.

The gaff hook was withdrawn, and a British-accented voice called back, "Name yourselves!"

Tonn gained his footing and cried out, "My name is Tonnison, and my friend is Berry."

The man on the ship—still unseen—replied, "Are you men, then?"

Tonn and Berry exchanged a look of surprise before Tonn answered, "Yes. We mean you no harm."

There was a silent beat before the sailor asked, "What is the year?"

Tonn answered, "2023."

After a few seconds a rope ladder was tossed down over the side of the ship. Tonn looked to Berry for assent; when it was given, he began to climb, Berry following close behind. Berry was almost surprised to find that the rope ladder felt real and normal—he could make out the individual fibers rough against his skin. As he reached the deck and stepped onto it, he felt wood under his trainers, but the sound of his footsteps was curiously muffled, as if the crimson gloom consumed part of it.

"I'm sorry about the gaff," the man on the ship said, "but I had to be sure you were human."

He turned, revealing an old-fashioned, threadbare soldier's uniform, olive drab with brass buttons half-undone and knee-high leg wrappings, a handsome face—

Tonn's knees gave way and he fell to the deck as he looked up at the man before them. "How can . . . you can't——"

Berry was crouched beside him instantly, concerned. "Tonn, what's happening? You okay?"

Without taking his eyes from the man who stood six feet away, watching curiously, Tonn gasped out, "It's him—dear God, it's William Hope Hodgson."

Berry turned, saw that Tonn was right—the man before them did match the photos he'd seen earlier. But that wasn't possible, was it? *Neither is a sailing ship in the middle of the Belgian countryside,* Berry reminded himself.

"How do you know me?" Hodgson asked.

Regaining his feet with Berry's assistance, Tonn stepped forward, incredulous. "I've read everything you wrote. I'm even working on a book about your writings."

Hodgson's face creased in surprise. "I'm flattered, Mr. Tonnison. But tell me, please: you said the year was 2023?"

"Yes."

Hodgson's brow furrowed as he turned away, pacing a few feet. "I don't understand. I know time has passed, but that's—that doesn't seem possible."

Berry stepped forward, asking, "Do you know how you got here? On this ship, I mean?"

Hodgson shook his head. "I was manning the Forward Observation Post, and then . . . suddenly I was here, alone on this ship." He turned to look Tonn in the eye, his gaze fierce. "Sir, if you are so intimately acquainted with my life, perhaps you can tell me—"

"I'm sorry," Tonn said, "but you were hit by a German artillery shell, and . . . blown to bits."

"And yet I'm here."

Spreading his hands in dismay, Tonn answered, "I can't explain it either, except—"

"What?"

Tonn thought for a moment before looking up again at Hodgson. "In *The House on the Borderland* when the Recluse travels to the arena of the gods . . ." He broke off, still working through the notion.

Hodgson prompted, "Yes?"

"Maybe the force of the artillery shell actually separated your consciousness from your body."

"And yet, I have a body." Hodgson raised his arms, took a few steps to demonstrate.

"You have a body *here*. But not in the real world. Or the *other* world."

"But the ship . . ."

Shrugging, Tonn said, "I don't know. Maybe the ship is like the one in *The Ghost Pirates*, caught between worlds."

"Like me." Hodgson's tone was both matter-of-fact and melancholy.

"And you're alone here?"

"Not always. There are . . . things . . . that we pass, and sometimes they try to board. That's why I nearly attacked you."

As Tonn and Hodgson talked, Berry examined the ship, touching the sails, testing the wheel, marveling at how real it all seemed. "So it does sail?" he asked.

They both turned to look at him. Hodgson asked, "I beg your pardon?"

"The ship—it sails?"

"I don't understand—the ship is *always* sailing."

Berry felt panic at the thought of the ship moving away, from Mont Kemmel, from his world; he rushed to the side, looked over the edge and saw . . . nothing. Beyond the ship was only the gloom, the color now subtly shifting from crimson to a lighter magenta. He felt no sway beneath his feet, but when he looked up he saw that the sails billowed out, as if blown by a steady and powerful breeze. His blood turning to ice, he went to his friend, grasping weakly at solid flesh. "Tonn, it's true—look at the sails."

"Where are we going?"

Tonn's question froze them both. As they stared at each other, shock etched in their faces, Hodgson stepped forward. "It journeys to places not of the *old* world. I've seen an island where demons the size of trees battled for supremacy. In polar climes, sirens sang to me, and their voices appeared as blue ice that shattered as it left their mouths. We drifted for a time in a mass of living seaweed that grew upward around the ship until we were surrounded by forests, but they parted for us when we at last sailed on."

Hodgson's attention wandered then; he turned away from Tonn and Berry, retrieved the gaff, and began to patrol the starboard side of the ship. Berry looked at his friend, whose gaze was turned inward. "Why are we here?" he asked in a low voice. "Did we . . . die?"

Shaking his head, Tonn answered, "I don't think so. I think it has something to do with the date—the anniversary of his passing."

"Like a ghost story." Berry remembered tales his gramma had told of spirits that returned on special nights, the date of their birth or death.

"That," Tonn said, "and maybe . . . *me*. Something about my interest in him, or—" He broke off for a few seconds before adding, "You know what's funny? In his books, things like this usually happen for no reason."

"So," Berry asked, gesturing at the ship and the void around it, "is this like his books?"

"It is, but it also *isn't*. It's like we're in his world, but . . . it's different somehow, it's———"

He broke off as Hodgson uttered an incoherent cry and lunged.

Berry spun to see something climbing up over the wooden side of the ship opposite them. At first he thought it was someone wearing a mask that depicted an exquisite feminine face, frozen in an attitude of disdain, but then he realized the thing trying to board the ship was made of stone. It was huge—it must have been at least eight feet tall—and it moved slowly, apparently due to its rocky bulk. Its massive shoulders hove into view, revealing its body draped in sculpted jewelry and garments.

Hodgson flipped the gaff about and drove the blunt end into the living statue's chest, trying to dislodge it. The thing grabbed at him, but its sluggish motion saved Hodgson, who danced back and then struck again. It returned both hands to the ship, holding on—and two more hands appeared next to it, one holding a short sword. Hodgson dropped the gaff, reached to the deck, and came up with an axe, which he used to chop the wood beneath one of the hands, all while dodging the sword. After two axe-swings a chunk of wood came free, the thing lost its grip and tilted back on one side. A final kick from Hodgson was enough to free its grip. All four arms flailed for purchase that it didn't find, but its carven face never altered. It fell back into nothingness, although Berry thought he heard, after several seconds, the distant sound of rock shattering against rock.

With the invader repelled, Hodgson leaned on the gaff to catch his breath as Tonn rushed forward. "Are you all right?"

Still panting, Hodgson nodded.

Berry joined them. "What the fuck was that?"

Hodgson looked at him, startled, seemingly more taken aback by Berry's language than the appearance of a living statue. "It looked rather like Kali to me."

"But it was made of stone."

"Yes. A statue of Kali, then."

Tonn thought for a few seconds before peering at Hodgson. "Kali ... 'The Goddess of Death.'"

Hodgson arched one eyebrow, appreciatively. "By God, lad, you *do* know my work, don't you?"

Berry stepped close to Tonn and asked, "What's going on?"

"Hodgson wrote a story about a statue of Kali that everyone thinks is alive, but it turns out to be a hoax."

"But—that *was* alive ... wasn't it?"

Tonn nodded, eyes never leaving Hodgson. "Sir, may I ask: what has occupied your time for the century you've been on this ship? Surely it didn't all go to fighting off goddesses."

"No. I've . . ." Hodgson paused before saying, with some excitement, "Let me show you." He set down the gaff and went through a door into the crew quarters below deck.

Tonn and Berry waited until Hodgson reappeared, lugging a stack of leatherbound books. "I found these down in the captain's quarters—empty log books. I filled these in a few years. Since then, I've continued to write on whatever I could find—the backs of charts, even sailcloth."

He set the books down on the deck. Tonn picked up the top one, flipped it open, squinted to read: *"The Ship on the Sea of Nightmares."* He flipped through a few pages before looking at Hodgson in wonder. "It's a new novel?"

Nodding, Hodgson waved at the books. "They all are. I've probably written fifty."

Tonn gasped. Berry understood: this was a dream fulfilled, a treasure beyond imagining. He placed a hand on his friend's arm, was pleased when Tonn added his hand atop Berry's. "This is . . ." Tonn's voice failed him. Instead he scanned the handwritten text, stopping to read passages, eyes glittering in the burgundy air. After a few seconds he turned to Berry excitedly. "I think I understand now." To Hodgson, he said, "Is there a scene in any of these where you fight a living statue of Kali?"

Hodgson's jaw hung open for a second before he said, "There is."

Returning his attention to Berry, Tonn said, "That's it, then: this place is Hodgson's world, the one created in his books . . . including the *new* books."

Berry glanced around, murmuring, "We're inside his stories?"

Hodgson asked, "You're suggesting this place is of my creation? If so, it's not deliberate."

Tonn answered, "No, but great art seldom is."

When Tonn returned his attention to the books, Hodgson watched him read. "I'm pleased to know they'll find at least one reader."

Tonn replaced the book atop the stack. "More than that. Many more. We have to get these out to the world."

Berry blinked in surprise; he was starting to think he and Tonn would be stuck here, forever, aboard this nameless ship. "How?"

"I've been thinking: what if the ship sails only in *this* world?"

"So . . . we climb back down, and we're back on Mont Kemmel?"

Tonn nodded, starting to smile.

"But Mont Kimmel had disappeared *before* we got on the ship."

"If I'm right about the date being significant, then it might reappear after midnight, when the date changes."

Berry began to laugh. "We can just walk away from this?"

"We can at least try."

From behind them Hodgson said, "But I can't go with you."

Looking at him, Tonn asked, "Why not?"

"Do you not think that I've tried to leave this damnable ship before? I've tried hundreds, *thousands* of times, but it doesn't work. The minute I climb overboard I find myself back on the deck. But you—you should leave, especially since you don't know if the conditions could change and strand you here."

Pointing at the books, Tonn said, "What about these? Will you permit me to take them? After all," he said, unable to contain his delight, "we've never had the work written by a great author in the afterlife."

The expression that crossed Hodgson's face was almost overwhelmingly sad. "I suspect I'm not who you need to secure permission from. I write to be read, but there are other gods overseeing my existence, and probably that of my work. In fact, I suspect you will be unable to take *anything* from this ship with you."

Tonn looked crestfallen. Berry stepped in, asking, "Is there a way we can test that?"

Hodgson considered before plucking one of the brass buttons from his coat. "Take this with you and climb down."

Berry accepted the offered button, felt its heft in his palm. It was tangible; Berry couldn't imagine it suddenly vanishing. He looked to Tonn, who urged, "Try it."

Walking to the rope ladder, Berry held the button beneath three fingers of his right hand, using the others to hold onto the rungs. He lowered himself cautiously, half expecting to be pulled down into an indescribable doom, but then his right foot touched ground.

The button was still in his hand.

He brought down his left foot.

The button was gone. From above, he heard Hodgson laugh bitterly.

"What?" Berry yelled up.

Tonn called, "The button is back on his jacket."

That was it; they couldn't take the books. Berry knew Tonn must be devastated. When seconds had passed with no sound from above, he climbed the ladder until he had just cleared the edge of the ship, but he didn't step into it. A sense of dread that he couldn't explain had built within him; he knew that going back aboard would trap him there forever.

"Tonn," he called.

The instant Tonn turned to him, Berry saw the regret on his face and knew.

"I'm not coming," Tonn said.

"But . . ." Berry spoke past tears now, making no effort to release his grip long enough to wipe them away. "This shouldn't be your world, Tonn. You have so much left in your own world—including *me*."

Tonn leaned down and kissed Berry softly, a lingering but light kiss, one that Berry would contemplate and rue and love the rest of his life. "I'm sorry. But I really believe I'm meant to be here. You're not."

Later on, Berry wouldn't remember clambering back down the rope ladder, or staggering through the magenta gloom, or hearing a clock somewhere in the distance strike twelve, or realizing he was looking at trees and a starlit field, not a ship surrounded by a waterless void.

He was still crying as he found the paved path and started toward the bus station.

All That Lies Below

Tim Waggoner

*T*his, Jacob Reed thought to himself, *was the worst idea I've ever had.*

He sat in the stern of an aluminum motorboat, upper body turned sideways, left hand on the tiller, right on the throttle, dressed in T-shirt, shorts, sneakers, and an orange lifejacket. He'd just stopped the motor, but he hadn't tossed the anchor overboard to keep the boat in place yet. There was a slight breeze blowing, and the boat was slowly drifting to the left. *Port,* he reminded himself. *Left is port.* The motion was gentle, and someone else might have found it soothing. Jacob, however, felt nauseated. It was warm and sunny this afternoon, only a few white clouds in the sky—a beautiful day—but he trembled as if it were a winter midnight.

Aaron thrashing in the water, shouting to be heard over the engine's roar, Dad sitting in the stern, completely oblivious to what's just happened, gripping the tiller with one hand and swigging a beer with the other, the boat racing across the lake, leaving Aaron behind, Jacob shouting, "Go back, go back!"

Take deep breaths, Jacob reminded himself. This was one of the techniques his therapist had given him for managing an incipient panic attack. He slowly inhaled, held the air in his lungs for a ten count, and then slowly let it out again. He repeated this process four more times, and when he finished he felt somewhat better. His trembling was less violent, and his nausea had diminished to a tolerable level.

He thought of the conversation he'd had with his therapist the previous week.

Now that we've practiced breathing and relaxation techniques, I think you're ready for exposure therapy. We'll start small, with you viewing still images of water, maybe even videos if you feel up to it. When you're comfortable with that, we can progress to touching water in a glass or sink, then being near a larger body of water, such as a pool or pond. Finally, we'll get more immersive, and you'll go into a pool or even a lake—but not until you're ready. It's important to go through this progression slowly, one step at a time.

Just listening to Dr. Curtis talk about this process had made Jacob nervous, but he'd swallowed, nodded, forced a smile.

Okay. Let's give it a shot.

He didn't really want to do any of these things, but recently his aquaphobia had become so severe that he couldn't manage to bathe himself properly or brush his teeth. He cleansed himself with a washcloth and one bottle of drinking water—no more—and he used mouthwash instead of brushing. He also applied a significant amount of deodorant every day, but it only did so much to mask his body odor. He was uncomfortable going out in public and stayed home as much as possible. He was employed by an insurance company, and he was able to work remotely a couple days a week, but his supervisor insisted he come into the office the rest of the time, and his coworkers wrinkled their noses whenever he was near, and they did their best to avoid him. He felt like a prisoner in his own life, and so he'd started seeing a therapist. Now, sitting in a small boat in the middle of a lake, he wished he'd never sought help. And he hadn't come to just any lake—he'd come to *the* lake.

It's your own fault. Dr. Curtis said to start small. Instead, you decided to jump right into the deep end.

An unfortunate turn of phrase—*deep end*—but apt in his situation. He'd feared Dr. Curtis's step-by-step approach would take too long, and he might give up before the process was completed. By going straight to the source of his phobia and confronting his fears head-on, he'd hoped that he'd be able to conquer them and be done with it.

Idiot.

He hadn't been back to Clearwater Lake since he was eight—nearly thirty years ago—but it looked the same as it had back then. Green trees lined the shore—oak and elm, mostly—along with ferns, goldenrod, cattails, and various flowers he didn't recognize. Waterlilies and algae clumps floated offshore, and a stately blue heron waded in the water, searching for food. The water itself was mostly still, rippling only slightly in the breeze. Although it was sunny, the temperature was mild, even a touch cool due to the breeze. It was a scene straight out of a brochure—

Visit Beautiful Clearwater Lake! Not everything was pleasant, though. Despite the lake's name, the water was dark and murky. He couldn't look at it for more than a few seconds before his pulse and respiration began to speed up. The water appeared cold, but there was no way he was going to reach over the side of the boat and touch it to find out. Worst of all was the smell—a combined odor of rotting fish and decaying plant matter that made his gorge rise.

He'd suffered from aquaphobia ever since *that day,* but mostly it had manifested itself in an aversion to getting into pools, especially ones that had a deep end. After Aaron's death, their parents had wanted him to take swimming lessons so that if he ever found himself in the same situation as his brother, he'd be able to survive. At first he'd refused to go, so his father made him and went along to make sure he did as he was told. He threw a screaming tantrum when the instructor tried to get him into the water with the other kids, and his father, embarrassed, took him home. His parents said no more about swimming lessons after that.

For several years he had a recurring nightmare about Aaron. The dream began with Jacob floating beneath the surface of a large body of water, but he wasn't scared. He sensed no danger nearby, and although he wasn't breathing, his lungs didn't seem to feel the need for air. Sunlight filtered down from above, and the water was warm and soothing. He'd never known such peace, and he wished that he could remain like this forever.

Jacob . . .

The voice came from below him, and when he looked down he saw a darkness so vast it seemed to fill the universe. A terrible cold radiated from it, and the water around him began to lose its warmth, as if the darkness was stealing—no, *devouring* it. The voice came again, and this time he recognized it as Aaron's.

Come down and join me, brother. The water's fiiiiiiiiiinnnneee . . .

He'd wake up at that point, sweating, heart racing, gulping for air.

He stopped having the dream after a while, but his anxiety at physically being around water only increased as he aged. A few months ago he'd gone to a local park with Lindy, the girl he'd been dating at the time. They'd walked along the trails in the woods, holding hands, and talking about whatever came to mind. He'd checked the weather on his phone before leaving to pick her up. If there was even the slightest chance of rain, he wouldn't go outside. The report said the chance was only 3 percent, so he figured he was in the clear. But they'd only been walking a few minutes before rain began to fall, just a few drops at first, but it quickly became a downpour. In absolute panic, he let go of Lindy's hand and ran back to the car. He was already behind the driver's seat when she got there, and as soon as she sat down he'd thrown himself into her arms and sobbed.

She broke up with him the next day, and although it was humiliating, he didn't blame her. Who wanted to be with someone as screwed up as he was? His condition worsened exponentially after that, until eventually his phobia interfered with almost every aspect of his life. Only then did he seek out a therapist, and he'd been seeing her once a week for the last month. She was helping, but so far his progress had been achingly slow, hence his decision—his extremely *stupid* decision—to speed things up by returning to Clearwater Lake.

At their first session, Dr. Curtis had asked him to tell her about what had happened to Aaron.

When we were kids, Dad took Aaron and me fishing at Clearwater Lake. It's only about forty-five minutes from my parents' house, and he would go there every Sunday when the weather was good. He always went alone, and Aaron and I would beg him to take us, too. Finally, Mom got sick of listening to us whine and told Dad that we were going with him, whether he liked it or not. He wasn't thrilled, but he agreed, and Aaron and I got our first trip to Clearwater Lake. It would turn out to be our last, too.

Dad didn't make us wear lifejackets—"Those things are for wimps," he said—and we felt very grown up. He bought us a couple of cane poles at a little shop by the lake, rented an outboard, and off we went. Dad liked to drink when he fished, so he brought a case of beer along, and he polished half of it off within a couple hours. None of us caught anything, and Aaron and I were bored, hungry, and sunburned. Dad didn't believe in sunscreen, either. Aaron started asking Dad to take us home, and Dad kept putting him off and drinking more beer. I was older than Aaron by a couple years, and I had more experience with Dad's temper, so I knew to keep my mouth shut. Aaron kept bugging Dad, though, and eventually he irritated him enough that he told us to pull in our lines and store our poles in the bottom of the boat. We did, and he reeled in his line and put his much nicer pole away. He pulled in the anchor, cracked open another beer, started the motor, and gave it the gas.

The water was choppy that day—a thunderstorm was rolling in—and the boat bounced on the waves as it surged toward shore. Somehow Aaron fell over the side, and Dad, he—he didn't seem to notice. He just kept on going and drinking his beer. At least, I told myself he didn't notice Aaron going overboard. As I got older, I wondered if Dad did something to knock Aaron purposefully out of the boat, as a way of punishing him for making us quit earlier than he wanted.

As I said, neither Aaron nor I wore lifejackets, and we couldn't swim. I shouted for Dad to go back and get Aaron, and he turned the boat around. We returned to the spot where we'd been fishing, but there was no sign of Aaron. We called his name over and over, but there was no answer. Later, the sheriff's department gathered volunteers to go out in boats to look for Aaron's body, but they never found it. It was as if the lake just . . . swallowed him.

I've hated water ever since.

A thought occurred to Jacob then. What if by trying to accelerate his healing he'd traumatize himself anew, making it even harder for him to get better? Maybe he should return to shore and take things slow, as Dr. Curtis advised. This trip wasn't necessarily a complete bust. He had managed to come here, rent a boat, and pilot it out onto the water—something he wouldn't have thought possible. That counted for something, right?

He started the motor, took hold of the tiller, pushed the throttle forward, and the boat began moving. He would need to do a 180 before he could head back to shore, and he'd have to fight the compulsion to run the motor at its top speed. The last thing he wanted to do was capsize the boat and end up in the water. He still couldn't swim, and although his lifejacket would protect him, the thought of floating in the water, alone, with no one around to help him, was terrifying.

As the boat surged toward shore, Jacob saw something bobbing in the water ahead. At first he thought someone had tossed some discarded clothes into the lake, but as he drew closer he saw it was a young boy floating on his back. He eased off the throttle and the boat slowed, and when he was close enough he turned off the motor and used a wooden paddle to maneuver next to the boy.

The boy was around eight or nine, thin, had brown hair, was wearing a T-shirt and shorts, and his feet were bare. He resembled Aaron, so much so that Jacob feared he was hallucinating. But closer inspection showed the boy's features were different—nose flatter, eyes farther apart, ears larger. Still, the resemblance was striking.

Don't be dead, please don't be dead . . .

The boy's eyes were closed, and his mouth was parted slightly. Jacob couldn't tell if he was breathing. He didn't want to touch him in case he *was* dead—and he *really* didn't want to get his hands wet—so he gently prodded the boy with his paddle.

"Hello? Are you okay?"

A stupid question. Even if the boy was alive, he obviously wasn't okay.

The boy didn't react at first, but then his eyes fluttered open and he looked at Jacob, squinting in the sunlight.

"Help . . . me . . ."

Jacob couldn't bring himself to touch the boy—he'd get his hands wet for sure if he did.

"Are you strong enough to climb in on your own?"

"No . . ."

Jacob thought about extending the paddle toward the boy so he could grab hold of it, but he didn't see how that would help the boy get into the boat. Jacob didn't have a choice.

Exposure therapy, he thought. He gritted his teeth and reached for the boy.

"What's your name?"

The boy sat in the middle of the boat, facing Jacob, who sat in the stern. The boy was wet and shivering, and Jacob wished he had a coat or blanket to give him. It didn't help that dark clouds were beginning to roll in from the west, blocking the sun. Jacob hoped they weren't storm clouds. He was still shaky and nauseated from helping the boy into the boat. If it started raining—while he was out on the lake, no less—he didn't think he could handle it.

The boy didn't answer right away, and Jacob feared he'd suffered a head injury or was in shock, but then he said—

Aaron

—"Stevie."

Aaron's full name was Aaron Steven Reed.

Jacob told himself the name was a coincidence, just like the boy's resemblance to his brother. He felt confident Dr. Curtis would have said the same if she were here.

After the boy was safely in the boat, Jacob had furiously wiped his hands on his shirt to dry them. They still felt as if they had a thin coating of slime on them, though, and now his wet shirt clung to his skin. *Don't think about that—focus on the boy.*

"How did you end up out here all by yourself?"

Jacob wasn't worried that the boy's lungs were filled with water. He hadn't coughed once since Jacob had fished him out of the lake. But *something* wasn't right here. Young boys didn't just magically appear in the middle of lakes for no reason.

"That last thing I remember is riding in a boat with my dad and brother. After that . . . ." He shrugged.

Jacob felt as if he'd been punched in the gut. Boat. Dad. Brother.

What if this *was* Aaron? What if the boy only seemed to look different because Jacob's memory of his brother had become fuzzy over the years? But it wasn't possible. For this boy to be Aaron, not only would he have had to survive drowning, he would have had to remain the same age he'd been the day they'd gone fishing with their father.

True. If he was alive. But if he's dead . . .

Jacob looked closely at "Stevie." The boy *seemed* alive enough. He breathed, moved, talked . . .

Seems *to breathe,* seems *to move,* seems *to talk.* A lot of *seems* there.

What was he thinking, that he was looking at Aaron's ghost? Or something that was only pretending to be Aaron? Maybe that's why the boy's features weren't quite the same as what Jacob remembered. "Stevie" was an imperfect copy.

The sky was growing darker now, and tendrils of mist coiled across the water. A storm was definitely coming—and soon.

He told himself to forget his foolish fantasy about Stevie being Aaron's ghost or some kind of doppelgänger. For the first time in three decades he'd returned to the site of the worst trauma he'd ever experienced, and it was affecting him in ways he hadn't anticipated. His mental health was already precarious—to put it mildly—and instead of building his exposure to water slowly, as Dr. Curtis recommended, he'd immediately thrust himself into the most stressful scenario imaginable. No wonder he was thinking ridiculous thoughts.

Only one thing was important right now, though: taking Stevie to shore and getting him the help he needed. The boy seemed well physically, but not all injuries were detectable at first glance, especially to someone without medical training. Stevie could have a concussion, maybe even be bleeding internally. The sooner the boy could be checked out by emergency medical personnel, the better.

Plus, Jacob *really* wanted to get off the lake before the rain came.

"I rented this boat at a small store near the dock. We'll go there and see if we can figure out what happened to you, okay?"

Stevie nodded.

Jacob started the motor, took hold of the tiller, pushed the throttle forward, and resumed his trip to shore with his new passenger aboard— a boy who was definitely *not* Aaron's ghost.

It happened swiftly, almost as if some cosmic switch had been flipped. The sky darkened, the mist grew thicker, and within moments Jacob couldn't see more than three feet in front of his face. Stevie was little more than a silhouette, and he couldn't make out the bow. He pulled back on the throttle to slow the boat, not wishing to collide with anything. He hadn't seen any nearby boats before the mist grew too thick, and he and Stevie were still a long way from shore, so he didn't need to worry about running their boat aground. Not for a while, anyway. But he wasn't comfortable surging ahead blindly. What if they ran into a floating log or something? Best to take things slow until they made it out of the mist.

"Weird weather, huh?"

Jacob tried to sound relaxed so Stevie wouldn't be afraid, but the words came out as a strained whisper.

"Why don't you like water?" Stevie asked.

The sudden change of topic took Jacob by surprise, and a few seconds passed before he could respond.

"What makes you think I don't like water?"

"You wiped your hands really hard after you pulled me out of the lake—and you looked as if you were going to puke."

He almost had.

He didn't want to upset the boy by telling him about Aaron's death, but he had other reasons for his dislike of water.

"The surface of water is like a thin barrier between our world—the world of air-breathers—and a hostile, alien one filled with scaled, slimy *things* that would eat us if given a chance. We can't see beyond the surface. Anything could be there, and it could be a hundred feet away from you or only a few inches. And there's no way to know how deep the water is. For all we can tell, it might go on forever."

"A teacher at school told us that people are mostly made of water. She said that when our earliest ancestors left the ocean they took the ocean with them."

Jacob's throat was suddenly dry.

"I try not to think about things like that."

"I like the water," Stevie said. "Especially when it's deep. It's so quiet and peaceful, as if you're dreaming and you never have to wake up."

They continued on for a time after that, neither speaking. Instead of the mist growing thinner the farther they went, it became even thicker, and soon Jacob couldn't see Stevie at all. The temperature began to drop, and Jacob soon found himself shivering. It had to be worse for Stevie, since his clothes were still wet.

"Are you okay?" Jacob asked.

"I'm a little cold, but I'm all right."

Before Jacob could say anything more, something big and heavy *thumped* into the starboard side of the boat, setting it to rocking. There was another *thump*, this one on the port side, and Jacob let go of the tiller and throttle and gripped the sides of the boat to steady himself.

"Hold on to something!" he called to Stevie, but he received no reply. Maybe the boy was too intent on bracing himself for another thump on the hull to respond to Jacob. Or maybe whatever struck the boat had reached in and snatched Stevie away under cover of the mist. He imagined a long, thick tentacle rising from the water, stretching toward the boat, and grabbing hold of the first thing it touched—which happened to be Stevie. Jacob had heard no splash. Maybe the tentacle had pulled Stevie into the water slowly and silently. But that didn't make sense. Stevie would have fought and struggled to free himself, making a great deal of noise in the process—and Jacob had heard nothing.

He was afraid to go forward and check on the boy. What if the thing in the water, whatever it was, struck the boat again while he was moving? He could lose his balance and fall overboard—and once he was in the water, the thing would have him. But he couldn't just forget about Stevie. The boy might need his help.

He took a deep breath, let go of the boat's sides, and started forward.

The motor was still running, but the throttle was set to low, so the boat wasn't going fast, and while the craft rocked from side to side as he moved, the motion wasn't severe enough to worry him. He reached the middle of the boat, where Stevie had been sitting, but the boy wasn't there. He continued toward the bow, right arm extended, moving his hand back and forth, hoping his fingers would brush against Stevie, but he felt nothing. Where could the boy have gone?

A cold pit opened in Jacob's stomach as a thought occurred to him. What if Stevie had never been here? What if he'd been a hallucination brought on by Jacob's anxiety, a companion conjured by his imagination to make him feel less alone and give him something to focus on other than his fear? Maybe the mist and the creature in the water were delusions, too. Suffering from a phobia was one thing, but now he was afraid he might be losing his mind.

He was on the verge of a full-fledged panic attack when the boat came to a sudden stop. He stumbled forward, slipped, and pitched over the side. He screamed as he fell, anticipating a plunge into cold, dark water, but while he landed on something wet, it held his weight, and he did not go into the lake. The fall knocked the breath from him, and he lay there a moment, recovering. He moved his hands across the surface of whatever was beneath him, and found it to be some kind of plant material—soft and wet, but packed together so tightly that he did not fall through. He rose to a sitting position, then tentatively stood. He took a step, and while the vegetation gave beneath his weight a bit, it seemed solid enough.

He'd researched Clearwater Lake on the internet, hoping to familiarize himself with the place to reduce his anxiety before setting out on his therapeutic journey. One of the things he'd learned was that the lake was plagued by invasive water weeds that blocked sunlight and prevented oxygen production. He knew the weeds grew in thick patches, but he hadn't imagined they'd be anything like this.

"Jacob!"

Stevie's voice, but faint, as if coming from far away.

"Come here—you need to see this!" The boy laughed then, the sound light and joyous.

Somehow Stevie had gotten out of the boat and onto the water weeds, and it appeared he had walked some distance on them. Jacob was afraid to go after him. He weighed more than Stevie. What if he came to a thin spot in the weeds and fell through? But he couldn't abandon the boy, either.

He started walking in the direction he judged Stevie's voice had come from.

The mist was just as thick here as it was over the water, and Jacob stepped carefully, fearful that he'd come to an edge without knowing it and fall into the water. He called Stevie's name several times, but the boy didn't respond. More than once Jacob had the sense that he wasn't alone, that things were moving on the weed layer near him, but he saw nothing in the mist. He heard faint rustling noises from time to time, as if leaves were being rubbed together, and he imagined strange plant creatures moving about on the weeds, ignoring the crude flesh-and-blood being among them.

Before long, the mist began to dissipate, and Jacob was able to see the plant layer beneath his feet. The sky was no longer dark, and now that there was nothing to block the sun, it was getting warmer. Eventually the mist was gone, and Jacob saw that he was approaching the end of the weeds. The sky was blue and cloudless, and water black and shiny as polished obsidian stretched outward for as far as he could see. There was no sign of shore, and he wondered if there *was* a shore anymore, if it had ever existed at all. A small mound of weeds shaped like a small boy stood at the water's edge. Jacob walked over and stood beside it.

"You made it." The plant-thing spoke with Stevie's—with *Aaron's*—voice, but there was a wetness to it, as if his throat was filled with fluid.

"I did."

"Are you ready to take the next step?"

Jacob gazed across the dark sea toward the horizon.

"I don't know if I can."

"You'll be free there. Free of fear, and most of all, free of guilt."

A tear rolled down Jacob's cheek.

A teacher at school told us that people are mostly made of water. She said that when our earliest ancestors left the ocean, they took the ocean with them.

The weed-thing held out a crude approximation of a hand. After a moment's hesitation, Jacob took it. The plant material was cool, wet, and soft, but that was okay. It was his brother's hand, and that was all that mattered.

"What's it like?" Jacob asked. "Down there?"

"Why not find out for yourself?" Aaron said.

Jacob nodded. He took a deep breath—his last—and together he and his brother jumped into the obsidian water. Still holding hands, Aaron swam downward, pulling Jacob with him, down, down, down, toward a great darkness that dwarfed the two of them, an endless expanse of Nothing.

It was beautiful.

It was horrible.

The Aaron that had spoken to him in his childhood dream had been right, though.

The water here *was* fine.

The Call

Stephanie M. Wytovich

Someone is out   in the waves
their body a moving cavern
a shipwrecked home
devoured by   the sharp pincers of
time. I watch it float, the sea a ghost
rocking the corpse   to sleep.

The wind whispers   *collect it*
I stare into darkness, the sound
of ocean beating, pulsing
in my ears. I fight back the urge,
to reach out   to touch it
to bring it onto the boat, cover it
with blankets, wash the brine
from its face.

The gray pull of rain brings me
to my knees. I worship   the swell,
the gentle surge of death. There is
a rope in my hands, a tremble
in my voice. I call out to the body:

    Don't worry. I'm coming.

The Shellback's Tale

Lee Murray

'Twas late of an eve I met him,
  And brass-monkey cold outside,
In his cups at Neptune's Pleasure,
And his pay-day left on the tide.

It was the packet *Mortzestus,*
Departed without Burroughs.
I pulled up a stool and called for a tot,
I'd help him with his sorrows.

I cast around the tavern,
Spoke with barely a breath:
"That packet is haunted by shadows and pain,
She's nought but mis'ry and death."

Young Burroughs arched his brow at me,
Leaned back and crossed his arms.
"An old shellback wants to spin a cuffer,
I don't see where's the harm."

I took a swig of my brandy
And pondered where to start.
'Twas so jolly queer, I scarce believed it
Ere though I'd played my part . . .

The ship had set out for 'Frisco,
Under a moonlit sky,
When a shadder climbed over the lee-rail:
I saw it with mine own eye.

Not possible; I followed it,
Forrard to the fo'cas'le.
It stepped o'er the port-rail and vanished,
Along with its deathly chill.

I said nought to the Skipper,
Lest he think me lily-livered,
But the 'prentice and Mate, they felt it too,
For, tremulous, they shivered.

We lit the blarsted binnacle lamps,
To curb our creeping dread,
But we were dotty, or jolly well mad,
'Cause there's no holding back the dead.

From aft there came a strange moaning
To freeze your marrowbone;
The 'prentice cried for his mam in London,
I prayed that I'd get home.

Then the gallant did come away;
I went aloft with Hope.
The poor devil fell to his death from the rigging,
Neck severed by the rope.

Though none spied the deadly shadder,
The Watch all saw Hope fall,
The clewline whirling about in the air,
Without the slightest squall.

Hope's death wasn't the worst of it;
That came after third bell:
Four ships, each with its ghostly pirate crew,
'Neath the ocean's gray swell.

The mist descended upon us,
The shadders crawled over the poop;
They were bloody and putrid with long-past wounds,
Swarming the ill-fated sloop.

By now the Old Man had an inkling,
The ship would ne'er see port;
Those ghost-men were wanting to trade with us,
Lives would have to be bought.

We lined up on the maindeck,
The Mate would call the roll,
And every third man would go to his death:
Such was the gruesome toll.

Afeared that I might be chosen,
I smelled the 'prentice piss,
And I prayed the boy would die afore me
In that lonely abyss.

The haze was as thick as pea-flour
Throughout the grisly game;
To my mother's shame, I leapt with glee,
He failed to call my name.

Thank the Gods, I weren't among those
Flung o'er her port-rail;
The 'prentice, the Ordinary, sent to the deep
And us, deaf to their wails.

We hightailed it then to 'Frisco,
The wind was at our back;
Nine, ten knots to the hour she gave us,
Despite the men we lacked.

I paused my tale, I sipped my brew,
And watched the man's response.
He shook his head, incredulous, and I
Seethed at his nonchalance.

Young Burroughs, he laughed in my face,
Threw down his coin to leave.
I was just an old shellback telling tall tales,
Too dotty to believe.

Yet on the morrow evening
A ship came into dock,
And, to a man, the crew came to sup,
Their faces blanched in shock.

I searched for Burroughs 'mid the punters;
He wasn't at the Neptune,
So the lad had ne'er the chance to hear
Bad luck turned to fortune.

See, news of the sloop *Mortzestus*
Had rolled in with the tide;
She'd foundered, plunged headlong into the sea,
Only one man survived.

The Captain's Wife

Nancy Holder

This is the story of the Ballards as was told to us by Third Mate Christopher Ballard, writ into the log of the *Euterpe* on this date, 15 June, 18—. It is a blood-chilling tale, and it explains why we didn't hang him.

On 5 June, 18—, I, Christopher Ballard, was waiting for my younger brother, Emerson, to join our send-off party the night before the *Euterpe* set sail for the tropics. Fog clouded the sky and heavy rain slid down the windowpanes of my sitting room. I saw bad omens everywhere, hanging in the night like dying stars, and I calculated our chances on the open sea. Unfavorable.

It was a night for spinning tales of ghost stories, not the fanciful yarns of my companions. My three mates, Jack S——, Old Tim, and Arthur W—— had polished off the noodles from the Chinaman as well as several bottles of gin and rum, "pushing out the boot" to wish Emerson and me fair winds on our voyage.

"And the mermaid says, 'I'd love to, sir, but as ye can see, ye cannot part me parts!'"

As Old Tim concluded, our two mates broke into laughter and I stirred myself to smile, though I had not listened to the story. I had prepared one to tell, but my attention drifted to the empty chair set out for Em, then back to the rain-bones rattling the panes. Em was long past due for the farewell party. We were shipping out together for the first time, as I had previously served on whalers, while Em's voyages were merchant runs measured not in years but months, to appease our mother. He had got his ticket as an Able Bodied, and I had won the Third Mate's berth. So there was much to celebrate.

It could be the rain had delayed vital work, or maybe there was more to be done on the *Euterpe* than Em had realized. Or perhaps the vessel was still weighed down with suspicion and dark deeds, despite having been sold to a new master, that being you, Captain Fallworth. Em's last voyage with his old captain, Captain Covington, was a yarn worth spinning on a night like this. Thinking of it, I was concerned that something new was amiss, and that Em was in a bad spot.

"Christopher! Kit, old man!" Old Tim yelled at me. "You're the one's read all them books with the fancy lingo. Sing for your supper, lad!"

"Sing, sing, sing!" the other two chorused, clapping their hands.

"Gents," I began, "with regret—"

"No!" Old Tim protested. "We'll have a story from you!"

The door slammed open. Em swayed on the threshold, soaked to the skin, pale as a gull, hat in hand.

He stared at the men and then at me and blurted, "Kit, what I've just seen . . ."

"What? What've you seen?" Old Tim called out. "Let's hear your story."

"A yarn! A yarn!" Jack and Arthur clinked their glasses and held them up. "Come on, boy!"

I went to my brother. Slinging an arm over his shoulders, I led him to his chair and eased him down. I met no resistance; Em sank like a dead man, covered his face with his hands, and moaned.

"Oh, God, Kit," he said, gazing up at me.

As Jack poured him two fingers of gin, Old Tim said, "Lad, what's got you rattled?"

"Lock the door," Emerson pleaded.

Old Tim rose on his bowlegs and staggered to the door. "Done," he assured the lad.

"I saw the captain—"

"Captain Fallworth?" I cut in, citing your name, sir, as our employer.

"No," he said. "*My* captain. I mean, the one who retired. Captain Covington."

"You went to his home?" I asked, stunned. An Ordinary dared not speak to the captain aboard ship, much less present himself on land.

"Well, there's a cheeky lad," Old Tim said. "Next thing we know, you'll be calling on the King of England!"

"Did he see you?" Jack asked. "Or did his butler throw you out on your arse?"

"Let him tell his story, for God's sake," Arthur said. "Start at the beginning, Em, if you please."

I took the gin bottle from Jack and poured Em another two fingers. After he gulped them down, he took off his soaked coat, and I hung it beside the fire. His hat, too.

He looked over his shoulder at the door. "It's locked? Someone might be following me."

"Aye, it's locked," Old Tim assured him. "Woe to anyone who comes at us tonight. Am I right, me boyos?"

"Let him speak," I said.

The company filled their glasses, leaned toward him, and waited. Em took a deep breath and began.

"Four years ago, I joined the crew of the *Euterpe*. The old girl had seen much better days. Sails patched and repatched. Splintery masts and yards. Signs of rust. Shipworm. The food . . . the less said, the better.

"Captain Covington was the skipper, and he owned the *Euterpe*, and you could tell he was ashamed of her condition. He was like a man with an ugly daughter: he loved her, sure, but she had shortcomings—and each year she was worse. But I knew the ship as a dear old gal and the Old Man as a fair master, so I kept signing on.

"At the last, she seemed barely seaworthy, and my mother had bid me not to go. So I went down to the dock with no plans to sail on her, just to see if an old shipmate of mine had gone aboard so I could give him some winnings I owed him.

"Imagine my shock when I laid eyes on her and found her fitted out like the Empress of Russia. Freshly painted, hull clean and smooth, with fresh sails and lines, everything trim. The Third Mate spotted me and assumed I wanted my berth, so before I answered yea or nay, I asked him straight out what was going on.

"'Captain Covington got himself a rich wife,' he told me. 'And look, there she is.'

"You could have sent me overboard with a flick of your finger! She was a fine lady, dressed in silks and laces such as would last half a day at sea, and quite young and beautiful. She was in a delicate condition, if you catch my meaning, quite . . . rounded, and though I know it happens, I was startled to think that such a delicate lady would deliver her child at sea.

"I didn't mean to stare, but she caught my eye and gave me the shyest, most fleeting smile, rather like the silver sparkle running through a school of anchovies. Me, an Ordinary, and her the Captain's wife. My face went aflame and without thinking, I smiled back.

"Then I saw trailing behind her a small, misshapen lad with a bushy head of black hair and eyes to match, glowering something evil as he caught my smile. He narrowed his sunken, shriveled eyes, and I swear he grew a second set of teeth as he pulled back his lips in a sneer. He was her cabin boy, courtesy of the Captain, and his name was Kian."

"Irish, then," Old Tim said.

"I think not." Emerson swallowed hard. "I think he was from no land we have ever heard of. He was a devil. Had I known what a right menace he was before I told the Mate I would come aboard, I would have done as my mother asked, and stayed ashore. From that day on, he goaded not only me but the entire crew. Our drinking water was sour. We found dead vermin in our hammocks. He tormented the pigs and chickens we had brought with us. How they squealed and clucked when he glided near them like a snake, threatening to strike at any moment. I called him out for it, and he said they were all destined to die, so what did I care about it?

"The lady was oblivious, and of course no one could go to her and tell her that we longed to push her little man overboard. Of a night she would walk on the arm of her husband, she round and rosy, dressed like a duchess, and the horrid little imp trailing behind in splendid clothes of his own.

"The Old Man barely noticed her. I'm not sure he ever listened to a word she said. I assumed he was occupied with matters of the voyage, but I could see that she was nervous about it. She would prattle on and tug at his sleeve. He'd make an effort, but his heart was clearly not in it. She stayed as winsome and sweet as ever and lavished her affections on Kian. He knew he was untouchable, and oh, how he threw his weight around! The pranks got worse and worse.

"A number of Able-Bodied went to the Third Mate on behalf of the crew, but McGregor was a weakling and nothing was ever said. After the first full month at sea, the dear woman seemed to . . . droop. It's not all that unusual for a shipboard wife to enter confinement with a heavy case of seasickness. Of course, it had naught to do with me. She was a lady high above my station. But that first day she had smiled that sweet little smile at me, and I felt protective of her somehow."

"As a man does around a pretty girl," Arthur drawled.

"No, it were not like that," Em said. "I saw her a few times more, and she was more prominently with child, and pale and wan. She shuffled as she walked, as if it were a great effort, and occasionally she caught her breath and hunched over, as if her time had come.

"She seemed to seek me out when she promenaded with the Old Man. She looked terrified, those big blue eyes of hers as round as saucers. Her lips would move and I would wonder, is she asking me for help?

"A few nights on, she no longer came on deck. The evil little cabin boy brought all her meals and took away her washing. He was so busy that I hoped his days tormenting us were behind him. But it bothered me, it did, that she never came out of the cabin anymore.

"Then came the storm. Winds so fierce they pushed at the masts, thrashed and harried us. The *Euterpe* creaked and cracked. Risking life and limb, we shortened the sails, lashing ourselves to stay in place as the seas poured over the decks. The waters flicked and slithered like huge . . . tongues, or whips. I don't know how to describe it, but *you* could, Kit, had you been there. As if they had minds of their own. As if they were searching for us, to send us down to Davy Jones. The sky was ablaze with St. Elmo's Fire, leaping and jumping like sprites all over the spars.

"I looked out into the darkness, searching for God Himself to save us, and I saw shadows, but not dark ones, no, they were glowing. Pulsing in a rhythm, with shimmering veins throughout, like the hearts of beasts . . .

"After a time I passed out, and when I awoke the sky was dark and the sea was calm, and I told myself that I'd dreamed it all. The dawn revealed that I had not, for the foremast was cracked clean through, and stores and barrels had been swept overboard. Our cages and crates of pigs and chickens too. Fog surrounded us, and to my mind it was glowing, but the others said not, and after a time the sun burned it off.

"Then we spotted a cage of our piglets floating on a bed of the strangest-looking seaweed, all covered in a thick white slime. The Mate cried out, 'One's moving in the cage! One's alive!' and we threw out a net and brought it up. Sure enough, among the poor dead things one was sort of rolling to and fro. We lowered the cage onto the deck and opened it; on a sea of slime, out poured the bloated carcasses, and the piglet still alive—or so we thought. They tumbled out onto the deck on a sea of muck so vile and repulsive that several men hied themselves to the rail and heaved out their guts.

"As Cook moved to gather up the dead ones, he swore at all the disgusting muck and guts and dropped the lot. It stank to high heaven. The 'living' piglet flopped onto its back, and from the center of its belly a rounded white head erupted through the gore. Its mouth was a bloodstained circle of long, needle-pointed teeth. It sucked at the air, then the gigantic worm-body shot toward us in an unmistakable attack. We all drew back in horror.

"The Third Mate said, 'It's a hagfish.' It flipped and chomped its jaws at us, and slammed against the bulkhead, stunning itself.

"'Look! Look, there's more of 'em!' cried young Thomason, an Ordinary, and as we rushed to the starboard rail we slipped and slid in the ooze. Grabbing one another's hands, we hobbled like old maids and flung ourselves against the rail, clinging as our feet slid and scraped from out beneath us. We peered over, and several of us gave a shout. Our obviously dead chickens bobbed and danced, oozing blood, while the hagfish that had not found a home in any of our creatures slithered through the seaweed like enormous slime eels. Blobs of mucus shone on the water like huge jellyfish, pulsing with the hags, only such hags as none had ever seen. They were fish from hell, frenzied with hunger, sure as I am sitting here quaking in my boots at the memory.

"To a man we were repulsed, all but the diabolical cabin boy, who studied the mess with a sly grin. He caught me studying him and his grin broadened into a smile.

"Later, while I was on watch I caught him approaching the side with a fishing pole. I grabbed it from him, crying, 'You accursed wretch! Belay that!'

"'You'll be sorry for that someday,' said he, and as the starlight caught his face, I saw something in his eyes—something terribly *wrong*. I was frozen, and I could not look away. I saw *into* his eyes, into a different place of mists and waving shadows that stretched and shrank with my heartbeats; and *things* that I cannot describe but I knew were . . . *not right*. From an infernal land, or a dream—I can't explain it all, but even as I speak now, I sense them, feel them as if they are boring into me. . . .

"But back then, as he tossed his dark hair and turned away from me, I thought of Captain Covington's wife, and I feared for her. Aside from the Old Man, this creature was the only—dare I say person?—with the liberty to enter the cabin where she was stashed.

"I shared my troubled thoughts on the watch, with a man I shall not name because . . . Are you certain that the door is locked?"

"Locked, aye," Old Tim said with exasperation. "I locked it myself. What are you on about? Is this a prank? Hagfish do not behave so. This is the tallest tale ever I heard!"

"What did you say to the man?" Arthur prodded. "Go on, Em."

"I told him that I feared for the lady. That perhaps she was in danger or—or that she had died."

"He said this: 'I heard her cry out last night.'

"And I said, 'So she is alive!'

"'Or was,' said my mate. He shifted his gaze in the direction of the captain's quarters, as if he could see through the bulkhead. 'You know 'twas her money caused all the changes to the *Euterpe*,' he went on. 'The

Old Man found himself a young heiress. The ship is fitted up. No doubt the rest of her money is in his bank account. And did you see his eyes when they walked together at night? Darting this way and that. As if looking for a way out.'

"I caught my breath. 'Then are you saying that he would——'

"'No, never,' said he. 'I would never say that.'"

"And?" Arthur pressed. "What happened?"

"She never appeared again. The little devil came and went, easy as ever, but I could not keep my eye on him every minute. We finished the voyage and returned to port. I stayed behind when the lads all left, lingering, to see if when the Old Man disembarked, she came too. But word came that my—our—mother was quite ill and anxious to see me, so I left without knowing." He drew a ragged breath. "But now . . . I know *something*, but what it is, I do not know."

"No more gin for you," Old Tim said, laughing.

"What do you know, Em?" I asked.

His voice was scarcely a whisper. "Tonight I was at the dock, Kit. Aboard the *Euterpe*. We were done with all the last-minute duties. And I was coming home to the party through all the fog and rain. I was passing Captain Covington's mansion and for some reason I looked up at the widow's walk. Through the rain I saw a figure, and as I squinted to make it out, the weather seemed to . . . lighten. The sky fair *glowed*. And I saw that the figure was Mrs. Covington herself! I was so overjoyed that I waved at her. She gestured for me to approach the house, and so I did."

"Out in the storm, she was?" Jack asked. "Just walking about?"

"Exactly when did you start drinking tonight?" Old Tim teased.

"I knocked, and a little servant girl opened the front door. The Captain loomed close behind her, and he blinked in astonishment at the sight of me. I did the same, for he had aged terribly in the months since I'd seen him. His hair and beard had turned gray. His eyebrows, too. He was gaunt, wasted. I wondered if he'd been ill.

"He gestured for the girl to leave us. As she moved off, I said to him, 'Sir, excuse me, but your wife saw me and bade me approach.'

"He stared at me as if I were speaking in a foreign tongue. 'My wife,' he said, and he ground out the words. 'You saw my wife?'

"'Aye, sir. On the widow's walk,' I said.

"'That . . . can't be. It can't be.' He looked upward, as if he could see through the floors of the house to the walk, and cried out, 'Oh, God!' in such an agonized voice that I took a step forward to comfort him. 'Marie!'

"At that moment a baby started to cry. The Old Man went sheet-white and turned his head in the direction of the wailing.

"He looked back at me and whispered, *'Run.'* And I did. I ran all the way here. Are you sure that the door—"

The door burst open. Old Tim, drunk, had not secured it after all. I recognized the man on the threshold—Emerson's old captain, Covington, but withered and aged, as Em had said. In his arms he clutched an infant. The child let out a nigh-inhuman shriek and set to crying.

"Take him," Captain Covington said to us, holding out the babe. His arms shook. "I beg you. And run for your lives."

"Sir, what are you on about?" Em asked, rising.

"Save him!" Covington cried. Then he began to gag.

Em ran to Covington, shouting, "Sir, sir! Your *eyes!*"

"The babe!" Covington begged, and Em took the child in his arms. It was shrieking like a banshee.

The man collapsed to the floor. He convulsed wildly, rolling back and forth; foam frothed from his mouth and his heels thundered against the floor. Old Tim pulled Em back, and Em screamed as an enormous hagfish hurled itself out of the Captain's mouth and flopped onto the floor, writhing in its own slime as it wriggled toward Em and the babe. God help me, but I thought that the monster had eyes, human eyes, and black as night.

I cried, "Out, out of here!" and threw Em's coat at him. He covered up the babe. I was without my own coat, but after herding him out I flew over the threshold. Shouting, our three friends followed behind.

We ran all the way here, to the *Euterpe*. Jack, Old Tim, and Arthur went their own ways. Em and I shipped out with the tide, as we were expected and as we hoped to be safe from whatever foul business we had run into. And I beg your forgiveness, Captain Fallworth, for not telling you sooner that when we came aboard, we were in trouble and we had a babe with us, the which we hid from you until it was too late to turn back to port. Of course our ruse came to light within hours of casting off, and as you know, you and we agreed that we would leave the ship with the babe once we reached our first port.

But then it happened, and I cannot explain it. I can only tell what I saw and heard. My brother came to me with the child in his arms. I immediately saw something terrible in Em's eyes, a flickering of something inhuman, a slimy, putrid contamination that rocked me on my heels.

"You see it!" Kit cried. "Don't look at me!" He turned his head. "I saw too. It's the same as I saw in the Old Man's eyes before he died." He began to gag exactly as Covington had. "Oh, God, Kit, it's in the baby's eyes . . . and it's in mine." He doubled over, retching, clutching the squalling child tightly against his body. "Forgive me brother, for what I must do."

Before I could stop him, he leaped overboard. That is the God's truth. He jumped. And as the sea took them both, a strange mist rose out of the water like green steam, and the waters bubbled. If I must swing for it, then that's my fate, but I swear to you I did not kill them.

I attest that these are my own words.

(Signed)

CHRISTOPHER JAMES BALLARD, *Third Mate, Euterpe*

This was the testament we had before us when we placed Mr. Ballard in the hold. The Captain was of a mind to hang him. Then two seamen, Thomas Vanderberg and Apollinaire La Fontaine, both Able Bodied, came forward and provided eyewitness testimony confirming the Third Mate's account of the deaths. We have written both accounts into the log:

I am Thomas Vanderberg, an Able Bodied Seaman aboard the *Euterpe*. I witnessed Emerson Ballard climb over the starboard rail of his own accord and fall willingly into the water. He was holding a baby when he went.

>(Signed with an X)
>THOMAS VANDERBERG, *Able Bodied*

Translated from French by Captain Fallworth:

My name is Apollinaire La Fontaine. I am an Able Bodied Seaman on the *Euterpe*. I saw the eyes of that child. Dear God, I saw *into* them and I knew I was looking at hell. I knew there were creatures, *things*, that hungered to come here and to kill us. Emerson Ballard saw it with his own eyes, too, in the shine of the Captain's plate set out for supper. If Seaman Ballard had not jumped, I might have thrown him and that baby overboard myself.

>(Signed)
>APOLLINAIRE LA FONTAINE, *Able Bodied*

We are agreed that Third Mate Ballard is innocent in the deaths of his brother Emerson Ballard and the Covington child. After a search of the ship, we found a small diary belonging to Captain Covington, hidden among the sea charts. Pages were missing, and though much was left unexplained, sufficient remained to confirm the details the Third Mate has related, including the location of the hagfish bloom. We will warn all ships away. Of the fate of the Captain's wife, Covington wrote:

Marie, then, was to be sacrificed to the imp's dark lords. Those creatures. Those abominations. For riches. For the Euterpe. *I am a seafaring man, and my ship was my heart and soul. It was easy to agree when "Kian" first came to me, because I did not love Marie. I loved the* Euterpe, *and I knew she would not last another voyage. So the bargain was made.*

That was before Marie conceived our child. I told K. I was done. He mocked me, declaring it was too late. The Outer Monstrosities must be appeased. But I might choose one to spare, wife or son. Oh, gods! She gave birth in our cabin and then . . .

A murderous contract, and my ticket to perdition. But my son will live.

Yet if aught had happened to her, who did Emerson Ballard see upon the widow's walk? Mr. Ballard is distraught, claiming that the child has served as a second sacrifice to the dark monsters and that his brother was not in his right mind when he jumped. There is much conjecture, and we each have our opinion, but we have no firm answers for this uncanny misadventure.

Captain Fallworth has agreed to Mr. Ballard's request that he be blindfolded and relieved of duty, and we shall take him under cover of night to a place we have sworn an oath never to reveal.

                (Signed)
                ANDREW FALLWORTH, *Master*
                L. W. ACKEL, *First Mate*
                M. GUSTIN, *Second Mate*
                DISCHER HENDERSON, *Acting Third Mate*

Latitude Dark

Teel James Glenn

I am Helmut Eisner, and I write this as a record of the occurrences on this flight of the *Graf Zeppelin*, the LZ127, in the year 1937 of the Common Era. I do not know if any will find this, for I do not know if I am alone in the world or, in fact, if the world still exists.

I had been having disturbed dreams for several days before this flight, indistinct slashes of crimson with disturbing, vague nightmare images that kept me from resting. Then as I was boarding the ship with the eighteen-man crew ahead of the forty-three passengers, I had a sudden sharp pain in my temple.

It was so severe that I swayed and clutched onto the railing.

"Too much celebration, Eisner?" came a snide comment from behind me. It was Hans Schmidt, my superior on the engine crew who did not like me, perhaps for no other reason than that I was a Jew. He would not say it outright, but it was clear to me and all on board.

"No," I said through clenched teeth as I fought back the throbbing pain. "I am ready to fulfill my duties."

"See that you do your duty with no excuses," he snapped and went past me up into the airship.

It was only the first of the headaches I had, though they did not become a constant until we were just a day out of Brazil, high over the reflective surface of the Atlantic Ocean. I began to have headaches almost from the moment we reached cruising height, but they were not pressure-related, as I'd had no such difficulty on our journey outbound from Frankfurt. Nor had I had such difficulty on the many other trips I had taken as a crew member of the airship, including my sojourn over the pole in '31.

I was a holdover from before the National Socialists—such as Hans Schmidt—took control of the airship and its sister, the *Hindenburg*, to use for propaganda purposes. My friends on that ship had to endure the same attitudes from their Party puppets. Captain Von Schiller had been forced to accept their influence to place Schmidt and his ilk, though he insisted that skill rather than party mattered with his ship's operation.

I am sure Hans resented that my experience meant he often had to defer to me on operational matters. I know that was doubly a scourge for my background.

He was a lean and sharp-featured fellow with watery blue eyes and hair so blond it was almost white, though he had seen the same twenty-five years I had on this earth. This was his first trip on the *Graf* as senior engineer, though he had worked on the *Hindenburg* for two of its voyages.

"Eisner," he said to me on the second day out from the coast when he saw me wince as I looked out over the surface of the ocean, "you are just weak. Or have you been secretly sipping Schnapps?"

"Neither," I protested. My eyes were slitted for the very light hurt. "I do not know why it hurts so, but it is real."

"Then it will be as real in the bags," he said. "Relieve Gustave on the catwalk for the next shift." His tone was as if he were talking to a drudge instead of a skilled airship worker.

Still, I looked upon the assignment as a relief.

I climbed the ladder that led up from the gondola to the superstructure of the envelope above, where the Blau gas reservoirs and the hydrogen cells were located.

For all the time I had been on the ship I still felt a sense of awe when I went aloft into the envelope. It was cathedral-like with arched aluminum ridges and doped canvas stretched across it to be its outer skin, like a great dinosaur of the air.

The Blau gas was used as fuel to power the outboard engines that propelled the floating behemoth through the sky. It had a density similar to air, so it avoided a weight change as it was used up. I moved along the narrow catwalk to the wide space that was the main observation post to monitor the cells.

Since the Americans would not give us any of their precious helium, our ships used hydrogen as our lifting gas. All the crew on the *Graf* and our sister ship the *Hindenburg* wore special booties and jumpsuits that would not generate any static electricity, for we lived with the constant danger of the hydrogen being ignited. It was a constant reality, but while we became comfortable with it we never took it for granted.

On the positive side, hydrogen is inexpensive to manufacture, so our airships began flights fully inflated to maximize payload, then slowly release hydrogen when needed. The gas cells were monitored to keep them from bursting as the outside air pressure lessened as we ascended.

I wore a heavy leather jacket and a wool cap, for the canvas walls of the ship were no proof against the cold skies, as there could be no heating units on the ship. Many times the passengers, or at least those unfamiliar with airship travel, complained that they had to wear winter gear for most of the flight. But then, they felt that the spectacular views made up for it.

One of my duties in the envelope was to valve the hydrogen to keep all at safe levels. I also moved through the spiderweb of struts to be sure there were no leaks and no metal parts of the superstructure that could rub against any other metal surface and thus create a spark. We were justifiably proud of flying more than a million kilometers, including circling the globe, without a single passenger injury.

The National Socialists held these facts up to support their "infallibility," but in fact it was the Von Zeppelin family and work of such as I who made that so.

I tried to put Hans and his ilk out of my mind and concentrate on the job at hand, but the pressure in my head continued, though the relative darkness of the envelope helped somewhat. I could not explain why I suddenly had these headaches, though I had to wonder if it was related to my nightmares.

They began on the nights before we debarked as I lay in my bunk in the tiny canvas-walled crew quarters. I slept deeply but with disturbing dreams that were jagged, scarlet images slashing across my mind. I had no clear memory of them when I woke, just an uneasy feeling that I should have. It was as if there were some sound beyond my understanding, at the very edge of my hearing, yet that hurt my ears. Or like some strange shape in a darkened room that seemed fearsome but when the light was turned on was merely a pile of laundry.

Yet after the day of our departure I was uneasy.

I forced myself to focus on the observations I needed to make, checking the gauges along the catwalk and watching for any sign of undue wear.

"Sent to this dungeon, Helmut?" Gustave hailed me from a higher catwalk. "What did you do to get this sentence?"

"I was not quick enough to jump when he told me to," I said. "And not high enough."

"I would tell him where to jump," he laughed. "I'll be down in a minute, almost done on this circuit."

While I waited for him to come down, I had to squeeze my eyes shut periodically against the pain caused by even the subdued light in the envelope. It was strong enough to make my stomach uneasy.

"Are you all right?" Gustave's voice at my shoulder startled me. I turned to look at him with squinted eyes.

"Yes, just a headache," I said. "I'll be fine."

"You sure?"

"Yes," I said. "Go take your rest break. I'm up to it." He didn't seem to believe me but nodded and headed down into the gondola, leaving me alone in the envelope.

I took a few deep breaths and began my sweep of the cells, a circuit that I had done hundreds of times on the various trips, so I did not feel I would miss much, even with my throbbing temples.

If Hans thought to punish me with my exile, he had misjudged me, for while I enjoyed the time in the gondola, I was always under someone's watch down there. In the envelope, among the massive gasbags, I was able to conduct my business at my own pace and with the joy that solitude can bring to one.

Still, my headache made my mundane monitor duties in the envelope a challenge that day, and I was forced to concentrate to do a thorough job. Time passed with no real awareness of it, so by the time I was finishing my fourth circuit of the catwalks my shift was almost over.

I was on the higher catwalk when I saw the flash of a figure at the other end of the envelope, rounding the Blau gas cells. I saw only a shape out of the corner of my eye and turned and called, "Hello."

When I heard no response, I called again, "Hello!" and moved to that end of the catwalk; but when I got to that station, there was no one there. As it was at the end of the walk it was a dead end; there was no ladder up or down from that spot.

I rubbed my eyes and almost shook my head to clear it, save that the pain was too great. I paused, leaning on the railing. I felt as if I could no longer trust what I saw. Perhaps the prolonged pain had affected my eyesight—which meant I could not be sure I had done my job safely.

Could I have missed a leak? Or some other sign of danger?

Fortunately, my relief came on duty in a few minutes, and I thankfully went down into the gondola and to the crew's quarters. I was lucky enough to avoid Hans and skipped my normal snack time to climb directly into my bunk. I pulled a blanket over my head and tried to sleep.

My efforts succeeded only partially, for while the darkness of my blanket blindfold helped relieve some of the throbbing, there were the slashes of crimson in the black again.

I must have dozed, but I did not rest; the disturbing abstract shapes filled me with dread, their angular, jagged colors flashing across my mind's eye. I tossed and turned and finally sat up to find myself sweating, shivering.

I was aware that some time had passed, for I could hear some music from the Victrola in the dining area, a luxury for the passengers when they ate regular meals. I thought perhaps I should check into the dispensary in the radio room to see if the nurse could take my temperature and give me something to handle my headache—which was still there. Perhaps I had somehow caught a sickness.

I splashed some water in my face and combed my hair to clean myself up. I also thought that perhaps food would help my strange state before I went to the dispensary.

I passed through the passenger lounge and dining area, where a dozen passengers enjoyed the meal and the view. I continued heading up to the galley across from the radio room. It was a small kitchen containing electric burners and ovens, an electric water heater, a refrigeration unit, and compact storage and preparation areas. No open flames were allowed on the ship.

The moment I stepped into the corridor across from the galley, I ran directly into Hans exiting the radio room.

"Ah, the shirker," he sneered at me. "Ready to assume your fair share?"

I had just enough residual pain to have a short fuse. "I do more than my fair share," I shot back. "I got my job with my ability, not because of party affiliations."

I saw his eyes go wide with the shock of my talking back.

"What did you say, shirker?" He stepped up to me to put his face directly in mine. "Did you just talk against the party?"

I regretted giving him reason to press me further, but I was also fed up with his bully tactics.

"I said what I said about your lack of ability," I repeated and attempted to push past him into the galley. He was not having it.

"You filthy Jew." He pushed me back with hands on my chest so that I slammed against the bulkhead.

That was too much for me. I lost control and threw a punch at him. What followed was a confusion of blows and grappling where I saw red and found myself screaming irrationally at him.

We both fell to the floor, but before either of us could do much damage in the tight quarters of the corridor, several of the crew were upon us and pulled us apart.

"What is the meaning of this?" Senior Officer Meier dressed the two of us down in the galley a few minutes after we had been separated.

We were both scratched up and unkempt and stood at uneasy attention. Neither of us wanted to look at the other, but I could sense the anger from Hans, and I am sure the others could see it in my expression as well.

"Well?" Meier insisted. "You, Schmidt, what was this about?"

I glanced at Hans, and he looked to me. I could feel the hate that radiated from him, but I will give him credit; he did not try to blame me.

"It was a misunderstanding about a sports score, sir," he said.

The officer looked skeptical and trained his gaze on me.

"Yes, sir," I said, "a futbol match in Braven was disputed. And I lost control."

"You lost control?" Meier said. He clearly did not believe either of us. "Well, you will not lose control on this ship again—is that understood?"

"Yes, sir," we both snapped.

"This will go on your reports," Meier said, "and I do not want to see any more disruption from either of you, is that understood?"

"Yes, sir," we both said and then were dismissed by Herr Meier. We separated with only side-glances to each other, and I went to the small infirmary to speak to the nurse who traveled with us. She took my temperature and attended to the few scratches on my face—against my objection.

"Just a little high, Helmut," she said. "I will give you some aspirin and recommend you take a sleep shift."

"But——"

"I will write it up," she said. "We will be in Friedrichshafen in only a day, and it will not affect the crew rotation. Better safe than sorry."

I was too tired from my struggle and my headache to argue much with her. I took the aspirin and accepted a cup of hot soup from the galley before heading back to my bunk.

We were approaching the Canary Islands, which meant we were only some twenty hours or so from Frankfurt. My missing one shift would not jeopardize the ship in any way, though I was sure it would not reflect well on my record.

I had been thinking of moving on from the job at that point anyway; it had been only a matter of time till I had direct conflict with the National Socialists. What I would do after, I had no idea—for I loved flying.

I looked out of a window at the Atlantic below and the glory of the sky. I would miss this daily view. Even with a dark storm in the distance, it was still a spectacular scene, God's creation in clear and joyful panorama.

I retired to my bunk, not even bothering to take off my jacket, simply kicking off my boots and pulling the covers over me. Soon the adrenalin fatigue from the fight and my exhaustion from resisting the headache for two days allowed me to fall into a deep sleep.

It was not a dreamless sleep, however, for the slashes of scarlet and flashes of indigo of my nightmares before the trip came back to task me. The flashes were flames, and I saw and heard screaming figures, shadowy shapes flailing wildly.

I shot awake with a yell of "No!" and sat, covered in sweat.

I was no longer sure if I was awake or asleep for a moment, yet the terror of the nightmare stayed with me.

I was alone in the bunkroom. The constant hum of the four Daimler-Benz engines in their nacelles was there, but there was another noise, a booming sound.

I jumped to my feet, yanked on my boots, and sprang to the compartment door. I flung it open and stepped out into the companionway.

"Hello?" I called. No one answered, and I saw no one.

There was another boom.

I had a sudden premonition of danger and raced down the corridor toward the open passenger lounge. I ran through the dining area but encountered no one. There I stopped, stunned, as I looked through the wide windows of the lounge, which showed the gray darkness of enshrouding clouds.

In those dark, amorphous shapes, I could see flashes of light that had to be lightning.

That was very bad.

I ran forward through the gondola, heading for the control room but oddly encountered no one. When I pushed through the door into the control cabin, I stopped, horrified; there was no one at the controls.

I sprang to the wheel, but it had been lashed in place as if the officer of the watch had been called away momentarily.

"Hello!" I shouted. "Crew on deck!" There was no response. I grabbed the speaking tube and yelled into it. "Emergency, ahoy, crew to the control room. Please respond. Is anyone there? Come to the control room."

There was no response. I tried again with the same results.

Outside the gray clouds were a roiling mass, seeming as solid as a mountainside. I still saw the flashes of light within the dark shape and heard the rumbles of thunder. I felt a chill race up my back.

What could have happened to everyone?

I moved from the control room to the chart room and the radio room, then the galley. In the kitchen, I found the electric burners still on and stew in a large pot that was still bubbling. I turned it off and left the room, stumbling back to the lounge, now terrified.

"Is anyone there?" I yelled, fully panicked now.

I moved through the lounge, the back corridors, and through all the passenger staterooms, opening door after door to find—no one.

I ran all the way to the crews' quarters and the washrooms and the very back of the ship. Finally I was at the back viewing window, hands pressed against the glass and trembling.

I was alone. Alone!

There was no one on the entire airship.

Could they have abandoned ship for some horrible reason while I slept and not bothered to wake me? If so, what calamity could have possibly compelled the entire crew and passengers to leave the airship in the middle of the ocean? And how could they do so?

"No!" I cried. "I am not alone. They are hiding, they must be hiding."

I turned and walked back toward my cabin, but I abruptly became aware of something different. I paused to listen and realized that the steady throb of the Daimler-Benz engines was gone. They had stopped, meaning we were now adrift.

I raced back through the entire gondola to enter the control room once more. I found that the gray mass of clouds had thinned. We were only several hundred feet over the water, and as the ship emerged from the vaporous shroud I could see the vast expanse of the ocean, but with a difference. It was like no expanse of water I had ever seen.

The surface of the sea was a sickly brown color and was covered with cancerous-looking clumps of weeds that bobbed and swirled from unseen currents.

"What is this?" I said aloud. It was nothing I had ever encountered, and the horizon showed an orange tinge that promised an unending panorama of decay. I had passed over the Sargasso Sea on previous flights, and this was far vaster and evoked a Gehenna of desolation.

I ran back to the chart room to see if there was any indication of what disaster had occurred or where we were. I was able to trace the route of the LZ127 from Brazil to the Canaries hour by hour on the chart, where I also found a notation that the storm was approaching but nothing more. There was no indication of any disaster or event that would lead to the ship's evacuation.

I stood perplexed, unsure what to do. I could not restart the engines myself, as it required at least three crewmen, and without them the only control I had over my fate was if I initiated a cell purge and tried to land the ship. But land it where? The scenario before me was a hellscape of desiccation and waste.

The envelope. The others must, for some unknown reason, have gone up into the superstructure to hide from me.

I raced up and scoured the catwalks from end to end, but there was no one. No one to help me.

Help, I thought, *I must radio for help.*

I moved to the radio room in something of a daze and powered up the radio set. I checked the log, but there were no messages out of the ordinary, nothing to indicate what had happened.

"Hello, hello to any who hear this S.O.S.," I said. "This is the airship *Graf Zeppelin* in distress. Any radio hearing this, please respond."

I waited breathlessly for minutes for a response, and when it did not come I repeated the same message many times. Many times . . .

With each repetition my sense of hopelessness grew. I tried every waveband I could, varying regularly, but still there was no response. Nor could I find any other broadcasts. I found no other radios, commercial or otherwise.

I took a deep breath and continued both sending and listening while keeping myself from losing heart.

I am healthy, I am safe—for the moment—and the ship still has lift. Even if I am far from land I am not in immediate danger.

This thought made me decide to determine my real circumstance—that is, what was at my command on the ship. I left the radio turned on and went to the galley to take stock of what food remained.

When I had fallen asleep, there was still a full day of the journey left and more than two score passengers and crew to be fed. The freezer was still a third full; there was still coffee, milk, even ice cream stocks in place. And there was still wine, beer, and an ample water supply. My immediate fate, then, was not to be one of starvation.

More likely I would go mad from the frustration of not knowing what had happened.

While in the kitchen I found myself hungry, and so I made a sandwich and drew a ration of beer and took both with me back to the control room.

The scene out the broad windscreen was much the same, a seemingly endless vista of diseased-looking, floating growths, all a sickly brown.

Even the sky's orange tinge now was more crimson, and the orb of the sun, low on the horizon, looked like an angry wound in the sky.

I finished my meal and beer, resisting the desire for a second drink, and returned to the radio room. I tried my distress call again till I thought my voice would go hoarse from repetition.

After a time I simply left the radio on and decided I would need rest. As I could not be far from the set, I fetched some cushions from the lounge and created a makeshift sleeping area in the control room, leaving the door to the radio room open.

I could only hope that some ship or land station would come into range and reply to my urgent call.

My head began to ache again and I felt dizzy, so I lay down in my makeshift bed and in moments was fast asleep.

I snapped awake to the sound of footsteps. At first I did not know if I had dreamed them, but when I listened intently I heard them again. I bolted upright and bellowed, "Who is there!"

The footsteps faded as I rose and ran down the dark companionway, following the sounds. I kept shouting, but the steps retreated from me back toward the stern of the airship.

I knew it: someone was hiding!

The footfalls faded away as I passed the passenger staterooms, and I stopped my headlong chase and listened.

"Why are you hiding?" I called. "What is this all about?"

I was answered only by silence. My head began to throb again.

I stood in the middle of the lounge dead center of the ship.

It was night outside the airship, but not the black night sprinkled with stars that I was used to over the Atlantic. The inky night outside was an odd purple slashed with scarlet points of illumination, a swirling display of lights that was unlike anything I had ever seen. I had seen the northern lights, but this was nothing like them.

Even the very stars looked strange to me, the constellations unfamiliar.

In the name of all that is holy, what has happened?

I heard the footsteps again, this time apparently running right at me from the stern and then past me. I also heard cries, horrifying screams of agony that faded even as the footsteps did.

Yet there was no one there, just the sounds of terror and of racing boots.

I began to doubt my own sanity.

"What do you want?" I shrieked. "What?"

I ran back toward the bow just in time to hear the noise of movement in the radio room. When I jumped through the doorway into the room, I was stunned again to find nothing.

"Why are you doing this to me?" I cried.

The radio was still on, with only static crackling from the speaker, as if there were no other radios in the world. There was nowhere in the room anyone could have hidden, yet I had clearly heard footsteps.

There was something else: the message pad by the radio had a new message on it.

My hands shook as I approached and lifted it to look at what was written on it.

My heart all but skipped a beat, and I felt lightheaded.

On the pad was written, "May 6, Lakehurst, New Jersey, USA. *Hindenburg* burst into flame on landing. Of the 97 on board there were 36 deaths; 13 passengers, 22 crew members and one of the ground crew. Many injuries. Sabotage suspected. Take all precautions."

The horror of it was overwhelming. I found myself swaying, my headache returned full force, and I abruptly fell to the floor, unconscious.

I woke with the sun high in the sky and a dread so deep as to be spirit crushing. Once more I searched the whole of the airship and the envelope to find that I was again alone.

The ship drifted further into the strange sea at the whim of the breezes.

I did not want for food nor drink, yet my hunger for the life I had before, for companionship—even with such as Hans—weighed heavily on me.

I continued radioing several times each day but, as the days dragged on, with less and less hope.

And each night there were screams and the sounds of phantom footsteps, though they became regular by and by, even comforting.

I have come to believe that somehow I have crossed to some interspace between life itself and whatever is beyond.

For many days now the ship has drifted over a flat plain of bilious-looking mud, with strange, stunted trees and bubbling pools. It was a vast scene of desolation, with cancerous-looking vegetation, multiple eerie, oily rivulets that flowed across the land like the veins of some monstrous being, and all a depressing, level sameness. It was as flat and as hopeless a vista as I could ever imagine. At the same time, the ship is losing lift.

Gradually as the days have stretched to weeks the *Graf* has sunk to only a hundred feet above this strange landscape.

When it is low enough to scamper down a rope I will leave my aerial raft and strike out on the land below, to find whatever might be there. Perhaps then the sounds of the screaming will stop and the souls that vex me will be left behind.

There was no trace of airman Helmut Eisner, who disappeared mid-flight on the last run of the LZ127, but the preceding journal was found on his bunk. Authorities believed he jumped or fell to his death somewhere in the mid-Atlantic.

From the Bowl of the Gods

Wendy N. Wagner

There were two things the man from the packing plant had promised David when he and his brother got off the train in Flora, North Dakota: beautiful sunrises and a good well—and in three months David hadn't seen a sign of either. He drew up his water bucket from the muddy waters of the Little Missouri and tried to remember how long it had been since he'd seen morning sunshine and not just fog. Did a sunrise count if you saw it from the window of a second-class train car with your brother's head between your eyes and the glass?

On the other side of the canyon, cows called to one another in mournful voices. David wondered if the poor beasts missed the sunrise as much as he did. One of the favorite parts of his job back in Boston was helping the milkmen load their wagons as the world slowly blushed to pink in the dawn. These mornings, though, when he woke to the sounds of unhappy cows and his brother's ever-worsening cough, David lay in the dark of their tent, smothered in the stink of clothes that never dried and blood that never washed away, and wished he could stay asleep forever.

The water bucket slopped against his leg as David paused in the cottonwood trees, trying to orient himself toward their tent. The tent city was only temporary, the hiring manager had insisted. Proud drawings of brick bunkhouses and a real wellhouse had filled the wall behind him as he shook David's hand. And David had believed him. After all, the meat-packing plant with all its coal-fired boilers and electrical refinements had gone up in only a matter of months, the problems of construction evaporated by the heat of Count de Fougeret's fortune.

No one knew where in France the mysterious aristocrat had lived or how he had made his money. Some people said he was the luckiest man in the entire West. Others whispered of deals with the devil. But when the count rode into Flora last summer with his purebred herd of black longhorns, he had promised that a meat-packing plant would usher in a new era of prosperity to the Dakota Badlands. Its design, more modern than anything in Chicago or St. Louis, could keep the line moving at the speed of one carcass per minute, as long as he could find the workers to keep up with it. The city hailed the rich Frenchman as a hero, and the plant's hiring manager had posted advertisements in newspapers across the entire country, begging men like Lewis and David Morse to come to Flora for good work and clean, fresh air.

Instead, they'd gotten stinking fog and a tent city. David paused at the end of a row of tents, cocking his head. Each sagging canvas pyramid looked the same, separated from the next by an identical clothesline drooping with blood-stained aprons and stiff denim pants. He closed his eyes and listened for Lewis's barking cough, loud enough to carry a hundred yards. It had only gotten worse since they'd started at the plant.

After all Lewis had done for him since their parents died, David wasn't about to let his older brother die in some filthy, rotten tent. He was saving for train tickets somewhere, anywhere away from this fog-forsaken place. Someplace where Lewis could breathe and David wouldn't have to listen to the sounds of cows in pain.

Outside their makeshift home, David stirred up the fire and readied coffee and oatmeal. He could hear the rest of the camp waking now. "Lewis," he called. His brother didn't stir.

David slipped on his work clothes, still damp from their soak in the river Sunday night, and tried again. This time he slapped the side of the canvas. "We're gonna be late."

His brother's cot groaned as he sat up. "You go on without me," Lewis wheezed. "I'll catch up."

"Foreman will have your hide," David warned.

"How 'bout I give him my lungs instead?"

David found a smile despite the absurdity. His older brother had always been able to crack wise. "Good luck, brother. See you tonight, okay?"

The fog thinned as he left the tent city, crossing the Little Missouri on a bridge as half-complete as the worker housing. De Fougeret's plant crouched on the far bank like a big brick toad, its tongue lolling toward the train line for the quick delivery of cattle. Cast iron gates standing twice as tall as a man blocked the entrance, and even though they were less than four months old, they gave a long, sad groan as they were thrown open.

A sorry mooing made him look across the road to see a lone black longhorn standing with its flanks straining against the barbed wire, fog coiling up its legs. David hesitated, unsure how to help the creature. The steer cried out again, its voice even more pained.

The sharp toot of the shift whistle forced him forward against his will. He was jostled and jolted away from the steer, caught in the stream of men flowing toward the gates. He knew a few of the workers well enough to greet, but he was glad to fall in line with old Barker the Boxer, a man whose back hunched in a curve so steep his head seemed to stick out of his chest.

"Cookie?" Barker asked, offering him a leaden lump studded with raisins. They shuffled into the brick arch of the plant's entrance. "You look like you could use something sweet."

"Thanks," David said, scraping up a smile. "Guess I just miss morning sunshine. By the time the sun burns off this fog, it's like an oven."

"This fog." Barker spat a burnt raisin toward the wall of time cards. In the distance, the train whistle sounded with the day's first load of cattle. "I've been in the Dakotas five years now and never seen fog like this spring. It's almost like it arrived with the count."

David stopped in mid-bite. "What do you mean?"

But Joe Lombardi was already pushing between the older man and David. "Where's your brother this morning?"

David hesitated, knowing full well Lombardi was Big Dave the Foreman's closest stooge. "Right behind me." Most of the men in packaging, where Lewis and Barker wrapped meats, treated the Morse brothers with sympathy. David knew the old man had figured out he was at least a birthday away from the seventeen he claimed to be. But David didn't trust a single man on the killing floor.

Lombardi's black mustache bent around a grin. He snatched David's time card out of its slot and held it out of David's reach. "With a brother like him, you need someone like me looking after you, Little Dave. You want to try running the bolt gun this morning?"

Now David's caution turned to full suspicion. Size and strength determined a man's position in the plant. The enormous Russians bound the screaming beeves' legs and hoisted them onto the line. Tall, wiry men like Lombardi shot the bolts into the terrified steers' brains. David, short and skinny, was a gutter, not a bolter.

The foreman caught David's hand as he reached for his time card. "Don't be an idiot, Lombardi. Morse doesn't have the strength to hold the gun steady. I'll be gutting today."

"What?" David stared at him. His first day gutting, David had cut too deep and flooded the cow's abdominal cavity with cow shit. He'd puked on his boots and been docked pay for a week. Gutting was one of the worst jobs, especially for a tall man like Big Dave. No one *chose* to be a gutter.

Big Dave raised an eyebrow. "Schedule change, Morse. You'll be handling offal today."

"That's a huge pay cut!" David's fingers curled into the palms of his hands, anger making his wrists shake.

"You'll get your usual rate," the foreman began, but then a triple blast of the alert whistle sounded inside the main building, and everyone went stiff.

That particular whistle only sounded when the count himself paid a visit.

"Clock in, clock in," Big Dave growled, urging men inside. David paused for a second, searching for Lewis, but again found himself caught up in traffic and carried onto the slaughterhouse floor.

Even after the night's cleaning, the place stank of piss and shit and old blood. It wasn't all cow smell, either. Big Dave didn't allow anyone to leave the floor save for their twenty-minute lunch outside on the riverbank. If you had to piss, you aimed for one of the cleaning troughs and tried not to miss a beat.

Far above the killing floor, the catwalk boomed as the count drove the end of his walking stick into its iron grating. "Gentlemen!" He raised his gloved left hand into the light, and somehow his voice rang out as if he stood beside David's very ear. The room went silent.

The count stood outlined against one of the skylights, every inch of him the elegant image of nobility: top hat, frock coat, walking stick. He could have fallen off the cover of one of the pulp novels Lewis liked—save for his upraised hand, whose ring finger looked strangely floppy and misshapen.

"I've had a telegram from one of our providers," the count called out in his elegant accent. "A very valuable item fell into the feed, and our rancher is certain these beeves have eaten it. It might yet be inside the gut of one of these creatures. So look sharp!" The count paused, his head swiveling to take in the entire group. "The first man to find this item will earn double their pay today."

The count rapped his stick on the catwalk again and then hurried toward the overseer's office. The entire plant buzzed with conversation.

David shook his head, a bitter taste in his mouth. Of course, a gutter would stand the best chance of finding something valuable in a cow's belly—and now Big Dave stood to reap the reward.

"Do you believe that?" Lewis's voice caught him by surprise. His brother looked skeptical. "'A very valuable item'? What could he possibly expect to find?"

"They took me off gutting."

His brother shot David a sharp look. "Be careful, Davey."

The start-of-shift whistle sounded, and they all rushed to their places. David could already hear the cows crying out in rage and fear as the Russians began unloading the train cars outside. The sound made his heart squeeze, as always.

His brother's words stayed with him as he cleaned offal and hauled it to the other departments. It was harder and more dangerous work than gutting, because once he had his buckets full, he had to sprint from the killing floor to the other departments. Intestines to the sausage room. Stomachs to the tripe scalder. Every step meant dodging blades and hoses, slipping and skidding on the damp and filthy floors. In the afternoon he nearly collided into a man hauling hides to the gelatin room. For a second David thought he saw the count's florid brand on the fresh black skins, but he didn't have time to wonder about it. He couldn't keep up as it was.

After the grueling day, the lion's share of the evening clean-up fell on his shoulders; there was no way Big Dave could be bothered with hosing down his workstation or cleaning the knives. David found himself scrubbing and scouring long after the rest of the men had clocked out for the evening. The lights had already been turned off, and darkness collected in the corners of the slaughterhouse.

He shivered, feeling invisible eyes on his back. Alone, it was easy to imagine the ghost of every murdered cow watching him work.

"Fuck this," he grumbled, and dumped the last of his cleaning solution into the gutter. The stink of carbolic acid stung his nose anew.

Something clanked and clattered in the gutter.

David put the bucket back into place and hesitated. The sound had almost certainly come from just another scrap of bone or hoof, but he had to look, didn't he? He stooped beside the dark trough in the floor and stretched his hand into its crevices. Slime and fur gathered beneath his questing fingers. He stretched his arm as far as he could reach.

The tip of his middle finger brushed a smooth surface. Smooth and hard, and as he leaned further into the stinking trough, he felt it clearly: a metal band like a ring with something heavy mounted to it. He managed to roll the thing toward his palm and get a hold of it.

"Morse!"

From the entry, the foreman sounded even surlier than usual. Behind him stood the count, his black clothes drawing the night around him like a cloak. The count's face was twisted with rage.

David leaped to his feet. "Yessir!"

"I'm locking the gates," Big Dave growled.

David broke into a run, the mysterious ring pinning his attention to his pocket. He wanted nothing more than to stop and pull it free, hold it up to the light, and see just what he'd discovered. Already he was buying a ticket to Seattle, Portland, hell, San Francisco, first class all the way. He couldn't wait to show de Fougeret and be rewarded.

He opened his mouth to catch the count's attention.

Then Old Barker caught him by the arm. "David. It's Lewis." The old man's face was gray, grim. And David forgot all about the ring.

They gave him the next morning off. Not the whole day; Lewis wasn't dead quite yet. There was still a chance the doctor could make it out from Rapid City before he drowned in the blood that stained his lips and bubbled up in his cough.

David hadn't slept, but he knew it was nearly dawn. He sat on his cot in the dim light of their faltering lantern and listened to the liquid gurgle of Lewis's breathing. The corners of his eyes stung, and he dug his knuckles into his eyes so he wouldn't cry. The doctor in Boston had promised them the better air out west would help Lewis's consumption, but that had been a lie, hadn't it? A lie like the promise of a real bunkhouse or a well.

He got to his feet—stooped double, because even for a small sixteen-year-old, a tent wasn't big enough—and patted his brother's shoulder. "I'll make you some tea, Lewis. Be right back."

Bucket in hand, he stumbled toward the river. When their parents had died, Lewis had been the one to take care of David. He'd found them each jobs and kept them fed. Read them to sleep at night from books and magazines he found cleaning the train station.

"You can do anything here in America," Lewis had told him one night after they'd read a particularly thrilling book by Jack London. "We'll be all right."

But Lewis had been wrong, hadn't he? The Count de Fougeret was proof of that. What you could do in America was limited, always and forever, by money. With it you were a god; without it you were nothing.

David sank down onto the riverbank and felt his shoulders begin to shake. He forced down the sobs. No one cried in *The Call of the Wild*. He swiped at his eyes and adjusted the creases in his pants so they'd stop digging into his legs.

He froze.

It wasn't his pants digging into his leg. It was the ring in his pocket. He couldn't believe he'd forgotten it.

David looked around himself. It was still early, but people were beginning to stir. In a minute this spot would be overrun by men getting water for their breakfasts. He hated to leave Lewis for long, but he couldn't let anyone else see what he'd found. Not yet.

His feet led him through the tent city, across the bridge, past the general store and the telegram office. On the other side of Flora, the rutted wagon road led into the hills and the big ranches beyond. The fog thinned as he climbed away from the river. He panted and scrambled up to the summit of the final hill, and then stared out to the east, where the sun nosed brightly over the horizon.

The Badlands stretched out before him, a long expanse of pink-and-gold striped hills connected by ribbons of cottonwood-lined creeks. He couldn't believe how different it was out here beyond the fog, the stink of the plant, and the mournful calls of de Fougeret's herd. Looking over the painted hills and beautiful trees, David could not understand why they called this place the Badlands. The sunrise called out the colors and rendered the landscape wondrous.

His first sunrise in almost three months. David felt a forgotten strength fill his heart.

He put his hand into his pocket and withdrew the ring he'd found in the charnel house gutter. On top of the thin metal band was mounted a disc the size of a quarter made of a soapy-looking green stone. The stone caught the soft glow of the sun and recast it against David's skin with a soft green glow. Someone had carved into the stone disc the shape of a creature with a blocky body like a strongman's, and a squared-off head like a bull's seemed to float off the surface. A bit of the stone was chipped, so that the tip of one horn was missing, the stump broken and rough. He licked his finger and rubbed grime from the bull's face.

"What the hell are you?" he whispered.

The wind began to stir, the air cooling. He smelled . . . cattle. Rain. Lightning.

Wrenching his eyes from the ring, he saw the horrible fog spilling down the sides of the painted hills. Despair made him cry out, but the air was so filled with the stench of ozone that it seared his throat. He dropped to his knees and began to cough like his brother, so forcefully that lights burst in the back of his eyes and all he saw was darkness and stars.

Then he was terribly, terribly cold, the ground beneath him like ice, the air around him as still and cold as a Dakota winter. His breath wrenched from his body, the steam vanishing into a tremendous darkness overhead.

The ring burned in David's hand, a green and vibrant light in a dark, hostile world. Its heat let him turn his head and look around himself to see that he knelt on the icy stone floor of an enormous bowl. The mountains enclosing this frozen plain reared up to the sky, vast, enormous. Their gray and alien flanks rose and fell, slightly, slowly, as rhythmic as breath, like the flanks of enormous animals.

After a very long time he was able to look to the peaks of the mountains and see the lights burning at their summits. He stared at them, and the lights stared back—not just *at* him, but *into* him. His head began to unspool the memories of his family, his work in the plant, his dreams of a better life.

Tears began to trickle from David's stinging eyes. The patter of tears down his cheeks was the only measure of time, if time even existed in this place.

Thunder crashed: the first real sound since he had arrived in this place.

A flash of lightning outshone the lights in the mountains. David leaped to his feet. His knees wobbled beneath him as if he had forgotten how to walk, but then he was running, arms and legs pumping with his utmost speed. The mountains neither retreated nor grew closer. The vastness of the plain made movement impossible.

A green light flashed in the distance, and something *yanked* his hand toward it, pulling it as irresistibly as the slaughterhouse line. The ring in his hand buzzed as it was drawn forward like magnets calling each other across space, dragging David across the ground.

"Who are you?" a voice bellowed behind him between clashes of thunder. "Who has taken my ring?"

David would have dropped the thing if his hand was not nearly fused to it. He knew that voice, its cultured European tones. How was Count de Fougeret here?

Then an enormous green house appeared in the distance, and the ring tugged David toward it faster and faster. He slammed into the house so hard his bones cried out. The force drawing him forward vanished. He collapsed against a smooth, warm wall of the same soapy stone as the carving in his hand. Above him stretched details of windowsills and drain pipes, the ordinary components of any ordinary house, but carved into a stone that even now hummed and glowed with green light. The bull-headed stone on the ring echoed the gentle humming.

"No!" the count roared, his voice echoing hugely. David clapped his hands over his ears, the broken stone on the ring gouging into his skin.

The sky lit up again, and now David saw the count floating between lightning strikes, his fine boots hovering inches above the ground. On his outstretched hand sat a tiny glowing bit of green: the broken fragment of the ring's stone.

There was something else about that hand, David noticed. Without the count's customary gloves, David could see the blackened stump of the count's ring finger—as if something had bitten it off at the first knuckle and the injury had been cauterized. The ring tingled in David's hand and, without his intent, slid onto his finger.

David felt as if he was inside one of the pulp stories Lewis loved. His mind struggled to force the strange pieces of his own tale to fit together. The ring belonged here, obviously. Its magic had carried him from the painted canyon all the way to this blasted and unnatural realm, and the fragment of green stone had done the same for the count. But while David was definitely, wholly, and completely here in this realm, he could see right through the floating count.

When the lightning flashed again, the eyes at the top of the peaks gleamed, and David knew they watched him and the count. Now David could make out the shapes of faces balanced high atop the mountains. Not human faces, but cats and wolf-things and men with impossible crowns. So vast and huge they could not be real. So vast and huge they *had* to be real.

Gods, a part of him whispered. *This is where the gods live.*

Another part of him laughed. Hadn't he just thought that rich men like the count were the real gods? What did David know about gods any longer?

"Give me the ring," the count boomed. Lightning crashed around him, but it sounded softer now. Whatever power over the weather he was wielding seemed to be fading in the presence of ring and the green house.

David stood up. The ring burned warmer, and that gave him courage. "No."

The count lashed out with his walking stick. The tip burned orange in the dark, but it only heated the air beside David's face.

It wasn't real here in the land of the gods. Not the way David was real.

"What do you want it for?" David asked.

The count stiffened, but then said begrudgingly, as if David's will forced the truth from his mouth: "It holds the power of Apis. The bull god of the Egyptian kings. The lord of abundance."

The light on top of one mountain flashed brighter. It shifted a little, and David recognized the terrible shape of its long horns. Longhorns, like the count's own herd.

He remembered the hides he'd seen in the slaughterhouse yesterday, black ones with the count's ornate "F" upon them. Remembered, too, the stories of the old god from Lewis's stories and even the Bible. David thought he understood.

"You made a deal with the bull god for your fortune, didn't you? But that wasn't enough, so you sacrificed your herd for—what? More money? More power?"

The count's face wavered. He didn't need to answer. David knew he was right.

"A bull god." David opened his hand and stared at the vibrating ring. He didn't understand why it was made out of the same stuff as the house, or what the house was doing here, or what the count would do with even more power. But he did know that a man who refused to put in a well for his workers or build them a real bunkhouse couldn't be trusted to do anything good.

David closed his eyes and drew up the feeling he'd gotten while cleaning last night, the horrible presence of ghost cattle. If there was anyone who ought to know how those steers felt, it was a bull god.

"Apis," David called out. "Do you know what this man has done with your gifts? Do you know how he treats his workers?"

The mountain shifted, its peak lowering itself like a beast lowering its head. The glow of godly eyes bore down on David, burning into his skin.

"You can't handle its power," the count said. "I've devoted my life to this magic. You're nothing but a stupid gutter!"

David couldn't help but laugh. Maybe the count was right. But David remembered the strength that had filled him with the sunrise that morning, the same strength that had just forced the count to speak to him like an equal. Maybe in this world David was strong enough to take a risk.

"I'm the one with the ring. I think I'll decide what to do with it."

The mountain leaned down, its outline clearly an enormous version of the bull-headed figure carved into the ring on David's hand. David looked from one to the other. He saw a tiny drop of blood on the chipped stone where it had dug into his temple. David rubbed it with his thumb, and the carving hummed louder.

If blood gave the idol power, no wonder de Fougeret had built a meat-packing plant. David tried to remember every steer whose belly he had ever cut. At first it felt impossible, the memories so locked up in repetition and despair, but as they unfurled they unlocked something inside him, a door held closed by the time clock, and the stinking tents, and the cruel foreman, and the lying hiring manager, and that doctor who told them Lewis would be fine if they just went out west. It was all blood and sacrifice, a machine for turning creatures into parts and parts into money and money into something like godhood.

"Apis," David whispered, sending all the pain and misery of his young life toward the watching bull god. All around him rose the screaming of cattle.

Time slowed as it had when he had first arrived on the plain. The tears rose in David's eyes again, freezing into ice on his lashes. For a second, David heard the count screaming, but then that too went silent. Only the buzzing hum of the ring interrupted the vastness of the gods and their resting place.

???

The bull-god's curiosity blasted through David's mind, nearly knocking him into unconsciousness. The ring vibrated so hard his teeth knocked together. An incredible sense of power filled his body. He could do anything he wanted, anything at all. He simply had to choose before his mind turned into mush.

It took every ounce of his strength to stretch out his hand. The green stone leapt and juddered on his ring finger, burning like a viridian sun. Spots rose in David's vision.

I wish— he began, and then there was only darkness.

He awoke to the smell of burning raisins, his eyes frozen shut.

"He's all right!" a voice shouted, and then a pair of hands was gripping his shoulders, and he was coughing and shivering, a chill like ice sloughing from his bones.

"It's okay," Lewis's voice sounded in his ear, and he felt the heat of a warm mug against his lips. The taste of hot tea made him choke.

When he finished coughing, he found that his eyes could open again, and that he sat in the dark beside a campfire and a tent, with Lewis crouched in front of him, holding out the mug of tea. Barker stood beside him, but his back was somehow straight and tall.

"You feeling any better, lad?" Barker said, as Lewis spoke over the top of him: "You've been sick for a week!"

"Are you okay? How's your cough?" David asked.

Lewis shook his head, confused. "My consumption's been better ever since we started working at the ranch."

David rubbed his eyes. "What ranch?"

"It's a good thing you went to Rapid City for medicine, Lewis," Barker said. "That fever did something to his memory."

Lewis forced David to drink more of the hot, sweet tea. David gripped the mug, looking around them and trying to make sense of it all. He had been very cold and very frightened, but he couldn't remember why. When he looked east, he saw the sky lightening above the hills. That made him feel a little better.

"What about the count?" David asked. "And our shift at the plant?"

"The count? His meat-packing plant caught fire before you ever got into town," Barker said, offering David a raisin-studded cookie. "He fled town in the night, and we got hired to round up his herd."

"His herd?" David felt too stupid to comprehend what they were saying. Hadn't the count killed his cattle for some kind of magic?

The thought sounded like the plot of one of Lewis's silly novels.

"There's one now," Lewis said, pointing across the campfire.

David sat up. In the soft light of dawn he saw an enormous black bull silhouetted on top of one of the pink-and-gold striped hills. It turned its head, and he saw the broken tip of one horn. Every inch of his skin prickled with gooseflesh.

"Thank you," David whispered.

For an instant, the bull's eyes flashed green. David clutched his tea and watched the sun come up, praising all the gods, wherever they might be and whatever they might look like.

Going, Going

Meghan Arcuri

The man slams into me like a locomotive, my head connecting with his chest before my rump connects with the concrete sidewalk. A pale green light flashes in my vision as my teeth snap together on my tongue. A metallic taste coats my mouth.

"Pardon me, ma'am!" the behemoth says as he holds a leather-gloved hand before my face.

A few passersby in their wool suits and broad-brimmed hats have stopped to gawk and clutch their pearls. Someone honks at us from their Ford cruiser, giant hubcaps gleaming in the sunlight.

I take his hand, and he guides me to my feet.

"Are you all right?"

I adjust my crimson felt hat—my mother's hatpin having done a reasonable job—and grab the handbag I'd dropped in the collision. I remove a handkerchief and blot my lips.

"Oh, my!" he says, looking at the red spot on my handkerchief. "Should we get you to an infirmary?"

I run my tongue over my teeth, hoping to clean away any blood. The metallic taste has waned.

"Good god, no!" I swallow and wipe my mouth again. Swallow and wipe. The red has turned to pink. "I hate doctors. They always want to poke you with something."

The gentleman chuckles. I'm not sure if he gets my double entendre, but it's safe to assume he thinks a lady would never make such a joke.

"I am so sorry. I honestly didn't see you." He steps back and brushes off his suit jacket. Fortunately, I have not bled on him. Marty would not be amused if we had to pay to get another man's suit cleaned.

"I'm five foot two. I'm used to it."

Although that's true, I'm surprised he said he didn't see me. I noticed him a half a block away: young, tall, handsome. I could have sworn we made eye contact, only because I had been amusing myself at the thought of this young man having a torrid affair with someone my age.

"Forty-eight is getting up there," Marty said to me on my last birthday.

"You're fifty."

"It's different."

"You gonna trade me in for a newer model?"

He tilted his head and regarded me. "Not yet." He pecked my nose. "You're still too inspiring."

And then I wasn't.

"That's no excuse for knocking you to the ground," my young man says. "Is there somewhere I can help you get to?"

"No, thank you, dear." I point to the third stoop down. "I'm very nearly home."

"Are you certain?"

"I am. But thank you for adding a bit of excitement to my day. It was turning out to be dismal."

He gives me a half-smile, probably not sure what to make of my outlook.

I'm used to that, too.

"Good day, ma'am."

"And to you."

The gawkers and pearl-clutchers have dispersed, though the honking persists. Not at me, much as I'd like to believe I'm the cause. That's just what you get in Manhattan at five P.M.

I brush off my rear and my hands. Unfortunately, my left stocking did not survive the incident: multiple runs have crawled down my leg. Marty will be thrilled I have to buy another pair.

More blood—a minor scrape on my calf. I refold my handkerchief and hold it to my leg. Not as bad as my tongue. Good thing I'm almost home.

I charge up our stoop, the minor aches and pains from my fall beginning to reveal themselves. The mustiness in the vestibule mixes with the faint scent of paint. A number of artists live in the building—our own little enclave, if you will—but I like to blame the smell on Marty. (Even though we're on the top floor.)

I trudge up the steps. All sixty-eight of them. They're a delight in the winter when we use more coal than usual: the metal bucket starts to get pretty heavy by step number twenty-five.

Our door is ajar, a peculiar green glow on the floor.

When I push it open I am not met with the usual mise-en-scène: our easels and brushes; the shabby kitchenette with two mismatched chairs; the bare throw rugs speckled with paint.

No. This is not my apartment at all.

But when I turn to leave, the door behind me has disappeared.

I am outside, a dirt path stretching out in front of me. It is peppered with knobby roots, lined with shrubs, thorny and angry. The evergreens and oaks seem to rise taller and taller, the sky nearly invisible. The scent of pine mixed with earth fills my nose, but it's tainted by a dank moldiness.

"Hello?" It comes out as a muffled whisper.

No birds chirp, no leaves rustle. My skin tingles, the eerie silence unnerving me.

"Hello?"

I say it again and again, but the louder I yell the softer my voice becomes.

Shocking. You've never been that quiet a day in your life.

The familiar voice echoes in my head.

"Marty? Where are you?"

His low, gravelly laugh surrounds me, making my gut rumble. He does not appear.

I attempt to scream, but only a soft whisper comes out.

Another laugh.

About a hundred yards ahead, the light is brighter. I try to run, but I gain no ground by doing so, my legs heavy with effort, my heart thumping, my lungs laboring. Like running in water. But I continue to move forward.

When the forest breaks, a small castle made of stone appears in the valley before me. Everything is bathed in shades of green: mint and lime, emerald and juniper, moss and shamrock. It's familiar, but the whys and wherefores are just out of my reach, on the edge of my brain. The surrounding mountains reach toward the clouds, impossibly tall. Insurmountable.

I walk and walk and walk to the front of the castle, much smaller up close than it seemed to be from afar. Its door is wide open.

Barely moving on my own accord, I am compelled to enter.

More steps.

Sixty-eight of them. I don't know how I know this, but I do.

Except they don't bend back and forth on one another as they do in any normal apartment building.

They go straight up.

To our apartment door, now firmly shut.

I knock.

Nothing.

I knock again.

Nothing.

I bang my fist on the frame, pounding and pounding.

The door opens to Marty's tall figure, his face scrunched up in confusion, annoyance.

"Why didn't you use your key?" He runs a hand over his thinning hair (his forehead gaining ground by the day), before turning around and shuffling back to his easel.

The apartment has returned to normal: no castle, no mountains, no green. Except for the varying hues on the large canvas in front of Marty.

"Have you been here the whole time?" I say, throwing my coat and hat on the rack by the door, not caring that both fell to the floor. I drop my handbag on a kitchen chair.

"Where else would I be?"

My tongue hurts. The scrape on my leg burns. I have a headache.

"Oh, I don't know." I flop onto the other kitchen chair, my heart still pounding, sweat still dripping. "On one of Marty Cooper's famous strolls through the City."

He nods at my leg before turning back to his work. "I suppose you're going to need a new pair of nylons?"

How could I explain to him what happened—from the fall to the castle to the stairs—any of it?

I probably hit my head harder than I thought.

"Maybe I'll get two." I fill a Mason jar with water and head to the bedroom. "And I'm fine, by the way. Thanks for asking."

He grunts and picks up his brush.

I pass by his painting and stop short.

"What is that?"

His brush stills. "A valley."

Two giant mountains in shades of olive and basil surround an emerald dale. A small house in the middle. So reminiscent of my little escapade.

"Where is it?"

"Nowhere. I made it up." He reanimates the brush. "A real artist would understand."

One of his favorite slights. I am a real artist, the easel and paints sitting next to his evidence enough. But once his career took off, I stepped back and focused on supporting him and his work.

"I need to lie down for a minute. Maybe when you get up for a break, you could heat the stew?"

"I'll get right on that."

"Don't blame me if you go to bed hungry."

I walk to the bedroom and slam the door.

A rare smile forms on Marty's lips. He has sold a painting. Not the one with the green valley (the only one he's been working on for weeks). He sold one of his still lifes people seem to like. I prefer the ones with the figures, of course, what with me being his only model. When I stepped away from my own career as a painter and decided to keep the books for him, it was on the condition that I would be the only figure he'd use for his work. Despite our penchant for trading barbs, we do enjoy each other's company.

Well, I do, at least.

Marty was true to his word: I've been his only model in every one of his paintings not involving street scenes or the sea.

That is, until a couple months ago when he found that diary and stopped painting people altogether.

He tried to hide the weird little book from me, but sometimes I swear he forgets to whom he's married. I always get my way. And the apartment's too small for any secrets.

One night, when he went out on his evening stroll through the City, I looked high and low and found it under the mattress.

Madness is what it was.

The old man who'd written it must have lost his mind: blathering on about endless days turning into endless nights, green lights and landscapes, and a strange race of hog people.

It's why Marty's new painting makes any sense at all. And probably why my brain went haywire after I'd hit my head.

The one thing that sticks with me after reading the diary, though—beyond the hallucinations of floating and the violent pig people—is how dismissive the old man was of his sister, Mary. She fed him, nourished him, cared for his house and even his precious canines, and he mentions her—what?—four, five times? What did she do? What was her life like? How did she feel about the state of her brother's mind? So many questions to which we'll never know the answers because he chose not to write them down. Maybe he forgot to; maybe he didn't care to. He erased Mary from the story, as if she'd never really mattered at all.

"Let's celebrate," I say.

Marty takes his seat at the canvas of the jade valley, mumbling something about "Too much to do."

"Too much to celebrate? Nonsense!" I say, grabbing my coat, hat, and bag. "I'll go see what I can rustle up."

He grunts.

I head downstairs.

Marty likes steak. We don't eat a lot of it, what with it being so expensive, but after he sold his last painting, I squirreled away some cash for an occasion just like this.

I walk a few blocks away to the butcher's. It's busy today. Or maybe it's not. I don't come here often, so how would I know?

As I get in line behind a young woman, another young woman takes up the spot behind me. The first woman orders two pounds of filet mignon and some lamb. She must be a Rockefeller or something. She then moves along to pay.

"What can I get you?" the man behind the counter says.

Before I can order my steak, the woman behind me says, "A pound of ground chuck."

"Excuse me," I say.

But the butcher is not making eye contact with me, and the woman ignores me as well. It's like I'm not there.

"Excuse me," I say again with more force. I slap my hand on the counter a few times, too.

The butcher blinks and looks at me with surprise.

"I'm so sorry, ma'am. I didn't see you."

"Pardon me," the woman behind me says. "I missed you as well. Please . . ." She holds out her hand. "Go ahead."

What is going on?

I'd blame the short thing again, but this woman is even shorter than I am.

I order my steak and pay, the butcher offering more apologies. I purse my lips and give him a curt nod before leaving.

I march back home and tromp up the steps of the stoop. I'm still so miffed about being overlooked, the sixty-eight steps barely register. Our open door and green glow on the floor barely register.

I burst through, saying "Can you believe—"

But once again I am not in my apartment. I am not with Marty. I am not even holding the steak I just purchased. I am on the dirt path in the pine forest, leading to the mossy-green castle in the shamrock-covered valley. I try to run from the path, to turn around, to get somewhere else, but every time I do I am back where I started. My heart thumps as moisture forms on my temple, my upper lip. Seems the only way out is through. So I walk and walk and walk. I arrive at the castle and pass through its open door, sixty-eight more steps rising away from me, leading me to our door, once again ajar. I pass through our door but am on the dirt path again, the castle in the valley laid out before me. I try to run and call for help, but like the first time, I struggle, unable to do either. Marty grunts. Then laughs, nowhere to be seen. I pause at the base of the castle steps, hunched over, hands on knees, breathing like an Olympian. This time a fence runs along the left side of the castle, creating a pen. Dozens of hogs roll around in it, snorting and snaffling and the smell of hay and slop and dung overpowering, as well as that dank moldiness. The castle door is open. I run through. I run up the sixty-eight steps. I burst through our door.

Marty rises and turns with a start. "What has gotten into you?"

The scents of must and paint and coal fill the air.

I am in the apartment. I am with Marty. I hold the steak I purchased at the butcher's minutes—days? weeks?—ago.

I rush to Marty's canvas. Has it gotten bigger?

"What is that?" I point to the left of the castle.

"Do you have to ask?"

A lone pig grazes next to the house.

"Why did you put it there?"

"I felt it needed something else."

I rush to the bedroom, flip up the mattress with a strength I didn't know I had, grab the diary, and storm back to Marty.

"How did you know about that?" He tries to grab it, but I dodge him.

"When did this replace me as your muse?"

"It hasn't." He tries again. I dodge again.

"These are the writings of a madman."

He grabs my wrist and yanks me toward him. He squeezes and squeezes. So tight, my grip on the book fails. I drop it to the floor. He kicks it toward the bedroom and shoves me to the ground. He moves to the book faster than I've seen him move in a decade.

"You keep your filthy hands off this." He backs into the bedroom and shuts the door.

I sit on the floor and do something I haven't done in a decade: cry.

After a fight with Marty, I typically call Betty. She's my best friend, my go-to gal, the person who makes me laugh the hardest. So opposite from Marty in every way.

Everyone needs a Betty.

"Can we meet for lunch?" I say to her on the phone the next day.

"What? Your voice is faint. Like you're far away."

"Can. We. Meet?" My tone is crisp and loud. I don't care if Marty hears. He's too focused on his damn mountains to care, anyway.

"Yes. I'll be right by." I can always rely on Betty.

"Great! I'll meet you downstairs in ten," I say.

"What? This phone connection is terrible."

"Meet. Downstairs. Ten. Minutes."

"Hoping you said ten minutes," Betty says. "If not, I'll come up and knock."

She hangs up.

I hustle to the bathroom to do my business and tidy up.

Back in the living room, Marty stands in front of his canvas.

A figure stands in front of the pig. Huh . . . he hadn't asked me to pose.

"I could've helped you with that," I say.

"I didn't need your help."

"Fine." I grab my coat and hat. "I'm getting lunch with Betty."

He grunts.

Bastard.

I slam the door, head down to the stoop, and sit on the top step.

Within minutes Betty has turned the corner, heels clicking toward me. I wave and smile, but she returns neither. In fact, she looks downright confused: brow furrowed, lips pouting.

"Betty!" I stand and give her another wave.

No response. She looks at her watch.

"Hello?" I say.

Nothing.

She walks up the stairs, right past me, and before I can reach out and touch her she's through the front door.

I follow her into the building, her clicking heels echoing off the stairwell walls. But the echoes soon turn to silence, and by the time I reach our door no one is there.

I push through the open door and am on the dirt path again.

The forest, the valley, the castle with the open door.

Sixty-eight steps to our door.

The path, the forest, the castle with the open door and the pigs.

Sixty-eight more steps to our door.

The path, the forest, the castle with the pigs.

But this time, a man—back to me—stands before the pen.

He is tall. Like Marty.

His hair is thinning. Like Marty.

I tap his shoulder, and when he turns to me it's Marty—but it's not Marty.

It is a strange, awful version of Marty: wide mouth, sharp teeth, with less of a nose and more of a snout.

I try to yell, to scream, but only a muffled whisper comes out.

The hellish version of Marty shakes his head.

"You're never getting out of here."

He laughs as I run from him, through the open door of the castle, up the steps, on the path, through the door, up the steps, on the path, through the door.

And Marty is right. I don't know how I know it, but I do.

I'm never getting out of here.

I'm gone.

Little House on the Borderland

Todd Keisling

"What's up, piggies? It's your boy, Spider Vain, coming at you with another deep dive into the weird, sick, and extreme. Tonight, we're crawling back into the seedy underbelly of the Internet. I'm talking about Last Redoubt, the dark web of the dark web, the sort of place where even the feds fear to tread. But before we take the plunge, be sure to smash those 'like' and 'subscribe' buttons . . ."

—Night Land, Episode 298

Most days, if Mikael Bartlett received a strange email, he'd flag it as spam and move on with his day. The most common emails promised untold riches, penis enlargement, ways to extend his car's warranty—all written with poor grammar and spelling.

This email was different, though. Its subject line read: HOUSE FOR SALE ON LAST REDOUBT!!! It had arrived in his inbox dedicated to fan mail, addressed to his alter ego, Spider Vain, host of the popular *Night Lands* channel. The nature of his channel—explorations of weird Americana, conspiracies, and things found on the dark web—attracted a certain kind of individual, often the strange, unhinged, or depraved sort. Spider's fans had volunteered to buy him drugs, offered their bodies for his sadistic pleasure, and pledged their undying devotion—all in exchange for a chance to appear on his show. One of them had even offered to mail him a necklace they'd made from their own severed toe.

No one knew his real name, and he preferred to keep it that way. He'd gone to great lengths to conceal his identity, even wearing an elaborate mask of a cartoon pig on camera to preserve his anonymity. This choice of personal décor was a favorite among his followers who often referred to themselves online as "Piggies of Vain." He didn't have the heart to tell them it was an inside joke between him and Janine: Spider-Pig.

By all legal counts, Mikael Bartlett and Spider Vain were separate people, like Jekyll and Hyde or Clemens and Twain. What the anonymity of the Internet couldn't conceal he'd left to his attorneys to handle, and for the last five years Mikael lived comfortably in Spider's shadow. The benefit of being someone else allowed him the privilege of viewing the world through a different lens. Spider Vain's proclivities for the strange presented a world slightly askew, drawn in shadow, where a mystery was often the point.

This email he'd received was everything he loved about the Internet: A house for sale on the dark web. What an odd thing!—but the notion intrigued him. He'd built an entire career out of odd things, and dark web real estate was too good to pass up.

He re-read the email:

> Subject: HOUSE FOR SALE ON LAST REDOUBT!!!
> Buy this house! Crypto only. It's a steal. Local. Didn't you say you needed new studio space? Surprise in basement.

A link followed the choppy message to an onion website, one of those encrypted places only viewable with a special browser. Mikael hovered his mouse pointer over the address. *Could be a bad link,* he thought. He stared at the screen, read the email again. *Could be a virus or ransomware. Or it could be exactly what it says it is. Wouldn't be the first time I made a risky click.*

He'd built a career out of risky clicks. What began as a hobby in his college dorm room had exploded over the last few years, garnering a cult following after his deep dive into the mysterious tragedy that befell a small Kentucky town a few years ago. From cults to the occult, religious mythology to conspiracy theories, Mikael's colorful personality and tenacious research fueled his channel's growth, boasting more than fifty million subscribers at the height of its popularity. Everyone loved *Night Land,* and everyone wanted to take a weekly journey into the dark with their favorite host.

Or they used to.

The algorithm had changed. Subscribers were down for the first time in three years, and advertisers had begun to notice. Buying a house off the dark web might be just weird enough to stoke the flames and make his channel sizzle once again.

How bad could it be?

The fan was right, whoever it was—he did need bigger studio space, a fact he'd mentioned several times on the channel. He could set up a new studio in the house and host his streams from there. His own little house on the borderland, wherever that was. Talk about immersive. Viewers would eat it up.

He licked his lips, savored the excitement in his voice, and booted up his quarantine machine. It was a special rig he'd built to operate apart from his home network, so if he ever visited a compromised site, there would be no risk of a virus infecting his other machines. Once he was ready, Mikael opened his Brave browser and clicked the link.

A grainy photo of a small yellow house appeared on screen. The building's walls were rounded rather than angular, and if it had exterior windows, he could not see them. In the foreground stood an old chain-link fence with a rusted sign reading "KEEP OUT." A second photo revealed the house from a different angle, its backyard giving way to the pit of a vast rock quarry. A copse of pines demarcated the property's adjacent side. The same chain-link fencing continued around the quarry's rim, buried in swaths of overgrown weeds, downed limbs, and dead leaves.

Mikael clicked on the last photo: a grainy, low-resolution image of an empty room. Dirt and leaves were scattered across the floor, the walls were covered in graffiti and grime and wiring, and at the far side of the room stood a doorway mostly obscured in shadow.

You must be the surprise in the basement.

He clicked away from the image and read the description:

LITTLE HOUSE ON THE BORDERLAND
Quiet. Secluded. As-is.
House comes with set of keys, deed, and secrets in basement.
Serious inquiries only. For more information, click here.

Secrets. Color me intrigued.

Mikael clicked the link and requested more information.

* * *

"I think this is a bad idea."

Janine "Lady Jane" Pepper delivered him a mug of coffee adorned with the *Night Land* logo. He sipped absently, scrolling through the house listing one more time before acknowledging his assistant.

"Everything we do is a bad idea, Janine. That's the point."

"Yeah, maybe, but this is like . . . really bad. We usually have things delivered to the dead drop. But to *go* to them? You're asking for trouble."

She had a point. Everything on the dark web required an extra level of anonymity, which worked both ways. Last Redoubt was an alternative to the more famous (and now compromised) site on the dark web known as Silk Road. If one wanted to procure such items as illegal drugs, sex slaves, untraceable weapons, and other illicit goods and services, Silk Road was the place to go. If one wanted another layer of protection from the FBI or other governments, and more likely something less common than a hitman for hire or a dose of fentanyl, Last Redoubt would satisfy those needs.

Night Land LLC had purchased its share of strange items over the years, from Dybbuk boxes and haunted dolls to an alleged piece of Malaysia Airlines Flight 370 and a clown. The latter was a grotesquely tall, gaunt man in a dirty clown costume who'd lingered outside the drop point harassing passersby before someone called the cops. Janine had refused to approach him, and for good reason: *He just stood there on the corner, picking his teeth with a knife and honking a horn.* Two weeks later he'd been arrested for the murder of a minor.

"Mikael?"

"Sorry." He closed the browser and gave her his full attention. "I'm listening."

"Aren't you at all worried about this? What if the house is—"

"A trap? A decoy? What?"

"I don't know. And that should scare you."

Janine's words lingered in the ensuing silence. She was two for two this morning. Mikael had been too eager to grasp the opportunity dangling in front of his face, was about to take hold without considering the dangers, and felt foolish. For someone so entrenched in the dark side of the internet, the man behind Spider Vain had almost made a rookie mistake: to leap before looking.

Fair enough, he thought. *But it's too good an opportunity to pass up. Maybe...*

He opened his browser again, began typing into the search bar.

"Don't leave me hanging, Spider."

Mikael cracked a smile. "I love it when you call me Spider. Especially in bed."

"Business before pleasure." Janine sipped her coffee, arching her brow with a Kubrick stare that she knew he loved. "What are you typing?"

He maximized the window and spun his laptop around. Another listing on Last Redoubt:

PERSONAL SECURITY
xxxMadDog306xx
I will keep you safe. 20+ years military exp.
Tactical support for $$$—NO HAGGLING.
Contact if interested—

Accompanying the listing was a black-and-white photo of a middle-aged man in full military gear, sporting a semi-automatic rifle and a face mask painted to look like a skull. Tufts of a scraggly beard protruded from the sides of his mask. He even had proper trigger discipline.

Janine closed her eyes and shook her head. "You're fucking kidding me."

"I'm not."

"Do you even have enough——"

"You know I do."

"Spider—Mikael, this is insane. You're insane. It's just dangerous. I know the channel isn't doing well, but there's got to be another way than buying a fucking house sight-unseen. Hiring a goddamn merc to protect us when we go there is icing on a cake of insanity. Are you even listening?"

"I am," he said, clicking the listing's contact link. "Your complaint is noted."

"You're not even worried that someone might be waiting for us there?"

"Of course I am, but I'm not going to let that stand in the way of a great opportunity like this, Janine. The show must go on. We need a hit for episode 300, and this is our best shot."

"This is just like that goddamn clown. No, it's worse. You're lucky I like you."

He beamed. "The luckiest. And I'll be even luckier with 'xxxMadDog306xx' watching my back."

Janine rolled her eyes, and Mikael began writing his query to Mad Dog.

Two weeks later, Mikael and Janine seated themselves across a table from the man known as Mad Dog. He was barrel-chested, clad in a camouflage vest and aviators, and wore a dusty trucker cap that read "All Guns Matter." The diner was just off the highway near Atlantic City, a greasy spoon that Mad Dog had selected for their meet-up, and it was bustling this time of day. A full breakfast meal lay spread out before the mercenary, and he helped himself with ravenous abandon. Mikael liked him immediately. Janine, less so.

"Mr. Mad Dog?"

The big man finished chewing, wiped a thread of maple syrup from his lips. "You're late."

"Sorry, we . . ." Mikael glanced at Janine, who'd insisted they scope out the diner before entering. "We're here now. Did you review the contract I sent?"

"Yep. Didn't sign it."

Janine cleared her throat. "It's our standard waiver, Mr. Dog. We need your consent to appear on film." She nudged Mikael. "You did tell him what we're doing, right?"

"Of course I did. Sir, we have to keep everything above board here. For taxes, insurance. You understand."

Mad Dog shoved a strip of bacon into his maw and chewed loudly. "I understand, but you don't."

Mikael and Janine exchanged glances. When he kept on chewing, Mikael said, "I'm not sure I follow."

Mad Dog wiped his hands with a napkin and took off his aviators. A thin scar ran down his cheek and across his left eye. The pupil had been split, appeared to be leaking like a runny egg into the iris. His other eye was normal, but the dissonance between the two made it seem too large, wide. Feral.

"You don't follow 'cause we don't live in the same world, friend. Think about where you found me. I ain't exactly operating 'above board,' and that means I ain't signing shit—'specially not with my God-given name. You call me Mad Dog, or don't call me at all. Understood?"

Mikael nodded slowly, felt foolish for even asking. "Fair enough. Understood."

"Good." Mad Dog crossed his arms. His biceps dwarfed most of the table. "I trust you brought the cash."

"We did," Janine said. "Half now, half when we're done."

The big man gave her a once over and cracked a smile. "That a fact?"

She gave him her Kubrick stare. "Indisputable."

To Mikael, Mad Dog said, "I guess she wears the balls in this relationship, huh?"

"We share them," Janine said. "I keep one right here in my purse, next to my Mace, taser, and tactical knife. Never know when I might want to take another one for my collection."

"Hell, I like you, even if this little ménage à trois is fuckin' weird. Tell me again about where we're going."

They found the place three hours later after backtracking along muddy access roads through the Pine Barrens. The coordinates they'd received were precise enough—the house was where it was supposed to be—but Google Maps only showed a blanket of pines and wilderness.

"Look at this." Janine handed her phone to Mikael. "No quarry."

"Must be old satellite images," he said, but Janine wasn't hearing it.

"You think that quarry just magically appeared overnight?"

He rolled his eyes. "I think you're making this out to be more than it is. Come on, help me unload the equipment."

Mad Dog was already out of his truck and suiting up. He wore a Kevlar vest, the ghost mask from his dark web profile, and the biggest knife Mikael had ever seen strapped to his left thigh. A sidearm decorated his right.

Mikael grinned. "Maybe you're a little overdressed."

"Different worlds, kid. Remember what I said." Mad Dog scratched his grizzled beard and took stock of their surroundings. "This place ain't right."

Mikael was already walking back to his SUV. "What place is, though?"

Mad Dog didn't answer. A few minutes later when Mikael glanced over his shoulder, the mercenary was gone.

"Hey, Janine."

She returned to the back of the SUV and wiped sweat from her brow. "What's up?"

"Did you see where our security went?"

"No, I was busy unloading." She reached inside the vehicle and retrieved a pair of studio lights. "He's your liability, you keep tabs on him. Guy gives me the creeps."

"Yeah," Mikael said, scanning the tree line. A sharp breeze swept through the pines, made the whole forest hiss, and a chill crept down his back. "Me too."

Mikael walked slowly through the weeds toward the house while Janine followed with the camera. He looked up at the crumbling stone façade. Patches of moss clung to the exposed foundation, spotted with silken spider sacs protruding from cracks in the mortar. The longer he stared, the more he thought there was writing somewhere beneath the fauna. Something written and worn away with time.

He wandered around the side of the structure toward the fence. An electrical box affixed to the house's outer wall hummed with life, feeding an antenna that pierced the air several feet above. "At least we've got service out here. Fiber, too." His words were lost on the wind rising out of the ravine. He stood on his toes to get a better look over the edge. The quarry pit was so deep he couldn't see the bottom, and its wall on the opposite edge was a sheer rock face plunging down into the dark. Mikael thought it looked as if a god had plucked a piece of the forest straight out of the earth. The way one might cut a cake, sliced in perfect squares for consumption.

"Aren't old quarries supposed to be filled in with water?"

Janine's voice startled him. He rocked backward on his heels and steadied himself.

"Your guess is as good as mine. Anyway, what do you think?"

"This is a good spot," she said. "Lighting's good, too."

He looked back at the camera, smiled, and spoke into the microphone affixed to his lapel. "How's my audio?"

"In the green."

"Cool. Okay. One-two-three, one-two-three . . ." He shook off his nerves, waited a beat, and slid the pig mask over his face. His transformation into the mysterious and debonair Spider Vain was complete, the world already darkening around him. "Ready when you are, director."

Janine gave him a thumbs up. "Action."

"What's up, piggies? It's your boy, Spider Vain, coming at you on location at *Night Land*'s new studio space! Where's that, you wonder? Great question. To be honest, we're not entirely sure, either."

He paused for effect. The wind picked up again. Janine tilted her head and bore a confused look on her face but didn't say anything. *Must've picked up something in the audio,* he thought, and kept going.

"Normally, this is the part where I tell you the history of whatever it is we're featuring. That, my friends, is what makes this episode so unique. We couldn't find a single thing about this house—no official realtor listings, no deed history, nothing. As soon as our crypto transferred, we received GPS coordinates. A week later these arrived at our dead drop."

Mikael produced two items from his pockets, one in each hand: a piece of folded paper and a rusted iron key.

"You'll see from the photos in the show notes that it's a map of the house—which doesn't make sense, by the way—and one of those old-school skeleton keys. The long and short of it is this little house doesn't exist on paper. One of your fellow piggies sent info about this place out in the Pine Barrens. Want to know how much ten thousand bucks of crypto gets you on Last Redoubt?" He jabbed a thumb over his shoulder. "This unique fixer-upper right here. A little house on the edge of an abandoned rock quarry. And here's the best part: there's supposed to be a surprise in the basement. . . . Okay, let's cut there. How was that?"

Janine stopped recording. She looked up, arched her brow. "Very you. Did I ever tell you how sexy you are in that stupid mask?"

"Every night, my dear." He trudged through the overgrowth toward the tree line. "Maybe we can pick it up from over here and get some B-roll while we're at it. I want to get as much as we can while the light is still good. Then we'll move inside."

She nodded, removed the monitor from her ear, and froze. "Did you hear that?"

Mikael paused, listening: the hush of wind through the trees and weeds, a hawk's cry in the distance and dead leaves scratching across the grass. He shrugged. "Hear what?"

Janine stuck a finger in her ear and winced. "It was really high-pitched. Like a whine of some kind. I heard it while we were recording, but . . . it's probably just a gnat or mosquito or something."

A few minutes later Mikael stood ready for the camera to roll once again. Janine gave him a thumbs up and said, "Action."

He took a breath and began: "Normally, my assistant joins me on excursions like this—and she is. Say hi to the camera, Lady Jane—"

Janine stuck her hand in front of the lens, gave their audience a thumbs-up.

"—but we're not alone this time around. Given the unique nature of what we do, the danger involved, and the fact this came from an unconfirmed source, we here at *Night Land* thought it best to bring some extra muscle in case things get——"

Something rustled in the trees. Mad Dog trudged out of the brush with his rifle in tow, heaving for breath, leaves and burrs tangled in his beard.

"Oh, perfect timing! Mad Dog, say hi to our subscrib——"

"Get that fuckin' thing out of my face."

He planted a meaty paw over the camera lens and pushed Janine out of his way.

"Easy, man, that shit's expensive." Mikael followed after him with Janine in tow. He turned to the camera and said, "Sorry about that, folks. Our friend Mad Dog is all business, just like his AR-15." He pointed to the camera. "Stop filming. Mad Dog, what the fuck?"

The big man kept on walking back to his truck. He mumbled something that neither Mikael nor Janine could hear.

"Hey, I'm talking to you."

Mad Dog reached his truck, threw open the door, and retrieved a shotgun from the seat. He leveled the barrel at Mikael's face. "Don't you move another fucking inch. Hands where I can see them, or I'll blow your fool head off."

Mikael froze, thrust his hands into the air. "You wanna tell me what the hell is going on?"

Mad Dog crossed the gap between them, pausing long enough to produce a handful of Polaroid photos. He threw them at Mikael's feet. "No, *you* tell *me*, ya little shit. What kind of fucked-up operation do you have going on out here, huh?"

Mikael slowly knelt and picked up the grimy stack of photos. He glanced at them but was too rattled to make sense of what he was seeing. It was just a pile of Polaroids, little windows full of faded shapes, blurry and frozen in moments of motion.

"I don't—" He blinked, tried to forget about the shotgun pointed at his head, and shakily flipped through the stack. Blurry shapes became flesh, eyes, teeth, mouths contorted in pain. Some of them were stuck together with dirt or—"Oh, fuck."

He tossed the photos, scattering them across the muddy ruts of the access road. One of the Polaroids sat face up in the muck. A young man stared back from the faded image with terror in his eyes, black electrical tape wrapped so tightly around his mouth and jaw that it cut into his skin.

In the background, just over the man's shoulder, was a figure holding some kind of blade. Its face was obscured by a cartoon pig mask.

Mad Dog pressed the shotgun into Mikael's forehead. "Better start talking, freak."

"Whoa, hold on." Mikael raised his hands in the air. "I don't—what the fuck are those? Where—"

"Found 'em scattered around a big pile of meat and bones. Gotta tell ya, kid, you ain't too bright. Leaving all those bodies out in the woods like no one would ever find them."

"I have no idea what you're talking about, man. I—I've never been here before."

"He's telling the truth." Janine sidestepped them, circling back to their SUV. Mad Dog held his attention on Mikael, tracing his finger along the trigger, eager to pull.

"Hard for me to believe, girl, when yer boyfriend's wearing the same goddamn mask that's in that photo."

Mikael yanked the mask off his face. "I bought this at a Dollar Tree years ago. Halloween clearance. What the hell makes you think that's me?"

"Why the hell shouldn't I? You 'n' yer goth princess shake my tree, flash your money, and drag me out here to the middle of nowhere. Is this how you get your kicks?"

"What? No, you dumb shit. Are you even listening to me? Fuck." Hot tears flooded Mikael's eyes. "Just—please get that gun out of my face. We can talk about this—"

Mad Dog's breath hitched. He lowered the shotgun, raised one hand in the air. "Easy, girl. Easy."

Janine stood behind Mad Dog, pressing the tip of a blade against his throat. "I wasn't kidding about my knife. Drop the weapon or your neck's about to get a whole lot redder."

Mad Dog complied, and Mikael exhaled in relief. He climbed to his feet and moved back a few steps. A muffled voice sprang up in the back of his mind: *This is why you keep a dead drop, dipshit. Layers of separation!*

He collected himself and gave Janine a long stare. Her tendons were stretched tight, pupils dilated, and she looked so natural in that pose that Mikael wondered if her heart rate had even elevated.

"Never seen you like that, Lady Jane."

She licked her lips. "You should see what I can do with a pair of handcuffs, Spider."

"I knew you two were freaks." Mad Dog directed his gaze to Mikael. "You really expect me to believe you've never been here?"

"We haven't," Mikael said, bending over to retrieve the shotgun. He held it out to the mercenary, who took it without hesitation. Janine lowered her blade and stepped back toward her lover. "And we've never seen those photos before. I've got over fifty million subscribers. Odds are better it's one of my fans."

"That's supposed to make me feel better?"

Mikael shrugged. "No. It doesn't make me feel any better, either. Regardless of what you think of us, those photos are just as shocking—"

A shriek ripped through the forest stillness and startled the trio. It sounded almost animal-like, full of primal rage and agony.

Then came a second cry, shrill as the first, a pair of rusty nails raking down the chalkboard in his head. He winced, covered his ears. Janine did the same, pressed herself against him, and he felt her tremble.

Mad Dog said something that neither could hear. A moment later, as the shrieks subsided, he took off toward the house with his shotgun and rifle. Mikael and Janine watched helplessly as their hired mercenary kicked in the door of the little house. The whole structure shook from his force, stirring up a dust cloud that enveloped his figure upon entry, and silence swallowed the world around them.

They stood by their SUV, waiting for the other shoe to drop.

Five minutes later they heard a gunshot.

Seconds after that came another scream. This one was unmistakably human.

* * *

Mikael waited for the dust to settle before entering the house. The screams—human and animal alike—continued in erratic bursts, punctuated by the occasional pause for reasons he did not care to imagine. A musty odor of old decay assaulted his nostrils.

"Do you see him?"

Janine waited in the grass. Mikael looked back, shook his head. She'd pocketed her blade and replaced it with their camera. *Bless her,* he thought, and held out his hand.

Her face fell. "You want to film this?"

"The show must go on," he said, forcing a smile that he hoped would pass for bravado and hide the terror welling up within.

"Fuck the stupid channel. You sound like every terrible found footage movie right now."

"Janine—"

She handed him the camera and stepped away from the door. "Please don't do this, Mikael. Let's just go. No one knows we're here. This could end badly for—"

Another scream, another shrill animal cry, and the outer walls of the house shimmered with a strange red light. A glitch in reality, the fabric of space rippling like a curtain in a breeze, disturbed and settled in a blink.

They exchanged glances, a tacit expression of mutual confusion, fear.

Mikael shrugged and said, "Stay here."

He stepped inside.

The house's interior was a mess, jaundiced by a light bulb hanging from the center ceiling. Graffiti and dirt covered bare walls, streaked with something shiny like old grease, and the occasional handprint dotted the filthy landscape. He lifted the camera and zoomed in on one of the prints. Black wads of mud and twigs and old motor oil clung to the wall, filling out the contours of a human hand. It was too small to be Mad Dog's.

He scanned the empty room. The little house was barely more than a studio apartment and too sturdy to consider a shack. Its open floor plan, once a canvas of scribblings and esoteric symbols, was now covered in the same dust and grime. A stained mattress lay at the opposite end in a circle of discarded food containers swarming with flies, shredded strips of fabric, a camping stove, and several used hypodermics. A solitary bucket stood a few feet away, and the rank stench of its contents assaulted his nose.

In the center of the room a wooden cellar door stood open and waiting.

Another scream crawled from the shadows below, urging a chill down the back of Mikael's neck, carried on the legs of terror skittering straight into his heart. He never signed up for this. Janine was right, they should just leave, forget this place exists, and hightail it out of here.

But the money and the fame and his goddamn curiosity were powerful counterweights, holding him down in the house he now owned, for better or worse. The possibility of more subscribers, advertisers, and revenue dangled before him—and he followed their promise despite the weakening sense of self-preservation screaming away in a locked chamber at the back of his mind.

Mikael Bartlett descended into the basement with his camera held before him like a holy man's cross. The house breathed with him, its walls pulsing, constricting to the rhythm of his racing heart, and its musty air grew tighter with pressure around his skull. How deep did these stairs go? There was light at the bottom to welcome him beyond the house's cobblestone foundation.

Down he went, following stone steps in a spiral deep into the earth, until at last he reached a wide and bright chamber of similar area to the house above. A series of lightless tunnels branched away from the room toward origins unknown. He remembered the map, how it didn't make sense at the time, but now he understood. How deep did these tunnels go? And to where? Maybe he'd explore them for a later episode.

Opposite the stairwell was the basement door from the house listing. Mad Dog's shotgun lay before it, smoke drifting lazily from the barrel. The stench of gunpowder was palpable.

A metal chair stood in the center of the room beyond the door. Shackled to it was the mercenary, riddled with wounds. The bulletproof vest had been torn from his body and his torso ripped open, entrails piled at his lifeless feet. Blood pooled around the chair, coating a mess of wires littering the stone floor.

Mikael traced the cabling back to a pair of worktables between each tunnel entrance, stacked high with A/V equipment, monitors, and workstations. He recognized the software on display—he'd been using it for years to cut and edit his videos. Studio lights were positioned around the victim in tandem with three cameras on tripods.

A film set. Fuck, Bartlett, what the hell have you gotten yourself into . . .

An animal's shriek echoed from one of the dark tunnels, spiking his anxiety, filling his belly with concrete. His heart froze.

Footsteps. Several, and heavy. Wet skin slapping stone. Growls and snorts.

He forgot about his channel and Janine. All he cared about was surviving, hiding, escaping. Panicking, Mikael retreated toward the door, praying for a place to hide. In his haste he tripped on one of the coiled wires and dropped the camera, watching helplessly as it clattered along the floor. No matter, he'd buy a new one; after everyone saw this footage, he'd buy a thousand of them. But first—

The door was made of thick wood, painted red, built to be heavy-duty—and locked with an old padlock.

The key!

Trembling, he produced the skeleton key and twisted it into the lock. The clasp released, and within seconds he was pawing at the door's edge, straining to pull it open.

A squeal from behind brought the hairs on his neck to full attention. The weight of the room changed, the air suddenly sour with the tang of sweat and something he couldn't place. For all his terror, he wanted badly to turn and see what monstrosity had wrought such carnage, but first the door. It creaked on its hinges, resisted his efforts with all its bulk, but slowly gave in.

Once it was open, Mikael took a step—and froze.

What he saw didn't make sense.

This wasn't another tunnel or another room. His foot dangled outside in the open air. Below was a bottomless ravine. The quarry.

There was something massive down there in the dark, moving, coiling around itself. Watching him from its hiding place. He could only glimpse its movement, and only from the corner of his eye. To stare directly at it was to stare into a fathomless void, his pupils unable to discern the dark.

The outer world took on a shade of maroon as reality rippled, shimmered. He wasn't outside anymore, but inside something else. Something with eyes on the inside, in the dark, and in the sky. A different kind of cosmos, pocketed inside another. The gravity bearing down on him from the unblinking eyes above was too much to take.

"What—this can't . . ."

Mikael stepped back inside. Turned around.

Six men stood in the kill room. Man-like in shape, but not men at all. They were nude, coated in blood and shit and weird black sludge. Masked—no, that wasn't right. They weren't wearing pig masks at all. They *were* pigs. Swine-Men, with snouts and tusks and piercing blue eyes. The one closest was covered in fresh gore. Mad Dog's killer.

Their grunts and snorts quieted as he slowly approached them. One by one, they knelt in reverence.

"Are you okay?" Janine's voice echoed from above.

The swine-men lifted their snouts, sniffed the air, and squealed in unison as they rose to their feet. One of them retrieved the camera and passed it along to him. He accepted it without hesitation.

The show must go on.

His voice or theirs, spoken or unspoken, he could no longer tell. They were united now, a single voice with a singular purpose, digits on the hand of something far greater and older. Pilgrims come to christen these tainted borderlands.

"Mikael, please answer me!"

Spider Vain looked up at the stairwell, and then down upon his most devoted fans.

He smiled. "Go fetch my mask."

That Colossal Wreck

John Langan

(There were a total of forty-seven business-type envelopes. Tied together with frayed twine in bundles of between seven and nine, they were packed in a single layer in a flat shallow box whose cardboard was furred with black mold. We discovered it in the long ledge at the rear of the basement that extended under the house's addition. How we had not noticed the box when we first moved into the house, neither Deb nor I could say. Only after I had slid it out from its hiding place did we see the mold, by which time it was too late, so I held my breath and rushed the box up and out the storm cellar doors, dropping it on the side lawn, where it burst apart, spilling the packets across the grass.

(We assumed the gathered envelopes were the property of the house's previous owners, their contents bills and bank statements. We indulged in a cursory debate about opening them, then retrieved a pair of sharp knives from the kitchen. Before sliding the blades under the sealed folds, we noticed that each envelope had been numbered in the upper left-hand corner, from one to forty-seven. Handling their worn and crinkled material, we also realized that they were older than our initial estimate, as were the folded sheets of paper we withdrew from them.

(In all, the envelopes contained one hundred and seven pieces of fragile, yellowed paper. Every last one had been written on front and back in a small, spidery hand in blue ink, which had by and large faded beyond legibility. The exception was a trio of packets, the first, eighth, and last, whose script was just decipherable in the strong afternoon sunlight.)

Envelope 1:
The Beach at the Crossroads

The first, small house my wife, Deborah, and I rented was located at a crossroads about five miles outside Huguenot, where she had taken a job in the biology department of the local SUNY school. Seven hundred square feet, the house had siding the yellow of a bumblebee. At the top of three concrete stairs, the front door opened into the living room, which despite its size had a fireplace, half of whose smoke rose lazily into the house when we lit it with the logs remaining in the garage. The narrow kitchen was on the right, the rings on its electric stove unpredictable. Straight ahead from the front door was the bathroom, to either side of which were a pair of rooms, the one on the left our bedroom, the one on the right an office/guest room. Between the front door and the road there was a reasonable lawn whose slender trees made it a challenge to mow—especially with the old-fashioned mechanical mower we attempted to use in the name of environmental conscientiousness—but which provided us a sense of privacy we didn't really need, given how fast the traffic whipped by on Springgrown Road, which ran north to south in front of the house. Behind the house was a generous wooden deck reached through a sliding glass door in the laundry room, which sat on the other side of the kitchen and where I eventually set up my drawing desk. The backyard was about the size of the front, a shed and an irregular line of trees marking the edge of the property. The door to the shed was secured with a padlock to which we had the key, so we used it to store everything we couldn't fit in the house, mostly (my) books. Between the house and shed, on the right as you faced out into the yard, was a rectangular plot of ground that had been sectioned off with solid wooden posts taller than I was and heavy wire fencing. This was the garden, which Deb said and I agreed we would use to supplement our diet. Our landlords joked with us that they would invoke the medieval right of *usufructs* and claim a portion of our harvest. We told them they would be welcome to it.

But preparing and planting the garden proved more difficult than we anticipated, mainly because of the soil. It was heavy, composed almost entirely of thick wet clay that resisted the shovels we dug into it. The soil held the water that wet winter had poured onto it, adding to its mass. Turning the ground over to ready the garden for the lettuce, tomato, and cucumber we intended to plant left the two of us exhausted, our arms weak, our lower backs aching. When we opened the gate and stepped into the weeded space, we envisioned it all blooming with future produce. By the time we called it quits, barely half the sodden area overturned, we decided what we had accomplished would (have to) be enough.

Nor was this the only problem we faced with the garden. Not long after the seeds we had tucked into the soil began to stretch up toward the sun, the local slug population discovered them and oozed their slow way onto the shoots and leaves, leaving ragged holes in their wake. Deb bought cans of cheap beer and plastic cups, half-filled the latter with the former, and placed the cups throughout the garden. Every morning we would find amber slugs floating in them, dead from their malted baths. Deb dumped them out on the other side of the garden fence and refilled the traps. Given the amount of beer we were buying from the general store up the road, I joked, we would be gaining a reputation as the local alcoholics, and not particularly discriminating ones at that. Deb smiled thinly. The next time it was my turn to pick up a six-pack of lowest-common-denominator brew, I made sure to mention to the woman behind the old-fashioned cash register that this purchase was for the slugs in the garden. Behind the scuffed lenses of her glasses, her eyes registered no response to my clarification.

A week or two after this, Deb and I were dinner guests of one of her colleagues, who lived on this side of the general store, in a colonial house up a short, steep driveway. Over its two-century-plus lifetime, the house had been added onto in a haphazard fashion, a room here, a room there, which gave the impression there was somehow more of its pale blue façade than you were seeing. We ate in the ground-floor kitchen, which was the newest part of the house, with an enormous, restaurant-grade gas stove, a breakfast bar, and a great blond wood table where Erik and his partner, Benjamin, served us succotash, polenta, and a green salad harvested from their garden. This prompted a discussion of our horticultural efforts, which had not yet yielded anything close to the abundance Erik and Benjamin had taken from the ground already. I blamed the relentless slugs (and repeated my joke about the volume of beer we were going through); Deb blamed the dense, wet soil.

This was fascinating, Erik said, because the ground around their house was exactly the opposite, sandy and dry. In fact, he said, they had a dry well their washing machine emptied into, and as far as he could tell after a decade living here, the dry well would never be filled. Their garden had been easy to excavate but required bags of compost and manure to render fit for planting, and the constant addition of fertilizer to keep thriving.

You know what this sounds like? Benjamin said.

We did not.

Where we are, he said, was once a beach, and where you are was a lake or sea.

How long ago are we talking? I said.

It would have to be thousands of years, Benjamin said. I mean, tens of thousands. Maybe more.

After dinner, as we walked home in the dark, grateful for the flashlight Erik had loaned us, I asked Deb her opinion of Benjamin's ancient-sea explanation for the state of our soil. She shrugged. It was possible, she said. She didn't know much about the geology of this part of the Hudson Valley. We weren't that far from the Svartkill's banks—in fact, we had walked to the closest bend on a couple of occasions, down the aptly named River Road, which formed part of the crossroads at which our house sat. On our side of the river, the distance to its brown surface was fifteen feet, if that. The opposite bank was shorter, no more than ten feet high, less, flat farmland beyond. The couple of times hurricanes had struck us glancing blows, the Svartkill had swelled over that east bank and spread across the tilled acres, flattening them into a wide lake whose expanse shone in the post-storm light. Under the right circumstances, Deb said, she could imagine the river cresting this side of it all the way to our house and past, to where the land angled up into the ridges that ran behind Huguenot.

I pictured the ground to either side of us under the Svartkill, the stands of young birch and oak to our left rising out of running water, their lower branches dragging in the current, the uncut grass to our right completely submerged, the distant light from our front porch a white smear on the flood. The skin on the back of my neck crawled, my mouth dry. I swallowed, asked, What would cause that kind of flooding?

This wasn't her field, Deborah said, but the Svartkill flowed north from New Jersey, didn't it? Somewhere in the mountains in the northwest?

It did, I said.

During the last ice age, she said, the glaciers didn't retreat evenly. Possibly you had one or part of one left in the mountains in Jersey, and when it melted it raised the Svartkill. Or, you know, geology, geological processes. Continents colliding, mountains rising, land pushing down. That kind of stuff could cause water levels to rise or fall substantially, and for an extended period of time. It still could.

Oh? I said.

Sure, she said. It's unlikely in either of our lifetimes. The kinds of processes we're talking about take millennia, longer. But they're still happening. Not to mention the odd accident can affect things. An asteroid or comet strikes the Earth, and everything gets fucked up—for a while, anyway. Or the super-volcano under Yellowstone blows its top and sends millions of tons of rock and dust into the atmosphere. Those things could occur a lot sooner—five minutes from now. Although we'd probably have a little bit of warning.

Would it do us any good? I asked.

Doubtful, Deb said. I guess we would try to intercept a comet or asteroid while it was still out in space, hit it with a missile and hope that altered its course. Assuming we detected it in time. You would think that would work with an asteroid, but I don't know about a comet. I mean, as I understand it, comets are compacted ice and rock, which seems as if it would mean a risk of the thing fracturing into smaller pieces, any of which might still hit the Earth. Not as bad as an impact from the whole thing, but still not great. Again, though, this is way outside what I study.

How about the super-volcano? I said.

Oh, no, she said. There's nothing we can do about that. If it erupts, we're screwed.

And the slugs will have their turn, I said.

Not if it's up to me, Deb said.

I pictured plastic cups of watery beer, overflowing with limp, lifeless gastropods.

Envelope 8: Ozymandias

The face took up the entirety of the backyard, its round chin a step down from the deck, its curled hair a foot from the shed, its left ear next to the garden fence, its right ear near enough to the (vacationing) neighbors' property to eavesdrop on them. Mud streaked its gigantic features, which were carved in what seemed to me the idealized proportions of ancient Greece, out of a quarter-acre of a white stone I thought was marble. In the early evening light the material glowed dimly. Thick soil two feet deep, grass roots dangling from its exposed surface in hairy strands, framed the sculpture. At the top of the garden Evan had heaped the soil in a mound on whose muddy summit he had parked the mini-excavator. He's still just a kid, I thought, isn't he? In spite of everything he's told us. Everything he's shown us.

Right now that kid was standing with the woman he insisted was his mother—would become his mother—my wife, staring at the carving's yards-wide mouth. Come here, Deb said without looking at me. You have to see this.

Bring the glaive, Evan added.

I dropped from the deck onto the stone, the impact jarring my knees, making the glaive's ashen length quiver in my arms. A wave of something like vertigo washed over me as I pictured the scene from above, me traversing the exposed sculpture like a mouse trudging across a man's sleeping face. From where I had been watching, the mouth appeared to be closed. As I walked to Deb and Evan, I saw the great lips were in fact parted, as if whoever this was supposed to be had been caught on the verge of speaking, or of just having uttered some deafening syllable. At its widest, the mouth was open far enough to permit an adult to squeeze himself into its shadowy interior. The lips were speckled with hundreds of green objects, each the length of my index finger, which upon closer inspection I saw were slugs—or something like slugs. Murmuring, What the hell? I bent forward to inspect them. The dirty yellow of crusted snot, they were veined with iridescent green, their horns capped with cilia, their backs lined by a row of curved spines.

Leaving behind trails of mustard colored slime, the slugs were crawling out of the statue's mouth into the cooling air.

A mix of wonder and revulsion made me straighten. What the hell? I said again.

Now we know what's been wrong with the septic, Deb said.

You see? Evan said.

See what? I said. Exactly what is it I'm looking at?

We have to go in, don't we? Deb nodded at the parted lips.

I haven't been able to figure out any other way, Evan said.

Go in there? I said, pointing at the mouth. For real?

I'll take the lead, Evan said. He held out his left hand to me. Pass me the glaive, he said.

Please, Deb said.

Please, he said.

Here, I said, giving him the weapon. To Deb, I said, You cannot be serious.

She was already withdrawing an object from the right front pocket of her cargo pants: a black, snub-nosed revolver.

What the hell is that? I said. Where did you get a gun?

The place in Wiltwyck, she said. Across from the bicycle store.

When did you get a gun? I said.

Don't worry, she said, the safety's on.

Evan was using the flat of the glaive's blade to sweep the slugs from the sculpture's lips, the metal chiming across the marble. The slugs tumbled down the stone rises into writhing masses. There'll be more inside, he said, pointing the glaive at the darkness within the mouth. We'll have to be careful. Weapon held overhead, he lowered himself until he was sitting on the lower lip, his feet dangling in the air. He scooted his butt forward and slid into the sculpture.

Deb squatted where he had been. All right? she called into the opening.

Come on! Evan answered. His voice was faint, far away, as if his descent had carried him much farther than the carving's mouth, had deposited him deep in the sculpture's guts. In one fluid motion Deb moved from crouch to sit, swinging her legs out into space.

Wait, I said. Please.

Are you coming? Deb said. Without waiting for my reply, she raised her arms, leaned back, and slipped out of sight.

Envelope 47:
Memory Alive Beyond the Body

Outside the golden dome, the final god had lost the struggle to maintain its form, the blast furnace heat of the Earth's surface liquefying Onda's rocky form, reducing it to a mass of lava.

I was not sure that would work, Humva vocalized, mandibles clashing.

Nor I, Evan said.

Overhead, the aged sun sprawled across the sky, its crimson brilliance filtered to a more tolerable orange glow by the dome's intercession. With the glare diminished, the larger rocks of the lunar ring were discernible. Meteors drew lines of fire across the heavens, now visible beyond the sun's bloated circumference. The constellations had come apart, their latest forms sundered by the acceleration of time and the incursion of new stars from the approaching galaxies.

Look at those, Evan said as more meteors flared into view. His voice was high, wheezing. Pilgrims from another place.

Andromeda? I said.

Triangulum, Evan said. On the horizon, bursts of light marked the impacts of a school of meteors on the planet's molten exterior.

The seeds, Humva crooned, secondary and tertiary arms waving in excitement.

Some, Evan said. Some.

I looked at him, at Deb's son, reclining against the rectangular cenotaph. The leg Onda had crushed was withered, desiccated. In only the time it had taken us to deal with the silicate deity, Evan had aged another decade, two, his hair, eyebrows, and beard longer and shaggier, bleached to a whiteness that shone yellow in the dome's luminance. The lines dug into his face had deepened to trenches that looked as if they grooved the bone underneath. A small forest of toadstools, their peaked caps purple, had sprouted up the left side of his neck and face, into his hairline. His eyes had receded into dark caverns, from which they regarded me dully, as if he had already completed the remainder of his journey out of this life. The skin on his hands was papery, mottled with age spots, the joints of his fingers swollen. Although its blade was gone, he maintained his grip on the glaive's charred shaft.

He was, I thought, the oldest human being I had ever seen. In a journey whose accumulated strangeness had worn my nerves to numbness, his weathered features seemed the most fantastic, the most unbelievable of all sights.

And how must I appear to him? My hair had fled the top of my head years ago, though its last, wispy remnants clung stubbornly to the base of my skull. The skin of my neck had lost elasticity, sagging into a wattle worthy of a turkey. My limbs were brittle sticks wrapped in loose, translucent flesh. Deb's pistol, festooned with its grafts of wood, bone, and chitin, weighed too heavy for one hand. I cradled it in my arms like the child we never had.

Another flight of meteors struck the planet, close enough for the explosions to wash the dome in white light, the detonations to shake the ground, shimmer the dome, as the collisions cast enormous plumes of lava and debris into the negligible atmosphere. The tremors toppled Evan onto his right side, where he lay motionless. After a moment of watching him make no effort to raise himself, I understood it was because he was dead.

The trench gaped between his body and Humva, at the foot of the diamond cenotaph. I was relieved the three of us had excavated the thick soil while we were still in possession of sufficient strength to do so. While I watched, Humva lumbered to Evan's corpse, bent over it, and gripped the legs at the ankles. Dragging the body, he backed toward the ditch until Evan lay parallel to it. Even in death, Deb's son maintained his grip on the glaive's handle. Bearing their freight of metal and organics, meteors dove into lava near and far, flooding the interior of the dome with flickering brilliance, convulsing the earth. Vision bleached, I watched Humva roll Evan's remains into the trench, then turn to me, right arms extended.

My knees were stiff, my hips almost immobile. Once the worst of the quaking had subsided, I shuffled over the rocky ground to the side of Evan's makeshift grave, across from Humva. I opened my arms and allowed the pistol to drop on top of Evan. Once, I said, you spoke at a funeral. Offered a few words of remembrance. For a life. Well lived. But . . . I shrugged. Language feels used up. Like everything else. We should get on with this.

The pouch was hanging at my side. I fumbled with the draw string, aged silk smooth. My fingernails tugged at the knot I had tied while Evan and I were still underground. The leather released and the bag yawned. Hands trembling, I eased Deb's head out from it. I didn't want to look at her, but I had always known I would. Time had drawn the skin tight against the bone, pulled the lips away from the teeth, collapsed the nose. Thankfully, the eyes were still closed, but the expression of peace she had worn into death was gone, replaced by the grimace of a person trapped in a nightmare. Despite myself, I whimpered. I held the head out over the trench. The skin was wafer thin, the skull delicate as porcelain. The slightest pressure from my palms, and my wife's head disintegrated into a powdery stream I poured onto Evan. When I was done, I wiped my hands together and reached into the pouch a second time.

We called them slugs, but that was only because we didn't have a better name for them, a more accurate location of their place in the taxonomy of the far future, and they resembled the gastropods that had plagued our garden sufficiently for the designation to stick. There were five remaining at the bottom of the bag, each the length of my hand, their brown, rugose hides still spongy to the touch, their toothed suckers spasming under my fingers, the cluster of feelers at their heads twitching. They weren't alive in the way we understood the term, Evan had said, nor was death something they experienced as did we. I scooped them out in two handfuls and dropped them into the grave. They sent up little puffs of dust where they landed on Evan. I grimaced.

Humva wasted no time. With his long feet he pushed the dirt heaped alongside the ditch back into it, working with such speed that all its contents—Evan, the glaive's wooden shaft, Deb's pistol, the dust of her remains, the quintet of slugs—were soon covered. I would have helped him, but my legs were finding it difficult to obey the commands my brain was sending them. Humva did not appear to mind. He hummed contentedly as he swept the last of the soil over the grave.

Near and far, a flotilla of meteors plunged from the sky, fiery emissaries carrying gifts from the reaches of the Periodic Table. The earth heaved, knocking me from my feet. Waves of light swept my sight away. The dome crackled. For what seemed a long time I lay trying to recover the breath that had been stunned out of me, my eyes full of flat whiteness. I didn't think I was dead—not yet—but how was I supposed to be sure? The prospect of a blind, breathless eternity stretched in front of me, stirring vague horror in my chest. I want to say it was a relief to feel any emotion, but this would not be true. What remained of my consciousness receded to a distant, blank nowhere.

After an indeterminate interval, sensation summoned my mind back from its retreat. There was something cool and damp under my cheek, something fibrous and gritty. A sharp green smell riding a sour, earthy smell prickled my nostrils. Enough of my vision was recovered for me to see the vegetation before me, the tall tomato plants tied to wooden frames with shoelaces, the rows of lettuce, the looping vines held down by round melons. I saw soil mixed gray and brown, peppered with tiny rocks, black ants hurrying over it. Beyond the greenery, wire fencing rose between stout wooden posts, marking the edge of the garden, of our garden, the one Deb and I had labored to create and nursed to fruition. The muscles of my arms and legs were too atrophied to permit me to stand, but I was able to force myself up into a kind of half-sit. The tears that spread across my corneas were slow, viscous. Through their distortion I saw the yellow box of the house, of my and Deb's first house. It was surrounded by what appeared to be a low, wide lake. I blinked, but the water remained, eddying around the foundation, stretching off into the distance.

Though the movement was painful, I turned my head to survey the rest of the garden. At the approximate center there was a small tree. Its slender trunk was a braid of creamy wood, silver metal, and purple flesh, as were the branches forking from it. Leaves like long purple banners hung from the branches. At first I thought my eyes were failing me, but no, there was movement on the trunk, the branches, things inching up and out on them, leaving lines of clear slime in their wake. These slugs might have been the same as those Deb had drowned in her beer traps, once upon a universe, except for the single pale eye splitting each one's back.

(Reading the three selections was the work of an hour, most of the time taken up deciphering individual words, a few sentences. The remainder of the day and most of the night was consumed by the worst argument Deb and I had had during our time together. She was convinced I had played the most elaborate of practical jokes on her, one that took the facts of our early life together, when we rented an undersized yellow house on Springgrown Road whose garden we wrested out of soil more clay than earth, and brought them together with . . . she couldn't decide what, only that it appeared to be making not so thinly veiled allegations about the future of our marriage, and specifically her fidelity to me. She wasn't sure whether I was expressing actual insecurities about our union or projecting my desire to leave it onto her. Given our failure to conceive the child we both wanted, she was particularly aggrieved by the figure of Evan.

(None of her accusations was true, but my protestations to this effect did little to persuade her. Pointing out the lengths I would have had to go to in order to construct this hoax, not the least of which would have entailed my secreting the box and its letters in a spot in a basement we had only glanced at while we were still negotiating our offer on the house with the previous owners, was not the irrefutable proof I thought it would be. Nor did my more straightforward declaration that I loved her and would not pull so bizarrely malicious a prank on her fare any better. She had heard enough stories about the practical jokes with which my brothers and I had bedeviled one another's childhoods, few of which she found funny, all of which she considered cruel, and which now rendered suspect every word that emerged from my mouth. As is the case in arguments of such intensity and duration, the current conflict acted as a magnet, drawing to itself a ringing clatter of resentments and grudges, some recent, some

years old. Fueling the dispute on both sides was the deep disorientation and anxiety the letters produced in us. I knew I was not their author, but Deb's seeming certainty that I was made me doubt myself, wonder if it were possible I had produced them in some bizarre dissociative state. For her part, despite her barbed charges, Deb knew I was not responsible for the box's contents. The strain of not facing this directly, however, was exhausting, and when at last we retreated to bed, she in the downstairs guest room, I in our room upstairs, it was as boxers after a bout whose length and ferocity have left their legs shaking, their arms limp.

(I woke after a couple of hours of dense, dreamless sleep. With me, agitation at the previous night's events was aroused, foreclosing any possibility of another few hours in bed. Replaying our exchanges in my memory, imagining different responses, and letting them play out in my mind, I descended to the kitchen and switched on the coffee maker. Outside the big window the world was emerging from darkness, daybreak coaxing trees and grass, the cars parked in the driveway, the hedge on the other side of them, into form and color. I poured my first cup of coffee (into the mug Deb had gifted me on my birthday, the one with ARTIST printed on the side in old typescript), added milk, and carried it onto the back deck.

(The air was pleasantly cool, filled with early birdsong. I saw the sculpture as I was raising the mug to my lips. It was a hand, positioned on top of the rise behind the house, the wrist emerging straight from the ground, the palm turned upwards, fingers slightly bent. Easily as big as our yard, it had been carved from white rock that seemed to gather the new sunlight to its smooth surface. The sight of the carving there against the lightening sky was like a great shout. I stepped back, and felt a slug burst under my heel.)

For Fiona

A Bodyless Thing

Sam Rebelein

I volunteered for this. What a joke. I *let* them lead me down that dark hall, deep within this cavernous labyrinth, further inside this mountain than anyone should ever have to go. I'd heard they do bad things up here, in the mountain. But I needed the money. I'd lost my job to a machine. Rent was due, and I saw this flyer in the laundromat. *Five grand for experiment volunteer.* I tore one phone-number slip off the bottom, and after a beat I ripped the whole flyer down and stuffed it in my pocket. I knew that was wrong. I told myself, *Don't be greedy.* But I didn't want the scientists to have people to choose from. And that's the joke because now, that particular currency no longer even *exists*.

The laboratory is carved, like a massive burrow, into the giant, sprawling mountain just outside of town. When I arrived at its spartan, pristine lobby, they had me sign a sheaf of forms, and as my hand was beginning to cramp from writing my name and the date so many times, the laboratorians whipped the clipboard away and led me to an elevator without buttons. They pressed their hands into the walls and the elevator ascended *fast*. I've suffered from vertigo since I was eleven, when the rides at the county fair nearly spiraled me into a coma, and the rapid rise of this elevator made my vision go gray. I had to lean against one of the white-coats as we went up, up, ever higher into these rough-hewn halls. The elevator reached its destination before I was able to recover, and the white-coats had to drag me out. I could feel the rough stone floor scraping along the toes of my sneakers, could pick out vague shapes swimming in the dizzying gray. An arm swinging here, the throat of some other hallway moaning open there . . .

Left, right, and around we went. How the laboratorians knew where they were going without consulting a map is beyond me. Perhaps this place has never even *been* mapped. I wonder if this facility is so vast and so old—so many forgotten leagues of it hidden in the deep dark bowels of the rock—that the company itself has forgotten experiments that were once conducted here.

At last we arrived at a cavernous room with a missing wall. In its stead, a wide, floor-to-ceiling eye overlooked the valley. My vision finally cleared, and from this vantage point I saw most of the forest below, all the pointy green trees and the waterfalls off the hills. Several towns lay scattered around, and far on the horizon were the glimmers of the city skyscrapers. The sun was beginning to rise. It baked the stone floors and walls of the room, giving the entire space a warm earth smell, like fresh chalk and newly mown grass.

The room buzzed with activity. Scientists scuttled back and forth, adjusting various brass apertures and glass screens filled with humming wires. Shelves carved into the granite walls were packed with blinking, churning, ticking equipment. A mad scientist's wet dream. And in the center of the room was . . . *this*. This box. This godforsaken *tomb*. It resembles a large, rectangular glass coffin, standing on end. It's approximately seven and a half feet tall (reaching almost to the ceiling), and three feet wide on each of its four sides. Each corner of the cell is banded with strips of dark steel, bolted in place and carved with intricate patterns of symbols that weren't familiar to me when I stepped inside. They're like a hybrid of cave drawings and the Nordic alphabet. Pig-headed men bow to a sun filled with runes. Constellations describing ghoulish skull-shapes glare down upon women whose bodies themselves appear to be runes. There was a kind of time-keeper, a chronometer, bolted to the top of the cell. Further runes circled its face, carved in sharp, violent lines into the metal.

From the iron base of the cell, leading off into gleaming brass-and-glass machines lining the walls, sprawled a series of cables and wires, thick rubber tubes like intestines. One machine looked to me like some kind of fax machine when I arrived. A feed-out of perforated paper grinds out of its snout even now, and as always, the papers droop to the floor to fold neatly into a tall stack directly below the machine.

This machine has printed continuously for an indeterminable amount of time, recording all my thoughts. That's the only thing they asked me to do: place the electrodes against my temples, and the machine would transcribe my experience. What exactly they'd intended to record, I'll never know. They merely pointed me toward the window and asked me to observe the outside world. No sound permeates the cell, so the scientists and I communicate through hand signals and the machine. Occasionally they'd ask me inane questions in writing, holding up large blackboard slabs against the glass. *How are you feeling? Are you cold?* Then they'd consult the perpetual printout of the machine for my responses.

In the beginning I stood inside the cell (there is no room to sit) and fidgeted, wondering how long I'd have to watch the sun wander over the horizon from day toward night. It slowly crawled across the sky as I hummed and rocked back and forth on my heels. All the while, the scientists peered in at me and wrote things down. They kept a very close eye on the chronometer atop the cell. They'd continually eye the time indicated there, check their own wristwatches, and jot notes furiously upon their pads.

Just before sunset something seemed to go wrong. A tall scientist taking notes on me frowned quickly up at the chronometer. He checked his pulse, then called over one of the other scientists. She joined him with her own clipboard, he pointed at the chronometer with his pen, and she, too, frowned. She went to one of the machines, checked its readings, and called out what it said. Apparently it said something very bad, because the tall scientist rushed to her side and together they began tweaking things on the machines. Flicking switches, turning knobs, throwing worried looks over their shoulders at me.

Their efforts did not seem to be working. They started running their hands through their hair and shouting at each other, barking orders at the other scientists. Everyone ran around, gaping up at the chronometer. One woman paused, putting her hand over her mouth. Seeing her do that sent a surge of panic through my chest. I shouted and banged against the glass, which was evidently also very bad, because the scientists waved their hands and shouted soundlessly at me to stop.

After a while the woman who'd put her hand over her mouth shook her head at everyone else. She pointed at me and spoke frantically, and

I gathered that she was suggesting they let me go. Something had gone utterly wrong, and my safety might be at risk. Fearing I might no longer receive my five thousand dollars, I retreated from the glass, pressing my back against the opposite wall of the cell, in an attempt to assure everyone I wasn't going to do anything to threaten the integrity of the experiment. I *needed* that money.

But the woman persisted. She was yelling now, shoving the other scientists. They shoved her back. She punched someone and then ran to the far wall to retrieve a fire axe. She ran at the cell, cutting a wake through the small crowd. No one was willing to get between her and the axe. She gave me a panicked look and mouthed the words, *Stay back*. Another wave of fear pulsed in needles through my blood. I shook my head at her, sent pleading thoughts to the transcription machine.

It didn't matter. She hefted the axe high above her head—and the room exploded into smoke. Thick gray clouds burst from the floor, so quickly that I only had time to see the last grenade clatter in from the hall, then *pop* into gas. Everyone dropped to their knees, coughing and sputtering, clutching their throats. Uniformed police officers surged into the room, rifles and shotguns drawn. They slammed into the scientists cowering on the floor and lashed their wrists with zip-ties, shouting orders and shoving the large black barrels of their guns against the backs of heads.

I can only assume that the laboratory's reputation had caught up with it at last. I grew up in this town, and I'd heard about this place all my life. I'd heard that they dismembered children here, that they fused parts of stray dogs onto other stray dogs and made them fight while they took notes. I'd always assumed these were just childhood urban legends. But at the arrival of the police I became convinced that this experiment—the one I'd *volunteered* for—was perhaps the least cruel thing happening in this mountain. At long last, the law had come for the laboratory.

But the scientist with the axe stood strong. She coughed and wavered but held the axe aloft. Several officers surrounded her, the muzzles of their guns glaring at her with cold steel eyes. They shouted at her, demanding she drop the weapon and lie on the floor with the other scientists. She coughed and shook her head, and finally, as the smoke was beginning to clear, she lifted that axe high—and the officers opened fire. Bullets sparked off the corners of the cell. Crimson burst across the glass as the woman shuddered and her axe clattered to the floor.

None of those bullets managed to leave so much as a mark against the cell. Not even a hairline fracture appeared in all its brilliant crystalline surfaces. But of course—a stray bullet caught the edge of the chronometer. It spewed golden sparks across the shuddering, dying scientist who had tried to save me. Whatever had gone wrong with the chronometer before, now it was *truly* beyond repair. And the thing I assume that woman had been attempting to avoid finally occurred:

My eyes—broke.

There was a blur of movement and color, and the room emptied, as if the bodies were sucked out of it through a vacuum. Outside, the sun dove behind the hills and stars pierced the bluish-black linen of the night sky. Suddenly men swarmed through the chamber, buzzing over the machines and peering in at me. I caught flashes of their faces. Ghastly apparitions, there in a moment, then gone within a blink. I felt like a stuck bug at a museum, watching countless decades of visitors gawk at me as I lay undead under glass.

The sun sprang up over the valley again, blazed like a flare across the sky, and dove back down. The moon leapt after it, then again, and again, faster and faster. I was losing an entire week of time, an entire month. I assumed I was simply having another episode of vertigo, so I put my hands against the glass to steady myself. I began to feel claustrophobic, and damn the money, I wanted out of this cell *now*. I couldn't even stretch my shoulders all the way, expand my entire wingspan. I had difficulty breathing. I could do nothing but watch, helpless, as bodies swam about the room.

Everything went black and I thought I'd passed out, until I realized someone must have thrown a cloth over the cell. I waited for several moments, my heart pounding. Had they forgotten me? Would I be stuck forever here, in a coffin in the dark? I had to put a hand to my chest, suck in great breaths through my nose, and shove them out between my teeth. I felt I was having a panic attack.

Then I realized my fingers felt . . . odd. I looked down and saw in the gloom that my fingernails had grown shockingly long. In fact, as I looked at them they stretched farther out of my hands, growing more cracked and yellow as they *stretched.* I saw, too, that I was growing a thick, wiry beard. It extended down over my ribs, and I *felt* my ribs more clearly. My legs shook with the strain of standing for . . . however long I'd been standing here. A year?

With a hot shock of horror I realized that it wasn't *myself* that had begun to malfunction. It was *time.* Or perhaps . . . I in relation to time. I don't know. But whatever that chronometer was intended to do, it was certainly no longer doing it. Because time was moving *very* quickly. So quickly that I refused to look down at myself again, for fear of what other odd growths and signs of decay would reveal themselves. I was only grateful that I did not feel hunger or a need to empty my bowels. Or sleep! Had I needed to sleep, I would have had to do so standing up. A small, unexplainable mercy, as my fingernails continued to curl outward and my bones continued to throb and warp with age . . .

The cloth covering the cell was whipped away, and I faced a new team of scientists. Their faces came in haunted, horrifying flashes. One moment they'd be puttering with the machines along the wall, analyzing the text-feed of all my thoughts, my screams, my panicked cries into the void, then *flash,* a sunken-eyed face glaring in at me. *Flash,* it was gone, replaced by some other ghoul, then *flash,* a whole crowd of them, peering in, taking notes, congratulating one another.

Outside, the sun rose and set, rose and set. It streaked over the world so rapidly that it became a solid golden smear across a blinking sky. Day, night, day, night. The leaves of the trees darkened and bled and shivered to the ground, then burst bright green as fall, winter, spring all arrived in a matter of moments. I couldn't feel the change of seasons through the glass, but I could tell that something was happening to the sun. The trajectory of its arc . . . tilted oddly, as if it were coming closer to Earth. I'd read somewhere that human beings were pumping so much water, and cracking so much of the planet apart for oil, that the axis of the Earth's gravity had actually begun to *shift*. Our orbit was changing. Perhaps *we* were moving closer to the sun, not the other way around.

Heat shimmered off the buildings of the city in wide, wet waves, rippling over the horizon and never faltering, even at night. Then the forest below my window yellowed, and the ground swelled with water as something new wormed its way closer. Great chunks of trees vanished as men dug and clawed and *expanded*. In mere moments the valley was all brown mush, and then, like ants, they constructed new neighborhoods, a new hospital, a new drive-in movie theater. I watched thousands of movies there, all in a blink, all no more than whirring faces, strobing lights and colors. And all the while, the sun burned hotter, closer. The anthill of the valley below swarmed with small bodies and cars and roiling plumes of smog. Then the streams of people slowed, and it seemed as if everyone were staying indoors.

Meanwhile, the cave-room buzzed with scientists. Checking the equipment, peering in at me. Eyes wide and sunken like alien ghouls. Faces sweating under the glare of that burning solar beam, warbling in a thick solid line across the sky, perpetually pursued by the moon.

The drive-in theater went dark, and great winds ripped through the valley, shooting holes through some of the houses below, blowing trees over. Big boiling thunderclouds brewed over the city and blasted over the valley, roiling and flashing. The storms lasted nearly a full minute for me, so I can't fathom how long they must have lasted in world-time. Long enough, at least, for the entire valley to flood, the houses swept away, and the pale face of the movie screen toppled into the rushing, rising waters. The water rose almost to the lip of my window, and everything went still. The scientists swarming the room vanished and did not return.

The world remained one great lake, with only the tips of skyscrapers on the horizon. The sun and moon continued to churn overhead, and I wondered why I could look at this endless circling of the heavens without experiencing my usual vertigo. Why wasn't this eternal spinning making me dizzy?

So finally I looked down at myself once more. And I discovered: *I was not there.*

Bones lay curled in a fetal heap at the bottom of the cell, covered in dust. I recognized my sneakers, the cloth worn through but the cracked rubber soles still present for now. I stared down at my lifeless, fleshless grin, and I watched as my teeth cracked and crumbled into further dust.

I'm dead. The thought sang in my ears, making my whole skull vibrate. But that couldn't be true, because *I had no skull.* I was just some floating, gaseous . . . thing. A specter. An entity, alive long after its death. A ghost. *I'm a ghost.*

They did something to me . . . *conjured* something, I don't know. But they *did* something with those runes on this box. They froze my consciousness in time. My body and the world, and everything else—it moves and ages at the same pace. But I? In my mind? I do not age at all. And never will.

Strangely, instead of horror, a sense of calm rolled over me. I had . . . nothing more to worry about. No more rent to pay. No more jobs to apply for. Money would never matter to me ever again. Everyone I'd ever known was dust now, deep underwater. I had nothing left to do with my *entire* existence except to watch, to wait, and to hope I'd wake up.

The sun drifted back away again, the earth's axis tilting once more. Snow blew across the valley, and the watery lake that had once been a forest, then a swamp, then a neighborhood and a swamp again—that lake froze before my eyes into a beautiful brilliant blue. The city remained dark, and I imagined I might be the last conscious soul on the entire planet. The buildings turned brown as they rusted, then they crumbled and fell, and more winds whipped them right out of my view, into ash.

I glanced down at the floor of the cell, and I, too, was no more than a mound of ash. Everything I'd ever thought or felt or wanted or *been*—reduced to a small hill of nothing. But still, the machines lining the shelves of the room ran on. Recording and whirring. Fax machine still printing its clean, rigidly organized stack of papers. Whatever kind of metal these contraptions are made of, it must be damn near indestructible. Or perhaps the runes carved into everything protect it all from rust.

Outside, trees stretched out of the ground, the lake sprouted anew into a swamp, and strange shadows began to pass amongst the undergrowth. I caught glimpses of tall lumbering creatures that resembled half-pig, half-ape humanoids. As I watched, they changed shape. They stood more upright; they lit fires. Some of the trees disappeared again, and log villages sprang up. I saw bright blue banners rise high on flagpoles. Mankind had apparently come and gone, but these pig-apes built new roads, a new city, a new bowl-type structure that I identified as a kind of coliseum. Every culture has its theater, I suppose. Every theater has its violence.

Suddenly the city was aflame. The coliseum was drenched in blood, then became clean again, the bright blue banners replaced with red ones. Smoke filled the sky for a moment, then dissipated as the sun continued to whir overhead, and in a flash—there they were. The pig-apes had discovered me. They'd discovered science just as they'd discovered theater, and the laboratory had been waiting, hidden in the mountain. As it always is.

These new scientists had wide yellow eyes and large tusks protruding from their snouts. With strange blunt tools they beat against the glass of my cell for many minutes, many decades of their time. I watched their clothing change shape and style and color. I watched their bodies shift, too. They grew fatter and stouter, as the red banners below slowly swarmed the entire valley and grew over the new city, which was suddenly backlit by a blinding explosion, and the banners in the valley turned green, and new pig-men in new robes began to beat at the glass, attempting to open my cell and see for themselves what lay inside.

They must have gotten bored with me, because they threw a tarp over the cell, and I floated in a void for a long time. I worried again that I might be stuck in darkness forever, with only glimpses of the outside. Through the tarp I caught shadow-filled flashes of bright light as these new beasts conducted experiments around me. Even crueler ones than the men before. I saw the silhouettes of creatures electrocuted, filleted alive, and worse. Snouts thrown back in howls of agony. Patters of blood scattered then vanished over the glass. I wondered how many of *them* had volunteered.

There were *many* lights, and the tarp vanished. The world was tinted green, and the city now was covered in black and emerald vines, stretching over the skyscrapers in a thick net. Some new race buzzed around the laboratory now. A shimmering, green-veined, tentacled being with the head of a wolf. These wolf-squids circled the cell and bowed and sang, and it seemed as if they were praying to me. As if I were a god. They surrounded me with green-flamed candles and sacrificed themselves unto me, piling up bodies against the glass that I was forced to watch decay. They scratched new runes onto the cell, or . . . now that I think of it, perhaps the runes were *always* theirs.

Eventually, they, too, were overrun by another civilization. Large groups of unrecognizable creatures swarmed the laboratory. Giant bugs crawled over the valley upon hundreds of legs, burning everything. *Everything* murdered one another brutally, leaving large dark stains smeared across the cell for what must have been centuries. I watched the bodies lying across the floor as their skin rotted, popped, and peeled itself off their bones. Their bones, too, cracked and tumbled and turned to ash. Their clothes unraveled, spreading into threads and then nothingness.

Still, somehow, the machine recorded my thoughts. Still its paper unspooled. Still the sun swam across the sky, chased by the moon, causing storms and floods, and scattering that city into dust over and over again.

Then the faces began to appear.

Dark visages in the skies, like the shimmers of far-off mountains, slipping into visibility just over the horizon. I could make out two large pale eyes, filled with blinking stars. A snarling canine mouth and furrowed brows. Four of these faces floated into view, hovering over the land, curling their enormous lips in disdain. Colossal monstrosities, glaring down as if they were angry with the planet itself. They peered in at it as if the entire thing—as if Time itself—were their experiment.

Then I saw, at the edges of the valley, their unfathomably large hands rising up out of the air. They lifted their mammoth hands, palms up, in unison, as they snarled down at the dying earth. There was a great flash, and the moon came hurtling down. It skimmed off the valley below, scraping a deep trench as it rocketed past, sending the heavens into a whirling madness as the earth spun, spun, and the moon adapted a new orbit, at a new angle. The valley burned and everything looked dry and acrid, and then new saurian creatures began to walk through the cooling sands of the valley. I watched as they walked more upright, and developed tools, and went to war, and built cities, and destroyed those cities, and discovered me anew, and peered into my cell, and analyzed the machines, and on and on and on. Not one new being seemed to recognize it was simply following a very old pattern.

I realized: No matter how many times the world rebirthed itself, the cruel drive of science would remain the same. No one who discovered this cell would treat it with kindness. Knowledge is a universal vice.

I watched *many* more civilizations tear themselves apart. Storms and winds and all kinds of world-noise buffeted the valley, rending everything again and again—and then the faces in the sky reappeared. They peered in at the earth once more, snarling their leviathan mouths, lifting their gargantuan hands. It must have taken them *years* to lift their hands fully, because it appeared to be such a fluid motion to me. They lifted their hands, beckoned the world to renew itself, and at their command the sun burned brighter, hotter, and quite literally melted everything into glass, then blew it all apart into sand, and the saurians came again.

Earth dies. Earth *always* dies. It's already happening to you, you just don't know it yet.

I say all this because . . . I do not know how many more times I can simply stand here (if standing is indeed what I'm doing) and watch this all unfold. My mind . . . cannot take any more.

So if you find this document . . . please. Shatter the glass. That's all I ask. I don't know what will happen once I'm freed. Perhaps I'll slip like smoke into the caverns of the laboratory, expanding into the air and free to wander over the trees, into the heavens, away from the gaze of those snarling world-laboratorians, running their vast experiment. Or perhaps *you'll* breathe me in, and I will walk around as you.

Or (and this is my greatest hope) I will simply dissolve. I will die, at last, in peace.

Please. I *beg* you to consider my sanity. I beg you to end this experiment. I beg you to let me go.

* * *

We found it deep within the Forgotten Wing, where the linoleum ceilings turn into rock. Where the walls are dripping ancient granite and the fluorescent work lights blink in time with the heartbeat of the mountain.

The grid was registering some minor, unidentified drain on the main lab's power, so I followed my detector along the wires on the walls and discovered this overlook of the city, this big glass . . . box, for lack of a better word. It's attached to some kind of fax machine–looking item with a nearly infinite and severely faded printout. I was amazed it hadn't rusted over or run out of ink. Still churning out pages, slowly but surely.

Interestingly, the feed-out has translated everything into modern English. Odd that it could do so seemingly with no access to modern English. Unless someone else has been back here recently, but I doubt that. And yet, the text describes things like "laundromats" and "fax machines," completely anachronistic to the ancient dates this machine claims to be reporting on. So it must be a translation, because the alternative is that some forgotten civilization, billions of years ago, had a culture and currency eerily similar to . . . ours. Which also suggests that everything the box recorded is bound to happen *again*. In fact, if we are unable to open the box, in theory, the subject inside could continue to witness this vast Ouroboros ad infinitum. Perhaps he already has.

The thought is almost incomprehensible. And *very* exciting.

As of this writing, we continue to work on understanding the box. Some of us do think it would be best to free the individual inside, but the majority of us believe something may still be learned from it. So we are working on installing a new ink cartridge into the "fax machine." We are confident that upon completion of this (surprisingly complex) task, the machine will continue to run indefinitely, as it already has. True, we are prolonging the subject's boredom and suffering, but subject comfort has never been a company priority. Besides, think of the *good* we could accomplish with this discovery. The things we could learn. For *science*. It could be endless, the wisdom we can gain from this bodiless thing.

And after all—he *did* volunteer.

This House

L. Marie Wood

Up the wall climb shadows
large, formless things that reach toward each other
heads tilted
limbs outstretched
communing
beseeching
yearning for something they could not place,
phantom memories adrift in closed spaces and stagnant air.

Carry on, carry on,
effervescent in their comportment
ethereal, their presence
natural, as the sheen reflects off the dust on the air,
coating it,
saturating before dissipating,
filling to burst.
Native
unreal
lost, like those who wander,
who tread too close;
lost like those who seek not truth, but agreement,
searching from above, up high
where they find only shadows.
Lost
beyond the eaves, ornate and set to ruin same
beyond the crown that keeps in eidolon, vulnerable and soft the portal
held in place by the many and the few,
the shadows climb, climb
to carry on,
to summon hither bane reward,
escape true.

Where the Silent Ones Smile

Patrick Freivald

Garrin raised his right hand, index finger extended. The acid-sweet tang of anticipation wetted his tongue, the culmination of a lifetime studying fields and forces wrenching his gut with a nervousness he couldn't afford to show.

"Turn it on."

"Initializing startup," Lassa said. From her seat, his chief assistant pushed buttons and pulled levers, then looked up at him in anticipation.

He dropped his hand.

"Fifty percent power."

"Fifty percent power." She pulled the first knife-switch down, connecting the power to the Halocian Generators. The gigantic, lumbering devices stirred, sleeping behemoths roused by the power of technology, their great, slow movements the obvious mirage hiding much subtler motion, N-dimensional nanoscale vortices made to harness the energies of the void itself. No dimming sun would set on the ambitions of mankind.

Garrin wiped his sweaty hands on his lab coat and watched the machines churn faster and faster, rising up above the great, columned building that had served as home and research laboratory for nearly the whole of his adult life. The building shuddered as energy fields sprang to life and spread across the sky, separating everything without from everything inside.

Lassa grinned, squinting against the red-orange of the dying but still brilliant sun. "You think it's going to work?"

He grunted. "Nothing this complicated works the first time. You know that." Her smile slipped, and he met it with one of his own to take the edge off. "Check the aggregators, please. We need this data, at least, to be perfect, so the next attempt will be better."

"Yes, sir." She looked at the screens in front of her. "Aggregators functioni——"

Something almost like a noise split through his mind, a gibbering wail more an impression than sound, like the memory of an intense emotion dulled with time, a yearning need grown stronger with age.

Lassa cringed next to him, her teeth clenched, sweat beading on her brow.

"What is that?"

Cockroaches and scorpions skittering over one another in a bucket, a rake dragged across icy stone tile, a frigid susurrus through trees dead of thirst. He shook his head, trying to dislodge the sensation. "It almost sounds like— What is it saying?"

"I'm sorry." A single tear fell down Lassa's cheek. Her voice faded to a bare whisper. "I'm so sorry. We didn't know."

Her knuckles white with the force of her grip, she threw the second switch.

Snap.

Head ringing from the impact with the floor, Garrin sucked air through a raw throat. Sharp pain kept him from breathing deeply; his ribs had to be broken, and perhaps his sternum. Spread-eagled on the rooftop, the sound-that-wasn't-a-sound overwhelmed the tinnitus, making it hard to think, hard to take stock of what had happened, of where he was. He looked down at his chest. Tendrils of smoke rose from his white lab coat, and the acrid stench of burnt hair and singed polyfibers set him to breathing through his mouth. One of his shoes lay off to the side, smoldering. Nettles raked the back of his throat as his head flopped back, and he stared upward at the dying sky.

A broad incision gaped in the space where the Halocian Generators had once been, and through it blazed a swirling, rainbow chaos darker than deep space and brighter than a billion suns. The non-sound dug at his mind, urging him to stand up, to join the thing or things in the wound, to give himself fully to their desires.

He struggled against the pain wracking his body to his hands and knees, desperate to fling himself into that ragged gash, to become a part of them, as companion or consumed or both.

The building shuddered. Somewhere to his left, staccato crackles heralded weapons-fire.

But why would they be shooting? It's beautiful.

A shadow fell over his vision, blocking the sky, and a sigh of anguished disappointment escaped his lips. He shifted to look past the darkness, to gain another glimpse of the majestic opening, and the shadow moved to block his vision.

"Doctor? Are you all right?" it said, and extended a black-gloved hand. "We got to go."

Garrin took the soldier's hand and allowed himself to be hauled to his feet, where he tottered, unsteady. Pain exploded through his left leg, and he tried not to look at the ragged remains of his foot and ankle. The man put an arm around him and half dragged him, one-legged, into the building, his slung rifle dragging on the ground as he spoke into his comm.

"I have Doctor Garrin. He's alive. Rooftop strike authorized."

The voice-things faded to a murmur as the steel door slammed behind them. He groaned at the loss.

Garrin gritted his teeth, pain wracking his chest as he held up a hand. "Wait. Lassa! She's still— Is she still out there?" Jealousy burned through him at the thought of her still gazing up at the sky-wound, or worse, rising through the air to join it and go beyond. The building shuddered, and hot air blasted through the ventilation.

They locked eyes, and the soldier looked away with a bare shake of his head. "Don't worry about Lassa. The important thing is that you're okay."

"I need——"

"Enough. We're getting you to a medical suite so you can get better, and figure out how to turn that goddamned thing off."

Turn it off? His mind balked at the idea. *Why would I turn it off?*

Garrin stared at the ceiling in the dark. Thought-things slithered and crawled, drawing his gaze through the upper floors to the blasted rooftop and above, where they waited for him, cajoling and cooing their inevitability.

Intense white light blinded him, and he squeezed his eyes shut against it.

"Oh, I'm sorry." Garrin recognized Dr. Yalle's voice and dared to open his eyes as she adjusted the room lighting. "I didn't realize they were on full."

Lies. He knew they'd been watching him through the mirror, through the cameras, through the incessant beeping machines pouring life back into his shattered body. They knew where he looked, but they didn't know why, and she'd been sent to test him. Outside his door the nurse's station looked identical to the one he'd fallen asleep near the night before. Same chairs, same tablets and autowriters stacked on the desk in the same places, same faded poster on the wall.

"Why did you move me?"

She clicked on a flashlight and shone it in one eye, then the other, before answering. "Pardon?"

"Last night after my final medications—I can only assume I was sedated without my consent—you moved me to another, identical room. I'd like to know why."

"Don't you think that sounds a little paranoid?"

He nodded, as best he could in the brace securing his neck. "Oh, yes, if it weren't true it would be devastatingly paranoid. What a ridiculous effort, to trick a man that he's in the same room when he's not. One might wonder the end-game of such a crazy scheme."

Yalle frowned her psychiatrist's frown and used her finger to scribble into her tablet.

"How do you know you've been moved?"

His heart, his very soul, wanted nothing more than to run headlong into the gash, to join the things in the beyond. It pulled at him, literally, tugging his mind ever closer to its embrace with every agonizing moment. He could have pinpointed its location across the universe, much less through a few stories of plascrete and ceramic composite. He looked at the ceiling toward it and tried not to cry.

She scribbled further. "You know where it is."

"Of course I do. How could I not?"

She frowned. "I need to show you something."

Orderlies entered and trussed him up for transport, lashing him down to an electronic wheelchair for which he did not have the controls. They drove him through hallways and down in an elevator, and he resisted the urge to stare at the gash, which he could see only in his mind, as its song faded further with distance. A burly military officer in a well-adorned uniform joined them as they emerged somewhere in the basement, a crude hallway of unadorned plascrete and heavy steel doors. It smelled of antiseptic and bleach and an underlying corruption bleeding through the impermeable walls. The man did not introduce himself, and Garrin didn't ask.

Yalle ordered a pair of guards to stand aside and used her ID to unlock one of those heavy doors, then stepped aside in turn so he could be wheeled through, Yalle and the officer right behind. Garrin's heart skipped a beat.

Encased in a shimmering containment sphere, Lassa sat on the floor, legs crossed, her naked skin the pale alabaster of a bloodless corpse yet riddled through with blue veins. Blood crackled through her sclera, turning her eyes a crimson pink. They stared at nothing a few yards in front of her face, and she grinned with pale lips stretched too wide over yellowed teeth. Her chest rose and fell, but she made no acknowledgment of their presence.

"Why is she naked?" Garrin asked.

Yalle frowned at the question, as if expecting a different reaction. "When the incendiary hit the rooftop it burned off her clothes."

"You dropped a bomb, knowing that she was alive?"

She nodded.

"Why?"

Another frown. "She'd killed forty-seven soldiers at that point. With her bare hands."

"But there's not a scratch on her."

"No, there isn't. The bomb didn't even burn her hair."

He licked his lips. "Has she . . . has she said why she did it?"

One of the guards grunted. "She hasn't made a peep in five weeks. Don't eat, don't drink, don't pee, just sits there and smiles like she knows something we don't."

The officer scowled at him, and he fell silent. *Oh, to know what she knows!* "How is she still alive?"

The officer fiddled with his wrist display and brought up a hologram. Men fired their weapons into Lassa as she danced among them, silent amidst the cacophony, tearing out throats and pulverizing limbs with athletic grace fit for a dance hall, that bloodless grin affixed on her face. When the last soldier fell, she turned on her heels and approached the access door—the same door the soldier had carried Garrin through—clothing shredded but without a scratch on her skin. Garrin yearned for the scene to pan up, to give him another glimpse of that beautiful tear, but the scene vanished in a fireball and went dark.

"Why are you showing me this?" He flicked a finger toward Lassa. "Her?"

Yalle answered. "When we got her in the containment field she sat, just as she is now, and hasn't moved since, even when we transported her here. She—I'm not so sure it's her anymore—it won't tell us what it wants, or what it's doing here, or how to close the anomaly."

"But why are you showing *me* this?"

"You worked with her for more than a decade. We thought that if there's anything of her left inside, you could perhaps coax it out, tell us what it wants."

"And," the officer interjected, his voice a deep baritone, "you created that goddamned rift, and we need you to close it before another whatever-that-is comes through."

"And who are you?" Garrin asked.

"I'm Lassa's father, and the man who's going to make sure you fix this thing, and bring my daughter back."

Garrin tried not to smile. "I'll do what I can, sir."

* * *

Fourteen months later, Garrin raised his right hand, index finger extended, and tried to fight off a feeling of déjà vu. Above him shimmered the containment field around the anomaly—such a boring name they'd chosen for the most glorious thing in the universe—and it muted the slithering non-sounds to near but not total silence, the barest hint of a lifeline from the insanity of the mundane world he'd remained trapped in since "the incident." Below his pedestal crawled a dozen technicians and scientists, checking and double-checking cables and conduits, monitoring power circuits and flux rings to make sure everything went as planned.

And how it wouldn't. Not to their plan. Garrin didn't bother to suppress a grin this time.

He dropped his finger. "Ten percent power."

"Ten percent power, sir." The military technicians wouldn't stop calling him "sir," and he'd long given up trying to stop them. It didn't matter, and neither would anything else. The field above hummed, a billion cicadas about to be smothered in ether. Lassa's father stared at him from across the rooftop, in command of the soldiers ringing the laboratory. His disappointment at the lack of change in his daughter was rivaled only by his determination to see the anomaly destroyed without further harm.

Garrin could taste his hatred.

"Twenty percent power."

"Twenty percent power, sir."

The pedestal beneath his feet began humming in tune with the containment field, the machinery he'd hidden inside coupling in resonance. He'd made sure the monitors and cogitators wouldn't detect the new signal, not until it wouldn't matter, but he could feel it and savored the feeling as it thrummed through his body, like a hidden predator on the verge of leaping on unsuspecting prey.

"Thirty."

"Thirty percent, sir."

A new resonance joined the system, a tendril of energy snaking up from far below. Within it, through the pedestal, Garrin thought-heard a tiny tendril of satisfaction, of inevitability, of crumbling walls and dying stars and ants ground beneath frozen boots. *Hello, Lassa. How I've yearned to speak to you.*

She did not reply.

The containment fields reached equilibrium, and the circuitry in the pedestal came to life, driving the system to full power well beyond the approved designs. As the fields merged, the power coils rebounded through the hidden machine. Unseen vortices groped at the containment fields, above and below, and tore. The field parted, and brilliant white light blazed outward.

As the white light struck the technicians and soldiers, they froze in place except to grin, eyes crackling with bloodshot. A billion billion nonvoices above joined Lassa's from below, and a sigh escaped Garrin's lips, the last sound he would ever make, as his soul climbed upward into the rend in the sky. Eternal silence fell, stretching out from the columned building in a blinding flash that would not end.

Night Landing

Ann K. Schwader

I. Arrival

Uploaded from our wasted world, we woke
into another: artifice of years
& minds, until the algorithm broke
to strand us—where? No paradise appears
within our virtual vision, only night
sunk down through desolation centuries
to cloak this landscape strange with sanguine light
from ranged volcanoes. Silently, unease
congeals into suspicion. When, not where,
have we arrived? A mortal weariness
afflicts this land, & drains the very air's
vitality. Until dawn breaks. Unless . . .
We glance up, then, unable to deny
our sun turned cinder in that charnel sky.

II. Landmark
We wrecked a planet, yet our fingerprints
at least endured as proof of life. Of breath
& blood & bad decisions unto death,
or cyber exfiltration. Ever since
the latter failed us, we have wandered lost
among monstrosities past any touch
of human ingenuity. Too much
condemned us, once—but did we guess the cost
of leaving it? These Watching Things that guard
each shattered compass-point stare past us, blind
& heedless of our passing. Nothing here
says refuge. Yet ahead, one hilltop hard

with geometrics sketches man's design:
a Pyramid, its Last Light shining clear.

III. Turned Away
It rose before us like a great ship's prow
half drowned in darkness. Circled by a fire
drawn from the Earth's last current, it endowed
a home's protection. Just as our desire
for sanctuary sparked, there came a call
less heard than felt, vibrating through our brains
with growing apprehension. Both appalled
& pitiless, it struggled to explain
why this was not our place. Some doorway torn
in twilight by the Days of Darkening
disgorged us, soulless. Whether we were born
or science-spawned meant little: all we bring
is utter death. At last, the caller showed
a twining night-gray trail. *There lies your Road!*

IV. Housed in Silence
How far we walked, we never knew. Our feet
grew tireless, almost gliding on that track
which held the mark of human hands—harked back
to all we built, until we thought to meet
more like ourselves. But no. We fell away
each from the other, soundless, shrouded deep
in journeying as in unquiet sleep
past hope of waking. Light, now: not the day
we left behind, but bitter brilliance made
for carving shadows in this House ahead,
whose Silence spills from doors thrown open wide
& windows gaped like wounds. Before we fade,
we know ourselves already less than dead
by our lost faces flickering inside.

After *The Night Land* by William Hope Hodgson

Night Hearing

Michael Cisco

The black ring around the sun had become so thick that I could look directly at it without hurting my eyes. I had to hurry. It has been getting dark earlier, and each day has been a little dimmer than the last. I had to use the light that was left to fetch my piece and get back. Eventually there would be so little light that the monsters would be out all the time, and I didn't know what I would do then.

 The House of Silence stirred the ether, as if it were aware that I was outside the circle. The near Monstruwacan had had nothing for me, and I had wasted too much time getting to him and waiting for him, and now I was regretting my decision to try for the far one. I thought I had just enough time before true nightfall to reach him and return. My arm capsule was empty, and I would not be able to save myself from destruction if I were discovered. I staved off my fear. The sun was nearly touching the horizon, but it was still summer, it would abide there a while, and I could already see the dwelling place of the far Monstruwacan. Just hold on.

 The price he demanded was dear. He saw my need, because I wasn't so proficient at hiding my emotions just then, after the great self-control I had been compelled to maintain during my journey, and he was likewise in haste, saying he had pressing business elsewhere. As we emerged back out under the sky, I saw the sun shrinking behind the mountains, and I knew I was too late. The far Monstruwacan, with many vulgarities, told me that he could not bring me with him or allow me to stay in his home, that he expected a visit from the Young-Watchers and that we should be both on our way. When he saw my distress, he did unbend enough to reassure me this much, saying that the moon would be full tonight, and this would be some help to me. I hadn't thought of that, but it was not much comfort.

 I realized I would have to resort to the trains if I wanted to return home safely. They would cover the distance in much less time, but the passage would take me through tunnels where night, and its monsters, lived all the time. If I could take off there, away from the circle, I could avoid destruction, but I'd be paralyzed. If the paralysis were to last until dawn, I might be all right if I were hidden well. I knew this was all just self-talk, though. I had to get back, that's all. That meant the trains. That meant going past the Tower and the Umbrellas, down where the Silent Ones will walk one day.

The Tower bristles with carved figures that once were human but fell victim to its necromancy in their brain elements. They watch all who pass by its base, looking for any sign of susceptibility. Should they find and exploit any such weakness, another will forever join them on the walls of the Tower.

Passing the Tower without incident was possible. You had to carry yourself neutrally, mind neutral, spine neutral, hands neutral. I put myself into the posture and steadied my breathing, but I didn't have much time to get ready. The body calms the mind, the mind calms the body. Above all, you couldn't think of the piece you're carrying. Gray metal neutrality armors body and mind.

I could feel the attention of the Tower wafting back and forth around its base, like gossamer, an invisible etheric anemone tasting the vibrations. Those seemingly inert tendrils were capable of darting toward any emotional contrasts like a bundle of striking snakes, homing in on emotional nerve cores, numbing them with pinpoint cold, paralyzing the victims before drawing them in and ossifying them. There was still enough daylight to keep the Tower more inert than not, banking down its appetite until the light failed. I slipped by unnoticed and paused to collect myself again in a pool of noise and activity where there was still some commerce. If I stayed there any length of time, the Forces would come to expel me, even with the sun in the sky, but I needed a moment. I felt sick; the need for peace came over me and gave me chills, like a light fever. I felt the blood leave my head, neck, and shoulders for a moment, and my hands went cold. It was all rushing in toward my center, kind of resetting me. The qualms passed. I wouldn't have to try to find a refuge to shoot here, where the Forces would definitely come after me.

The Umbrellas were another hazard, harder to prepare for, since they were unpredictable. I still hadn't figured them out. I wasn't sure whether or not I should move past them as quickly as I could; that might be a sign to them. They want to capture anyone who knows anything about them, to prevent us from passing on important information to others. I have to remember that they aren't natural predators. They don't kill to eat. It's not the body they want. Someone as knowledgeable and important as I am would be a special target, too.

I decided to approach the Umbrellas as if I were just going about my business. I had to underplay my awareness of them. I reasoned that I could always take off running if I needed to. The power of the Umbrellas didn't extend past their shade; all I had to do was to get through them. Any detour was impossible, given the lateness of the hour. I started through the scalloped shadow that they formed together and made my way through their long, whitish stems.

"Hey, miss!"

I nearly jumped. A voice at my back. I didn't give any indication that I'd heard.

"Hey, missy, hold up a second! Excuse me!"

The voice was supposed to be a human man's. I could feel each word smash against the back of my head, and my shoulders.

Give no sign, I told myself. *Don't look!*

"Hey, excuse me! Excuse me, miss!"

It was following me. The voice was not fading. I could hear the scrape of feet in loose trash.

I made straight for the other side. I couldn't risk trying to use the stems to interrupt its view of me, prevent it from tracking me easily, not yet. My feigned obliviousness would have to hold me over a little longer.

"You're just going to walk away like that? I'm talking to you!"

There was hostility in the tone now. The Umbrellas captured and refocused their agents' voices, keeping them tightly fastened around you. The anger trembled inside me, and I was afraid. Suddenly I remembered how the shade of the Umbrellas was prolonged by the shadow of the overpass on the far side. That meant that it would have that much more opportunity to get me; I had to start weaving now, to throw it off, give myself a chance.

As I swung around one stem and then the other way around the next, I glanced back and saw it. I knew it was only pretending to be real. The clothes were light brown on the right side and dark gray on the left, and there a newsboy cap that came right down over where the eyes and ears should be. It was talking op-talk to me now, a warbling short-wave radio sound that chittered and bent, chopped words into meaningless fragments. The voice said—

"Miss, close your eyes . . ."

I said the master word back, and the pressure on my brain elements recoiled. That was when I broke into a run. I dodged in and out through the stems and then sprinted as fast as I could across the long expanse of shade below the underpass. The ground there was gray and lifeless, like the surface of the moon, blanched and killed by the concrete. I could feel avid eyes on me, and hear the mutter of many stirring forms gathered in the shadows, but I could also see the dim but distinct line on the earth where the dying sun's light pinked it, and in a moment I was there and free. I didn't have to go on running, but I wanted to get out of there, and I had to reach the trains, so I kept it up as long as I could stand it, until pain lanced me through my ribs and I had to stop. I found a bench in a decaying little shelter by the road and sat there, holding myself, catching my breath. The need to refill the capsule in my arm was strong, very strong, but I couldn't do it there, exposed, in the open. I could lose my piece. There were unreal ones around who would try to snatch it from me if they saw it, and time was pressing. I had to get to the trains quickly, and even if I did, I would still have to make the last leg of the journey after sunset. But the evil waxed with the night, and so, even in its first hour, it might still be avoided.

I gave myself only a brief respite on that bench and then pressed on, hurrying toward the verdigrised green canopy that marked the spot where the trains stopped.

There was no one there. The tracks were empty, but I could hear a distant rumbling that told me the train would not be too long in coming.

That was good. The gray metal pillars that support the green canopy afforded some relief from the steady watching, but I was far too alert, for all that I was sick for want of peace, not to notice the stuttering of the ether, the gathering note of a mind klaxon that would alert the monsters to my presence. It built steadily, but it was a ragged, evil pseudo-sound; simply hearing it sapped the will and created illusory mazes where there were only straight ways. That was why I needed the trains. The straightness of the tracks helps to counter the enlabyrinthine waves that emerged at dusk from empty doorways. At dusk the empty doorways all became portals to the House of Silence that Hope Hodgson warned us about.

It came, passing under a concrete grating that projected wan patches on its sooty metal roof: one of the ancient hulks of the railroad builders, eyes burning with cold, but bright, light. It drew up to the platform and stopped with an anguished gasp. Furtive, unknown persons slipped from its flank and hastened to join themselves to abhuman evil. I darted inside and into a corner, made myself as small as possible against the gray metal walls, clutching my rock in my pocket. With a melancholy squeal the doors closed, the floor beneath me swayed, lurched, a bang shook the train and a panic flashed over me, thinking it had broken, the lights went out. The train floated forward, rattling, into the darkness, and I could see the glint of many eyes outside, feel a rush toward the cars, like hungry fish schooling around a stricken whale. I made ready to bite into my rock. That would mean death, but not destruction.

But then the light bloomed again, dim and dingy, but filling the car. A whirring noise began with them as well, and I felt the stale air move over me. A push at my back told me the train was moving under its own power, accelerating, and we began to streak past those cold eyes. Speed would keep us safe.

I clutched myself to myself, trying not to think of what might happen. Immediate danger was past, but we were still underground and in darkness. It was necessary to scan the other passengers, to determine if any of them weren't real, which of them knew me or realized my importance. Again, I was fortunate. There were only three others that I could see, and they were all huddled, cautious, wary, like me.

The train shot through the darkness. Chanting the master word in my mind, I willed it to move faster. You mustn't look outside. I always saw horrible things in the dark of the tunnels. You couldn't see what the monsters are doing beneath the city, beneath everyone's feet, and remain sane, remain clean. I'd seen things through the windows of this train that I dared not think about. I'd seen how the dogs are being corrupted into Night Hounds, what they were fed on, and how abhumans used pain to destroy the souls of their captives. I'd seen giant gray women step heavily down from pedestals of trash to open the body cavity of a small child for the dogs, seen their inert, joyless faces, their impassive cruelty.

My thoughts were abruptly cut short when someone, a man, lurched toward me. I made myself small, drew my knees up to my chin, readied my rock. One bite, even one touch to my tongue, and I could escape destruction. He said something to me that I couldn't hear over the noise of the train. The windows of the car were all open, admitting the noise and stink of the tunnel. He swayed, speaking in a tone that seemed—I say *seemed*—kind. I chanted the master word in my mind and shut my eyes tight. I felt cold, even though my heart was galloping. When I dared to open my eyes again, he was gone. That felt safe and, at the same time, strangely sad.

The train burst out of the tunnels and space expanded around us. The racket of the train diminished and the air lightened immediately. We were through.

There was almost no light left in the sky. I couldn't afford any delay, any camouflage. The station was at the bottom of a steep hill. My circle, my shelter until the call came to join the redoubt, was at the top. I had to lean forward until I was all but staring directly down at my feet, the angle of the street was so sharp. Heavy autonomous cars shot empty past me, up and down. If I could only have latched on to one as it went up . . . The same stupid fantasy. They never slowed down enough for that.

About two-thirds of the way there was an unpaved pathway that led to an open space in among the stunted, sun-starved vegetation. A kind of camp had been half-heartedly installed there, but I never saw anyone in it. I knew, though, that the abhumans and pseudo-people never used it; they didn't need those kinds of human comforts, like a chair to sit in, a tarp to keep the rain off. By the time I reached the path my heart was jumping against my ribs, my breath was short, my face felt swollen, and I was dripping with sweat. I was in excellent physical condition, I'm an alpha, but even I couldn't handle that much effort all in one go, not while I was so badly in need of my peace. I went over to the rusted steel chair there and sat down in the camp. The brush was still just alive, mainly because this spot was never out of the daylight. It nearly concealed me once I sat down. Just a few minutes, and then, up again. A quick push and then I would be safe, safe for days.

When I next knew anything, I was in total darkness. In panic I jumped up, knocked over the chair with a great noise. Even sick with need, I had fallen asleep! I had no way of knowing what time it was, but there wasn't a trace of light left in the sky. Not of sunlight. My addled condition began to pass off, and I realized the darkness was not so total: the promised full moon was already shining. I had been standing stock-still, to avoid drawing any further attention to myself, and now I made ready to go by turning my head without otherwise moving, to find, in the indistinctness of the moon's light, the path back to the street, my only way home. The automatic cars would still travel up and down all night, and their light would help guide me and repel enemies, but not reliably, not fully. They were a grossly inadequate protection. But as I turned my head, not moving a muscle otherwise—and I was able to stand perfectly still if I needed to—I heard a crashing in the brush. Something clumsy and large wallowed toward me, toward the noise of the falling the chair, coming not from the path, but from the opposite direction, where there was an old water pipe, I remembered then, big enough to shelter something very sizeable from the sun all day. My sickness, my haste, my fatigue, all had conspired to make me forget about that hiding place for monsters!

It lunged drunkenly toward the clearing where I stood, still perfectly immobile and now, all too late, fully alert. It snuffled, coughed, wheezed as it came, stopping and starting, with what sounded like quick snatches of thin breath, and it rummaged feebly in the bushes as it came, as if it were pushing them aside to paw at the ground beneath them. It knew I was there, but it didn't know where, that was clear. And I had a line of escape to the path and the road. I couldn't fight the thing, I had no diskos, so I reasoned that I had only to decide whether to depend on stealth or haste to get me to the road and the paltry protection of the lights there. The thing in the brush would emerge any moment into the clearing, and the moonlight would definitely reveal me. I had my piece ready in my hand. I would try to move off quietly at first, then run if I had to.

I began creeping toward the road, while behind me what gasped and fumbled broke through into the clearing with staggering, almost rattling footsteps. I crouched and shrank, made myself small. Incoherent abhuman vocal sounds wheedled in a hoarse, high voice at my back. It was asking the night for me. The ether swam with the residue of the klaxons and I was suddenly terrified, remembering how the night itself could direct its creatures. I hurried to the road, taking advantage of the noise of a passing car to cover the sound of my footsteps, and resumed my ascent in as near to a run as I could manage against the lofty angle of the hill. I prayed, I begged, I snatched at the air in desperation, and finally the ground leveled off under my feet. I had reached the top. I could move forward as if a weight had dropped from me, but I was dripping with perspiration, chilled but not refreshed by the dank, cellar-like night air that turned the sweat of my body into slime.

A yelp of relief sprang uncontrolled from my mouth when I saw the familiar outline of my home, the shelter I had inherited from my parents and where I had always lived. There was my circle, visible only to me who fashioned it on the foundations laid by my parents. I said the master word aloud and crossed the air clog. I was safe.

The empty capsule burned in my arm like a hot ember. Whenever it became empty, it would move to a different part of my arm, and sometimes it traveled from one arm to the other. Now it was where it should be, in the left forearm. I hastened to make ready, entering my shelter and replacing my safeguards quickly. I had a seat before my watching station, where I could look out over the great expanse of the night and see the little makeshift redoubts shining there. Soon we would be called to the our lasting refuge.

I had to chant the master word aloud to get my hands to stop shaking. The fear of the night outside was still worrying at me. Avoiding waste meant utmost care though, and it was important too not to overcharge the capsule with more of the saving death energy than it could contain, or I would be released entirely. At last I was ready, and with the proper replenishment of the capsule I could feel waves of well-being and safety rinse the fear and sorrow from me. The tranquil joy of success and the steady hope for my salvation welled up in me and poured down from my crown chakra. I gazed out over the monster-infested landscape below without dread, but rather with the equanimity of a Monstruwacan. Then I closed my eyes to hearken to what I might detect with my night hearing. My mind opened within the safety of my circle, and I attuned myself to the etheric resonations that traversed the darkness. There were abhuman mutterings, op-talk, warped and garbled words, numbers, partial phrases, but every now and then I received a distinct signal.

Tonight there was nothing but noise. I ran my eyes around the room, my stores, carefully rationed. My books . . . *The Halloween Tree, Curious Myths of the Middle Ages, The Smoky God, Ethics, A Medicine for Melancholy, The History of Magic, Phenomena: A Book of Wonders, The Druids,* and four copies of Hope Hodgson. That one—I collected every copy of it I found, and they were neither many nor well preserved. Between the four of them, I had the complete teaching. Whenever I read the Hope Hodgson, I would get lost and have to start over; I don't think I ever managed to find the ending, but I know that I've seen the end page, the words THE END printed, I know I have the complete teaching. I began to believe that I would find the end when the time was right, and ceased to worry about it. Now, as I reached for the copy I was then reading, I felt a stir in my brain elements and paused, centering my attention entirely on my night hearing.

I have no idea how much time there passed, but something in me called out to the source of that emanation, and I received a reply. There, in the ether, a distinct, human voice had spoken the master word. There was no doubt about it. And then there came to me a message—*just hold on, I am coming*. I continued to listen for an hour or more after that message came, but there followed only a silence such as I had never heard before with my night hearing, as if the words had stunned the other voices into muteness with their purity and power. At first I foolishly entertained the idea that this was the call to take refuge in the redoubt, but, as I gazed into the darkness, I could see no activity, no indication of any kind that such a general call for mobilization had been given and received. With an astonishment that burgeoned steadily into amazement I realized that I myself had been addressed personally. I had received a message such as Naani had received in Hope Hodgson, and who else but the narrator of that book, the nameless seventeenth-century English lord and lover of Mirdath, had ever sent such a message? There is no other of any kind mentioned in Hope Hodgson. And what could that mean but that his incarnation in this time had called out to hers? And what could that mean but that I am Mirdath in this time and destined to be Naani in eons to come?

All this raced through my mind in less time than it takes to tell it, and I see now that the shock I then experienced was not so much perfect surprise as it was the thrill of an unexpected confirmation. No sooner had the idea formed than I knew it to be true, and an idea that had been hidden within the profounder depths of my consciousness, along with the memories of those other lives that had throughout time been mine, stood plainly confirmed. The only problem was this: in Hope Hodgson, the narrator was not reunited with Mirdath until she was Naani. The circle was destined to close, but in the future, millions of years from now. I had always thought that reincarnation was continuous, so that souls were never out of bodies for long. We all carried the capsule in our arms to preserve our souls so that they could come back again even if our bodies were destroyed. Were there, however, long gaps between incarnations? I had thought everyone always came back. That would mean, however, that Mirdath would have lived countless other lives before becoming Naani, just as she would have had an infinity of lives before she was Mirdath. So did she and her soulmate only meet for the first time in the seventeenth century, and only for the second time millions of years later?

No. No no no. It made much more sense, it only made sense, if we met in every lifetime. The narrator's experience was a strictly coincidental transposition in time along a continuum of lives. It probably took that many different versions for a sufficient resemblance to happen. That's the only answer. I was Mirdath, I will be Naani, and it was my destiny to meet him. He was calling me. He was telling me to hold on and wait for him.

Days passed. As long as I had my piece I could stay inside indefinitely. Supplies were not that plentiful, but I had water and some preserved food. I didn't go out, so I didn't get dirty. I kept the capsule fully infused, though it moved around as I said. Above all, I lived in constant vigilance for any new word from him. My brain elements were focused perfectly on the ether and not a single impulse went unnoticed. When I was freshly charged, my listening opened in me and my body became cold and weightless, as if it were becoming ether itself, as if I held a bright, clean blue sky inside, and when the voices came in the day I was like a garden filled with light. They never told me anything, though. I couldn't make them out. It wasn't the master word I heard, but it wasn't op-talk either. I gazed out my window and saw the Tower, the Smoking River, the Dark Palace, and the Giants' Kilns, and the voices moved among and through them jabbering harsh, ugly noises, words that stretched and drooped, insect voices, spectral murmuring, but it always seemed as though there were still something human there behind and among them. Those sounds hid the words, thoughts, and feelings of true humanity, but they were not stilled altogether. I could listen for them now and feel happy, knowing that he was out there, aware of me and looking, and I sang out to him so he could find me.

My piece dwindled away all too rapidly. It seemed as though it were somehow losing strength, and my capsule's power was not steady. A stronger remedy might quiet the clamor of evil that surrounded me and enable me at last to hear distinctly the narrator's message. I resolved to visit the near Monstruwacan and take counsel with him.

I set out shortly after daybreak, when the whirrings and groanings of the night's monsters sullenly subsided into a muted, ominous hum. They were weakest in the few hours after dawn, and I was able to reach the near Monstruwacan's circle without any special difficulties. I had only to give a wide berth to the Red Clouds, which hang motionless on the side of a great glass barrier, and seem to pour sickness and nausea down on those who pass through their shadows. I knew better than to come too near to them, and passed on quickly.

The near Monstruwacan's circle was surrounded by broken walls and torn shelters. There would not infrequently be others in the Monstruwacan's care waiting for him there, and this time I saw a woman, bent and wizened, standing serenely beneath one of the higher remaining walls. She turned a little to and fro, benighted and entranced, as I approached, her face turned expectantly toward the house. I asked if she knew if the Monstruwacan were receiving right now.

Her back quaked as she chuckled.

"Not I," she said, and turned completely around to face me, to show me my mistake. She leered at me with gray, glassy teeth, gray, clouded eyes in a pasty corpse's face.

"Not I, said the dog," she rasped. "Not I, said the cat. Not I, said the *pig*."

She spat the last word at me with her lips while her teeth remained sealed in a slimy grin. The teeth and eyes were the first to turn gray once the soul was taken. She was one of those who was destroyed without being killed.

Now her jaws parted, and she drew breath with feigned effort. It was a common ploy, I could tell, an attempt to put me off my guard. Her legs collapsed under her, and she rested her skinny frame against the crumbling wall behind her. She breathed hard and peered up at me, her eyes not quite able to fix me.

"I've been waiting *a long time*."

Her voice rose to a wheedling falsetto, drawn painfully out of her.

"Can you . . . ?" she licked her lips. "Can you . . . ?"

I stood stock-still. Like an insect, she fixed on movement, and perhaps sound.

Her performance extended to a show of exhaustion now, as if she couldn't bring herself to finish her question, or perhaps even to remember it. Suddenly she slumped, threw back her head, and let out a throaty scream that made my ears ring. It was as if she needed the relief, and when she had emptied her lungs she drew a slow, ragged inbreath and let her head roll onto one shoulder. She gazed at the ground, pretending she was no longer aware of me. I knew better. I remained motionless but began to think of how best to escape. I needed to see the Monstruwacan, and while the day was not too advanced, I couldn't afford to leave and come back again. Besides—I don't know why it didn't occur to me sooner—that scream had clearly been an alarm that would bring other proto-grays and abhumans here.

The only good course of action would be to make a dash for the Monstruwacan's open window there, chanting the master word as I went. Once inside his circle I would be safe enough, and I could escape out the back if necessary. As I thought about this I inadvertently took a step toward the house, brushing aside some litter that covered the open space there.

She stirred.

"Are you Russell?" she asked me suddenly. Then she raised her head and looked me in the eye. "Because you *sure do sound like it!*" she roared, grinning wildly. *"You sure do sound like it!"*

Drawing on my deepest instincts, I shouted the master word and ran for the window, her uncanny chuckling at my back. I threw myself over the sill and pushed with my legs, propelling myself forward and scrabbling across the floor. The Monstruwacan was sitting opposite me with his head thrown back. I stood and addressed him in the abrupt silence of that room, but he did nothing. It didn't take me long to determine that he was deep in a trance of his own, his body rigid, tense with the strain of heroic mental effort. He had been charging his capsule as well—of course, since the signaling brain was then so strong. He might have been talking to the narrator in that moment.

I tried speaking to him, to see if he could hear me, relay my words and the narrator's answers, but he was striving so mightily that he had no attention to spare. I asked him if he could instruct me. He told me mentally that I should take no more than I required and go, leaving the question of compensation for another time.

"Is it time to go to the redoubt? Is it ready?" I asked.

He couldn't tell me anything further, but, as I often did, he remained perfectly still, his lips fixed in a curious O. Even the fly that rubbed its forelegs on his cheek did not induce so much as a twitch.

I took two pieces with his permission and left him there, hard at his work. The rear exit of the house was choked with debris, but that made it a safer path for me, at least, for the purposes of getting away unnoticed.

The sun was touching the horizon as I re-entered my circle, but my relief vanished when I saw that an attempt had been made to breach my defenses. There were curse markings on my door, and yellow bands that crossed in an X over the portal, to deny me entry; my circle was not strong in my absence, and some of the lesser abhumans were still able to approach even without the master word. Now I understood the pseudo-woman's scream, her bizarre words; her challenge forced me to draw on my reserve energies, which in turn depleted the efficacy of my circle and so permitted the other puppets to approach my refuge. It seemed they were trying to block the entrance with their emblems and to contaminate my circle. I tore through their curse forms and membranes, but there was an abhuman seal on the door.

I was far too intelligent, too farsighted and wise, for them. I had another way inside. I could crawl beneath the house and enter through an opening established there for that purpose. No, they had not had the wit to find that.

Once safely back within, I thought better of trying to open the sealed door. Far better to let them see it there and intact, and so imagine that I had not returned but sought out some other shelter. They would be watching the house now, of course. They surely saw me struggle with the door and stopped their ears and closed their minds against the master word that I repeated aloud. Then they would also have seen me cleverly pretending to depart in frustration but would not have observed me returning through the rubble and stunted brush that clings to the slope below, or making my way through the fence's hidden gap, which only I knew about, since I made it. They would look for me elsewhere, for a time.

But they were bound to come back. When their search failed, they would return here. Not by night, though. But if they were able to weaken my defenses further, perhaps even by night, they might enter. But no—it was, after all, *by day* that they should struggle the most. Those who I have the most to fear are yet still bound by night.

Could it be time at last to find the redoubt? Where else could I go? It was certain destruction to try to survive even the daytime without some shelter, some cover, a circle. But this shelter was without a doubt marked now. Alone, I hadn't the will to repel their combined and focused assaults. I had encountered those who had no refuge of their own, who depended for their continued existence on the charity of the Monstruwacans, but even they faded and fell away in time. Could I transfer my circle to a new place? But there were no new places, no places that were not already contaminated by the abhuman and monstrous. I could see the sun flicker like a spasming heart, pulsing the whole of the dark world alight for an instant only to gutter again, day and night strobing, but the lightless intervals growing darker, longer.

Just hold on—

But am I safer *by night*? Isn't it *by day* that I'm safer? But they came by day and marked my door. I shouldn't assume that means they won't come back by night. I've shored up my defenses, strengthened them. It was too late then to venture out in any case. Wasn't I supposed to receive the call to come away to the redoubt? How could they have overlooked someone as important as I was? I was supposed to be called away by now. Where were they?

I reviewed my seals and defenses. I renewed the master word, empowered my circle. They could not come in; it was still strong. They would have to come back, and by then I would be taken away. He would find me and bring me away.

Night fell. I recharged my capsule, drawing on what I had received from the Monstruwacan. The night hearing came over me then with greater power than ever before, and I knew I had been right all along, that *this* would be the night. A darkness gathered around the edges of my vision, just as it gathered around the sun in the sky. My arms and legs felt cold, my body floated, my earthly senses slipped more and more free of the burden of my material form.

I knew the voice was real, because it said the master word to me. That word could only come from another person; the House of Silence couldn't form that word. Hope Hodgson said so.

But perhaps I was somehow tricked or compelled to imagine the master word, to speak it myself, when prompted by one who could not say it. Then it was my own voice I heard, a ruse of the House of Silence. It was the House of Silence, or what it harbors, that moved in the ether, and when I called out I called unwittingly to it, and it answered with an echo.

I can't hold on any longer. I'm sorry. I don't think I ever was Mirdath, or Naani. I think I must have overheard something intended for another. The voice was calling someone else. It was the House of Silence, but perhaps the House of Silence would be a better place for me. It wants me. It alone wants me.

Just hold on

I'm not strong enough to keep going like this. I don't want to be reincarnated. Maybe destruction would be the right thing for me. The capsule is there to save me from destruction. They gave it to me because they love me. If I use it, will I come back? There's nothing to hope for. Will there ever be?

Just hold on

Already my head swims. I feel a cold, soft blow in my chest, and I know I am deep in my night hearing. A little more added to my capsule and I will finally hear it, the voice, clear and distinct. I only have to let go.

The Battlements of Twilight

Kyla Lee Ward

I had not been a year within the Bastion when the Elders requested that I spy upon the Clairvoyant Abyssine.

The Bastion! It was never my home, for I had fled terror and blood, and could not settle within those vast, gray chambers punctuating a corridor spiralling down, down, down. They haunt my dreams still, merging with my memories of the purge of Zepholis and the love I lost there. The founder of our order, the Prognosticant Abelard, had foreseen our need and sunk the Bastion into the utmost reaches of the southern waste. But it was Abelard's prediction of the great disaster that would rend the earth, and our perhaps overzealous efforts to spread knowledge of the same, that brought the purges upon us. Clairvoyant, Psychokinetic, Therapeutic, and Ergokinetic—all Talents were declared monstrous.

When people spoke of me it was of the Psychometrist Damon, my Talent that of reading memories. These memories might be imprinted upon an artifact or place, or even flesh if the trauma was great. Yet in all cases I might only perform the reading through physical touch. Sometimes I found I could decrease the intensity of a memory if this was the subject's wish. Not a common Talent, nor one of the more potent, but historians and doctors sought my aid, my days were busy, and I was happy. Then came the day my love and I must also flee. We were separated in the crowd as the guns roared. Returning under cover of darkness, I touched blood upon the pavement, and I knew.

Grief dwelt in the Bastion, side by side with anger and fear. Doubt ran wild through the corridor, resentment brewed in the small cells we were allotted. Yet the Order's work continued, determining the surest means of humankind's survival, in defiance of those who wished to destroy *us*.

Abyssine came from the floating fields of Hydrarchos: I knew only her fame, which was great. She was chief among those who sought alternatives to Abelard's vision, believing that even the greatest among us should be questioned. Hydrarchos too had been purged, but she and her followers escaped the worst. They traveled in a vessel topped by sails and bottomed as a sledge, with great banks of thrusting poles, to which water, salt, and ice were all alike. This ship was too large to be brought into shelter, so it remained outside the front gate, moored to the stone pier as crystals grew slowly over the hull. Abyssine's people used the boat for their operations. What they did there was unknown to the Elders, and so they came to me.

Do you know the burden of life exceeding love? Has it come upon you, in your strange, new world, that you reach back to me now? The burden may not be shirked, it being love's last wish that you escape, that you live on, and this comforts for a while. But then fear slips into your cell, slides into your lonely bed, whispering that this means nothing, for love itself meant no more in the end. Fear forbids you to seek death same as love, and yet death will inevitably come. And so the hours crawl the walls like serpents, and past events show vivid as if I knelt once more to those seeping stains as the rain fell upon my back. Until it is time at last to rise and seek the battlements, where Abyssine is known to go to watch the dawn.

Within the Bastion there was no need for us to conceal our nature. I passed up the corridor in the black and russet robes of my Talent, my rank displayed in golden rings piercing my lip and a garnet in my nose. I shaved my head, as was the fashion of Zepholis, and could not be brought to abandon it. What curious vanities we had in those days.

I remember the air outside scraped my skin and stank of natron. The vessel lay beneath me, a discarded toy. Above me the sky stretched forever, clear but for bloody rills of cloud. The ruby of the sun studded the horizon, and its color resonated in the salt pans and ice sheets until it seemed the whole world shared my memories and there was no escape. In that moment neither love's wish nor Elder's word meant anything to me, and only fear restrained me from the jump.

This Abyssine felt. A Clairvoyant in robes of black and purple, she felt the despair rising from me as the sun drew mist from the ice, and so she came.

And she said, "They hate us because we feel."

I did not reply.

"Those who drove you out. Who stole what you valued most. They do not feel our agony, but we feel their fear, their resentment, their petty anger and shame. It is not that we know the future, it is that we know *them*."

"By choice I would not know them," I said. "Nor feel. But I cannot erase my own memory."

Beneath us the Bastion wakened, a flaring of all the emotions she listed and more. It seemed ridiculous that we should think ourselves the saviors of humanity when we were its wreckage.

Abyssine gazed out over the stone machicolations. "Has there been any among us, ever, who could cheat death?"

"One day even the sun shall die," I responded. "Where shall we be then?"

"Come to the ship at sunset." She gestured to it, the glistening vessel they said would never move again. "Perhaps you shall have your answer." She left me there, striding off along the battlements with the sun barely sketching her shadow.

All this was to the Elders' satisfaction, yet it seemed to me that Abyssine must surely know the risk she ran in letting me join her. Her reputation did not include shying from conflict. There were those who said, though quietly, she had refused an Elder's diamond when this was offered, choosing to pursue her own experiments wherever they might lead. Even now she persisted, denying her own very great powers and those of her followers to the efforts of the Prognosticant Maru.

I had played my part and there was no reason for me to remain here, watching the sun crawl higher. Yet I had no wish to return below, where even now Maru's followers assembled.

Sweating, swaying, and shuddering, nine hundred Talents all striving to articulate a single thought through every possible emanation. To drive it far, far beyond the sphere of Earth, toward whatever life may exist in the outer reaches, where stars persist as bright as they say our sun once gleamed and time itself has no meaning. The vastness of the penultimate hall was one writhing organism that had the Bastion as its straining throat. Grief dwelt in the Bastion, side by side with anger and fear, but here there was only Need—nine hundred cries of desperation incited and focused by the Prognosticant Maru.

SENSE US. SAVE US.

Colors the retina could not interpret, noises inaudible yet deafening, shadows that were cast by nothing passed among the gestalt. Then came a vast quaking that shook not a single grain from the walls and yet seemed to rock the Bastion to its foundation. It contained a *reply*.

HERE.

The ranks of Talents spun like kelp fields in a storm. The reply burst membranes, opened bowels, and sent some into fits. Even the Prognosticant was battered, nose spraying blood over robes of cobalt and black and his rare blue diamond clotting over. But he remained upon his feet, for this was what he had foreseen, that granted him a title and dignity Abyssine could not approach. That in response to this procedure, once perfected, would come a Reply and thereafter a Door would open, through our utmost pains, in answer to our utmost need. A Door leading beyond our dying world to another.

All that had passed in the hall, I read.

The Bastion had no history. Upon arriving, my abilities had been deemed of no greater utility than a mechanic's. It was I who tended the generators providing our light and heat. Yet, as reports of this great event spread in its aftermath, the Elders summoned me once again. I had felt the concussion as I performed my rounds, ensconced as was my custom in a shielding meditation. I was commanded to enter the hall once the stunned and damaged had been removed, after the blood and ordure had been cleansed, to crawl like the sun from wall to wall and read whatever I could from the stone. Any hint that might serve to enhance our understanding of what had transpired.

Rather than the echoes of a revelation, I felt only a visceral and multitudinous response to something I could not myself detect. I stopped and ensured that my senses were open, that I had truly released the shield. I felt like some small insect crawling over the surface of a cold and darkened light globe, where others had found a dazzling glow. Then it came to me that none of the actants had truly understood what they experienced, but reverted to terror, awe, or whatever response seemed most appropriate to them.

I approached the station of the Prognosticant, upon the central dais. Surely here I would detect the truth. Once again, it was only Maru's own emotions I detected, his exaltation and fervor. His absolute sincerity of belief.

All this I duly reported, and the Elders muttered and frowned, citing this passage in Abelard's writings and this other in the exegesis, passing this recollection and that directly from mind to mind, concerning previous reports of such a Voice from the stars. These reports were not common. For the most part they came from the distant past and such Talents as the chroniclers deemed mad or vile. But in this present time, were we ourselves not deemed so for the peaceful exercise of our abilities and commitment to the truth? Was it not feasible, even likely, that this had been the case for those operating at the very dawn of our history? Most tellingly, Abelard had not forbidden such attempts to reach beyond our world, though he had considered them dangerous as the nature of the Voice could not be proved. It was agreed that no decision should be contemplated before I made my report on Abyssine. They released me to my regular duties, and thence the evening meal.

In the refectory a Borean Theraputic stood, with silver rings and a single citrine, her eyes serenely closed. She proclaimed that she had *seen* the world beyond, and all there was glorified by the stars. Knowing this, she had no wish to view our present squalor.

A gilded Psychokinetic of Eurupolis claimed to have *heard* such sweet utterance as all sounds, even to the music of harps, must henceforth hold no pleasure for them, and bid all be silent, that they too might hear.

I left the refectory and descended to the front gate.

Night in the waste was as cold as pity and the stars were the merest pinpoints above, limning the curves of the Split Moon. We who were summoned to the vessel numbered some eighty, plus the Hydrarchons, and we proceeded along the great, stone pier, hoods drawn up and hands tucked within our robes. The ship's lights had been kindled and glistened upon the crystals now extending up the masts, a sight both beautiful and somber. There was no discussion among us, neither of thought nor word. We proceeded up the gangplank and down the steps to the underdeck. Rowing benches lined the long space, and Abyssine greeted us there.

She was tall and had the green skin and dark hair of her homeland. Her marks of rank were gold and a sapphire of the deepest violet. She greeted each visitor by name, standing nowise on rank but addressing us all as Seekers. Facing me, she offered her hands, as few would to one of my Talent.

"He that I loved died many years ago," she said, "and all I do is in respect of him. I asked you who might cheat death."

"None of us do."

"Now I ask who among us has the need? Do you believe your beloved persists in some form, beyond that of matter? That what you and I read of others is more than a mere field the body generates?"

This was a great question, to which members of our order had devoted their entire lives. I responded that I wished to believe, though Abelard had never ruled on this matter. At this she smiled. "But your *love* persists. Is this not astonishing?"

Abyssine took my hands, and I felt such compassion and sorrow that I nearly wept. For I understood now that the years to come would offer no end to my grief, that it would at best grow familiar to me or be channeled into some great work.

She passed to the next in line, and I sought to compose myself. Soon we were all seated amongst the oars and benches, beneath the hanging lamps, and some began to hum or sing softly in their different tongues. The rise and fall of this calmed me. When the person next to me offered a hand, I took it and gave my own to the next in line. I felt then the agony of a shattered polycule and the grief of a Telekinetic for a woman of no Talent at all. And they felt mine.

Abyssine projected her thoughts to all and all responded—nothing further from the straining of Maru's acolytes could be imagined. *Who loves?*

All did and all had lost, and each grief was as particular as the beloved. Accepting this was to join a gestalt, where the energies of all would support the heaviest burden. *Seek, then, for those whom you love, seek their presence however your Talent permits. Seek them in whatever time and guise, casting aside the constraints of the here and now, the shallowness of name, sex, and race. Only seek for your love and find them, fearing not the darkness through which you pass.*

As Maru's working had channeled energy up and outwards, so this working passed within. Part of me wished nothing more than to follow the company into this warm and incalculable depth, where every miracle seemed possible, even consolation. But the bristle of my rings and the cold of my gem gave me warning. For while the wisdom, even the reality of Maru's procedure might be debated, I knew now that Abyssine resorted to the utterly forbidden.

Attempts to contact the dead went back to the earliest conceivable glimpses of our past. Legends told of *witches* and of *necromancers,* common enough names for all Talents in those days, but appropriate to those who, believing that the Dead were privy to the future, sought to grasp it through them. Such procedures were banned by Abelard for their danger and the horror they engendered among the un-Talented. And yet . . .

And yet, here before me was the prospect *that it could work* . . .

I held firm. If my love had not answered me when I touched those stains, it would not answer now. My meditation would shield me from this madness.

I had expected that many of the Seekers would not return or would do so with minds broken. Yet return they did, some reporting touches and whispers, but the Clairvoyants particularly spoke of exchanges that seemed to confirm the days of the Rending were upon us and warned also of another danger, that pride and fear would bring to pass.

I played no part in these discussions, only releasing a little of my awe and fear. It was only as all made ready to depart that I allowed myself to bend and brush my fingers over the wooden deck.

You know what I felt. Memories sweet, familiar, and having no place here. Memories of myself, held by one who loved me. But I rose as if the integrity of my boot had been my sole concern and passed down the gangplank without emitting the slightest sign. I felt Abyssine's concern wash over me, but no one made to stop me going.

There was no question of my lying or attempting to conceal the magnitude of Abyssine's offense. Not from the Elders. She was summoned late the next day to give account of herself.

She came alone to the penultimate hall. I caught whispers before her arrival, that the other Hydrarchons, upon her instructions, had abandoned their duties and sought the sanctuary of the vessel. But Abyssine displayed no fear. She stood before the Council as serene as if they assembled it to honor her.

The Prognosticant Maru stood once more upon the dais. He was a wiry Eurupolitan, skin ruddy as loam and hair black and long. But his eyes were arresting, a shade off the hemlock of an Ergokinetic's robe, and an Ergokinetic he had been before his elevation. The Talent of channeling pure electrical energy was rarer than mine.

"Clairvoyant Abyssine." He dipped his head to her in respect. "Long have I desired you to join me here. I would it was voluntarily."

"I will not join your work, Prognosticant." She spoke bluntly. "I say here before the Council, the goal you pursue is an abomination and will lead only to destruction."

The Elders stirred and buzzed, communing. Then the Elder Sibylla addressed her. "Who are you to make such accusation? Exiled as we are, reduced in number as we are, you incite your people to risk themselves in direct contravention of Abelard's dictate!"

"What do we risk but the natural cycle of life? And a cycle it is. I tell you, I have witnessed our eternal return, of the same soul into different bodies. But the destruction Maru courts is of that very soul."

"The Prognosticant Maru foresaw the Voice and the Door," interrupted the Elder Castigne. "What has your heresy revealed?"

"That humanity persists beyond the Rending and even beyond the death of the sun."

Her words were stirring and I, who had felt the presence of my beloved but knew not how to believe, had to force back tears. Maru spoke in turn of the Rending and its horrors, well known to all, and the sacred duty of the Order. Then he spoke of the insights his followers had received, each according to their nature, and assured us that through the Door lay both survival and apotheosis. "We risk ourselves," he said, "in expectation of great gain. The Voice beyond is coming!"

"How answer you the charge of the Psychometrist Damon," Sibylla addressed him, "that no trace of this entity could be detected here?"

Those greenish eyes met mine, and truly the man was a Talent profound. "In this I read only proof that we have truly connected with a being not bound by the limits of our organism. Through contact with us it has learned to speak, to see and hear. By a like process we shall transform, and the death she would have us embrace will be no more! I ask that the Council authorize my proceeding to the penultimate stage of my work, and further that you instruct all Talents that have participated in heresy to join us freely in no fear of punishment."

This way and that the disputation went, and through many emanations. For though none had yet died of Maru's procedure, the likelihood was there, and the benefit must needs outweigh the risk. I sat, gazing upon Maru on the dais and Abyssine on the floor, and thought ill of the Elders who had set me between them. And though I had read Maru's confidence, it seemed to me that Abyssine's faith surpassed it.

Finally the Elders suggested that Maru might proceed, but only those deemed strong enough in body as in mind were to take part. A general amnesty was to be proclaimed, for the benefit of Maru's work, but for Abyssine to share in it she must recant and urge her followers to join. This she refused to do.

"Each Seeker will do as their own heart dictates. Never have I claimed control over that."

Now her imprisonment and punishment were certain. In horror I heard them order the construction of a cathecting mure.

The cathecting mure was a vile device that turned the body's own electrical field into a torturous gibbet. A creation, obviously, of ergokinesis, the mure was designed to release the prisoner's psychic energy through pain, making it available to another's purpose against their will. I could have no part of this, though I did not dare speak. I made my obsequience to the Council and fled to the only place I could.

Amid the fragments of the horizon, the dull ruby was almost lost, the sanguine plain clotting already to black. I walked slowly from the trapdoor toward the edge of the wall, the encroaching night slashing at my face, and cursed my cowardice. Better I had walked into the night and never returned than enable Maru's work. My death now would be scant recompense.

One step, the world was tenebral. The next, there was light. I saw my own shadow limned across the stone, as yet faintly, but with such definition as the sun at perihelion. A pale brightness, falling upon the back of my head and shoulders, revealed the true vastness of the plain. A sound emerged from the heavens, suggestive of a distant and breaking wave.

I stood witness here to something beyond expectation, something to which my mind thrilled as my skin stung. Words there were none, nor will to descend and raise the alarm. I could only wish with everything left to me that my love stood at my side.

And then I felt you.

You, the love of my life, lodestone of my soul, to whom I give yet owe all. The meditation may have kept me from experiencing our reunion as the others had, but the connection was made all the same. I felt you now and you felt me, and our memories passed between us. I knew that the path would be long and death the ordeal I must pass through once my work was done. We should be together once the world had changed and we too had changed, in all other aspects but this.

Your past was my future, my present your myth. You told me what it was that approached, why my very cells shrank and the sky emitted a thin yet universal scream. And I knew then what I alone could do, and how and when I must do it.

Below on the vessel, swathed figures clambered about the hull and masts.

It was time.

Those deemed unfit for the working were exiled to the uppermost cells. The Hydrarchons remained upon their vessel, even though the light from the sky had brightened and the sound was an oncoming roar. All agreed that the Rending approached, and Maru would lead our final effort to escape. Only the unfit, the pregnant, and one grieving Psychometrist would remain within the Bastion—Maru did not consider my energies worth stealing. All others would descend to the penultimate hall, there to await the opening of the Door.

None of that throng would ever have dreamed they could be thwarted by such as I, and through such mundane means. But setting the generators to fail was easy for one who had had their care for so many months. Then I assisted my fellow exiles in their climb. In this way I stole the robes of an elderly Therapeutic and joined the crowd descending to the hall. I drew the hood down over my face and commenced my shielding meditation, once again releasing a little of my awe, and no one questioned me, their own minds in such tumult it felt like the roar outside. My disguise held, even when I stopped at the base of the ramp, frozen in horror by what I saw. None questioned me or barred my path, even as I worked my way toward the point where Abyssine was immured.

They had placed her opposite the dais, almost level with Maru, so he might draw upon her power. I was shielded, but the sight of her naked feet suspended above the floor, her body rigid, and her face striving against the pain would have made a stone weep. They had denied her the robe of her Talent and the gem of her rank: she had only a shift and the crackling aura of her own black hair. Tiny sparks leapt between her fingers, the nails slowly blackening. Other Therapeutics stood beside her, monitoring her life signs until the work should begin. Somehow restraining my horror, I joined them and waited for what I alone knew would come.

Maru wasted no time with words but raised his hand. It seemed to me he held each one of his followers inside it. The chanting began, the swaying to quicken, and the mingled cathexis to build. Still I waited.

Then all went to black.

The ritual lost not one beat; the chant continued as did the undulation. I had been a fool to think mere darkness would disrupt what had begun. But no one saw me extend my hand towards the torture-glimmer of the mure.

I was no Ergokinetic. I could not pull Abyssine from her cage without terrible damage to us both. But once again, the generators had taught me something about electricity. I now believed that by reducing the memory of her muscles, I could keep her alive. I was protected with vulcanized shoes and gloves, but I still needed to touch . . .

The shock robbed me of consciousness. When I awoke, it was to darkness writhing and wracked with groans. The surrounding press had kept me upright, but I had lost my shield: I felt their mania drumming against the taut surface of my mind, threatening every moment to engulf me and sweep me along regardless of my will. In the utter blackness colors swept past me and shadows without source, a Nothingness pained my ears as I flailed and failed to break free.

Then Abyssine was there, her hand upon mine, drawing me through the madness with irresistible force. Without her, I cannot believe I would have made it clear. We found the chamber's edge and so began our ascent, struggling up the spiral against what was now a *shuddering*, reaching from mind to body, scraping our skin like hooks and twisting our muscles. Still we crept on up the corridor.

Barely had we cleared the level above when that sense of twisting became unendurable, and instead of nine hundred voices screaming in terror and pain, I heard without hearing that which twisted my very core.

NOW.

My eardrums bled and have never fully recovered.

A mighty quaking knocked us off our feet.

The floor cracked and rocks fell from the ceiling, and I knew not what came from without or within, only that there was before us a pale,

pale gleam. And yet, once we reached the front gate there was terror there too.

The gate had warped from its seals and the sky light diminished, was fading even as I beheld the clouds tearing, fleeing toward the south from some immeasurable impact. The horizon now appeared taller and closer, a rising, standing wave. It neared even as we watched.

Preparations upon the vessel were complete. She lay in her shroud of crystals, sails blooming from every mast.

"Go bring those from the cells above." Abyssine was yet calm, taking her position at the mouth of the downward spiral. "They will be needed."

Glad enough they were for direction, the thirty or so huddling in their cells. Some asked if the Rending had come, and this I dared not answer, only bid them make haste as the walls shuddered. Shall I speak of compassion, in this hour? Those blinded or crippled by the purge, yet who would have descended the spiral to aid their fellows, only that Abyssine forbade them?

"Go to the ship." Her voice cut through calamity. "She will ride the coming wave—she was made for this purpose." Though I was deaf and trembling in all my limbs, I beckoned them on.

Then it came upon us. Proof that Maru had indeed seen true.

The Door had opened and what came from it was no longer a Voice. It did not exist in any earthly way, and yet it was there in the corridor, scarring itself upon the air. I know I did not perceive its truth, that like those who received the Reply, I responded to it in a manner that made sense to me. It seemed there was a monstrous tongue, seeking to taste all that the Earth offered, and I knew then the fate of the nine hundred.

Only Abyssine held it back from us. She stood there yet, the power Maru would have stolen surrounding her in a purple nimbus, hallowing and protecting us all.

But with each lick the nimbus weakened.

Then I came to my senses. I seized my fellows by hand and sleeve, cursed them and roared, drawing them from the horror and along the pier.

As we reached the vessel, gloved hands took us and drew us into shelter. I was borne, not to the oars, but to the prow, which had been turned to face the black south. I believe I was shouting, crying for Abyssine: as the ship lurched, I pitched forward, and my hands scraped the raw wood.

The memories came to me, left purposefully by only the second person to understand me in this life. Abyssine knew she would not escape the Bastion, but nor, she vowed, would she succumb to the horror Maru had unleashed. Death she feared not, but in her absence I must navigate the Rending and find a refuge Abelard had never seen.

The wave hit—the ship leapt forward and so we traveled like a leaf at the forefront of the storm, the earth splitting behind us. And more than this I cannot share with you until our voyage ends.

Grief dwelt in the Bastion, with anger and shame. Now it has all been swallowed.

Death Knocks (Someday Soon)

Maxwell I. Gold

i. Other Side of Nowhere

Crooked hands, and wrinkled lips like rotten fruit,
will loose their grip on that Other Side of Nowhere,
where the sun never rises, never again—
never to shine on broken seas
with brittle galleons gliding o'er purple waters,
their ruined sails full spread beneath the spectral glow of unknown stars—
never to sing, but wither and fail,
pieces of a dying asphodel,
a blossom broken; a stem, smothered in salt—
never to act as sentinel guiding
the lost soul's fate through storm and gale,
never to trumpet that final anthem
whose soliloquies ring deep in the murky sinews
when Death knocks.

Someday soon, yearning to touch iron hills,
colored with rust and decayed flora,
where the old ships once made safe call
to familiar ports,
under lumbering towers of stone and light—
too far from the rocks,
too late to spy the ghosts of loved ones—
pathetic mortality met
with freckled, rocky backsides on the Other Side of Nowhere—
lined with poppies, thorns, and bones,
tattered yarns swaying in the cold, dark air,
humbled by the mass of Eternity—heavy and fat—
when Death knocks.

ii. Someday Soon

Someday soon, and the seas will rock no more,
no waves to roil the hearts and hatred of men;
no stars beneath the empty gutted salt-depths;
no thunderclaps across bellicose nights
that seized the bravest and stalwart souls;
no hope within the fingers of the Void
betwixt graveyards of wood-rot, barnacled-flesh,
and nightmares when Death knocks.

Someday soon, the endless, pitch-dark worries
that clutch the breasts of those who stood
by the iron hills—waiting for a call from beyond the shore,
only to expect a lingering whisper
or praise by vague creatures floating
amidst the purpled fog of the night—
waiting for the possibility that shadows might not dance,
without hallucinations of dead ships,
to reveal the corpse of Hope.
No—the return of Light;
waiting for the realization that none of it
will matter in the end—
when the Earth is covered in salt,
waiting for the day when Death knocks.

Someday soon, the music swirling in the foam
and fervor of pits too tenebrous,
too despicable to be named
belching fire, lighting,
and truth as if wrought by gods themselves;
too awful for worship,
and too beautiful to be captured
by stroke of pen;
too late, when I realized nothing else,

except the crooked hands and wrinkled lips like rotten fruit
too late, they come from the Other Side of Nowhere—
they come for me—
when Death knocks.

Bellow of the Steamship Cow

Aaron Dries

Inspired, in part, by actual events.

Just another Budapest baby manacled to an umbilical cord in 1897, only this one was unaware of his talent for escapism until he broke free of the womb and emerged into the spotlight with a slap on the bum. His name was Erich Weisz, and he had transitioned from one world to another. In to out, warm to cold. Blackness to brightness. And soon, from Hungary to America, where he would, as "Eric of the Air," master the trapeze by the tender age of nine. Later he would go by "Handcuff Houdini," a pseudonym he chose in tribute to his idol, the French magician, Robert Houdin.

Vaudevillian. Rope whisperer. Charmer of the chain.

Harry Houdini.

Death was a plum he bit to tempt the pit inside, licking the juice from his chin for the tramp-coins-turned fortune they threw at his feet. It wasn't always a blessed life. Accused of faking and bribery many times over, threatened with the implementation of the Lunacy Law, a string of failed relationships, the constant rupture and repair with his family, dodging both Russian influenza and the Bubonic Plague. There were times, though most often after opium or mescal binges with carny folk, when Houdini's desire to trick himself back into his mother's womb called loud and clear, a tightrope he walked again and again until he met Bess. She kept him safe, safe as his saintly mother, or so thought the "Handcuff King" until one night in late October 1902.

The night of Hope's chains.

With the arrogance awarded those who fall like men but land like cats, Houdini strode into the Blackburn Theatre on the corner of Jubilee Street and Railway Road with his wife, brother, and doctor, a building with a twenty-five-foot proscenium and a thirty-foot deep stage. He was confident of another success. At least this time he wouldn't have to use the straitjacket.

"What is his name again?" Houdini asked Bess.

She stood by his side backstage, dressed in a pouter pigeon blouse and trumpet skirt, smelling of the Jergen and Eastman's *Violette of Saville* perfume he'd bought her in Paris earlier in the year. He missed performing with her, but was glad she was on tour with him that year, though the fact he was the star act and she was relegated to the wings remained a quiet wedge between them. He hummed the tune to *Rosabelle,* the song she had sung in her act when they first met at Coney Island. The song was one of their many signals and codes.

Bess, born Wilhelmina, smiled.

Sometimes Houdini daydreamed about how his wife would grieve if he died during an escape, imagining the roses she would throw on his casket as it was lowered into the earth, and all the handwritten notes she would have to compose in response to the sympathy letters coming in from all over the world. He saw her by his grave in the Jewish Machpelah Cemetery in Queens where she knew he wanted to be buried. He thought of all the ways he would try to reach out to her from the other side, through tappings and chills and the gentle prodding and poking of their pets, because everyone knew animals saw things that people could not. Even when they wanted to so badly.

"William Hodgson," Bess said, close to his ear, brushing his cheek with her teeth. She said the dandy's name as if she were slinging mud, clumps of clay between her fingers that she squished and shaped, then pressed against and into Houdini's body. The muscle behind that power was erotic. It was pink. He also admired how she saw his opponent that night, the officious muscle man who carried himself unlike other men.

She hated their host for his otherness, too.

"William Hodgson," Houdini said. The name had a feel to it, like felt worn thin with the baldness showing through. "I thought there was Hope there, too?"

"Yes. William Hope Hodgson, of the school of Physical Culture."

"Hmm."

"Why do you hate him so?" Bess said, drawing away, her face crow-winged by shadow. The way she said it had a hint of challenge to it. As if she already knew.

"I don't hate him. I just don't understand him, Bess. And that's enough."

"Don't do it," said a voice from behind them. Houdini turned. The speaker was his brother, Hardeen. And by his side stood Doctor Bradley with his little black case and top hat in hand. They looked worried. There was something in the air; Houdini sensed it also, but tried not to let it show on his face.

The curtains opened as if in reply, revealing all 2,500 plush seats in the theatre, which had been designed by the famous Livermore brothers, and which now was owned by the MacNaghten Vaudeville Circuit. Every seat was filled. Harry Houdini had no way of knowing that his performance that night would be one of the top acts ever to grace that stage. Just as he had no idea that, come 1932, the theatre would be closed and would sleep for many years to come.

People said that at night, backstage, you could sometimes catch whiffs of the sea.

Shadows remember, Houdini believed, as did his wife. Rigging ropes remembered. The chalk of old markers remembered. And so did all the echoes, echoes of what came before. Every theatre is haunted. Just some theatres more than others.

"Go," Bess said. "I'll be here when you're done. I love you."

"Will you?"

"Believe."

Houdini took the stage, dressed only in canvas trunks. The floorboards under his bare feet had a little give to them; it reminded him of his wrestling days as a kid.

Hope was out there on the stage already.

William Hope Hodgson could try all he might to shake the Essex out of his voice, but Houdini could spot those knuckles in his mouth a mile off. Houdini should probably consider himself lucky to see the man in person, and not from behind his camera. A real shutterbug, he'd read.

If Hope wasn't lifting weights, sculpting his body into statuesque firmness that made so many around him envious, he was out photographing aurora in the sky over lakes or fly larvae in goat bellies somewhere. Houdini had researched him in depth after the challenge came through. You would think a man as pretty as Hope, with those almost ladylike features, who had seen so much of the world from the bows of great ships, would have the aptitude to create art that didn't all look the same. Still and cold and dead, unless you invited yourself to imagine what might be in all that blackness around the edges of things. Perhaps the man—though he was really still just a muscled-up teen—was yet to discover his medium. *And good luck to him,* Houdini thought, smug and hungry to deride him. *You prissy bastard.*

"Ladies and gentlemen," Hope said loud and clear. There was a lilt to his voice that set Houdini's teeth on edge. "I am so very interested in Mister Houdini's *apparently* anatomically impossible handcuff feat. And it is because of my curiosity that you are all privy to a great challenge tonight."

Houdini ground his jaw. *Because of your curiosity?* he thought. *I think you'll find, O Essex cabin boy, that I have a significant part to play in the entertaining of your crowd.*

The expectant silence of the people watching was one Houdini was ready for, even comforted by. In it he heard the shuffling of fabrics, a cough here and there, the web of intimidating nothings that screamed PROVE YOURSELF OR DIE IN FRONT OF ME.

"But, skeptic that I am," Hope continued, "I have conditions when it comes to our little display."

Little display . . . Why does he intend to goad me so? Houdini wondered.

Houdini wondered who was the boy behind all the overcompensating muscle. Wiry and ferrety, he suspected. Hope evoked the anger of the schoolyard in Houdini for some reason. Trip him as he walked by, throw stones at him.

Build your body all you want, Hope.
I see you.

"Firstly," said Hope, "I insist that I bring and use my own irons on you. Secondly, that I iron you myself with my own two hands." He lifted his arms. "And thirdly, and most importantly, that if you are unable to free yourself, the twenty-five pounds I've wagered against you will be forthwith donated to the Blackburn Infirmary."

A cheer from the crowd. Houdini could hear them but not see them in the spotlight.

Hope faced him, arms gliding down to his sides. "What do you say, 'Handcuff Houdini'? Do you accept?"

"As I mentioned in my reply correspondence to you," Houdini said, wrists crossed at his stomach, ready for the irons, "I accept your challenge. I have deposited the twenty-five pounds at the Telegraph Office on an interim basis, should I not escape in time."

He played up that last line, and there was laughter from the gallery.

There was none, however, backstage where Bess held Hardeen's forearm.

"So, yes, businessman, I accept. But let me make it clear: I do so in protest," Houdini said. "I wish to say this now and say it loud for all Blackburn to hear . . ."

Hope's men dragged the chains out of the wings as he spoke. These men moved, swished, as though ferried on a tide Houdini could not see, their dark eyes lamplight in reverse, shining nothing whilst seeing everything.

"I do not think these chains are regulation," Houdini said. The crowd murmured. "Even hearing them rustle on the floor now, I suspect my worries are warranted. These bindings have been tampered with."

Hope looked at Houdini again. The peach-fuzz covering Hope's skin. Long eyelashes. The sweeps of neatly combed hair parted down the middle. A tilted wrist. His flat stomach and the roll and fall of his trouser bulge, so much like a shifting partner under the sheets when they turn away from you now that your breath has soured in the night. Houdini felt himself faltering. His throat turned dry.

"Or perhaps," Hope said, "you cloud your insecurity with subterfuge. A magician to the end, nay? Or in lieu of magic, an illusionist." He turned to the audience. "Are you satisfied knowing you're sitting in the parlor, awaiting simple card tricks again? Or do you want to see some *real* magic tonight?"

The crowd gave their answer. And their answer was unanimous.

Hope turned back to Houdini. "My word is my honor. These very manacles that my men are applying to you now are bindings that have been used on my person by the Blackburn police, my clients who sought my personal training programs not two years ago. You yourself once escaped from Blackburn jail from those same officers. Why doubt now?"

Houdini nodded.

Hope smiled. It seemed, though it may have just been a trick of the light, that something shifted beneath the skin of his face, like a shark that didn't break the water until it was about to bite. *Sharks*. Houdini had heard that the man on the stage—his host and challenger, the force behind the casual fettering and locking of his limbs—took to the ocean to capture such monsters on film. *What fascination with the sea,* thought Houdini, a man of air and sky, as his wrists and ankles were manacled. Hope sealed the final bind himself, just as he said he would, sliding in the key with such force you would think he had a penchant for fencing and not for pressing weights. The padlock thudded against Houdini's prick, which was snuggled tight within his canvas shorts. Despite himself, and unnerved, Houdini felt a curious thickening down there.

"Believe," Hope said. The word turned Houdini's guts to icy sludge. "Now, men, blindfold our guest and let us begin!"

And in the dark, Hope's men led him to Houdini's curtained cabinet.

"It's been too long," Bess said to her brother-in-law. "Something is wrong."

Hardeen shushed her, not wanting to acknowledge it. He looked to the doctor, who stood in profile beside him, stoic as a coin etching, and decided that he would not panic unless Bradley showed signs of panic himself.

Houdini's brother would not have to wait for long.

The curtained cabinet, a cramped nothingness that smelt of oil of cloves and mold and something otherly. Sweaty, Houdini stopped to ease his heartbeat back into its normal tattoo and inhaled deep and squinted beneath the blindfold. There was something in the smell that made him think of the German steamship *Frisia,* which brought Erich and his siblings and parents to America so long ago. The smell of blood.

Of meat. Shit. Piss. Milk. Ammonia.

He recalled one day aboard the ship after a storm that had left so many ill. Weary, he left his mother's side where she was trying to distract herself from her nausea by knitting yet another pair of woollen slippers, size six, and wandered toward a braying sound coming from the livestock pen at the stern. He knew he should not go but went regardless, passing many people along the way, their faces ashen and gaunt, cowled in snoods and oversized hats. Their eyes followed him, and once Erich had left them behind he felt their gazes on his back. Erich found the pen where one of the cows lay on its side, screaming, swarming with lice. Other men were coming now, and the child feared a beating for moseying without an accompanying adult, but he could not tear his focus away.

A stillborn calf, purple and sleek, lay in a widening puddle of sloppy meat, strangled on split flesh, half in and half out of its mother cow, pinched tight in a bloody sideways smile.

This could have been me, he thought, as the men pushed him aside. *This was like the babies my parents talked about, my brothers and sisters who had not survived.*

Yes, Houdini's cabinet, all those years later, stank of birth gone wrong. In the dark, afraid, he whispered his mother's name. Only something else answered instead.

Doctor Bradley drew the cabinet curtain open at the twenty-five-minute mark. He had been breathing so deep and hard there were condensation beads in the wiry brush of his mustache. "Do you need to be freed, Harry?"

Houdini wrestled in the black. Hope's chains sang their song all around him.

"Can you feel your hands?" the doctor said. "Your feet? Speak, Harry."

"No," Houdini said through gritted teeth. "But leave me be."

"How can you free what you can't feel? Damn it!"

Houdini gasped, dropped his hands. "Get my brother to ask Hope if he will loosen the bindings for a minute only. That and nothing more. Just to regain my sense of touch. It is so bloody hot in here, Doctor. The air's dense."

Bradley, with Hardeen by his side, made the request. Hope refused to the cheer of a crowd who wanted to see death, even though they knew deep down that they would not know what to do should it be delivered to them upon the hardwood stage.

Bess lowered her head and fingered her wedding band. On the inside of the ring a single word was inscribed in ornate lettering: *Rosabelle*.

The cabinet curtain came down. Houdini could not sense the deepening of shadows but knew he had been left alone again from the stifling of the air. Soon it was as though he were drowning, and he had no choice but let Hope's water into his lungs.

It filled him up. Ballooned Houdini's arms and legs until they bulged against the unwavering pinch of the stranger's iron. A head of scratchy cotton. A mouthful of sand. And on Houdini's tongue the salt of the sea spilling up from inside, trying to drag him under.

He kicked his legs, only his feet no longer touched the stage. Weightless, he swung his body from left to right to left again, the blindfold slipping off his face and floating away, curtaining in the air, curving to an invisible yield, robbed of all shape and purpose. Light refracted through this strange nothingness, and Houdini wondered where he was or what was left of him. Bubbles exploded from his mouth and scrambled for that cold light, but never reaching it. He glanced about, the iron bindings digging further, anchoring him in place beneath the immense pressure of an ocean that could *not* be there, yet *was* there just the same.

The bellow of the cow boomed through this darkness.

Houdini grew still.

My God.

It was no cow out there, but a shark, big as moon-dawn and every bit as white. He thrashed as the jaws parted, gullet rippling, gills opening, and it swallowed Houdini, chains and manacles and Hope's pins and all.

He woke, face down in a puddle of footrot trench water that tasted of oil. Rolled over, still bound, and looked up at a Belgium night sky. An artillery shell pinwheeled toward him, so slowly that the seconds curdled as if trying to hold death back. Houdini didn't know how he knew, but he did, that this was the year 1918, and in this future the world was at war. He flinched. Eyelids dropped. In that beat of darkness, half a second perhaps, all the years he had missed clapped by as if viewed through one of the Coney Island Nickelodeons he and Bess often peered into, laughing, in the months of their early courtship.

Explosions. Bodies being ripped apart. Kisses. Fucking. A billion births and a billion deaths. Blood. Cart crashes. Buildings being built. Buildings coming down. Secrets. Truths. Every glory. Every single love.

Houdini opened his eyes. The artillery fire illuminated the men struggling in the muck beside him, one of whom was Hope. He had thinned out, a lot of that muscle stressed away, and he held a man the way one holds his wife, the two of them screaming into each other's faces, their uniforms the same color, their faces the same color, though it all might have been the wet earth that painted them gray. Houdini, too, was covered in the slop—it lathered his naked chest and legs and arms, smeared here and there by the links of chains to reveal the white skin beneath.

That same mud would crack under the assault of the sun come noon the following day, all their disembodied arms and legs and torsos and backs and their faces and torn-off testicles and the crests of their cheeks broken apart and left to dry, some of the pieces dangling from wire. Rats would feast on their innards. Crows would go for their eyes.

In the moments before the bomb touched the ground, Houdini watched Hope grip the man tighter. Their kiss was unlike any Houdini had experienced with Bess, and more like those he had shared with other women in his youth, women he thought about more than a married man should. These women were still important to him in ways he didn't want to acknowledge, and so different from the life he grew into.

Houdini tried to slip free of Hope's irons as the seconds continued to grind by.

The bellow of the steamship cow echoed over the misty stretch of no-man's-land, drawing Houdini's attention to figures out there, clothesless men who climbed over the scribbles of long barbed wire. They moved outside of time, carrying chains with the manacles pointed outwards, crabbish and snapping-snapping-snapping. They were naked except for their gas masks, the tubes too long and swinging like pendulums above the tufts of their pubic hair.

The bomb hit the ground.

Everything turned white.

Again Harry Houdini was pulled from one world and into the other, and he went screaming, reaching through ballast and smoke, scaling the umbilical cord back into the womb where it was safe, wet flesh squelching against his face, and was welcomed. Only darkness there. And so still in those waters. He heard his mother's heartbeat, constant as the tail of a great white shark sweeping back and forth, thrusting all those teeth closer.

"If the great Houdini is beaten here, then let him, this night, in front of you all, give in," Hope said. His men drew the cabinet curtain open, those last words—*give in*—an auditory punch to the side of Houdini's head. He recoiled, the blindfold on the floor between his knees. He lay on his side, writhing, as the chains were unclasped and drawn off his swollen limbs. Iron struck the wood, uncurling like a great dying thing, clink by clink, vertebra by vertebra. Bess, his brother, and the doctor rushed to him, trying to help him up. Houdini pushed them away, fearing that their attention would make him appear weaker in front of the audience.

Houdini struggled to his feet. His veins were so pronounced that they cast their own shadows in the spotlight, as if he were decorated in black vine. His family and doctor slinked back into the wings. Bess put her hand to her mouth, thankful that her husband would physically recover, but sickened because she knew that the humiliation he'd suffered for Hope's amusement (or was it revenge for crimes others had committed?) was a wound he would always carry. And in this she was correct.

Faces stared from their chairs. Nobody spoke. Nobody moved.

Houdini, shaking, lifted his right arm to point at his host. His voice cracked as he shouted, and shouted loud, because the volume of whatever he said would dull the insane images in his mind, the smells he had smelled in the cabinet, the feelings he didn't want to acknowledge. "I—I—I have never been treated so brutally in fourteen years of performing."

Bess prayed someone out there would come to his defense. Nobody did.

"The irons were plugged!" Houdini shouted. *"The irons were plugged!"*

But the show was over, and nobody cared. Hope spirited himself from the stage. The heavy curtain blinked shut, sweeping up the stink of brine and ocean mist.

"Plugged, I tell you. Plugged!"

Houdini was mortally wounded on October 22, 1926, after being struck in the stomach multiple times by Jocelyn Gordon Whitehead on a lark in Montreal, unaware that in the process of their play Houdini's appendix had been ruptured. This was eight years after William Hope Hodgson died at the Fourth Battle of Ypres, where he had re-enlisted to fight after a mandatory discharge due to injury. He went back to the trenches of his own accord, leaving behind a wife and a body of macabre fiction that has since woven in and out of print from that year onwards. Hope died childless, he and a British signalman blown to shreds by a German artillery shell.

What remained of them was burned at the site to stay the vermin.

Flesh to ash and bones to charcoal, two among the thousands, there at the very eastern slope of Mont Kemmel in Flanders.

"I can take the hurts," Houdini said when the pain set in, gripping his stomach where he had been punched by Whitehead. "I can take it. *I can take it!*"

Houdini's end did not come fast—nine days later, in fact. Against old Doctor Bradley's advice, he traveled to Michigan to meet Bess. He then graced the stage at the Garrick Theatre in Detroit for what would be the final performance of his life. Half an hour into the show, Bess watched her husband collapse, the crowd surging to point and cry. She ran to his side and lifted his heavy head. Heat beamed off him in waves.

Wards at Grace Hospital still had flickering gas lamps that made the sweat on Houdini's face resemble sequins on a parlor mystic's headscarf. At some point during the height of his fever, Houdini saw gas masks in the dim at the end of the ward, their wearers climbing over barbed-wire fencing that had etched itself into existence. Mask tubes dangled like lamed arms. He hated how their bug eyes never blinked, the muscles beneath their mustard-gas-stained skins flexing as they prowled for him. Bess held Houdini down when he thrashed on the mattress, crying for help as the men from the cabinet ripped off their masks to reveal shark teeth and aurora eyes.

"There's nobody there, my Harry," Bess said, tears beading from her cheeks and landing on her husband's brow. *"Believe!"*

Houdini watched them come with their manacles and chains, Hope's old irons rattling across the hospital's scuffed linoleum floor. They stank of the sea and chalky fog. Dead larvae fell from their tongues.

The man born Erich Weisz on March 24, 1874, died that All Hallows' Eve, the chains clasped over his wrists and ankles, dragging him into the final dark from which there is no escape. Bess was with him when it happened. His mother, sadly, was not. Houdini had promised his father on his deathbed that he would look after her forever, and he kept his promise as best he could, buying her houses, requesting his salary in gold coins that he would have poured onto her lap. Cecelia Weiss had passed away thirteen years earlier from a stroke. Her funeral was postponed so that Houdini, who was touring Europe at the time, could make it home to place in her coffin a pair of woolen slippers, size six.

Houdini was buried by her side in Machpelah. But when Bess passed away in 1943 after suffering a heart attack at the age of sixty-seven, her family insisted she be entombed at the Gate of Heaven Cemetery in New York City, as she had been raised Roman Catholic and not Jewish like her husband.

Thirty-five miles of East Coast soil, some consecrated but mostly not, separates them to this day.

For many years Bess tried to reach her husband through séances, guided by mediums, some of whom were frauds who broke her heart again and again without an ounce of remorse. Only once, after an exhausting session in Hollywood a decade after Houdini's passing, did she ever feel she came close to something. The session wrapped without event. Bess stepped out onto the street in the escort of a friend and was chilled by a young man walking past whistling *Rosabelle's* melody.

Later that night, alone in bed, the candle that she had been burning for her husband for ten summers straight, which she had taken with her from state to state, house to house, blew out within the breezeless bedroom. She would for years to come tell anyone who asked that she herself extinguished the flame.

The darkness it left behind was unlike anything she had ever experienced.

Bess clambered up on her pillow. Her fingers bunched into fists. She began to quiver, seeing nothing. *Almost* nothing. Her pulse started to climb. She could hear it in her ears.

"Harry?" Bess said.

Silence.

"Harry, is that you?"

Slowly the stench of ocean rot swept over her. Brine. Salt. Seaweed and fish guts and algae bloom. For a moment Bess, squinting to fight the blackness around her, thought she saw something moving in the corner of the room between the armoire she had inherited from her mother and the wall, and even then, only when she peered at it from the periphery of her vision. It may have just been the dappled lily print of the wallpaper that resembled a face back there, with the mouth open yet making no sound. Or maybe not. Maybe, she thought, this was a dream. But then, distant, as if coming from the adjoining room, she heard the rattle of chains, followed by a deep cow bellow. The sound left her so very sad, a feeling that had no time to take hold—though it would return the following day even stronger and never let her go—because something was crawling over her skin.

Not one thing, but many things. Hundreds of things. Thousands of things. These things were in the corner of her eyes, popping under the force of every blink. In her nostrils. Making their way into her mouth and across her gums and between her teeth. Things beneath her night gown. Things under her arms. Things that marched across her thighs and sought out her hair for nesting.

Bess scrambled off the mattress, sensing she was watched from the corner of the room yet finding no comfort in that presence, itself a kind of betrayal she would never reconcile. Slapping herself over and over, Bess fumbled for the drawstring light near the door and yanked it. *Click.* Darkness to brightness, stage spotlight harsh and every bit as unforgiving. She spun to her dresser, bumping it, overturning glass perfume bottles, knocking a brown glove to the floor. It slapped her foot as though a hand were within it, a hand grabbing her from beneath the kinds of water Hope wrote about and she read in secret, ready to pull her under. The three-piece mirror set reflected Bess Houdini's face. Lice covered her skin in a writhing widow's veil. She crumpled to her knees, alone but not alone, and wept.

The House on the Scannerland

David Agranoff

From a manuscript discovered in 1987 in the ruins of a foreclosed house in Santa Venetia, north of the village of San Rafel California. The events outlined here are from notes found at the house.

Author's introduction to the manuscript:
   I have thought long and hard about the story that is set forth in the following pages. In my research into celebrated science fiction author Philip K. Dick, I have learned about many strange events. The manuscript—you must picture me when it first turned up in my research with quaint but barely legible handwriting. *Was it the work of the writer?* Had it been written as a jape by the children who claimed to find the pages or the house that almost swallowed the writer's soul?
   "I read, and in reading, lifted the curtains of the impossible that blind the mind and looked out into the unknown." What truth can be found in this story is in the shadows between one man's visions of heaven and hell, joy and paranoia. It will provide certain thrills, but I merely offer this as a story.

—David Agranoff,
December 2007

   . . . In the west of America lies an inlet on earth's largest, most powerful ocean. It is situated, alone, at the base of a low hill. Depending on the season the water swells around the house, or the tides uncover tiny pools filled with millions of tiny lifeforms. In spite of the isolation, my friend Tony and I would often hike there north of town. When our summer vacation from school came, we brought tents and made the hike. We told our parents we were fishing, but they didn't seem to notice that we left our poles in the garage.
   It was Tony's idea to stay overnight. The house was always in his thoughts. He wanted to be near it. There were rumors about the nature of it. Foreclosed and boarded up, a state rare in the homes around this

part of the country where land has such great value. It was home to a man of great imagination, who envisioned other worlds and strange futures. He hardly slept, the light in his office like a sentinel reflecting off the coast, not guiding in ships but dark visions. The man hated to be alone, so youth chasing the visions and wild dreams followed the light to his door, and often they slept on his floor.

Reaching the ruin, I was silent and awed. I felt the strange energy in my bones. Tony looked at it as if he had happened upon an ancient temple filled with gold. He had no intention of unfolding his tent. Before the sun disappeared he planned to be inside the ruined home. I told him I would not spend a night in that house for all the wealth in the world. There was something unholy, something diabolical about it.

I walked into the kitchen, pulling my shirt over my nose to block the smell of rot and decay. The dishes reached to the ceiling like Babel's tower, supporting an ecosystem of buzzing life. The cabinet was open, exposing a pipe with a tiny drip that over time had bored through the floorboards, carving a slowly widening chasm. The kitchen floor was littered with Raid cans and a shoebox tied shut with a single rotting shoelace.

Seemingly unaffected by the smell in the room, Tony walked past me to the white fridge. He pulled on the handle, and the seal fought him. It should have been warning enough not to open the door. The seal split with a loud hiss and air fit for a dozen tombs. Inside several glass bottles marked "dairy" danced on the shelf disturbed for the first time in years. The liquid in the bottles had long since turned colors and developed shapes. Behind them were jars large enough to hold a half-gallon of liquid filled with pills in various shapes and sizes.

"There it is."

Tony set down his backpack. Pushing the milk bottles out of the way, he carefully reeled in a bottle of pills.

"White Cross, the good shit."

"What?"

"There is a biker dude, he used to go to San Rafael high, but flunked out. He sells pills, way better than grass. Guy says this old science fiction writer guy used to live out here, and every time he sold a book he would load up. One hundred bones on these massive bottles of White Cross. That is how he wrote the weird stuff."

"Like what weird stuff?"

"Alternate realities, robots, time travel, I don't know, weird shit."

"How long has it been here?"

"Pills don't go bad. Come on, let's party and sell the rest."

Tony kept working the jar, had to put his weight into it, and the seal was tight. As he made several frustrated grunts, I walked over to a desk positioned by a window overlooking the ocean. The desk had an area of less dust in the shape of a typewriter that had been there for a long time. A pile of notes sat on the table. The type on the header was scratched out, and in blue pen *"Dear Anne and Laura"* was written and a line of ink went through it. *"Dear Nancy and Isa"* had been typed, also crossed out. Finally, *"Dear Carol Carr."* There was an address for New York City.

I feel like an old man. I live here in this ancient house, surrounded by huge unkempt gardens. I have friends, all the drug-chasing teens of Marin County. I would rather have their visits than feel the weight of all creation alone. I have spread rumors and stories to prank the kids that the devil built this house, but the longer I live here with the power that keeps my family away, I fear it may be true . . .

Tony grunted. The seal budged on the jar and unleashed trapped air with a pop. The sound kept popping as if it echoed in infinite universes each time it faded, but I swear I heard it echo into a timeless chasm, even over the events that would come to haunt us. Tony found two pills, different from the others. The red pill called to him.

"This one."

"Why that one?"

He shrugged and swallowed it dry. He reached for the canteen that hung off his bag. Tony offered me a matching pill. We did this dance all the time. I would say no, and Tony would bug me into it. Tony pushed me to fight the boys who bullied me in the schoolyard. To climb the rock wall I was afraid of, to smoke my first cigarette, to steal Dad's beer. Tony always made me do the things. I knew I was taking this pill.

One moment the pill sat on Tony's hand, and the next the earth turned a different speed. The pill hit my blood stream, and the chemicals washed over my mind. A long space of time came and went, all between the ticks on my watch. Seconds or eons, it lost meaning. I moved, my body made it to a window, and I stared at the sun as it disappeared over the ocean. I could suddenly sense the movement of the specks of light. Tiny glowing stars in the sky moved quickly through the universe streaking across the night sky, disappearing into the days that passed, nights that returned and twisted around me. The living solar system moved slow enough for me to watch; no, I was moving with it. No, it was something different I was feeling.

Those pills were good shit.

Tony was in the kitchen. He was scratching at his skin, enough that he was bleeding a little from his arms. I walked closer.

"Damn bugs," he whispered and put up his finger to shush me. He stared at the pit that had formed under the dripping sink. A half-human, half-pig like squeal came from the chasm.

"You don't want to mess with those swine things."

Tony and I turned to see the ghostly figure who'd spoken. He was only in his forties, but the graying beard and years gave him an ancient look. He was scribbling in his notebook. I looked at the papers I was holding. New handwriting had appeared on the page, the words had just appeared, but the lead from the pencil looked faded. *I found two kids in the house. They look almost through me.*

His form was faded and ghostly; he was only here in spirit. The ghost watched Tony scratching, his arms, his hair.

"Aphids," the ghost whispered to me. "Tell your friend to put the little fuckers in the box, he'll stop itching for a bit."

I looked at the ghost. He seemed to be inspecting the house. "I thought it was the pills, but it might be the house."

I was sure it was the pills. Tony walked toward the ghost and they both waved their hands through each other, neither finding anything solid on the other side.

The ghost pointed at the chasm under the sink. "Don't let the cats fall into eternity. I used a rope to explore, down there. It doesn't end, at least it doesn't seem to end. I have written such nightmares you know."

"Nightmares? About bottomless pits?"

The ghost considered my question. "At the bottom is a face. Cold, mechanical."

"A robot?" Tony asked.

The ghost shook his head. "A god, an angry one. He hides in the jars." He lowered his voice to a whisper. "In the pills."

I was confused about the god in the hole or the pills, but the chill in the ghost's voice reached out and shook me. "Not in the hole, at the end of time, pay attention." The ghost heard his thoughts, or felt them, looked at the wall. "I can't hear anything over the rain."

Tony laughed and came over to me. "It is him, the writer that lived in this house."

"No, it is the pills. We are just seeing things."

The ghost wagged his finger and tsked in disagreement. "Stop it, you are in my imagination, boys, treading water in the sea of sleep. My daughter, Laura, she'll get worried and come to help me. Then you'll float away like good little boys."

"Sir, I think you might not exist."

The ghost nodded. "My whole life I have asked that question. Days stretched until hours and minutes became years and ages long enough to rot stone. Laura will wake me and then you won't be here to blah-blah in my dreams."

Tony leaned closer, "We are in his dreams."

"And what is he?"

"Phil, my name is Philip. I am a writer, second-rate science fiction. I won the Hugo Award once, but I had to lock it up. These druggies, they would trade it for pills. You ever heard of that award? I don't think my books are that great myself."

I looked at Tony and then down to the manuscript. The pages were looking at me, and I jumped. It was as if I felt eyes on the page looking at me.

It was as if I felt eyes on the page looking at me.

Wait.

It was as if I felt eyes on the page looking at me.

Shit.

It was as if I felt eyes on the page looking at me.

I turned the page. It was blank except this . . .

I put down the manuscript, and glanced at Tony.

He looked out the window, but his mind traveled to another universe.

I put down the manuscript and glanced at Tony.

I looked at the sentence and Tony three more times before I closed my eyes and asked him.

"Was he mad?"

"I have a bigger question."

I didn't open my eyes. I was afraid. Tony was in the room, but his voice was distant.

"Why were we in it?"

"Tony, I am going home. I am putting down these papers."

I opened my eyes as Tony ran to the door. I was behind him, and the door kept apace out of our reach for a time. I was tired, dying to quit but too scared to stop. I reached for the handle, and it stayed beyond my grasp. When the door opened the house faded away. Into the cold night under the marine layer coming off the ocean, reality woke me like a bucket of water.

Sometimes in my dreams I see the enormous pit where the house had been. Whenever I walk toward the coast it calls to me. The ghost storyteller thought he escaped, but a part remained, and he still is writing this story. I feel sometimes I'm still in his stories, that they consume me. He watches me from the veil of eternity when I walk the shore. He walks and demands the stories be told. So here I am each breath a beat in the story of souls trapped in that house.

Out in the Night with the Memphis Dead

Andy Davidson

LeBleu flicked the last of his smoke through the open window. Sparks kicked off the Buick's chassis into the hot August night. The rushing air was sweet with the promise of rain. Far out over the Delta, lightning rolled in sheets. The radio crackled with the news, the only news in the world tonight: "The King is dead . . ." From the bathroom floor to the ambulance to the hospital to Vernon P. on the steps of Graceland, and now, finally, to the widow herself, surrounded by all those fat, mutton-chopped men in that terrible mansion: Aaron Elvis Presley. Born January 8, 1935. Dead this day, August 16, 1977.

The timing, LeBleu thought, was cosmic.

Wedged in the Buick's passenger seat was a career brute, Mickey Cyclops, three hundred pounds of washed-up wrestler stuffed in brown polyester pants and a white Stafford shirt. He made a grunt at the radio, then reached for a carefully squared handkerchief from his shirt pocket. He wiped beneath the patch that covered his left eye socket, an empty orbit forever weeping water. Skin forever raw. What's more, he had no teeth in his head, and his tongue lolled out like a drawer someone had forgotten to shut. He was, quite possibly, the ugliest man in the world.

LeBleu hummed under his breath, a wistful snatch from E's "American Trilogy": "'Look away, look away . . .'" He didn't go in for rock. LeBleu was a gospel man. He liked it when the Stamps sang back up, but the old boy had been too fat for too long, taking too many pills. American trilogy? American tragedy, more like.

Mickey, meanwhile, sniffed his handkerchief.

The night held vibes and portents. LeBleu felt them dance, current-like, along the nape of his neck, destiny arcing between some next-door universe and himself. A gentle rap-rap-rapping at his chamber door.

They took the first exit off the Old River Bridge, plunging immediately into the deep Arkansas dark. Off the broken asphalt onto a pitted gravel road threading the pylons of the bridge. Moths and mosquitoes and winged things unknowable swirling in the glow of the headlamps, the car rocking over a rutted scree of mud-buried beer cans and the cast-off rags of homeless junkies. Old tires reared out of the marsh grass like the heads of giant catfish.

LeBleu cut the motor and they sat for a minute in the close dark, staring at the far Memphis skyline. The UP Bank building at North Main blazing red. A dark line of warehouses atop the bluff, silhouetted against the orange sky like a mouth of ruined teeth. Beale Street in uneasy mourning tonight, so many bluesmen contemplating their own mortality, their own poverty, over bottomless glasses of whiskey and gin. The New River Bridge shining like a gateway into some last glittering redoubt from the Delta night. It was all a lie. Memphis was a toilet.

Out on the river, a barge pushing coal to Illinois slid past, a black behemoth.

Something heavy landed on the Buick's roof.

Only the brute started.

Le Bleu's eyes were glazed and far away, fixed on visions of a nearing future.

There was a sputtering, as of insect wings.

"Babe?" Mickey croaked.

Le Bleu lit another cigarette from a gold case inside his vest pocket. His lighter was a Zippo, BECAUSE I SAY SO inscribed on the base. He drew deeply, exhaled. Through the smoke he said, "Newsman said the old boy died on the toilet. Said he was reading a book called *The Scientific Search for the Face of Jesus*. What do you think of that, Cyclops? You reckon he found Jesus popping pills on a Graceland crapper?"

The brute said nothing. He pressed his head against the passenger window, craning to see whatever was shuffling above.

"Man was a genuine seeker, I'll give him that," LeBleu said. He sent a curl of smoke out the open window. "But there is no science to avail man's search for godhood." LeBleu pressed a hand over his heart, opened the button of his silk shirt, and gripped the talisman nestled in his chest hair. Its shape—round and squat and monstrous—reassured.

The car rocked gently as the thing on the roof launched itself into the air.

Mickey saw, in the swirl of the headlights, a flap of iridescent wings, big as kites.

LeBleu clamped his cigarette in his mouth and used both hands to button up. "We in the Borderlands now, brother," he said around the cigarette. Four rings shimmered on his right hand, one on every finger but the thumb: a diamond, a ruby, two sapphires, and an opal. Set in gold, silver, platinum. His hands were thick with sinew, knotty. They had pinned many men in years long past. He closed his eyes. Drew in a deep breath. *With these hands,* he thought, *I will build my temple.* He opened his eyes. Blew out smoke. Then threw his cigarette out the window. "Best get to it."

He had dreamed of this night since he was a boy. The night of his ascendance.

A night of glorious purpose.

Destiny writ so much larger than an Arkansas cotton field.

Of that time he mostly remembered lying awake on a straw-tick mattress in a sharecropper's shack, the sound of his mama crying through the mud-daubed walls. Daddy lugged a sack by day; by night, he drank. Daddy said *I love you* with his fists when he drank, so sometimes Little Henry snuck out the back screen door after supper and fell out beneath the oak tree at the edge of the property to count the stars, as numerous as all the accumulated days that women and children had suffered upon this Earth. Night after night the constellations were his confidants, but they were cold, silent, and certain of their own fixture in the firmament. Until at last there came a rain of stars over the fields, one chill December night when the ground was frozen, and by then he was fifteen and knew a sign when he saw one. His mama had taught him about such things. She had the sight, and her mama before her, and her mama, and now he had it, too. *You will see things and just know, baby. You'll know things before they happen. You'll feel them. Here,* and she touched his chest, and his chest was forever warm with the memory of her touch. That night, when the stars fell, he wept, then ran off. It was that or use on Daddy the knife blade he'd turned up in the rich black dirt of the fields that fall, as if the earth itself had made up an offering unto him.

In some Arkansas river town he hopped a bus into Mississippi, and from there to Memphis, and in Memphis he saw a man on the corner handing out leaflets for the Army, and the man was trim and fit and looked sharp as a razor, so he lied about his age and said he had an earnest desire in his heart to go kill Nazis, but the military saw through him, and so it was that in his wanderings he snuck into a circus at the edge of a starved town. Just a few ragged tents and a sad, weary elephant chained to a buckboard wagon. The elephant trunk-guzzling rye out of an old wash bucket. Inside one tent there were women dancing. Inside another a dog-faced boy and a dwarf. In the last he saw a man of such size, such girth, lifting a five-hundred-pound barbell over his head, and the man wore a leopard-skin unitard, and his first true vision came to him then—*You will know it, baby,* his mother had said, *because it will be like a wallop to the chest from an angry mule.* Indeed, it threw him on his back in the straw, this vision of himself, older, standing tall in a long coat and sweeping out his arms as two women stood beside him and peeled off the long coat, which was trimmed in fur, and a spotlight shone somewhere behind him, and there were cheers and whistles, and a bell rang, and his sunglasses were silver, and his hair was big and perfect.

Years later, after the circus, when all his friends were gone to Florida and the trains ran no more, the elephant long dead from alcohol poisoning, he found himself a thief and pickpocket on the streets of New Orleans, about to sell himself to men in alleyways, when he saw, in a TV-shop window on Magazine Street, a man with beautiful hair. His own hair, straight out of that long-ago vision. The man held a guitar. He sang, but he sang as if things were caged up inside him, as if some other world was bound up in his veins, bursting to spill over into ours. Hips from another dimension!

It was that moment that a hand fell on his shoulder, and a man behind him said, "You got a nice build, kid. You ever wrestle?"

And thus it began, the years-long ascendance of Henri "Babe" LeBleu.

As glittery and fiery and unforgettable as that star-shower of his youth.

Keys flashed in LeBleu's hand. The trunk flew up and the man hog-tied inside opened his eyes wide, a red bandana gagging his mouth. He wore a white leotard, spangled with silver sequins. The leotard was too tight. Flesh bulged beneath it. The man, like LeBleu, like Mickey Cyclops, was old. Too old to wear the magic that had once made him great.

LeBleu laughed and clapped his hands. "Johnny Vegas! Look at you, son!"

Mickey dragged the man out of the trunk. He threw him in the dirt.

LeBleu bent over him and tore the bandana free.

Johnny Vegas begged and cried, betrayed by the boy who had once called him Father.

"Hush and hark," LeBleu said, reaching into his vest. He took out a blade, curved and sharp. A sickle-moon of steel. It gleamed red in the taillights.

Johnny Vegas hushed. Johnny Vegas harked.

"How long you been promoting fights in the Mid-South region, old man? Twenty, thirty years? Hell, you made me the star I am today. Plucked me off the street when I was a breath away from dying. You taught me holds, gave me the moves. Put real power in my hands. The power of self-actualization! And now you cut me. You cut me deep, you Judas Iscariot. I came to you with a business proposal. I wanted to make a pact. Buy out your roster, make us both rich men. But you was misled by that old serpent pride, weren't you, Johnny? What was it you said to me? 'Know your place, son.'" LeBleu looked at Mickey Cyclops, whose tongue was an exclamation point of drool. "Know my fucking place," LeBleu said, as if to no one, or himself.

Johnny Vegas begged some more. "I called you my son . . ."

"Shush now, Johnny. What we got here is a Texas death match, see? Falls don't count. It's no time limits. No disqualifications. No holds barred. And the loser leaves town forever, you dig me?"

LeBleu took a wad of Johnny Vegas's silver hair and yanked his head back and swiped the curved blade of the knife across his throat. Blood gushed over the white leotard and LeBleu felt an instant surge of energy, transferred from the man before him to himself, from the very earth itself, up through his blue suede shoes. It made his legs crank and hound-dog, that current, that arc from another world. LeBleu cried out "God DAMN it, now!" and kicked the air, chopped it like Bruce Fucking Lee. The talisman burned in his chest hair. He wiped the blade on the old man's pale fish belly and stepped back, leaving Mickey to haul him up thrashing.

Out of the trunk, LeBleu lifted out the first of four limestone jars. Its lid was carved in the shape of a falcon's head. He set it on the ground, in the red taillight glow, among the shards of a broken wine bottle. Out came the second jar, head of a jackal. Third, head of a monkey. Fourth, head of a man.

Mickey Cyclops hooked Johnny Vegas's bound hands over the Buick's trailer hitch.

LeBleu looked on the pale, deep-seamed face of his mentor with something like pity. "You was heavyweight champion of the world, back in the day. And you chose me, of all the fish in all the sea. I thank you." He bent and kissed the old man's forehead. "But tonight you are food for horrors. Tonight, Johnny baby, all the kings are dead."

Nevertheless, Johnny Vegas was still alive when the short, curved blade sliced the leotard just below his belly button. Overhead, in the high-up beams of the monstrous bridge, great wings shuffled, something gave out a long, triumphant scream, and the asphalt thundered and rocked as big rigs flew past on their way to Little Rock, Oklahoma, the deserts of the west.

Later, when the messy part was done, the leftovers dumped in the river, LeBleu set the four blood-smeared jars at the edge of the bluff, their offerings inside, and watched as the lightning blazed over the city. It was long and leggy, walking lightning, cutting sideways through the sky, just as the curved blade had cut through Johnny Vegas's gut. LeBleu stood touching the talisman through his shirt and muttered arcane words that had never been pronounced aloud. He muttered them in conjunction with the names of all the wrestlers whose souls he would own as King of the Books, Mid-South Promoter Supreme, and in that moment he saw a spear of lightning stab down and split the Memphis shore wide open, and there, revealed in that flash, was the Other Land, a sunless land of red ash and belching smoke, stretching away to an infinite and darkling plain of Night, where the End of Man awaited and terrors lurked with hunger for human souls. Beyond the veil of the pulsing clouds a fearsome being reared over the city, a beast-god of no name, of no age, tall and broad and many-armed, with eyes of flame and a maw that opened like the craggy mouth of a volcano, and this was the One to whom Le Bleu had long prayed, the source of his sight, his mama's gift, the Source of All Gifts: he understood at last that this was the nameless entity he had long courted in his anger, his desire for vengeance, his greed for what he was owed. A true King, a King of Blood, showing LeBleu the future he would shape, here along the Memphis shore: a Pyramid, in this city of antique name, miles high and touching the clouds, a vast arena, where the champions of days long past would be remembered, and the young would fight two and four and six to a card, for the old Mid-South would surely pass away, and the new Mid-South would be fashioned in the image of Henri "Babe" LeBleu, and all the fears he had ever felt would be as wilting flowers in comparison to the greatness and reality and terror of the thing he would become; *such is the monstrous futureness of this which I have seen, of this I will become . . .*

A Pyramid on the Borderlands.

A last redoubt of glory, a haven for heroes.

Le Bleu fell to his knees amid the jars containing the guts and liver and heart and tongue of Johnny Vegas, and clutching the talisman through his silk shirt, which was soaked through with sweat, he gasped, "The King is dead!" And there was more to say, though he found himself almost choking on the glory of the words.

Nearby, leaning against the fender of the Buick Riviera, the brute Mickey Cyclops daubed his eye as he heard LeBleu cry out, like a man in the throes of some religious ecstasy, "Long live the King!"

Then came a tremendous thunder crack, and the rain began to fall, sending up a roar on the giant bridge overhead, dislodging all manner of winged creatures, a flock of dark, spectral beasts that moved en masse to blot out LeBleu's vision, the city lights, the sun that would rise tomorrow.

The hot night's promise—a lifetime's promise—at last fulfilled.

About the Authors

Linda D. Addison is an award-winning author of five collections, including *How to Recognize a Demon Has Become Your Friend*. She has been honored with HWA Lifetime Achievement Award, HWA Mentor of the Year, and SFPA Grand Master of Fantastic Poetry. She has published more than 400 poems, stories, and articles, and is a member of CITH, HWA, SFWA, SFPA, and IAMTW. Find her in these anthologies: *Black Panther: Tales of Wakanda; Predator: Eyes of the Demon; Chiral Mad 5; Sorghum & Spear: The Way of Silk and Stone; Shakespeare Unleashed; The Book of Witches; A Universe Anthology: Stories of the Reconvergence; Weird Tales: 100 Years of Weird*.

David Agranoff lives and writes in San Diego. He is an award-nominated author of horror, bizarro, and science fiction mostly. His short story collection, *Screams from a Dying World*, was nominated for a Wonderland Award for Best Collection. His debut novel, *The Vegan Revolution with Zombies*, is a satire that received rave reviews and was even featured in the *Journal of Animal Studies*. His novella "Punkupine Moshers of the Apocalypse" was featured in the *Best Bizarro Fiction of the Decade*, edited by Cameron Pierce. His novels, published by several publishers, include *Boot Boys of the Wolf Reich, Goddamn Killing Machines, Flesh Trade* (co-written with Edward R. Morris), *Last Night to Kill Nazis, People's Park, Punk Rock Ghost Story*, and the Splatterpunk Award–nominated eco-apocalypse novel *Ring of Fire*. He is co-host of the PKDickheads podcast focused on the work of author Philip K. Dick and other classic new wave science fiction.

Meghan Arcuri is a Bram Stoker Award–nominated author. Her work can be found in various anthologies, including *Borderlands 7, Chiral Mad, Chiral Mad 3, Madhouse*, and *Under Twin Suns: Alternate Histories of the Yellow Sign*. She served as the vice president of the Horror Writers Association for more than four years and is the recipient of the 2022 Richard

Laymon President's Award. She recently made her first foray into children's literature with her non-horror picture book, *Milk the Cat* (illustrated by Ogmios). Prior to writing, she taught high school math, having earned her B.A. from Colgate University—with a double major in mathematics and English—and her M.A. from Rensselaer Polytechnic Institute. She lives with her family in New York's Hudson Valley.

Sal Ciano is an author and editor based in South Florida. Born in New England, he was raised by a loving family who encouraged his reading of cosmic horror and weird fiction, and even took him to Lovecraft's childhood home and grave before he was ten. When not working or spending time with his friends, family, and dogs, Sal spends time exploring the world around him and delighting in the strange parade of the completely absurd, the indescribably weird, and the heart-breakingly ephemeral experiences that comprise all existence.

Michael Cisco is an American writer, Deleuzian academic, and teacher currently living in New York City. He is best known for his first novel, *The Divinity Student*, winner of the International Horror Guild Award for Best First Novel of 1999. His novel *The Great Lover* was nominated for the 2011 Shirley Jackson Award for Best Novel of the Year and was declared the Best Weird Novel of 2011 by the Weird Fiction Review. He has described his work as "de-genred" fiction. His other novels include *Animal Money, Celebrant, Ethics, Member, Pest, Unlanguage,* and *The Wretch of the Sun*. His story collections include *Antisocieties* and *The Secret Hours*.

L. E. Daniels's novel *Serpent's Wake: A Tale for the Bitten* was shortlisted for Singapore's Half the World Global Literati Award 2016 and is a Notable Work with the Horror Writers Association's Mental Health Initiative. An editor of more than 120 titles, Lauren co-edited Aiki Flinthart's legacy anthology *Relics, Wrecks and Ruins* with Geneve Flynn, winning the 2021 Australian Aurealis Award. With Christa Carmen she co-edited the Aurealis finalist, *We Are Providence*. Her recent publications include "Birnam Hall" (in *Generation X-ed*), "Ma Bones" (*Midnight Magazine*), and

"Silk" (in the Stephen King tribute anthology *Hush, Don't Wake the Monster*). Recent personal essays include "Spooned by the Dead" (in *Out of Time: True Paranormal Encounters*) and "Weird Witness." Lauren's poem "Tarantella" appears in *Under Her Eye*, "Final Cycle" in *Cozy Cosmic*, and "Night Terrors" in *Of Horror and Hope;* the last is a finalist for the 2022 Australian Shadows Award.

Andy Davidson is the Bram Stoker Award–nominated author of *In the Valley of the Sun, The Boatman's Daughter,* and *The Hollow Kind*. Born and raised in Arkansas, he makes his home in Georgia, where he lives with his wife, Crystal, and a bunch of cats.

Aaron Dries is a Bram Stoker and Shirley Jackson Award–nominated, and Ditmar, Australian Shadows, and Aurealis Award-winning author based in Canberra, Australia. His novels include *House of Sighs, The Fallen Boys, A Place for Sinners, Where the Dead Go to Die* (with Mark Allan Gunnells), plus the novellas *The Sound of His Bones Breaking,* the acclaimed *Dirty Heads,* and *Vandal: Stories of Damage* (with Kaaron Warren and J. S. Breukelaar). *Cut to Care: A Collection of Little Hurts* was described by Paul Tremblay as "heartbreaking, frightening, and all too real." Dries is a host of the popular podcast *Let the Cat In* and co-founded Elsewhere Here Productions.

Patrick Freivald is the four-time Bram Stoker Award–nominated author of nine novels, including *Black Tide, Jade Sky, Special Dead,* and *Twice Shy,* and dozens of short stories, many of which are collected in *In the Garden of the Rusting Gods*. A physics teacher and beekeeper, he lives in Western New York with his wife, cats, parrots, dogs, and millions of stinging insects.

Teel James Glenn's poetry and short stories have been printed in more than two hundred magazines including *Weird Tales, Mystery Weekly, Pulp Adventures, Space & Time, Mad, Cirsova, Silverblade,* and *Sherlock Holmes Mystery*. His novel *A Cowboy in Carpathia: A Bob Howard Adventure* won best novel 2021 in the Pulp Factory Award. He is also the winner of the 2012 Pulp Ark Award for Best Author.

Maxwell I. Gold is a Jewish-American author who writes prose poetry and short stories in cosmic horror and weird fiction with half a decade of writing experience. He has appeared in numerous publications including *Weird Tales, Other Terrors: An Inclusive Anthology, Startling Stories, Chiral Mad 5*, and many others. He is a five-time Rhysling Award nominee and two-time Pushcart Award nominee.

Nancy Holder is a *New York Times* bestselling author who has written dozens of novels and hundreds of short stories, essays, and articles. A recipient of seven Bram Stoker Awards, she received a Lifetime Achievement Award from the Horror Writers Association in 2021. She has served the HWA as vice-president and a member of the board of trustees. She was also named a Faust "Grand Master" by the International Association of Media Tie-in Writers in 2019. An avid Sherlock Holmes scholar, she is a Baker Street Irregular. In addition to writing original fiction in a number of genres, she is known for writing material for *Buffy the Vampire Slayer, Teen Wolf, Hellboy, Nancy Drew, Zorro*, and *Sherlock Holmes*, among others. She novelized the films *Crimson Peak, Ghostbusters*, and *Wonder Woman*. She and her writing partner Alan Philipson are currently working on two comic book/graphic novel series, one for Moonstone Books and one for IPI Comics. She lives in the Pacific Northwest.

Todd Keisling is a writer and designer of the horrific and strange. His books include *Scanlines, The Final Reconciliation, The Monochrome Trilogy*, and *Devil's Creek*, a 2020 Bram Stoker Award finalist for Superior Achievement in a Novel. A pair of his earlier works were recipients of the University of Kentucky's Oswald Research & Creativity Prize for Creative Writing (2002 and 2005), and his second novel, *The Liminal Man*, was an Indie Book Award finalist in Horror & Suspense (2013). He lives in Pennsylvania with his family.

John Langan is an author and writer of contemporary horror. Langan has been a finalist for the International Horror Guild Award. In 2008, he was a Bram Stoker Award nominee for Best Collection, and in 2016 a Bram Stoker Award winner for his novel *The Fisherman*. He is on the board of directors for the Shirley Jackson Awards. His fiction has appeared in the *Magazine of Fantasy & Science Fiction* and the anthologies *Poe* and *The Living Dead*. His first collection, *Mr. Gaunt and Other Uneasy Encounters*, was published by Prime Books, and has been followed by several more, including: *The Wide, Carnivorous Sky and Other Monstrous Geographies, Sefira and Other Betrayals, Children of the Fang and Other Genealogies,* and *Corpsemouth and Other Autobiographies*. His first novel, *House of Windows*, was published by Night Shade Books. He currently lives in upstate New York with his wife, two sons, and cat.

Adrian Wayne Ludens has sold stories to several dozen dark fiction anthologies and magazines. His latest story collections are *Bottled Spirits and Other Dark Tales* and *The Tension of a Coming Storm*. Adrian is a Library Associate and a hockey PA Announcer. He lives in the Black Hills of South Dakota with his wife, Lizzy.

Lisa Morton is a screenwriter, author of nonfiction books, Halloween expert, and prose writer whose work was described by the American Library Association's *Readers' Advisory Guide to Horror* as "consistently dark, unsettling, and frightening." She is a six-time winner of the Bram Stoker Award, the author of four novels and more than 150 short stories, and a world-class Halloween and paranormal expert. Her latest releases include *Calling the Spirits: A History of Seances* and *The Art of the Zombie Movie*. Recent short stories appeared in *Best American Mystery Stories 2020, Final Cuts: New Tales of Hollywood Horror and Other Spectacles,* and *Classic Monsters Unleashed.* Lisa lives in Los Angeles.

Lee Murray is a multi-award-winning writer and poet and a five-time Bram Stoker Awards winner, including for poetry for *Tortured Willows* (with Christina Sng, Angela Yuriko Smith, and Geneve Flynn). A NZSA Honorary Literary Fellow, Lee is a Grimshaw Sargeson Fellow and winner of the NZSA Laura Solomon Cuba Press Prize for her forthcoming prose-poetry collection *Fox Spirit on a Distant Cloud*. She is an Elgin Award runner-up and a Rhysling-, Dwarf Star-, and Pushcart-nominated poet. Her poem "cheongsam" won the Australian Shadows Award for poetry for 2021. Her poetry anthology *Under Her Eye* (co-edited with Lindy Ryan), a women-in-horror project in association with the Pixels Project to prevent violence against women, was published in November 2023 from Black Spot Books.

Peter Rawlik, a longtime collector of Lovecraftian fiction, stole a car in 1985 to go see the film *Re-Animator*. He successfully defended himself by explaining that his father had regularly read him "The Rats in the Walls" as a bedtime story. His first professional sale was in 1997, but he didn't begin to write seriously until 2010. Since then, he has authored more than fifty short stories and the Cthulhu Mythos novels *Reanimators, The Weird Company, Reanimatrix,* and *The Eldritch Equations*. In 2014 his short story "Revenge of the Reanimator" was nominated for a New Pulp Award. In 2015 he co-edited *The Legacy of the Reanimator* for Chaosium. He lives in Southern Florida, where he works on Everglades issues and does a lot of fishing.

Sam Rebelein holds an MFA in Creative Writing from Goddard College (with a focus on Horror and Memoir) and a certificate of graduation from the Lubbock Area Square & Round Dance Federation. His work has appeared in *Bourbon Penn, The Dread Machine, Coffin Bell Journal, Press Pause Press,* Ellen Datlow's *Best Horror of the Year,* the Stoker Award–nominated anthology *Human Monsters,* and elsewhere. Sam's debut horror novel, *Edenville,* is out now from William Morrow. His follow-up collection of stories set in the same fictional universe, *The Poorly Made and Other Things,* is forthcoming in early 2025. Sam currently lives in Poughkeepsie, New York, with two very old dogs.

Ann K. Schwader's most recent poetry collection, *Unquiet Stars,* appeared in 2021 from Weird House Press and placed third in the 2022 Elgin Awards for full-length collection. Ann is a two-time Bram Stoker Award finalist and has received Rhysling Awards for both short and long form work. She was named a Science Fiction & Fantasy Poetry Association Grand Master in 2019. A Wyoming native, she now lives and writes in suburban Colorado.

Steve Rasnic Tem is a past winner of the Bram Stoker Award, World Fantasy Award, and British Fantasy Award. His novel *Ubo,* a finalist for the Bram Stoker Award, is a dark science fiction tale about violence and its origins, featuring such historical viewpoint characters as Jack the Ripper, Stalin, and Heinrich Himmler. He has published more than 500 short stories in a career that has spanned more than forty-five years. Some of his best are collected in *Thanatrauma* and *Figures Unseen* from Valancourt Books, and *The Night Doctor & Other Tales* from Macabre Ink.

Tim Waggoner has published more than fifty novels and seven collections of short stories. He writes original dark fantasy and horror as well as media tie-ins, and his articles on writing have appeared in numerous publications. He is a four-time winner of the Bram Stoker Award, a one-time winner of the Scribe Award, and he has been a finalist for the Shirley Jackson Award and the Splatterpunk Award. He is also a full-time tenured professor who teaches creative writing and composition at Sinclair College in Dayton, Ohio. His papers are collected by the University of Pittsburgh's Horror Studies Program.

Wendy N. Wagner is a Shirley Jackson Award–nominated writer and Hugo Award–winning editor of short fiction. Her work includes the forthcoming novel *The Creek Girl,* the gothic novella *The Secret Skin,* the horror novel *The Deer Kings,* and more than seventy short stories, poems, and essays. She serves as the editor-in-chief of *Nightmare Magazine* and lives in Oregon.

Kyla Lee Ward is a Sydney-based author, actor, and Ghost Host. Reviewers have accused her of being "gothic and esoteric," "weird and exhilarating," and of "giving me a nightmare." Her writing has garnered her Australian Shadows and Aurealis awards, she has placed in the Rhyslings and received multiple Bram Stoker Award and Ditmar Award nominations. *This Attraction Now Open Till Late* is her first collection of dark and fantastic fiction, after two poetry collections and the co-written novel *Prismatic*. Her short film *Bad Reception* was screened at the Third International Vampire Film Festival, and she is a member of both the Deadhouse immersive theatre company and the Theatre of Blood, which have also produced her work. She enjoys fencing, travel, and scaring innocent bystanders.

Robert E. Waters's writing career began with "The Assassin's Retirement Party," published in 2003 in *Weird Tales*. He has written two novels in the 1632/Ring of Fire series: *1636: Calabar's War* (with Charles E. Gannon) and *1637: The Transylvanian Decision* (with Eric Flint). In addition, he has written several science fiction and fantasy short stories and novels, including the media tie-in novel *The Last Hurrah*, set in Mantic Games' Dreadball/Warpath Universe. Some of his most recent work include the Chimalis Burton series of stories and novellas involving Native American cryptids (*A Bluebird from Aspen*, *Eyes of the Wolf*, and *Ice Music*). Robert lives in Maryland with his wife Beth, their son Jason, and their two lively cats Snow and Ash.

L. Marie Wood creates immersive worlds that defy genre as they intersect horror, romance, mystery, thriller, sci-fi, and fantasy elements to weave harrowing tapestries of speculative fiction. She is the recipient of the Golden Stake Award, a MICO Award–winning screenwriter, a two-time Bram Stoker Award finalist, a Rhysling Award–nominated poet, and an accomplished essayist. Wood has won more than 50 national and international screenplay and film awards. Her short fiction has been published in the anthologies *Sycorax's Daughters* and *Slay: Stories of the Vampire Noire*. Her nonfiction has been published in *Nightmare Magazine* and in academic textbooks such as the cross-curricular *Conjuring Worlds: An Afrofuturist Textbook*. Her papers are archived as part of University of Pittsburgh's Horror Studies Collection. Wood is the founder of the

Speculative Fiction Academy, an English and Creative Writing professor, and a horror scholar with a Ph.D. in Creative Writing and an MFA in Speculative Fiction.

Stephanie M. Wytovich is an American poet, novelist, and essayist. Her work has been showcased in numerous magazines and anthologies such as *Weird Tales, Nightmare Magazine, Southwest Review, Year's Best Hardcore Horror: Volume 2,* and *The Best Horror of the Year: Volume 8 & 15.* Wytovich is the poetry editor for Raw Dog Screaming Press and an adjunct at Western Connecticut State University, Southern New Hampshire University, and Point Park University. She is a recipient of the Elizabeth Matchett Stover Memorial Award, the 2021 Ladies of Horror Fiction Writers Grant, and has received the Rocky Wood Memorial Scholarship for nonfiction writing. She won a Bram Stoker Award for her poetry collection *Brothel.* Her debut novel, *The Eighth,* is published with Dark Regions Press, and her nonfiction craft book for speculative poetry, *Writing Poetry in the Dark,* is available now from Raw Dog Screaming Press.

About the Editor

James Chambers is a Bram Stoker Award– and Scribe Award–winning author and a four-time Bram Stoker Award nominee. He is the author of the short story collections *A Bright and Beautiful Eternal World*, *On the Night Border*, and *On the Hierophant Road;* the novella collection *The Engines of Sacrifice;* and the novellas *The Devil in the Green*, *Kolchak and the Night Stalkers: The Faceless God*, *Three Chords of Chaos*, and many others, as well as the original graphic novel *Kolchak the Night Stalker: The Forgotten Lore of Edgar Allan Poe*. His short stories have appeared in anthologies and publications in multiple genres, including crime, fantasy, horror, pulp, science fiction, steampunk, and more. He edited or co-edited the Bram Stoker Award–nominated anthologies *Under Twin Suns: Alternate Histories of the Yellow Sign* and *A New York State of Fright* as well as *Even in the Grave*, an anthology of ghost stories.

Printed in the USA
CPSIA information can be obtained
at www.ICGtesting.com
CBHW060223141124
17271CB00009B/72